David

and

Goliath

The Guardian Angel Chronicles

David and Goliath

A Novel

Bryan Hathaway

WinePress **WP** Publishing

WinePress Publishing (PO Box 428, Enumclaw, WA 98022) functions only as book publisher. As such, the ultimate design, content, editorial accuracy, and views expressed or implied in this work are those of the author.

Unless otherwise noted, all Scriptures are taken from the *Holy Bible, New International Version®, NIV®*. Copyright © 1973, 1978, 1984 by Biblica, Inc.™ Used by permission of Zondervan. All rights reserved worldwide. WWW. ZONDERVAN.COM

Scripture references marked NASB are taken from the *New American Standard Bible*, © 1960, 1963, 1968, 1971, 1972, 1973, 1975, 1977 by The Lockman Foundation. Used by permission.

Scripture references marked KJV are taken from the *King James Version* of the Bible.

ISBN 13: 978-1-60615-015-3
ISBN 10: 1-60615-015-4
Library of Congress Catalog Card Number: 2009928732

To my children Brianna, Brandon, Brittany, and Brooke; may they realize that character is defined by their actions and not through their words. It takes years to develop a reputation and seconds to lose it.

To my brother, Todd, for reasons I cannot express.

Acknowledgments

Special thanks to my wife, Bonnie, my sister, Hope, and my daughter, Brianna.

They believed in me.

Chapter One

MARY'S PULSE RACED. She did not know if the short climb up the stairs to the nursing home, or her feelings of guilt, triggered the acceleration of her heartbeat. She had placed her father at The Waters, a senior care facility, three months earlier. Today was his birthday. She was not sure how he would respond to visitors, but knew it was time to see him. She held her child's hand; her husband followed reluctantly.

"But I don't wanna see Grandpa today," the small boy whined.

"We've been through this already, Jimmy," Mary snapped at her son. "Today is Grandpa's birthday. Don't you think he'd enjoy a visit from his favorite grandson?" Mary glanced to her husband, Joe, for support.

"Favorite grandson, huh? Jimmy is his *only* grandson, not that your father's even aware of that. I don't know why you insist on visiting your dad. I think half the time he doesn't know who you are, either." Her husband's remark stung.

"Grandpa doesn't know you, Momma?"

Mary glowered at her husband and said to her son, "Your Grandpa is a wonderful person. I don't think it would be fair to leave him all alone on his birthday. That's no way to celebrate. You understand, don't you, honey?"

Jimmy mumbled a feeble, "I guess so, Momma."

Joe grabbed Jimmy's hand and tugged him up the staircase. "Come on, Jimmy. Maybe Grandpa will tell us about one of his great adventures."

Jimmy's laughter echoed off each step.

Mary wiped the moisture from her eyes. She managed a thin smile and followed her boys up the stairs, hoping her anxiety would leave the moment she saw her dad.

David and Goliath:
The Guardian Angel Chronicles

David Liberty slumped in his chair, gaping lifelessly out the small window. His body was broken. No longer did he demonstrate the ability to control movement, and he knew his life would soon leave him as well. His mind was still intact, but no one would ever know, for his body had failed him. Why was the world so willing to go on without him?

He sat in silence, trapped in a body that had betrayed him, a body that had become a living tomb. He could recall almost every aspect of his seventy-five years, including each agonizing loss of strength, function, desire, and lastly, hope. He remembered each moment of the day his family decided to place him here at The Waters. The walls that surrounded him were as much of a prison as was his failing body.

Where had the man gone that he had struggled for years to build? More importantly, where were the lives he had touched now that he needed help? Was this how God rewarded him for years of a life lived as a role model to others?

David's despair was interrupted by a gentle knocking on his door.

"Mr. Liberty, you have guests here to see you." The nurse's aid pushed the door open.

Light flowed into the small and dreary room as Jimmy and his father came bouncing in.

"Howdy, Grandpa. Happy birthday!"

"Yes, happy birthday, David. It's good to see you," Joe said.

Mary entered last, walking slowly to where he sat by the window. She knelt in front of him and tenderly tried to lift his chin. "Hi, Daddy," she whispered. "How are you doing on this special day?"

Jimmy crawled into his mother's lap and placed his small hand on David's arm. "Grandpa? Do you have any stories to tell me?"

He could see the look of anticipation in his young grandson's eyes and felt the tender love in his daughter's touch. If only he could reach out and hug Jimmy—to hold him, play with him, and tell him about Mary and the rest of his family. If only he could tell his daughter, or even show her, how proud he was of her and how much he loved her.

He could not reach; he could not talk. His eyes did not convey recognition. In those few agonizing seconds, David Liberty put all his remaining energy into delivering his feelings. His head slumped forward, out of Mary's hand, the only response he could muster. His body betrayed him.

"Is Grandpa gonna talk, Mommy? Does he still love you? Am I still his favorite grandson?"

Of course I love your mommy! David's thoughts shouted. *I love you too, Jimmy.* He wanted to be alone. He wanted to die. He couldn't take it anymore. *God, please end this madness!* Why was this happening to him? *I love you, Mary. I love you, Jimmy! Just leave me alone and let me die. I can't stand seeing your faces.*

Mary gently placed Jimmy on the bed. Then returning to her father, she entwined his fingers with hers. "Happy birthday, Daddy." Tears welled in her eyes. "I hope you feel better soon."

Joe helped his wife stand, gently patted David on the shoulders and said, "David, it was good to see you again. We'll be by again on Thanksgiving."

He turned to his son. "Jimmy, say good-bye to your grandfather."

"Do we get to go to McDonald's now, Dad?"

Joe flushed mildly and nodded. "Jimmy, say good-bye to—"

"Good-bye, Grandpa, see ya 'round." Jimmy hopped off the bed and tugged his father out the door.

Mary followed her family but paused and whispered, "Bye, Daddy. I miss you." She pulled the door softly closed, creating a dismal hue in the room.

Good . . . just leave . . . and don't bother coming back. I don't want to see any of you again.

The car ride home was long. Mary stared out the passenger's window, longing for the past, when her father was much healthier. She found herself recalling those moments. Flashing back to her past brought a smile to her lips. A spot of moisture formed on her cheek.

She truly had a blessed childhood, growing up with her three brothers and two parents. She adored her father. She was always excited to see him when he returned from business trips. Later on, Mary joined her father on some of his company trips.

Her father had been a motivational speaker. David Liberty was recognized throughout the United States as a man who could change small businesses into large, successful companies.

Businesses from around the country sought his strategies for goal setting, customer service, and interpersonal relationships. Even more exciting, he was instrumental in saving couples' marriages.

David's listening skills and genuinely good heart helped him form a bridge between struggling newlyweds or older couples. He always stated that the rewards of his work were proportional to the size of the smiles he helped create.

Mary's father was also an exercise nut. He not only exercised his body, but also his mind. He felt it was just as important to exercise the brain daily as it was the body. His charts and exercise graphs could be found in nearly every room of their home.

Mary treasured her father's discipline and tender touch. However, he was not always there while she grew older.

Mary knew her father's decline came from the inside out, rather from the outside in. The breakup of his marriage with her mother, the loss of his oldest son, and other events in his life weighed heavily on his soul. David placed the blame on God. Mary tried to tell him it was OK to be angry with God, but her father always changed the subject.

Mary sighed. She was sure he did not have much time left here on earth. She only hoped he would go quickly and quietly, so he would know no more suffering.

David lost track of time while he agonized in his despair. He heard a click, and the door to his room opened. Whether it had been mere moments or days since his family had left, he was unsure, but a melodious voice brought him back to his maddening reality.

"Good afternoon, Mr. Liberty." A woman's voice sang as she drew up his shades and spun his chair toward the door. "My name is Joelle. I'm your new physical therapist. We're going to see what you can do here on your own. What do you think of that?" Her smile was impish, and her eyes twinkled when she pulled out an ambulation belt.

I think you are a freakin' loon, lady. David's thoughts burned. *If I could move or walk do you think I'd be here?*

Joelle leaned David forward and expertly slipped the ambulation belt around his waist, humming cheerfully. Once the belt was secure, she placed David in an upright position.

"Time to begin the evaluation. Are you ready, Mr. Liberty?"

Sure am, you stupid idiot. Can't you—?

"I see in your file that you've lost your ability to speak. Can you move your head?"

Can you shut your mouth?

Chapter One

"Or blink your eyes?"

Drop dead.

"Let's see if we have any movement in those arms and legs, Mr. Liberty."

I wish I did, lady, 'cause I'd drop kick your butt across this floor.

Joelle moved each of David's extremities, checking his range of motion and overall muscle tone. She continued her cheerful humming and asked him questions, but David was too irritated to hear or to mentally scold her any longer.

Finally, the incessant humming stopped. The physical "terrorist" seemed to be finished. Joelle was busy writing in his file. She finished, closed the chart, and placed her hands on either side of his face.

David felt a strange tremor throughout his being as Joelle cradled his head. His whole life played before him in an instantaneous slide show. He nearly lost consciousness from the barrage of emotions that clung to his life's pictures.

As his senses recovered, his eyes refocused on his tormentor, who tapped the end of his nose with the tip of her finger. "Mr. Liberty, we're all done today. I'll see you tomorrow to begin your physical therapy."

What the heck did you just do to me, lady? You need some mental therapy if you think this body can do anything. And shut the dang drapes before you go.

Joelle retrieved the belt, gathered her things, and left David to his now-lightened prison. The door remained open.

Close my door, you—

"One more thing." Joelle popped her head back into the room and grabbed the door. "I'll drop-kick your butt across the floor if I hear 'freakin loon,' 'stupid idiot,' or any other derogatory remarks from you again. You got that . . . David?"

Before he could think a response, the door slammed shut, and he was alone. His mind struggled with what her words implied. Did she know what he was thinking? He tried to recall their exact conversation, but his body failed him. He fell into a dreamless sleep.

Chapter Two

DAVID WAS RUDELY awakened by the floor nurse. "Time for your medicine."

It was Clara, an uncaring, underpaid registered nurse. She poured liquid into a medicine cup, tipped David's head back, and roughly fed it to him. "Looks like you've been in your chair all night," she said. "Wait 'til I tell that poor excuse for an aid about her screw up. At least I don't have to lift your sorry butt out of bed and into the chair." She turned and slammed the door behind her.

While David tried to shake the cobwebs out of his head, the door opened. A musical note touched his ears, and his eyes observed the energetic form of Joelle. "Here we are again, Mr. Liberty. Are you ready for some fun?"

David's head reeled. *What do you want with me?* His thoughts rang clear.

Joelle straightened his slumped form and placed his hands squarely on the armrests of the chair. "You do realize that sitting like this is extremely bad for your spine."

Can you hear my thoughts?

"I think I'll start by working with your legs, massaging and tapping to see if we can get those muscles to respond."

Right. My mind is going bonkers as well. I'm going crazy, and now I've got this pyscho therapist to push me over the edge.

Joelle worked on his right calf and spoke softly. "You're not going crazy."

In his mind, David froze. She *did* respond to his thoughts. She had heard them yesterday! *Who are you?*

"I told you my name is Joelle, and I'm here to help you rehab."

I mean, who are you? How the heck can you read my thoughts? I don't understand what's going on here.

Joelle stopped and gingerly placed David's leg down. She glided over to the window, peered out, sighed, and turned to address her patient. "There are rules to be followed, David."

What rules are you talking about?

"Rule number one: Only I ask the questions."

What are you babbling about, woman? I—

"David, if you don't follow the rules, I won't come back."

That would just break my heart.

"I'd think that you might actually enjoy the ability to converse with someone. How long has it been, Mr. Liberty, since you carried on an intelligent conversation? Three weeks? Three months? Or has it been a number of years?"

I don't know what you're talking about. Why are you doing this? What's happening to me? I don't—

"David! Do you really want me to leave, or would you like to have the opportunity to find out why I'm here?"

David did not respond right away. Everything was too confusing. He had been tired of living and tired of his body failing him. Most of all, he was tired of being lonely. His loneliness—and body that had become his prison—was enough to make him want to die.

The intrigue of the current development quelled his self pity. He settled his thoughts and stilled his emotions. In the span of a few seconds, he weighed the pros and cons. It did not take long.

Rule number two?

Joelle's impish smile returned. "That's a question, I believe, Mr. Liberty. Are you in agreement with rule number one?"

Yes. But once my sanity returns, I'll make some rules.

"Sane or insane, I ask the questions. As for rule number two: I'm always right."

Typical woman. If David could, he would have smiled. The burden he was carrying felt a little lighter. He was no longer alone.

Mary could not tolerate how she had left her father. What haunted her more than anything was the lack of life or recognition in her father's eyes. David had been losing himself for a number of years; she was sure of that. The one thing she always believed, however, was that the man from the past was residing somewhere beneath the surface. She could see it when she looked into her father's eyes. Not daily, but there were moments that she thought he could be rescued.

Mary finished the last of the breakfast dishes and entered her bedroom. She had a feeling there was not much time. She delicately pulled a small cross out of its hiding place. It hung on a thin, gold chain. Both cross and chain still held their shine after all those years. She and her brothers had purchased the cross for a Father's Day gift. Later in the year when they had saved more money, they bought the chain for Christmas and gave it to their father.

Her father's eyes and smile had been radiant. After many hugs and kisses, he placed the chain around his neck. For years she never saw her father without it. On the beach, at the gym, or just around the house, it was a part of him, like his wedding band. Until his decline began.

Mary was not sure, exactly, when she found her father's wedding band in the toilet bowl. She was still in high school. The cross and chain she found in his sock drawer. It was sometime after Tommy, her brother, had died.

Mary wrapped the trinket in a wad of tissue and tucked it in her purse. It was a three-hour drive to the nursing home. If she left now she would be home in time for Jimmy's bus. She grabbed the keys to the car. Time was running short.

Feelings follow actions.

"Explain what you mean by that."

Joelle's questions had been never ending for two hours. For the first hour and a half they appeared meaningless and wandered from subject to subject so aimlessly that David was sure that his mind had failed at last.

Most people wait to feel something before they act, David said mentally. *That's not reality. Our feelings come after our actions. For example: If you start to act happy, such as smiling, laughing, joking and so forth, you will feel happy. It's a simple example and holds true, even in more complex situations.*

"The same for love," Joelle said.

Yes, it is. Love . . . David answered too quickly. He paused and realized the depth of her reply. It had not been a question, but a statement that carried an accusatory tone.

His thoughts were interrupted by a knock on the door. It swung open. His daughter stepped into the room. She appeared flushed and disheveled, looking as if she had just rolled out of bed.

"Oh. Hi. I'm Mary, David's daughter."

Joelle looked panicked. She turned toward David to hide her expression and the coloring of her face. "All right, Mr. Liberty. That's all for physical therapy today."

"Oh, thank God they have found someone to help you, Dad."

"Hi. My name is Joelle." She extended her hand.

Mary enclosed the extended hand and hugged Joelle. "I hope it's not too late. We've been lobbying for various services." She stepped back, keeping both hands on Joelle's shoulders. "When was this approved?"

David's glass struck the floor. Liquid flowed across the floorboards. David lifted his arm from the tray to his chair.

"Daddy, you moved your arm!" Mary broke her engagement with Joelle and raced to his side, laying her head against his chest. "Oh, Daddy, I saw your arm. It actually moved!" She looked into his eyes.

David stared ahead and managed a single nod. Mary buried her face in his chest and sobbed.

Joelle slipped quietly out the door.

Chapter Three

DAVID WATCHED JOELLE leave without saying good-bye.

"Daddy, I'm so proud of you," Mary chimed. "I brought something for you. It's important that you wear it. In fact, I want you to wear it for me. I'll talk to the staff to make sure no one removes it."

She reached into her purse and removed the chain from its fragile protector. Then she hung the necklace around David's neck. Delicately she adjusted the cross against his chest.

David screamed in his mind. *No, Mary! I'm not ready for this. I don't want to remember. I can't remember Tommy or you every day. It hurts too much! Please take it off. I don't want to remember* Him, *either.*

Mary stepped back to admire her work. "Now, that's my father." She moved forward and embraced him.

"Knock, knock, Mr. Liberty. It's time to see the doctor," a stout nurse quipped and entered the room. "Good morning, Mrs. Mathew. Didn't I see your name on the guest list just yesterday?"

"Yes, you did, Wilma. I needed to see Dad again today."

Wilma pushed a wheelchair over to David as a young aid also entered the room. Both women made preparations to transfer David into the wheelchair. "I'm sorry to cut your visit short, dear, but we have to take your father down to see Dr. Stevens."

"Oh, no, that's quite all right. I've got to get going anyway. It's delightful to see you have a physical therapist on board. I'm sure she'll be beneficial. Especially with Dad. He—"

"Physical therapist? What on earth are you talking about?"

"Your staff physical therapist. I met her this morning. She was helping Dad. I saw him move his arm."

"Therapist, huh? Are you aware of any P.T. on staff, Michele?" Wilma addressed the young aid.

"No ma'am, I'm not."

"Here we go, Michele. One, two, three, and lift." Two pros, the caretakers transferred David to the chair and wheeled him out the door.

"I'm not sure who you met this morning, Mrs. Mathew," Wilma said. "As far as I'm aware there is no therapist on staff. I'll double check. What did you say her name was?"

"I . . . I'm not sure . . . I don't remember. In all the excitement of Dad moving his arm, I guess I forgot."

"That's all right. Don't you worry; I'll see what I can come up with. Have a good day. I'll call you this evening."

The women escorted David down the hall, leaving Mary behind.

David wondered who Joelle really was. He thought any sane person would be fearful of such a stranger, especially since he could not defend himself or run away. Instead of a feeling of alarm, however, David was energized. It had been a long time since he felt any excitement.

He wanted to console Mary, for he believed that Joelle did not mean him any harm. Instead, he was still powerless to communicate his thoughts to his daughter, but he *had* moved his arm and his head. What an interesting day! When would he see Joelle again?

"Michele, I don't know who was in Mr. Liberty's room, but I intend to find out," Wilma stated while the trio continued down the hall.

"Maybe we do have a new therapist on staff," Michele said. "Dr. Stevens is new. He started this week."

"No, I don't think so, dear. We've not had any plans of bringing a therapist of any sort on staff. More overhead, you know. Can't have the big wigs shelling out any of their profits," Wilma huffed. "And speaking of Dr. Stevens, I don't like the man. I think the board made a poor choice by hiring him. He shouldn't be practicing medicine in this setting."

"I think you're being a little old-fashioned, Wilma. Medicine isn't what it was when you first started working."

"We pursued a career in medicine because we cared about people. Dr. Stevens doesn't seem to care," Wilma insisted.

"Listen to you. You better keep your voice down, or somebody might hear you."

"Sweetie, at my age I just tell it like it is."

I hear you, sister! Fire both them barrels. David normally tuned out conversations. The events of the day however, had changed his awareness. For the moment, he was very interested in what was going on around him.

"Mr. Liberty, here we are." Michele came to a stop in the small treatment room. Wilma placed David's records on the counter and patted him on the shoulder. "Dr. Stevens will be here in a moment. Don't you run too far away."

Funny. Try not to get your butt stuck to a chair, either.

No sooner had the women left when a man entered the room. He was young for a doctor. He sat on a stool and opened David's file.

He flipped through the pages, and occasionally paused and scribbled. For several minutes he didn't acknowledge there was another person in the room. Head down, he was absorbed by the file. He paused. Turning slowly, he focused his attention on the patient in the wheelchair. He stared at David intently.

Whadya looking at, smiley? You've got the personality of a door knob, David's mind said.

All of a sudden, the doctor lunged and reached through David's collar. His fingers grasped the chain Mary had placed around David's neck. With a quick jerk, he snapped the chain and held it in his clenched fist. He shook it only inches from David's face. "You won't need this any longer."

David, stunned by the pain, reeled in agony. The throbbing came more from his chest then his neck. He watched the doctor place the chain in his pocket and exit the room.

David's hands tried to clutch at his chest as he collapsed forward in the chair. The pain was searing. *What have you done?* His mind wailed in anguish, *That's mine. It's from my children. Give it back to me!* A stench of sulfur interrupted his thoughts.

Then everything went black.

Chapter Four

MARY WAITED UNEASILY by the telephone that evening. She had had a difficult time driving home. Her mind played out hundreds of scenarios that could explain the therapist she met in her father's room.

The phone rang and she scooped up the receiver. "Hello, this is Mary."

"Hello, Mrs. Mathew. This is Wilma from the nursing home."

"I've been waiting for your call. What did you find out?" Mary asked.

"I'm afraid I have some bad news. After your father's medical checkup, we found him collapsed in his wheelchair. Dr. Stevens reexamined him and thinks he suffered a seizure."

"Oh, no! Will he be all right?"

"Dr. Stevens is not sure how your father's body will handle the stress. And Mrs. Mathew, there is something else."

"Something else? What? What else?" Mary's heart pounded.

"We had to restrain your father. He began clawing at his neck and chest."

"What? I don't understand. Dad hasn't been able to move his arms for a long time."

"I don't understand either, dear. Something happened, but we're not exactly sure what."

"I'll be there as soon as I can, I just have—"

"No, Dr. Stevens says he shouldn't have any visitors for the next few days. He's afraid any more stimulation would be too much."

"But what can I do?"

"Just sit tight, hon. I'll keep you informed."

"Wilma, what about the physical therapist?"

"That's the other thing. I don't know who you saw, honey, but there's no therapist on staff. I checked with everyone. We're not even looking to hire one."

"Then who was in Dad's room this morning?"

"I don't know. But I'll take extra care of your father. Don't you worry."

"Thanks, Wilma." Mary struggled to maintain her composure. "Please call me as soon as you know anything."

"Will do, dear. Sorry about the news. Good night."

"Good night."

After Mary hung up, she sobbed. She had always known that at some time she would lose her father. She was just not prepared for it right now. Her father wasn't prepared for it either.

David's head reeled as he gradually awakened. The burning in his chest was less intense, but its presence brought a sudden recollection of the encounter with Dr. Stevens. His chain and cross had been ripped from him. Stolen! He tried to rub his chest and realized his arms were bound. Nooo! He was trapped.

David's head sagged, but no tears came. His one brief moment of hope and excitement had been followed by a blast of reality. He did not know if he could endure the torment.

His body had failed over the years, but what had been the cause? He had received no answers from any of the specialists he had visited. One or two of the quacks actually stated that his perceived failure was due to a psychological shutdown.

His mind searched for answers. When had it all started? Things had gone downhill sometime after Tommy died. At first, David's legs slowed. He stopped exercising. After being confined to a wheelchair, he stopped reading. Eventually, he stopped communicating and wished for death.

The intrigue of his female visitor had stirred buried thoughts. He now felt alive. There was no rational explanation for the feeling. The only reason must be based on his simple interaction with Joelle. He did not know if he would ever see the strange therapist again. His heart burned with a desire for Joelle to return.

Chapter Five

DAVID WAS NOT sure how long he had been restrained. What he gathered from the conversation around him was that Dr. Stevens had left strict orders that he was to be restrained at all times. Apparently the good doctor was falsifying his accounts that he examined David regularly.

Something began to change in David. He did not fully understand the mechanism of the change, but he desired life. His freedom had been taken away. He now realized that his old prison had been one of self-limitation. His new prison was imposed by someone else. Perhaps his need for justice or retribution fueled his need for life.

Through the days that followed, Wilma was a blessing. The kind nurse checked on him frequently during her shift. She talked to him as if David could understand everything she was saying. Of course he could, but he had regained only the ability to nod his head. He was unable to turn right or left; therefore he could respond only with a "yes." Wilma caught on quickly and continued to soothe and talk to him.

Wilma told him that she talked to his daughter every day. Mary would come as soon as circumstances allowed. David guessed Dr. Stevens was the driving force behind her not visiting.

"I don't like that man one bit, Mr. Liberty," Wilma said.

Yeah, I scratched his name off my Christmas list too.

"He is insulting and demeaning; a regular wolf in sheep's clothing, if you ask me. Thank the Almighty we're getting a new resident."

What? What did you say?

"She's supposed to start tomorrow. Our good Dr. Stevens has not been around the last few days, so the board brought on a new physician. I hope she can demonstrate some compassion."

Great . . . but how will I ever get my cross and chain back?

Wilma finished fussing over David, kissed him lightly on the forehead and said, "I'm sure we'll get you out of those restraints soon, Mr. Liberty. Maybe the new doctor will show us how evil Dr. Stevens really was."

Evil? I'd definitely say there's something wrong with that man.

Wilma left David deep in thought. He hoped the new doctor was proficient enough to see that he was not a threat to himself. He had frantically tried to demonstrate that his necklace had been stolen. His waving and clawing raised alarm with the nursing staff, who thought David was trying to inflict harm to himself. They had quickly restrained his arms.

He did not understand anything about his encounter with Dr. Stevens. Why or how did he know that David was wearing a cross? More importantly, why did he rip it off? What had triggered the return of his arm mobility? David stared up at the ceiling. *I miss my family.*

"Why, that is so nice to hear, Mr. Liberty," the musical voice chimed.

David's heart leaped. He stared at Joelle, who knelt beside him. *Where did you come from? I mean, where've you been?*

"Tsk, tsk. Rule number one, Mr. Liberty."

If David could, he would have laughed out loud. His surprise rapidly turned to joy and relief when Joelle released his bonds. His arms were free! He inspected the backs and palms of each hand. He could move!

David recounted to Joelle the events that had followed the day Mary had interrupted them.

Joelle listened to his thoughts as David explained what had transpired in the exam room. She squeezed his hand. "I'm sorry, David. I know these dealings have been confusing. I don't mean to brush aside what has happened since our last meeting, but there are questions that I must ask you. Is that OK?"

Yes, as long as you promise not to leave—I mean disappear—again.

"That is not for me to decide."

David felt his heart sink, but he did not want his companion to leave just yet. *Fire away.*

Joelle's warm smile returned. "Here we go, Mr. Liberty. I know about your past, but I'm unclear on certain details. You spoke to hundreds of business people in hopes of improving their profitability and success. What was your main premise?"

Be a servant.

"What does that mean?"

It's simple. Serve others. This applies not only to your customers, but to your co-workers, employer, and suppliers, as well. By taking a servant's attitude, you make others feel important. We all want to feel special. If you increase others' feelings of self-worth, you strengthen the relationship. Strengthen the relationship, and you improve profitability.

"You also counseled married couples. What tended to be your main principle?"

Live each day as if it were your last. Selfishness destroys a marriage. As humans, we ironically tend to give more to others when we know our time is short. We studied terminal patients. A large percentage of them grew closer to their loved ones. Their knowledge that time is short changed their actions. When we act like we love one another, the feeling of love follows.

Most difficulties come later in marriage. Our actions have changed. We do not put our partner first. With changes in actions, the feeling of love will fade. It is recommended that each morning we should actively decide to love our spouse.

"That is how you lived your marriage?"

The question caught David by surprise. He struggled momentarily with a memory that he tried to suppress. *I . . . I'm not sure.*

"So you taught these principles but did not live them."

Now, wait! That's not entirely accurate. I—

"You did not practice what you taught. You spoke of actions and how they affected relationships, whether in a marriage or business, but you never followed your own advice."

What are you talking about? It was not my fault—

"Are you familiar with the story of Adam and Eve?"

The change in topics confused David. *What? Yes, I'm familiar with the story.*

"What was Adam's sin?"

David's focus was not entirely on Joelle's question. He was flustered by the accusation that he did not "walk his talk."

"Mr. Liberty, what was Adam's sin?" Joelle's second attempt with the question penetrated his defenses. Her voice echoed through his body.

He . . . he ate the fruit from the tree of knowledge.

"How was that sin?"

David racked his brain. Had it been so long that he couldn't remember the simple story of creation? *I think it was because he disobeyed the Lord.*

"So, his sin was one of disobedience?"

David felt a trap close around him. *Yes.*

"But this was not Adam's first sin of disobedience, was it?"

David drew a blank. The strange feeling of being led down an unwanted path continued, and he was unable to run away from the uncomfortable confrontation. *I'm not sure.*

"What about the fact that God placed Adam in the Garden of Eden to care for it, to cultivate it, to protect the garden? Yet Adam stood by as the serpent threatened the garden and his wife. Adam stood by and did nothing. He did not stop his wife from taking the fruit and did not call for help from God when the serpent stood before them. Adam was disobedient before he ever ate of the fruit. By failing to act, he committed a sin against his Lord."

Confusion and bewilderment flooded David's mind. He did not understand what Joelle was saying.

"You stopped praying. Your lack of action led to your love for God to dwindle as well. You became disobedient. Like Adam, you sinned against God with your lack of actions."

He took my son. If there really was a god, how could He have let that happen to me? I was faithful. He was not. David closed his eyes. He did not want to think of it again.

Joelle seized him by the shoulders. The strength of her grip was startling, causing David to pop his eyes open. "You listen closely, David Liberty. Don't you think that God, being a Father, felt your pain? Don't you think He remembers the pain of losing His own Son? That He consciously turned His back while His Son was tortured and crucified. What makes you think you are so special not to share that pain?"

David shrank in his chair. He struggled to break free from the fiery gaze that held him. He wanted to run away from the questions. More importantly, he wanted to avoid the answers.

"What do you want, David Liberty? What do you want?"

What kind of question was *that*?

What's wrong with you? He was unable to break her grasp or look away from the stare that held him.

"You turned your back on God. At first, you were just angry with Him, but then you shut Him completely out of your life. What makes you think that He won't turn His back on you when you stand before Him?" Joelle stomped out of the room and slammed the door. Her words echoed within his head. *What do you want?*

An incredible amount of energy left the room with her. David's heart raced faster and faster. The thought of salvation and eternity frightened him more than the prospect of life merely ending.

What if there really *were* heaven and hell? If death was truly a new beginning and not an ending, was he willing to risk eternity? What would happen when he died? It was easy to accept death as an end. It was far more difficult

to accept there was more after death. It could imply that there were consequences for actions or the lack of actions.

What if his own selfishness was the causative factor in the failure of his
marriage or in the death of Tommy? He cried throughout the night, chest
and shoulders heaving, but no tears fell. His thoughts and memories kept
him from sleeping. David was not sure what he wanted.

David waited anxiously for the return of Joelle. He was unsure which
words he would use, but his night of reflection had stirred something deep
inside his being. As his focus shifted from the window to the door, a familiar
form glided into the room.

"Good morning, David." No smile or enchanting song escaped Joelle's
lips. Her face carried an intense look of determination. Power radiated in
the room, surrounding her. "Your answer?" She crossed her arms and stared
through David.

Terror gripped David. Doubt and confusion engulfed him. His defenses
went into action. *I want to live.*

"You call this living? All men must die, David Liberty. What do you
want?"

I don't want to die.

"All men die, but only a few truly live their life. Why don't you want to
die?"

*I'm afraid. I don't want God to be angry with me. I want to have time to fix
my relationship.*

"Words. Merely words. It is no longer the time for words; now is the time
for action."

*But . . . but . . . I can't earn salvation! Salvation is a gift, a gift borne of faith.
I want time to ask forgiveness.*

"Do you have faith in God?"

I did. I mean . . . I can again.

"Faith of itself, if it does not have works, is dead."

David was stunned. *I can't act. I have only my arm movement. I can't walk
or communicate. How can I demonstrate my faith?*

"I will ignore your question and ask mine anew. What do you want?"

I want to be healed. I want to love again. I want to live. David paused and changed his answer. The self revelation came without difficulty. *I want a second chance. I want to see my son. I want a second chance at life.*

Joelle's countenance softened. She knelt beside David. "Mr. Liberty, are you asking God for a second chance?"

David's thoughts raced. He dreamed about reliving his life and correcting his mistakes, to touch, to laugh, to sing. *I guess I am.*

"He must love you very much, to give you such a chance." Joelle paused, as did David's heart, "This chance carries a heavy price and consequences. It is a battle you will fight for your very soul. You will also be fighting for the souls of others; therefore, it is a war you cannot afford to lose. There will not be another chance. Is that understood?"

No . . . I mean yes. I'm not sure what you're telling me. Who or what, exactly, are you?

She ignored the question. "You will be sent into the lives of others to demonstrate your faith and commitment to the Lord. You will get your second chance. Your body will be born anew, but your speech will be impaired. You will use actions to assist those in need and to demonstrate your beliefs. No longer will you be able to use meaningless words to teach; now you will *do*.

"You will take the role of a face in the crowd. The essence of who you are shall not be lost. You will have the knowledge necessary to interact with others in your host body. Your trials may not be obvious at first, but all of them must be completed. Your actions or lack of actions will be judged by others."

What? I don't understand. How—?

"You will be judged by the people you come into contact with. Their verdict will determine your eternity. You are your brother's keeper. If you are able to win back their lives, then yours will not be forfeited."

David's eyes widened; his heart raced. He could not believe what he was hearing.

"Any decision not to complete the trials results in failure. Failure means an eternity away from your heavenly Father, and you will never see your son again. Your trial has begun.

"I've been sent to tell you that life does not end with death. Your past life was incomplete. You were not obedient to your Father, and this new path is now your atonement. Do you understand what that means?"

No, but I'm sure you'll tell me.

"I *have* been telling you, David. It will be your apology for lack of obedience. You will demonstrate to God through your actions that you believe and love Him. You will ultimately help others so they will not lose eternity and you, therefore, will gain yours. Your actions will reveal your soul."

But that's not what is written—

"Don't tell *me* what is written! I have read the Scriptures. Even the fallen one believes in the existence of the Lord, but that does not grant him eternity. To you it will be revealed through others and the Word. With the discrepancies in your world on the interpretation of Scripture, don't be so naïve to think you know the mind of God. He has chosen you for a second chance. Feel blessed and make the most of it."

David sat in bewilderment. The weight of what was happening tore at his remaining sanity. Everything had been more acceptable just a few days earlier. He'd had no hope. He'd had no fear. His only desire had been to escape life—life that mocked him while his spirit failed. Now, his soul stirred. It cried out for life. It cried for the opportunity to be rejoined with something that had left. It was a cry that could not be ignored.

"David, there is one more thing." Joelle's voice softened, and David began to lose consciousness. "Satan will be trying to win people's souls. He takes great delight in destroying the Lord's children. His minions will be your adversaries, and you may not recognize them. Beware! The ability he has to distort the truth and tempt humanity is great. Once Satan identifies you, your mission will—"

Will what? David's world blackened around his unanswered question.

BOOK ONE

"Pride goes before disaster, and a haughty spirit before a fall. It is better to be humble with the meek than to share plunder with the proud."

—Proverbs 16:18–19

Chapter One

DAVID BENT FORWARD to pluck the irritating weeds from the luscious landscape. With rake and hoe in hand, he turned over the sun-baked earth. He stooped and broke the smaller clumps of dirt with gloveless hands.

Exhausted, he leaned heavily on his tools. Taking his last sip of water, he wiped his chapped lips and sweaty forehead on his shirtsleeve. The afternoon sun beat down relentlessly in this part of California. His job as the Barnes' caretaker was as thankless as they come. "Whether a business owner or an employee at McDonald's, take pride in your work. Give one-hundred-and-ten percent effort and your hard work will pay strong dividends in the future. Serve others in whatever capacity you are employed. Servitude and humility will attract new customers and keep the old ones returning. Strong relationships are built with this principle. Relationships are the key to success." David smiled inwardly at the words from one of his first seminars. His self-reflection was brought to a disrespectful end.

"Hey, Mr. Dirt Digger. Tie my shoes!" The rude command was uttered from a twelve-year old boy standing defiantly on David's bag of collected weeds. Three of the boy's friends stood by, gawking at their friend's bravado.

The young boy, Sam, turned to his friends and said, "Watch what I can make him do!" He glared at David. "I said, 'Tie my shoes!' And I want double knots."

"Aww, come on, Sam, let's go back and play some more ball." One of Sam's playmates looked to the ball field.

"No, wait," replied another. "Let's see what happens."

"This dumb oaf has been working for my dad for only three days, and I can tell him whatever I want." Sam's expression looked like that of a conquering war hero. "Fact is, he can't talk or nothing. Big, stupid, girly gardener. I said, 'Tie my shoes!'"

25

David bent forward to the laughter and amazement of the four boys. He expertly tied both shoes. Then smiling, he stood and rubbed Sam's crop of red hair. Sam's hair became stained with a brown highlight from the dirt on David's hands.

Sam's friends laughed all the more when the dirt trickled down the front and back of his shirt. Sam's face turned crimson. He stepped away from David. "You'll be sorry you did that!" He grabbed the bag of weeds and dumped them out. "There, how about some more work, dirt-digger?"

Sam and his friends snickered while they ran away, leaving David alone in the garden.

David collected the mess and stuffed the weeds into the plastic garbage bag. He wasn't sure how or when he'd arrived in this new environment. As far as he could tell, he was the gardener or caretaker for the estate of John Barnes, a professional baseball player for the San Diego Padres. His actual "boss," however, was *Mrs.* Barnes, who gave him his daily list of chores. She also signed his small paycheck.

David was amazed at the transformation his body had undergone. He figured he was somewhere in his early thirties. Strong, tall, and defined, his body moved with a grace that had long been forgotten. The sights, smells, and sounds of this place made him feel like he was in a new reality. It had been decades since his body had felt this good.

David felt awkward but decided to say a short prayer. It had been a long time since he had prayed. *Here I am, Lord. I'm not sure how I will be needed or tested. Joelle implied there would be more than one trial. I ask for strength to carry out this task. And . . . ah . . . thanks for this second chance.*

David raised his eyes toward the sky and waited for a response. No reply came. He sighed and finished his work in the garden. *This is a far cry from being a motivational speaker,* his thoughts echoed while he walked across the lawn to dispose of the garbage.

Something struck his foot, followed by a loud voice. "Hey, dirt man, throw that ball here."

David saw that he had wandered into the outfield, near where his young tormentors were playing baseball. Picking up the ball, he tossed it into the air a number of times. He enjoyed feeling the seams of the ball and the ease at which it floated up and down.

"Hey, I told you to throw that here!"

A grin stole across David's face. He reached back and snapped his arm forward. The ball left his hand with sharp revolutions. *Here it comes, you spoiled brat. I hope your father taught you how to catch a curveball.*

Sam's glove moved toward the incoming ball. The ball's course changed and it broke sharply to the left, missing the glove and striking Sam squarely in the stomach. He doubled over with a muffled cry and fell to his knees.

David's stride carried him across the outfield. He leaned over Sam, who was having difficulty breathing. Sam squeezed out some tears between his gasps for air.

David tried to tell Sam to breathe, but no words left his lips. He took hold of Sam's legs and pumped them toward his chest and back again until Sam regained his breath.

Sam's small posse of friends arrived on the scene.

"Hey, Sammy, you all right?"

"Yeah, Sam, why didn't you catch that ball?"

"That dirt guy was trying to get back at you, right, Sam?"

David picked up the ball and held it out in his palm.

Sam stared defiantly at David and then snatched the ball away. "Come on, guys, let's go finish our game. First one to home plate is pitcher."

All four boys raced across the field, but Sam stopped and turned back to stare at the new caretaker. "That was a curve ball, wasn't it, mister?"

David nodded.

"Maybe you could show me sometime?"

David, smiling, shrugged his shoulders. He winked at Sam and left the boys to their game.

Sue Barnes and her son, Sam, sat at the dinner table alone, which was the norm during the long baseball season. Even during a long home stand, Sam's father was rarely at home for a family meal. Meetings, training, treatment, or business were among the list of reasons Sam heard his father tell his mother as an excuse for not being around.

"Where's Dad playing tonight, Mom?"

"He's playing here, in San Diego. The Padres are playing a make-up series with the Phillies."

"What? He has a home game and I'm not there?"

"Sammy, it's a school night. You know the rules."

"Dad would've let me go."

Sam was right. Too many times Mrs. Barnes had to play the disciplinarian, a role she usually played solo. "Sammy, you'll see your dad play this weekend. Now, eat your supper and tell me about your day."

"Me and the guys played some ball."

"You play ball every day. How was school?"

"Aww, it was OK."

"How did you do on your math quiz?"

"Mr. Stone said I could take it another time. I told him I wasn't ready for it yet."

"Samuel Barnes! Are you offering Padres tickets for favors in school again?"

Sam's complexion matched his hair. "No, Mom. I didn't!"

"You march right upstairs and get your math book, young man. I'll let Mr. Stone know tomorrow that you're ready to take that quiz."

Sam stood and smashed his chair against the table. "I wish Dad were here!" He raced out of the kitchen.

Sue heard her son's door slam shut. "I wish your dad were here, too." She cleaned the dining room table and placed the dishes in the dishwasher. She was concerned that her husband, John, did not know his son. John was too enamored with his own success. This year had been the best of his career, and it was the final one of his contract. The money he could demand would be unmatched throughout the major league.

The man Sue married had slowly disappeared over the last few years. John was all about John. No one could hit, throw, or play defense like John could, and he was not afraid to let others know about it. He had alienated most of his teammates and the few friends they had. The only friend he possessed was his new agent, a Mr. Stevens.

She did not care for Frank Stevens. He constantly told John how great he was, and John believed him. Frank told John that personal stats were more important than the outcome of the game. The Padres would not reach the pennant anyway, so John should pad his stats to increase the size of a new contract.

Sue no longer felt as if she were in a marriage. John wanted only the physical part of intimacy and no longer seemed to desire the emotional aspect of the relationship. Sue and John were no longer in a healthy union. She sighed while she scrubbed the plates free of food and recalled a time in the past when things were less complicated.

When they were first married, baseball had always been a priority, but not the most important part of John's life. His family and the Lord had come first. Sue's main concern had always been family and church. Now both these areas were suffering.

She promised that she and Sammy would help out at church this weekend during their fall fundraiser. She sighed. Maybe the new caretaker would take Sammy to the ball game while she fulfilled her part of the promise. She bowed her head and prayed that God would change her unhappy life.

Chapter Two

DAVID AND SAM were both unhappy with the company they shared. David had hoped to spend the day relaxing, not babysitting a spoiled child. He was waiting for God to reveal his test. Sam made it clear that he wanted to go to the ball game with his friends, or even his mother. Anyone would have been better than the speechless dirt digger.

Sam insisted on sitting in the left field seats. As the son of the famous John Barnes, he had seats reserved right behind the dugout, but Sam wanted to sit behind left field. His father was on a homerun streak, and Sam wanted to catch what would be his father's four-hundredth career homer.

Their seats were in the second tier. "Hey, dirt man, why don't you go get me a hotdog and Coke?"

You got it, little big-man.

"And bring me some fries, with lots of ketchup. Make it snappy!"

Some extra hot sauce coming right up.

David returned to their seats carrying fries, a hotdog, and drink.

"Hold my drink," Sammy ordered. "Hand over the dog and fries."

David handed over the food, but in the process of sitting in his seat, he spilled Sam's drink. *How careless of me.* He struggled to repress a grin.

Sam stuffed a handful of fries in his mouth. Suddenly, his expression changed from contempt to surprise. Spitting his fries in all directions, he gasped. "Hot . . . hot . . ." He fanned his face and sucked air in and out as quickly as he could.

David bent to the stadium floor and scooped up a handful of the spilled ice. He held out his hand.

Sam shoveled the ice into his burning mouth. He chewed on the ice cubes and surveyed the spilled food and drink strewn around his seat. His baseball shirt was stained with hot sauce, and there was plenty of laughter from the surrounding fans. His eyes narrowed. "You did that on purpose."

David shrugged. *Maybe you'll learn a lesson.*

Sam smacked his lips. "I still need a drink." His tone was more of a plea than an order.

David nodded and used his hands and mouth to demonstrate chewing.

"No . . . no thanks. I'm not hungry."

David descended the stairs. With the distraction of the incident, David and Sam had missed the top of the first inning. Apparently the Padres had quickly retired the Phillies' batters. He hoped to return in time to see John Barnes hit the ball.

The line was long at the concession stand, and David missed Sam's father at bat. He plopped in his seat and handed Sam his drink. He pointed at Sam and swung an imaginary bat. He followed the swing by placing his hands palm up with a small shrug of his shoulders.

"No luck. Dad grounded out to third, but he had a foul ball that he crushed over there." Sam pointed in the direction where his father had hit the ball.

In the bottom of the seventh, John was at the plate again. The Phillies were leading, five to three. The Padres had a runner on first and third, with nobody out. When he stepped into the batter's box, the home-plate umpire stood and waved his arms, signaling a time out.

The third-base coach trotted over to John. It was evident by their body language that the two men were arguing. Finally the coach threw his hands up in the air. He stalked back to his post at third base and crossed his arms.

"What was that all about?" Sam asked David.

David had played his share of baseball during his life. Although he was no professional, he understood the coaching aspect of the game. He placed his hands out as if holding a bat, turned, and slid his right hand down the imaginary shaft.

"What? They won't have him bunt. Dad's too good to bunt."

David shrugged. *He isn't a team player, kid.*

The third-base coach resumed delivering his signs to the runners and batter.

A loud crack resounded throughout the park when John Barnes's bat connected with the pitch. The ball shot sharply to the outstretched glove of an alert third baseman. The Phillies' player quickly touched third base, doubling up the runner who had just left, and gunned the ball to first base. Just like that, the Phillies recorded a triple play. The inning was over. The stricken fans gazed at the opposition returning to its dugout.

The third-base coach kicked the dirt and stomped to the dugout.

John calmly retrieved his glove, and walked out to shortstop.

Must be too good to hustle, David thought.

Sam muttered. "Dad will hit that homerun next time. I just know it."

John Barnes came up to bat in the bottom of the ninth inning. The Phillies were leading the game, five to four. The bases were loaded, and there were two outs.

The pitcher delivered a throw, searing toward the outside of the plate. John swung at it, and sent it flying to the left field wall.

The crowd stood up and watched the ball soar toward the wall. Time slowed while hungry fans extended their arms toward the sky in anticipation of catching the homerun blast. The ball descended into the ecstatic crowd, and the frenzied fans fought to possess the prize. When the pushing, yelling, and hysteria settled, one person raised the ball in triumph. The crowd applauded when David Liberty lifted the ball in hand, high above his head. One fan, however, did not share in the applause.

John Barnes strode to the podium for the post-game press conference. Multiple voices calling his name and flashing cameras greeted him when he reached the microphone. He pointed to one of the reporters. They were all prepared with pens and recorders.

"John, how's it feel to be the youngest player to reach the four-hundred club?"

"It feels like the numbers and facts tell the story," John replied.

"What do you mean, John?"

"It's quite simple, I'm the best."

Many of the reporters nodded and murmured in agreement. Although the statement lacked any modesty, it was the truth. No one had accomplished what this superstar had.

"Hey, John," another shouted, "do you see yourself in a Padres uniform next year?"

"If they give me the best offer, then you'll see me here next year."

"Would you rather play for a team that's a contender?"

John chuckled. "I'd rather play with the team that has the biggest checkbook."

"Seriously, John, how does tonight's accomplishment add to your legacy?"

"As I said, gentleman, the stats don't lie. With a gold glove and the batting crown besides, I don't think there is another player in the league with my talent."

"Or with your humility," one reporter quipped. Then he said, "John, Stan Brooks from the *Sun-Times*. Can you tell us about the seventh inning?"

"Seventh inning? What're you talking about?"

"You know." Stan smirked. "When you apparently missed the bunt sign and hit into a triple play?"

"Bunt sign, my aching head, man! You don't ask the league's leading hitter to bunt! I'm the reason we won. What kind of question is that?"

"I thought I'd prepare you for when your teammates ask you the same question."

"Are you kidding me?" John's voice rose, and his face warmed. "They're happy about the outcome. This moment isn't about them; it's about me!" He stood defiantly, waiting for the next question. When no more questions or flashes came, he stepped down from the podium.

John heard a variety of good-byes from the reporters. "See you next game." "Great hit John!" "Hope you're here next year!" "Way to go, Johnny!" "Mr. Four Hundred." The comments meant nothing to him. He stomped out of the room. It was supposed to be a time of celebration, but he was not in the mood to be happy. His next thought was of calling his agent, Frank Stevens.

David and Sam fought their way through a mob to get to their vehicle. They got lost in the crowd and avoided being interviewed about their retrieval of the homerun ball. Once they hit the parking area, it was easier moving. The mob still flocked outside the main gates looking for the person who had caught the ball. David shook his head. He didn't know how they had managed to slip past all those watching eyes.

The doors to the limousine opened, and David and Sam climbed into the back seat.

Sam had not said two words since David caught the homerun ball. He stared out the window as the vehicle pulled out of the lot.

David welcomed the silent treatment and marveled at his good fortune. With any luck, Mr. Barnes would sign and date the baseball. David could not begin to imagine the worth of the ball. He could sell the ball and leave his current employer. His old entrepreneurial spirit weighed out the options.

His euphoria dampened when an inner voice interrupted his thought process. *What are you doing? How is this being a servant of anyone but yourself?* David reached into his pocket and gripped the seams of the baseball. It was real. He knew it. His mind struggled while his fingers rolled the ball over and over.

His thoughts drifted to his conversation with Joelle. His new task was unclear. Help people who needed help. Demonstrate his faith with his actions. He wondered what type of control existed on his actions. Could he be plucked out of this dream if his actions were detrimental to himself or others? Joelle's words danced in his mind: *You will be judged by those you help.*

Before he knew it, they had arrived at the Barnes' estate. David realized he had to focus his actions in the right direction.

When Sam exited the vehicle, David grabbed the boy and spun him around.

"What do you—?" Sam snapped.

David turned Sam's arm over and placed the homerun ball in his hand. He closed Sam's fingers around the ball.

Sam did not say a word. He stared at David.

David winked and ruffled Sam's hair.

Sam smiled and sprinted toward the house.

David waved. *I think I might catch on yet.*

Chapter Three

MONDAY AFTERNOON DAVID worked beside Mrs. Barnes. She had asked him the previous night if he would help her with the landscape she had designed. A local landscape service brought many plants to the Barnes residence, but the proposal for the cost of planting the various shrubs, flowers, and vegetation was outrageous.

Mrs. Barnes proved to be a great coworker. She was not afraid to get her nails dirty, dig holes, or lug heavy plants to their destination. Her enthusiasm was infectious, and David attempted to whistle while they slaved in the hot sun.

"Mr. Liberty, I want to thank you again for taking Sammy to the game. He's been in seventh heaven since he caught his father's homerun ball. Can you imagine that? Sammy catching his father's four-hundredth-homerun ball?"

David smiled and shook his head. *Why that little runt!*

"You know, he's so proud of that ball. I wish his father hadn't taken it from him. John claimed that it was his by right, and Sammy turned it over to him without an argument. He wants so much for his father to be proud of him." She sighed and dug more vigorously at the roots she was fighting. "Sometimes I wish I had never seen a baseball.

"Oh, never mind my belly-aching! You really must not talk so much, Mr. Liberty. We'll never get this work done with you running your gums so." She laughed at her attempt to make a joke and tossed a clump of dirt in his direction.

David grinned and scooped some lose dirt at Mrs. Barnes. He was surprised by the speed at which the sod and weeds suddenly pelted his body. She tossed everything within reach toward him, both arms spinning like a windmill. David recovered and returned fire. His aim was true. The sod caught his adversary in face and hair.

Mrs. Barnes could not hide her smile. "You're gonna pay for that!" She grabbed the watering can and headed toward David.

David dashed behind a flagpole. Mrs. Barnes ran to the right. David moved to the right. She moved to the left. David moved to the left. One thing was certain—David was not going to get wet.

David smiled and made funny gestures, indicating that he had persevered in their little game. His heart raced. He was mesmerized by the woman across from him. How long had it been since he had enjoyed the simple company of a woman? He was unaware of the jibes and threats that Mrs. Barnes was playfully yelling.

David ducked just in time. The watering can sped near his forehead. Mrs. Barnes stood still. She placed one hand on her hip, turned out her lead foot, and shook a pointed finger at David.

He did not hear a word. Her posturing and whole demeanor caught him off guard. *You are so beautiful.*

"Hey, Mom! Whatcha doing?" Sam's voice brought David out of his enchantment.

Mrs. Barnes's glance scolded David as she replied, "We're digging holes for the new shrubs."

What am I thinking? David turned away from mother and son.

"Yeah, right, Mom. Looks like you're having a water fight."

"Sam, what do you want?"

"Actually, I was wondering if David could play ball with us. We need one more player."

"We still have a lot of unfinished work to do, Sam."

"I just thought if you're done playing with him, maybe I could have a turn too." Sam's tone was innocent, but his eyes twinkled with the mischief of a seasoned prankster.

Mrs. Barnes's face flushed. "Go ahead, David. We'll finish this tomorrow."

David hesitated while he watched Sue Barnes leave. He hustled after Sam, relieved to escape the encounter with everything intact. He hoped.

Nine boys waited to play a baseball game. Sam's guest made their number an even ten. The boys could not agree on how they wanted to play. Where should the fielders play? Should the batting team supply the pitcher? Maybe David should be the all-time pitcher. They argued back and forth until Sam felt a tap on the shoulder.

"What?" Sam looked at David.

David tapped his index finger to his temple.

"You have an idea?"

David nodded and bent to the dirt, where he scratched the shape of a ball field. Through gestures and frustration, the boys managed to figure out what David was trying to tell them.

Everyone seemed OK with the format, and the game was soon underway. David and Sam were on opposite teams; for the boy had made it clear he did not want David on his side. Sam's team was in the field first. "You won't win," he said and took the pitcher's mound.

The game was never close. Sam's team members were methodical and precise in playing the game of baseball. They won the game by a significant margin, but Sam did not appear happy. He glared at David.

David captivated his teammates. They played hard and still lost. They laughed and cheered and enjoyed the game of baseball. The score of the game was not congruent with the way David's team celebrated. David noticed Sam frown and shake his head.

David waved good-bye to his young teammates, and they emphatically returned his wave.

He walked over to Sam and gave him a thumb's-up—"good game."

"Yeah. You too. Nice game."

Sam and David made their way back to the house. Sam stopped and studied David. "Who are you?"

David frowned.

"I mean, where are you from? Have you ever played baseball professionally?"

David smiled and shook his head.

"Will you play again tomorrow?"

David shrugged and swung his outstretched arm around the premises.

"Yeah, I know you have to help Mom, but will you play with us again? Please?"

David was taken back by the plea in the last question. He smiled, patted Sam on the back, and nodded.

Sam smirked. He waved good-bye and rushed up the steps and into his house.

Chapter Four

"SAMMY, TIME FOR dinner!" Sue hollered to her son.

Sam entered the room and plopped down in front of his plate. "Hi, Dad! What're you doing here? No practice tonight?"

John Barnes did not glance at his son and replied, "I've a meeting after supper."

"Maybe we could play some catch before your meeting."

"I doubt I'll have time."

Sue noticed the disappointment play across her son's face.

John lifted his head from the papers he was studying. "Sam, we'll have plenty of time to play ball once my season is done."

"Yeah, OK, Dad. I already played some ball today, anyway."

"Did you win?"

"Yeah, and I crushed the ball a couple of times. The other team even had Mr. Liberty on their team, and we still beat 'em."

"Who's Mr. Liberty?"

"You know, Dad. He's the gardener."

John made a noise of disgust. "The gardener? He is a gardener for a reason, Sam. When you have no talents or brains, that's the kind of life you lead."

Sue felt her cheeks warm. Her son came to David's defense before she found the words to reprimand her egotistical husband.

"I don't know, Dad. He definitely can play ball. You should've seen him out there. He even got Mark to hit the ball. There was something about the way he played. I can't explain it. It's almost as if he motivated his team to play better."

"I thought you said you won the game."

"We did, but we always win. I don't know. There was something different today. Anyway, Mr. Liberty might play again tomorrow, if he gets his work done around the house."

John looked at his son. "He might know how to play ball, but no one plays it like your old man."

"Yup, you're the best, Dad."

Sue noticed the tone that the statement carried, but her husband went back to reading without further comment.

"Mom? Do you think Mr. Liberty will get his work done tomorrow?"

"I'm not sure, Sam. We've got a lot of work to do."

"Yeah, well you wasted time with that water fight—"

"Sam." Her voice strained as she glanced over at her husband. "If you want to help us out, then maybe Mr. Liberty will get the chance to play."

"Fine." Sam placed his fork on his plate and stood up from the table. Giving his mom a dirty look and his father an imploring one, he left.

Sue stood as well and cleared the table. She noticed John glaring at her.

"Water fight?"

"It was nothing. A harmless water fight. It was so hot, and we were . . ." Sue fumbled for the right words.

"Were what? What were you, Sue?" John's temper surfaced.

"John, it was nothing."

"Nothing? You call flirting with the gardener nothing? I can't get my wife to sleep in my bed, and now you're flirting with another man? I just—"

"What about *my* needs, John?" Her voice rose. "Where's the man I married? The one who was going to be my partner and companion? Where did he go, John?"

"I'm out there providing for my family."

"You play a game, John. How does that provide for Sam and me, when you're always playing?"

"A game? Is that what you said?" John's voice grew eerily calm.

Sue knew it was too late to take her words back. "John, I'm sorry. I just think we—"

Her statement was cut off by another voice. "Hey, John! Is anybody home?" Frank Stevens walked into the dining room. "I hope I'm not interrupting, but the door was open, and I do have other meetings."

John's icy stare lingered on Sue for a few seconds before he turned to address his agent, "No, Frank, you are not interrupting at all. We're finished here." There was finality to his statement. "Let's go out to the gazebo."

Sue stood there as her husband turned his back and left the room without another word or look. Mr. Stevens paused. Sue was stunned by what she saw. His gaze was fixed on her eyes, and she stood paralyzed. A small grin crept to the corners of his mouth—an eerie look. A cold sensation trickled down her spine as she watched Mr. Stevens turn and leave.

After dinner, David returned to the garden to work on the landscaping. He figured if he could get enough of the work done this evening, he would have time to play baseball with Sam tomorrow. The sun was setting, but even in the twilight, he could accomplish much. He knelt, pulling weeds and scooping out dirt, and heard voices approaching from the house.

"I don't know about that, Frank." John Barnes's voice filtered to David's ears.

"I'm telling you, John, this is what you must do."

The second voice was distantly familiar to David. He dug and toiled in the earth and continued to eavesdrop in order to tag a fleeting memory.

"What about Sam?"

"If you show she is an unfit mother, you will get custody of your son."

David stopped digging and watched the two figures enter the gazebo. They did not notice his presence. David shifted more into the bushes and closer to the men.

"I've never believed in divorce," John said.

"Listen, your marriage is spiraling downward. It's only a matter of time before Sue asks you for a divorce. If you file for the divorce now, she won't be entitled to the contract you'll be signing. You remember the contract? The one that will make you the highest-paid player in the history of the game?"

The hair on the back of David's neck stood up while he listened to the voice of John Barnes's companion. His mind sounded an internal alarm, and David's heart thumped. He needed to get closer.

"Frank, I don't know. It seems so drastic."

"Are you really willing to throw away all you've worked for?"

David's quick breathing matched the pace of his heart. His muscles inched him closer to the gazebo, against the urge to retreat into the darkness. A strong smell of sulfur threatened to reveal his hiding place, forcing David to cover his mouth and nose to prevent him from coughing.

I need to get a quick look.

"John, your wife doesn't share your dream. Besides, you can have any woman you want. No one would turn down a date from John Barnes."

David cautiously parted the branches of the cedar bush where he was concealed. He could see John's face clearly, but Frank had his back turned.

"I really *could* be with anyone I wanted," John mused.

"That's right. Someone who appreciated your accomplishments and who was willing to put you first." Frank turned, offering David a view of his profile.

David squinted and stared hard, trying to make out Frank's facial features. Although the voice rang clearly in his mind, the man's silhouette offered no recognition. His imagination must be running wild. He sighed and relaxed.

"Did you hear something?" Frank twisted, scanning the surroundings.

"Just the wind. When should I serve Sue with the papers?"

Frank did not answer. He continued to search the shadows. He raised his head, as if testing the air. "I have papers in my car. You can give them to your wife tonight."

David heard no more of the conversation. Instead, he slipped back into the darkness. David pondered. There was something wrong about John's agent. It was more than the fact that Frank was persuading John to divorce his wife. David had felt—for a brief second—something evil radiating from the person standing in the gazebo.

David entered his small guest house and gathered his things. He stuffed his few belongings into a duffle bag and prepared to leave. *I have to get away for a while. Sam will be all right until I return. So will Sue.* Something fell out of his belongings and clinked on the floor. David reached forward to retrieve the small metal object. He stared at a wedding band. His eyes misted, and he struggled to hold back the tears.

Dear God, it can't be! What is this, how—? David dropped to his knees as the revelation struck. It was not Sam or Sue. It was John. John needed to be saved. *How could I have missed that?* David trembled. Things had gone too far. He couldn't help John now. *Dear God in heaven, what can I do?*

A voice echoed in his mind to answer his question. *David, listen to me. Listen to your heart.* Joelle's voice sang from a far-off place. *Look at your hand.*

David studied the wedding band in his palm. The marriage—that was the key. He panicked at the realization of what needed to be done. The covenant that John and Sue had made was where he needed to start. *How can I save their marriage when I couldn't save my own?*

With God all things are possible. Was it Joelle's voice or his? *What God has joined together, no human being must separate.*

David and Goliath:
The Guardian Angel Chronicles

David collapsed onto his bed. He had been unable to salvage his own marriage. His pride had kept him from reconciling with his wife. How could he keep John from making the same mistake?

As the tears spilled over, David prayed. He did not know what to say and was ashamed at his feeble attempt. Words did not formulate. The need was there, but he had so many needs, he did not know where to start.

With anxiety, David knelt beside his bed. He reflected on the situation and blocked the question of his own sanity. Wherever he was, whenever he was, all he could do was accept the situation. These days of feeling alive had been a gift beyond repayment. His new lease on life could be canceled at any second. He knew it was time to focus on others. He did not want another person to experience the agony he had felt with the breakup of his family. Be a servant.

A simple prayer left his heart. *Your will be done, Lord.*

David sat in the silence and waited for an answer. He could hear the crickets chirp in the night, and his mind remembered the times with a family, a family God had blessed him with: laughter, smiles, and love. He saw children running, playing "bean ball" with their father and mother; a wife that entwined her fingers with his and looked into his eyes like no other could.

David saw a family playing kickball in the backyard, children calling each other names, sometimes in jest and sometimes not; a puppy chewing on soft, pink hands; the campout in the yard, an emptied tent, and children nestled warmly in their own beds. Christmas morning and presents neatly wrapped under a tree, to be quickly shredded by excited fingers. Church on Sunday. Bedtime prayers.

The birds sang when dawn broke through the horizon. David opened his eyes and knew it was time to save a family. Arrogance and pride had formed some deep roots, and it was time to do some weed control. David stood. An answer boomed in his soul, causing him to stagger.

Play ball!

Chapter Five

SUE BARNES DRIED her eyes with a tissue. She had waited in her husband's room last night, determined to show John that she loved him. John never appeared; at least he had never entered the bedroom. However, he *had* returned to the house sometime during the night. She held the proof in her hands. Divorce papers greeted her in the morning, resting neatly on the kitchen counter. She hoped her son had not noticed them lying there.

Sue could not decide when John and she began drifting apart. Now, she felt defeated; knew the situation was hopeless. She folded the papers and stuffed them into her back pocket. Then she took her work gloves and headed outside.

Sue headed to her landscaping project. Her mind and body felt numb. She had always considered herself a strong woman, but she did not know if she had the strength to survive the coming storm.

Sam's voice brought Sue back to her surroundings. He and Mr. Liberty were diligently working side by side. She stopped and stared in amazement at her son. He placed a juniper in the ground and packed the red soil around its base.

Sue cleared her throat.

Sam turned and flashed his mother a big grin. "Good morning, Mom. Are you ready to dig in? Get it? Dig. In?"

"Sam?" Sue shook her head in disbelief. "What are you doing?"

"I'm helping you and Mr. Liberty. You said if you got the work done we could play baseball."

"Baseball!" Sue's anger surfaced. "Let me tell you something, young man—"

Before she could finish the sentence, David knelt before her, holding a single white rose.

"Mr. L-Liberty, what are you d-doing?" Sue stuttered.

David stood up. He gripped the rose in a closed fist and made a small circle with it around his heart. He handed the rose to Sue and pulled a baseball out of his back pocket. David pointed to himself, Sam, and then directly at Sue.

"What? Are you mad? I'm not going to play some silly game. It's absurd! I've had enough baseball to last me a lifetime."

David strode over to where his shovel leaned against a shrub. He grabbed the shovel and tossed it to the ground, folding his arms across his chest.

"Oh, really? You're going to quit if I don't play? Is that it?"

David nodded.

"Fine. You're fired." Sue turned her back on him.

"Mom, don't!" Sam hollered.

Sue felt something on her shoulders and a strong grip spun her around. "Mr. Liberty! What are you—?"

David reached around to Sue's back pocket. He pulled the divorce papers from their hiding place. He intently stared into Sue's eyes.

"Hey. How did you—what are you doing?"

David returned the papers to her pocket and pulled the baseball out again, displaying it in front of Sue's face. His gaze became imploring. His other hand gripped her shoulder, transferring calm and confidence with his touch.

Sue's eyes misted. "I don't understand."

David placed the ball in her palm. He pointed to himself, to Sam, and to Sue, tapping her outstretched ball in hand.

"You really want me to play baseball with you?"

Sam piped in, "Come on, Mom. It'll be fun."

Sue could not comprehend what was happening. Her yardman was insisting she play baseball. It made no sense. How did he know about the papers in her back pocket? Had he secretly been watching her, or had he been with John when the papers were placed on the table? What disturbed her was that David knew the content of the papers. She was sure of it.

"I'll see how I feel after we finish our work."

Her response seemed to appeal to David. He picked up the shovel and returned to his project.

"We'll get the work done, won't we, Mr. Liberty?" Sam scrambled back to his work.

David nodded and playfully tossed a shovel load of dirt in Sam's direction. Then he turned his gaze toward Sue, as if to say, "Everything will be OK."

The three of them worked side by side throughout the morning. By lunchtime, the work Sue had planned for the day was completed. It was impossible that so much work had been finished in so short a time. She looked around in awe then mumbled, "I guess after lunch we can play baseball."

"All right, Mom!" Sam hollered. "Did you hear that, Mr. Liberty? Mom's gonna play ball with us!"

John swung the bat and whiffed.

"Come on, John! You're pulling your head every single time. Keep your head with the bat and attack down on the ball."

John's focus was not on batting practice. He had not been able to convince himself that a divorce was in his best interest. "Shut yer mouth. I know how to hit the ball. Everybody knows I can hit the ball."

"Stop foaming at the gums and show me you can back up your talk," John's batting coach replied in disgust. He mumbled under his breath, "Arrogant jackass."

"What did you say to me?" John chucked the bat against cage, where his coach stood. He stomped over, grasped the net and placed his face near the barrier. "You got something you wanna say, Ron?"

Ron crossed his arms and stewed in silence.

"Yeah. I thought so, you fat bag of wind. Trying to teach me, when you never played in the big leagues."

The rest of the batting participants stopped to observe the confrontation. They milled closer to hear the two combatants and witness the outcome. The Padres' manager tossed down his clipboard and walked over to the batting cage.

Ron flushed and responded, "Yeah, Mr. Big Shot. You think we all got to bow at the feet of the great John Barnes. Truth is, not one guy on this team likes you."

"Likes me? Who gives a rip if they like me or not? I can hit the ball."

"You're not a team player," Ron said. "You used to be, but you're not anymore."

"Are these guys gonna help me get a new contract, Ron?" He swept his arm, signaling at the rest of his teammates. "Nah, I don't think so."

"Yeah, we're all hoping you get a new contract. And a new team to go with it."

John snapped. He scrambled to exit the batting cage with the intent of tearing Ron apart. Before he could get to his antagonist's throat, a blow froze his diaphragm, and he was driven to the ground. John fought to free himself, but too many hands prevented him from moving. His teammates smothered him to the ground.

"Johnny, settle down now." The voice of the manager filtered through the bodies that restrained him. "Just settle down, will ya?"

John's chest heaved, and his muscles became rigid with the stress of being restrained. He tried to flail and head-butt his assailants. Once he realized it was useless to continue to struggle, his body went limp. "All right. I'm OK now. Just let me go." His head drooped.

"Johnny, why don't you call it a day and hit the showers?"

"Yeah. Sure, Skip." John felt the hands slip away, and he was free to move. He kept his head down and headed for the lockers.

Emotionally and physically, John Barnes was exhausted. He slumped against the tiled wall and let warm water beat down his neck and back. He could not remember ever feeling so low. He was on the verge of receiving the biggest contract of his career. Frank had told him the numbers the Giants had proposed, but John was not sure he even cared. He slammed his hand against the wall over and over again in frustration. Facing upward, with eyes closed and the shower striking his skin, he shouted, "Help me! Please help me, dear God!"

He continued to stand in the shower, waiting for some type of revelation. There was none. John turned off the shower. He dried himself, dressed in his street clothes, and left the locker room.

Frank was leaning against a Mercedes-Benz®. "John, I think I have another offer on the table. Looks like the Dodgers are interested in your bat and glove."

"Hmmph. Are they interested in *me*?"

"What? What kind of question is that? Stop sulking and get your head in the game. Let's go to the house and finalize things with your wife. We don't want any loose ends."

"How much?" John wanted to know.

"We haven't agreed on a solid number yet. You still have six weeks left in the season. You need to set yourself apart from the team even more. The more you stand out, the more money the Dodgers will spend."

"My numbers are already tops."

Frank smiled and slapped John on the back. "Yes, indeed they are. Come on, let's go tie up those lose ends."

The car ride was a blur. Frank continued to talk, but John did not listen to a single word. He struggled with his own unhappiness. He was the best at what he did, so why was he so distraught?

The car pulled into the estate, and John noticed a ball game being played on his personal field. "Looks like Sam has another game going. Pull down there. I want to see my son play ball."

"You can watch Sam play anytime. Let's take care of business first."

"Come on! Just a few minutes. I wanna to see my kid hit." John could not remember the last time he had seen Sammy hit the ball or the last time he had not blindly followed Frank's lead. "Five minutes. Then we finish our business."

"Deal."

The two men exited the vehicle and walked over to where the boys were playing, except the boys were not just boys. A man and a woman were playing too—Sue and the gardener.

John's face heated as he watched another man interact with his wife and son. All three were laughing and carrying on without him. He clenched his fists at his sides and remembered the "innocent" water-fight story. A stranger was playing ball with Sammy and hitting on his wife. "She's still my wife!" John hissed through clenched teeth.

"Ah, yes. Looks like your wife didn't waste any time mourning her loss." Frank smirked.

John did not reply. He strode across the field, walking at first, but then his legs carried him faster and faster, causing the boys to stop playing. "Get away from my wife!" John shouted. He shoved David hard, slamming him against the bench.

"Dad! What are you doing?" Sam hollered.

Sue screamed and confronted her enraged husband. "John Barnes! What on earth are you doing?" Sue glanced toward David. "Sammy, is he all right? Are you all right, David?"

"*David*, is it?" John growled. He pushed his wife to one side and towered over the collapsed gardener. "You're fired, mister. Get up and fight, you home-wrecker!"

"John, what has gotten into you? Are you insane?" Sue grasped John's arm and tried to tug him away from the fallen man.

"Dad! We're playing baseball, just playing baseball. Mr. Liberty was going to teach me how to be as good as you, Dad."

"*I* should be teaching you, Sam. Not some dirt digger."

Sue's voice remained hard. "You're never here for your son. Go ahead and teach him, John. Teach your son how to play baseball."

John glared at his wife. Tears streamed down her cheeks. Her eyes pleaded with him while she braced her palm against her husband's chest. John remained infuriated. He did not move, but his eyes took in the scene of young boys anxiously watching. One young boy was helping the gardener to his feet. It was his *son*! He gritted his teeth.

Sam helped Mr. Liberty up and stood defiantly in front of the gardener like an impenetrable shield.

"Sue." John's voice trembled. He pointed at David. "I don't want him here any longer, around you or Sam."

"You don't even know this man," Sue protested. "He means us no harm."

"Boy, it doesn't look that way to *me*, John." Frank stepped up and clasped his hand on John's right shoulder.

David's heart skipped. For a moment, his whole body froze, and he broke out in a cold sweat. Recognition flooded through him when he saw Frank Stevens in the light. *Dr. Stevens!*

"What?" Frank turned to David. His eyes narrowed. "Why do you call me by that name?" He studied David's face. "You! What are you doing here?"

"Huh? Who are you talking to, Frank? Do you know this man?" John nodded in David's direction.

"Fire him, John. As your agent and your friend, I'm ordering you to fire him."

Sue came to David's defense. "John can't fire David. I'm his employer."

"Sue, stay out of this," John ordered.

Frank Stevens stormed past John. He pushed Sue and Sam out of his way and confronted David. "You shouldn't be here. What are you doing?"

Playing baseball. David's body no longer trembled. A strange calm controlled his emotions. *I recognize you, Frank. Or should I call you "Dr. Stevens"? Where's my cross and chain?*

Frank ignored David's questions and continued the conversation mentally. *Do you really think you can stop what I have set in motion? You're too late. John Barnes is mine. I care nothing for the other two. I can collect them at another time in the future.*

You have no claim on him, David challenged.

Ah, but you're wrong. John is willing to sell his very soul to be the best there is. And I am willing to buy it.

David was puzzled. *I don't believe you.*

Ask your Lord. He allows me to take him.

Something was amiss. David could not fathom how to argue or battle with Dr. Stevens. His knowledge of the Scriptures was weak.

I will finish what has begun. Stevens turned to leave.

Play me for him. David's words came without hesitation.

Stevens turned and smiled. He spoke aloud. "What do you propose?"

Baseball. A game of baseball. Your team against mine.

"And where is your team? This team of boys?" Frank extended his arm toward the boys around him. "This is your 'team'?"

David nodded.

"What are the stakes?"

If we win, I become John Barnes's agent. If we lose, you remain his agent.

"I'm his agent now. What are you willing to sacrifice?" Stevens opened his arms and hands to receive a gift.

David shivered. His mouth felt dry. He licked his lips. *You will take me for your master if we lose.*

Stevens nodded. "It is done. We play tomorrow tonight at seven at PETCO Park®." He walked away.

David remained still, stunned at the agreement. That was not enough time! He collapsed to his knees. *Dear God, have I done the right thing? Joelle? Can you hear me?*

Sam interrupted David's thoughts. "Mr. Liberty? What's wrong?"

Sue helped David stand. "That was strange. Frank was talking to you as if you were responding."

David responded with the first words his lips had uttered in a long time. "I was." Hearing his own voice was as much of a jolt to himself as it was to the people around him.

"Mr. Liberty! You can talk!" Sam exclaimed.

"What the heck just happened?" John's voice boomed. He shouted at Frank Stevens, "Where are you going? What's going on?"

Stevens waved his hand, got in his car, and drove away.

David reached out and touched John on the shoulder to get his attention. He went straight to the point. "Mr. Barnes, my name is David Liberty, and I would like to be your agent." David had no time to wonder about the return of his voice, but knew he needed to make the most of the gift.

John laughed. "What are you, crazy? I *have* an agent. I thought you couldn't speak. What are you trying to pull, anyway? Get your hand off me." He swatted David's hand aside and went into a defensive position.

"David," Sue asked, "What's going on? Have you been able to talk all along? Were you deceiving me all this time?"

David looked into Sue's eyes and then at the faces of the boys around him. "John Barnes, I challenge you to a hitting contest."

John looked surprised. "What? You're crazy! I think you've been struck once too often with a baseball bat, buddy."

"I don't think you can beat me." David attacked John's ego.

"You're on, dirt boy! I'll take you to the cleaners."

"You will take the best of three hits. I will take only one."

"Did you say I get to take the best of three, and you only get one attempt?"

"Yes. Sam will toss the ball, and Sue will mark the hits." David winked at mother and son. "Is that acceptable with you two?"

Sue and Sam frowned, but nodded.

"So, what do I win?" John's question was smug and direct.

"If you win, I quit. If I win, you play for my team tomorrow tonight and hear me out. That's all I ask."

"Deal," John snapped. "Let's get this show on the road." He walked over to the bench, picked out a bat, and strolled to the batter's box. He did not question the conditions of the wager. "C'mon! Let's give you a taste of humble pie."

David grabbed the balls and handed one to Sam. "Sam, throw your dad good pitches he can smash."

"Mr. Liberty, what are you doing?"

David placed a finger on Sam's lips. "Just trust me."

"But you can't outhit Dad!" Sam shook his head and took his place on the mound. The other boys moved out into the field. Sue directed where they should stand to help her mark the ball.

"Hey, David!" John bellowed, "Is it where it hits or where it stops rolling?"

"Where it hits," David answered.

"All right. Sue, did you hear that?"

Sue waved her hand in answer.

"Son, toss me a ball and watch your old man crush it." John mechanically signed the cross and got into his batting stance.

Sam tossed his father a pitch.

John smacked all three balls. Each successive hit traveled farther than the previous one.

Sue and the boys marked the longest hit.

John went out to gloat over his performance. "Sammy, this hit would have been way out of any ballpark in the majors. I bet it traveled over 600 feet! Maybe farther than Mickey Mantle's record." He turned and hollered at David, "Might as well throw in the towel, buddy. Ain't nobody on this planet beating that mark."

David politely waved, whispered instructions to Sam, and walked toward the batter's box.

Sam trotted to the outfield. "Mom, Mr. Liberty said you better back up quite a bit from where Dad hit the ball. He doesn't want you to miss the mark."

John laughed. "What game is that fool playing?"

Sue nodded and moved deeper out in the field.

"Yeah, hon, that's it. You keep walking backwards. I think I'll move up toward the infield." John strode to shallow left field.

Sam returned to the mound. "Are you ready, Mr. Liberty?"

David nodded and smiled. "Give me some speed, Sammy."

"If you say so." Sam went into his windup and mumbled, "Hope you know what you're doing."

David swung and met the pitch. The ball shot out fast, carrying well over John's head. The ball continued to rise and rise. When it reached its apex, the ball descended, accelerating toward the ground. Sue dashed across and out of the field to meet the ball. When the ball struck, she was only seconds behind and stood to mark the ball.

The small group eventually surrounded the ball. No one spoke. David arrived last. He bent down, picked up his prize, and placed the ball in John's hand.

John was too stunned for words. He looked at David and then at the ball. Gingerly he rolled the ball over in his hands and gaped at the words: "John Barnes 400th." His gaze flicked from the ball to David and finally back to home plate. Then he dropped to one knee and held his stomach.

David placed a hand on John's shoulder and said, "Through God, all things are possible. It's time for us to talk. Plus, we have a ball game to get ready for."

"A ball game?" John shook his head. "What on earth just happened? Did anybody else see how far he clobbered that ball?"

"Tomorrow evening at seven, we play a baseball game at PETCO Park®. Everyone here will—"

"Wait a minute. All these kids get to play?"

This time, when David opened his mouth, no words were formed. Taking a deep breath, he tried to speak again. Nothing. No more words left his lips. He could only nod in affirmation.

Sam was quick to notice. "What's a matter, Mr. Liberty? Did you lose your voice again?"

David shrugged and nodded. He struggled to hold back tears of frustration.

"Hold on! Just hold on for one minute! How the heck did you hit that ball so far? No one could hit a ball that far. No one!" John shook his head. "I saw it and don't believe it. And with my baseball, the one I hit my four-hundredth homerun with. It's under lock and key in my showcase. I don't understand."

Sue stepped beside John and slipped her arm around him. "John, it must be a sign."

"A sign? What kind of sign?" John sounded confused.

Sue tightened her grasp on her husband and glanced at David. "You want all of us to play in this ball game, David?"

David nodded once, with deliberation and need.

"What is the importance of this game, David?"

David approached John and Sue. He took Sue's left hand and firmly but cautiously grasped John's left wrist. He laced husband and wife's hands together and enveloped them with his own hands. *Come on, Sue!*

John tried to disengage his hand, but David held him fast.

"Does this have something to do with our marriage?" Sue whispered.

John continued to struggle. "Sue," he hissed, "what did you tell him?"

David ignored John and nodded at Sue. Letting go, he stepped back and raised his index finger, signaling "wait." He motioned for Sam to come forward. David placed his hands on Sam's shoulders and faced him toward John and Sue.

"Sam?" John asked. "What does Sam have to do with this?"

David's eyes narrowed. He pointed at each family member then brought his hands together tightly.

John said, "Yeah, but what . . . ?"

David ripped his hands apart and brushed them three times.

John stepped backwards.

Sue understood. "Our family will be broken." She turned to John. "Is this what you want for your son?"

"Dad, can we all go play?" Sammy did not remain quiet anymore.

There was a long moment before John answered. He scratched his head and said, "I *did* lose the bet. Might as well play some ball together."

Chapter Six

JOHN WAS PERPLEXED about everything that had transpired. None of it made sense. There were too many questions without answers. The lowly gardener wanted to save a marriage. David had outhit the best hitter in professional baseball and acted like it was no big deal. There was no cheering, no gloating, and no self-admiration. David had expected to outhit him. Who was this man that struck a ball farther than possible for any human being? And how did he get the ball from John's showcase?

John realized he wanted to play in the ball game. He did not know why, but something stirred within his being. Things had not felt right since leaving the divorce papers on the dining room table for Sue to find.

He slipped into his night robe and made his way, rather slowly, across the landing to the door of his wife's room. His heart pounded. Beads of sweat dripped off his forehead and blanketed the palms of his hands. He stared at the barrier, unsure what to do. Try as he might, he could not reach forward to grasp the doorknob or knock against the solid birch door. It had taken all his courage to make it this far; he had no energy left to continue the journey.

The door swung open, and he stared into the eyes of his wife.

Sue gasped. "John! You startled me!"

"I . . . I'm sorry," he hesitated. "I didn't mean to scare you. I thought . . . well, never mind. I just wanted to—"

"Wanted to what?"

John looked away. "About the papers . . ."

"Let's not stand where Sammy might hear us." Sue walked into her room. "Come in and shut the door."

John's heart continued to hammer but he found the courage to follow Sue into her room and shut the door. "Sue, about the papers . . ."

She whirled. "Is that what you really want? You don't want to be married anymore?"

John could not meet his wife's eyes. He was so sure the night before that he wanted a divorce. What Frank said made complete sense. It was time to cut the ties with this marriage, time to get out now, before he signed a big contract.

Before he could find a way to answer her question, Sue asked another. "Don't you love me?"

Startled, he looked at his wife's face, but remained speechless, unable to answer her.

"Let me hear you say it," Sue said. "Tell me you no longer love me, and I'll sign the papers right now."

Her poise enhanced her beauty. John struggled to say the words that would not come. Sue coolly waited for him to say something.

"That was some hit the gardener had, wasn't it?" he blurted.

Sue smiled. "Yes, I'd have to say it was the greatest hit I've ever seen."

"I don't think it's possible for a human being to hit a baseball that far."

Sue moved closer. "Maybe Mr. Liberty isn't human."

John forced a nervous laugh. "What? Are you crazy? What kind of statement is that?"

"I mean, I think his hit was some kind of a miracle."

"Miracle? Why would you call it that?" John wetted his lips, and his wife inched closer.

"After the emotional roller coaster I've been on today, I think it's a wonder we're standing here right now." Sue placed her hand against John's chest. "To think that a simple man could outhit the best hitter in baseball."

John's face warmed and he removed Sue's hand. "Sue, I'm really confused right now. I don't even know what I want." He studied her face. Tears filled her eyes and she looked away. "I'll see you tomorrow. At the game. I will honor the bet I made with the gardener, although I'm sure it has nothing to do with you and me."

John retreated from the bedroom and shut the door. He longed to embrace his wife. He wanted his family to remain intact, but he was afraid that nothing would be the same again.

David communicated the best he could during the van ride to PETCO Park®. He was pleased that the players knew the signs, the positions they would play, and their order in the lineup. He was, however, unable to convey any more about the meaning and importance of tonight's game. He smiled while the team sang, "Take Me Out to the Ball Game."

He would pitch and John would play catcher. Sue would take first base, using her reach and glove skills to anchor the position. The rest of the boys would cover the infield and outfield. Three adults and seven boys made up the team. David wondered what kind of team Stevens had assembled.

David and his hodge-podge team entered the first-base side dugout. They were the home team.

John mumbled, "I'm going to take the boys out and warm them up."

David nodded. He emptied the equipment bag and organized the bats, helmets, and catcher's gear. He hung the last helmet and glanced out to the mound. There stood Stevens, waiting impatiently.

David forced his legs to carry him at a normal pace. He did not want to seem overanxious. He passed his players and heard Sam talking to his friends.

"Look, Mark. There's Gary Smith. He's playing catch with Stew Jackson. And there's Drew Jones and Cliff Henderson."

Stevens had brought professional players. How he was able to get them on such short notice David had no idea. He climbed the mound and faced his opponent.

"Sooo . . . what do you think of my team?" Stevens smirked.

I see only six players, and you need seven.

"I will be the seventh. We don't need a full team. Your boys and woman are non-factors. Why is John out there with your boys?"

I think you are forgetting Someone.

Stevens' countenance darkened. "He has no power here. To interfere would breach the covenant of free will. Would it not?"

I know you would lie if it suits your cause.

Stevens glowered at David. "You have much to learn. It will be my pleasure to teach you after I win this game. I will instruct both you and Mr. Barnes what it means to serve me." He strolled off the mound and into the third-base dugout.

David clapped his hands to get the attention of his team. Boys and adults hustled over to the mound.

"Are we really going to play ball with these pros, Mr. Liberty?"

David smiled and ruffled Sam's red hair. The boys did not realize that this event was much more than just a baseball game. David knew it was best that way. The boys would feel no pressure. The pressure would be on *him*.

David stabbed his fist out and the team gathered in, slapping their hands on top of one another.

John glanced at David, "OK boys. On the count of three, we shout 'team.' One, two, three!"

"Team!" they chorused together.

The boys sprinted out to their positions. Sue and John remained on the mound with David.

"David, I hope there are no delusions of grandeur here. There's no way our team can play at the level of these pros. I hope you're planning on just enjoying the game and not winning. It would take a miracle the size of your hit to beat this team." John kept his voice low. "I made a bet and will honor it, but don't think I will enjoy this."

David felt twinges of despair. If he could only talk! He was sure he could motivate the team to give one-hundred percent, but even one-hundred percent might not be enough.

He tapped his glove hand on John's shoulder and pointed to John's and Sue's hearts. He then pointed to the sky.

Sue glanced at her husband, who simply shrugged. "We don't understand, David. Maybe we should forget this part."

David grimaced. He motioned Sue to take off her baseball glove and hold out her hand. In one quick movement, David snatched her hand and tugged her wedding band from her finger.

"Give that back!" Bewilderment rang in Sue's voice.

John shouted, "Hey, what are you doing?"

David acted as if to throw the ring away, causing both husband and wife to yell, "No!"

He stopped in mid-throw and placed a hand to his ear. *What?*

Sue grabbed David's arm and wrestled to retrieve her band. "Give me my ring!"

David brushed her aside and held the ring up in front of John's face. *Take the ring*! David's thoughts shouted.

Paralyzed, John stared at the wedding ring inches from his face.

Sue stopped struggling.

Take the ring! David pushed John backwards and held the ring in his open hand. He kept Sue braced behind him with his other arm, glared at John, and nodded at the ring.

With shaking fingers, John reached out and took the ring from David. He held it up, staring until his eyes misted. John blinked through the tears and his gaze found his wife.

David held Sue in front of him and splayed out the fingers of her left hand.

John's body trembled and he stepped to Sue. He removed David's hand with his own and looked into his wife's eyes. Tears streaked down his cheek and he placed the ring on her finger.

David embraced the couple and placed his forehead against Sue's and John's. He gently split up their reunion, winked at Sue, and nodded toward first base. He watched her wipe her face on sleeve, smile, and hustle over to her position. David spun to face John. He grinned and nodded toward home plate.

John returned David's grin and hurried to the catcher's position. He faced David, slammed his fist into the mitt a few times, and crouched into his stance. "All right! Let's play some ball, boys!"

David retired the first three batters. The speed and control of his throws rivaled any of the major league pitchers.

In the bottom of the first inning, David stood by first base, acting as coach. Sue was the first batter. She took three practice swings before she stood in the batter's box.

Frank Stevens crouched in his catcher's position, waiting for the pitch. "Hey, sweet cheeks, let's see how lucky you are at the plate."

Sue watched the first pitch, all the way to the catcher's mitt.

"Strike one!"

She stepped out of the box, swung the bat back and forth, took a deep breath, and stepped back into the box. The second pitch was on its way—speeding like the first—and it smacked into Stevens' mitt.

"Strike two!"

"So I heard you're available." Frank's tone was laced with sarcasm. He tossed the ball back to the pitcher's mound. "How about you and I going out after this for a victory celebration?" He squatted and made the noise of a kiss with his lips.

Sue's temper flared. She swung blindly at the next pitch.

"Strike three!"

She clomped back to the dugout, and the ridicule of Stevens' laugh followed like her shadow.

Sam did not fare any better his first time at bat. Three pitches and three strikes made the second out. When Sam returned to the dugout he said, "Dad! There's no way I can hit one of those pitches. They're way too fast!"

Mark was up next. David waved him over for some quick advice. David took Mark's bat, then squatting low, got into a batting stance. Mark nodded in agreement and hustled to the plate.

Their ploy worked. After six pitches, Mark was on his way to first base. The pitcher was unable to throw the ball in Mark's small strike zone. Mark was still trembling with fear when he stepped on the base pad. He managed a grin when David ruffled his hair and thumped him on the back.

John stood calmly at home plate. He looked at David, who went through a variety of hand movements.

The defense shifted their players. They knew John's tendencies.

"So, your wife said she'd go out with me tonight, champ," Frank said.

"Is that the best you got?" John replied as he made the sign of the cross and went through his pre-batting ritual.

Frank's face darkened. "I'm sure my best will be better than yours."

"Watch and learn, rookie."

The pitch flew toward home plate. John hesitated a split-second then accelerated the bat, smacking the ball toward short stop. The ball glanced off of the fielder's glove and sped toward the center-field wall.

Mark ran as fast as his young legs would carry him as the ball rolled to the fence. He made it safely to third base. John stood at second.

It was David's turn to bat. He walked up to home plate and examined the field. This might be one of the only times during the game his team had a chance to score. He was determined not to waste the opportunity.

"Are you ready for an eternity of servitude?" Stevens asked, squatting behind home plate.

Why don't you let me know how you're *preparing for it?*

Stevens stood up from his crouched stance, removed his catcher's mask, and glared at David. "I'm not sure who you are, exactly, or why you're here, but I will relish having you tell me all about it, after you lose this game."

I'm not here to lose. David was confident. For the first time in years, he demonstrated an act of faith.

Stevens did not reply. He returned to his crouched position, replaced his mask, and signaled or the pitch.

David watched the first pitch zip across the plate.

"Strike one!"

The second pitch was a mistake. David uncoiled and launched the ball to deep left field, where it struck the wall and bounced back into the field of play.

Mark and John both crossed home. The boys cheered as David dashed around third base.

David sprinted toward home, where Stevens stood blocking the plate. David lowered his shoulder right as the ball smacked into the catcher's glove. Stevens landed hard on his back.

David reached instinctively for the plate. His fingers touched the corner, but to no avail. The catcher had the ball.

"You're out!" the umpire screamed.

David bounced to his feet and offered a hand to assist Stevens. *Need some help?*

Stevens ignored the gesture. He stood, handed the umpire the ball, and walked away. "There will be no help for you."

David brushed off the dirt and ran, clapping his hands in celebration to the cheers from his team. Two runs. Would they be enough? His team grabbed their gloves and ran out to their positions.

Top of the second inning Stevens batted while a runner stood on first base. He spoke to John, who crouched behind the plate. "So, why are you playing against me? I have the power to negotiate the biggest contract in baseball history as your agent. I thought that was what you wanted."

"I'm not sure what I want. Let's finish this game, and then we'll talk. Besides, I lost a bet and I'm honoring the payment."

"Things may change after this game."

"Why?"

The pitch traveled toward John's outstretched glove, but it never touched leather. Stevens sent the baseball flying over the left-field wall.

One pitch and it was a tie game.

The top of the third inning no runs were scored, but the opposing team connected with more of David's pitches.

David jogged off the mound and was met by John. "Is your arm going to make it?"

David shook his arm out and made small circles with his shoulder. His elbow remained bent and his fist closed. He tilted his head to the side and shrugged his shoulders.

"If you get to the point where you're done, give me a thumb's-down."

David nodded, but he prevented John from going into the dugout by grasping his forearm.

"What?"

David nodded to the bench, where a bunch of dejected boys sat, some with chins resting in hands; others had their hat brims pulled down to cover their face.

"Uh-oh. Looks like we need to give 'em a pep talk, right, coach?"

David nodded and poked John in the chest with his index finger. *You'll have to; I'm still unable to speak.*

"Are you nuts? What do I say to them? 'Don't worry, boys. They're pros. You're not supposed to be able to hit the ball.'"

David sighed. He tugged John into the dugout and clapped his hands repeatedly, getting the team's attention. He signaled with one finger to "wait a minute," and stooped to take the shoelace out of his shoe.

John addressed the boys. "What's the matter, gang?"

Sam piped up. "Dad, none of us can hit those pitches. They're way too fast. We can't all squat low and hope for a walk like Mark. You'd think they'd toss the ball slower for us. It's just a game."

"I know, son, I'm afraid there's—"

David interrupted John by resting a hand on his shoulder. In his other hand he held the loose shoe string. David strutted around with hands tucked into his armpits, flapping.

"What are you, some kind of bird?" John asked.

David nodded and raised his finger to indicate "wait." He got down on all fours and acted as if he were howling into the sky.

"Now a dog . . . right, Mr. Liberty?" Sammy asked.

David nodded.

"Are we doing charades?" asked Sue, perplexed as the rest of the group.

David nodded an emphatic "yes." He pointed at John then himself, and got down on both knees. He demonstrated with his hands that John was very big and that he, David, was small. David took the shoelace and twirled it round and round over his head. He abruptly stopped, picked up a small stone and carried it to John's forehead. He glanced hopefully at his observers.

"You're shooting something from a helicopter?" John asked.

David frowned and shook his head.

"David and—" Sue started.

"Goliath!" Sam finished eagerly

David nodded.

"I get it." Sue verbalized her thoughts. "We are David, and the other team is Goliath."

"And David beat Goliath, right, Mom?"

"Who are David and Goliath?" Mark's inquiry saved others from the team from asking the same question.

"They are characters from a story in the Bible," John answered. "David was a small farmer of sheep, and Goliath was a giant soldier in an army. Goliath challenged any man from his enemies to fight him. All were too afraid except the boy David. David took his simple sling and went out to fight the giant soldier."

"And he won?" Mark interrupted.

"Yep, he won. He wore his shepherd's clothes and faced an armored soldier. The story states that David won with the help of God."

Nobody spoke. The boys looked at each other, unsure what to make of the analogy.

"Batter up!" the umpire yelled.

"Mr. Liberty? Are you saying we can hit the ball and even win this game with help from God?" Sam asked.

David clenched his fists, pumped his arms, and nodded. He went over to Sam for a "high five." Sam hesitated then grinned and struck David's open palm. David journeyed down the line of boys, receiving energetic slaps from their outstretched hands.

The boys hooted and hollered their excitement, bouncing around and slapping each other with high fives. They yelled encouragement to Rob, their center fielder, who chose a bat and ran to the batter's box. "Here we go, Robby. Here we go!" Two claps and two stomps followed the cheer.

Rob struck out. He managed to foul three pitches and showed the boys that contact could be made with the speeding fastball.

"He's not so fast," Rob said, receiving slaps of congratulations and "good job" as he returned to the dugout.

It was back to the top of the order and Sue's turn to bat.

Stevens squatted behind the plate. "Your team seems awfully happy, especially for one that's going to lose."

"I don't think we're going to lose." Sue was positive. "And why are you so intent on winning the game, anyway?"

"Oh, I don't know. I think winning the game will be rewarding to me in the long run. Plus, my dear, your faith is severely misplaced. Your pitcher is beginning to tire, and we have six innings to go."

Sue readied for the pitch. "As is my husband's faith in *you*." She whipped the bat when the ball flashed in. Wood connected with cork, and the ball scooted safely between the short stop and third baseman. She stood safely on first and nodded at her cheering team.

Sam hit a slow grounder to third base, sacrificing his mother to second base. An errant throw and Sam stood on first, his mother on third.

"Great job, son!" John hollered. He looked over his shoulder, pointed his bat at Sam, and nodded with a wink and grin.

He stepped into the batter's box.

Frank asked for a time-out and strolled out for a conference with his pitcher. He returned and bent to his position. "Good luck. Try not to hit the ball to Cliff."

John swatted the first pitch right to Cliff, who made a casual play to second, forcing Sam out. John beat the throw to first, avoiding a double play.

David stepped to the plate to bat left-handed.

"Just full of surprises, aren't we?" Stevens' tone was laced with venom.

David watched the first pitch sail wide of the plate.

"What if we make the wager more entertaining?" Stevens waited for a reply. "Mmm, not speaking to me now, huh? I thought if you knew more of the details of what will happen when I win, you would feel less pressure."

David let the next pitch go by.

"Ball two!" the umpire hollered.

Steven's voice pierced David's mind. *Not only will John sign a huge contract with me, I will make sure I bring along the boy and his wife as well. I was only interested in his soul, but now I have been inspired to collect theirs. And then I will find your family. You will lead me to them.*

David stepped out of the box. He surveyed the field, swung the bat back and forth, and stared defiantly at Stevens. *You've already lost.*

"Try not to crack under the pressure." Stevens slapped his fist into his glove and signaled to the pitcher.

David's knuckles went white as he gripped the bat harder and harder. He took a deep breath and stepped back in the box. A distant memory tickled David's mind. "The Lord is my refuge; of whom am I afraid?"

David hit the next pitch to the right-field wall.

Two more runs were scored that inning, and David's team retook the lead.

The ball game continued to seesaw back and forth over the next few innings. Both teams were able to put runs on the board. David's velocity continued to fail and the young boys' confidence continued to grow. Neither team seemed to gain the advantage, although Stevens' team had neutralized John's power. Every time John went up to bat, Stevens strolled to the mound. Then John hit the ball directly at the shortstop. Whether the ball was in the air or on the ground, the outcome of the hit was always an out.

The game entered the bottom of the ninth inning. Steven's team led nine to eight.

The first two boys failed to reach base and both recorded an out.

The next batter, Rob, walked so the tying run was aboard. The boys stood at the chain link fence, fingers entwined in the loops, shaking it and cheering their team.

David smiled and clapped his hands as Sue stepped to the plate. The boys' enthusiasm had never wavered since the third inning. They had made a game of it.

Sue steadied herself.

Stevens sneered. "Are you ready to make the last out for your team?"

"Nope, I think your pitcher is tiring."

"Have you signed those divorce papers yet?"

An awkward swing placed Sue behind in the count.

"Strike one!"

"I think John is eager to start dating other women again."

The ball zipped by. "Strike two!"

Sue backed out of the box and looked imploringly down to David.

David motioned for time-out and hustled down toward Sue. John came out of the dugout to meet with them.

"He's getting in my head. I don't think I can do this!" Sue's said.

"C'mon, hon, you can do it! Just ignore him."

Sue did not say anything. She bit her lower lip, keeping her gaze away from her husband.

David reached into Sue's back pocket. The papers were still there. He pulled them out, unfolded the divorce agreement, and handed it to John.

John looked at the document. "What's this?" When John recognized the paper, he ripped it in half. "Sue, it . . . these . . . it was a mistake. I don't want a divorce. We . . . I . . . may need some help, but I know I never wanted this." He continued to tear up the papers.

"Batter up!"

Sue's eyes glistened and she stood tall. She returned to the batter's box.

"Did you have a touching reunion?" The smugness in Stevens' voice was palpable.

The crack of the bat was her only reply when she hit a line drive over the second baseman's outstretched glove.

There were base runners now on first and second with two outs.

Sam grabbed his bat, placed his helmet on, and raced out of the dugout. A hand gripped him at the shoulder, causing him to stop and turn around. "Hey! What the . . . ?" Sam looked up into the face of his father.

"Sam, get up there and take your swings. Don't let them cheat you out of that. You get your swings."

"Got it, Dad!" He turned to go.

"And, Sam?"

"Yeah, Dad?"

"I want you to know I've had a great time playing ball with you today."

Sam beamed. "Me too, Dad." He jogged to the plate.

Sam struck the first pitch high into the air. Its descent carried it near the first baseman. Sam lowered his head and ran toward first. He glanced up to see the fate of his hit as the ball came down toward the open glove of the first baseman. Then ball and fielder disappeared when the second baseman crashed into his teammate, knocking him down. The ball dropped harmlessly to the ground.

Everyone was safe and the bases were loaded. The home team was down a run.

Stevens stormed out to the pitcher's mound, yelling at the two fielders. He pointed a finger at each of them, shaking and threatening that they had better not screw up again. He slammed his mask and helmet back onto his head, and stomped back to his position. He stopped abruptly when he noticed John waiting at the plate. Stevens turned around, went back, whispered something to his pitcher, and returned to his place.

John placed one foot in the box and glanced at David.

The boys were going crazy in the dugout. Bases were loaded and the best hitter in the game was up to bat.

David touched the brim of his hat and then his right ear, signaling John to bunt.

"Time!" John hollered and ran down to meet David. "Are you nuts?" he whispered harshly. "You want me to bunt? I'm the greatest—"

David stopped John by placing his fingers against John's lips. He stared at John and shook his head.

John sighed. "All right, I admit it. They know what to expect and how to pitch to me."

David nodded. He pointed toward the dugout and the runners on base.

John surveyed his teammates. The boys were shouting and jumping up and down. "They really want to win this game, don't they?"

David bent down and plucked grass from the ground. He took one blade and pulled it easily in two. He counted out nine, bound them together, and failed to pull them apart. He slapped John on the back and returned to his spot near first base.

John entered the batter's box and looked down toward David.

David gave the bunt sign. *Come on! You've got to trust me.*

John stepped in and awaited the first pitch. A fast ball, low and inside, came tearing at him. John swung with all his might and missed the ball. He missed the ball badly.

"Nice swing there, Shirley!" Stevens mocked.

The second pitch was fired in the same location, and John squared away and dropped a bunt perfectly down the first-base line.

Time slowed while everyone reacted to the bunt. The base runners sprinted toward the next destination, while the fielders were caught off guard by the ball trickling down the baseline.

Stevens and the pitcher met simultaneously where the ball had stopped. Stevens pushed Gary aside with his glove, bare-handled the ball, and whipped it down to first base.

The ball reached the first baseman's glove the same time John's foot struck the bag.

The umpire hollered, "Safe!"

The tying run crossed home plate.

"What? Are you blind?" Stevens shouted and charged the umpire.

While Stevens ran toward the umpire, Sue stole home for the game-winning run. She leaped off the plate and into the arms of the boys who were yelling and jumping.

Sue fought her way through the excited group of boys and into the arms of her husband.

"Great job, Sue," John said. "Way to keep your head in the game."

"Awesome hit, dear. They never saw that one coming," Sue replied.

John laughed. "No, not even I saw *that* one coming."

David walked past the celebration to the mound, where Frank Stevens waited.

Stevens' appearance hid any reaction to the outcome of the game. "So, you've won this round."

This round?

"John Barnes is no longer under my claim . . . at this point in time, anyway. You won. You are his new agent." Frank dumped a folder of papers on the ground and walked away.

David picked up the folder and glanced at the paperwork, all of John's contracts and agreements. David's team had won. He strolled over to where everyone was celebrating, interrupted John and Sue's embrace, and handed them the papers.

"What's this?" Sue asked as John leafed through the papers.

"It's all my contract stuff. I guess Frank no longer wants to be my agent."

Sue encircled his waist with her arms. "That's a good thing. I never liked that man."

"So, David, I guess this means I'm in the market for a new agent. It seems to me that with all the crazy things that have happened today, you'd be the best man for the job. What do you think?"

David glanced at the many faces that were awaiting his answer. He smiled, and his response was broken up by Sam's voice.

"Hey, look, you guys. There's a lady out there in center field. How'd she get there?"

All eyes turned to take in the form of an elegantly dressed woman standing alone in center field. The celebration quieted.

A shiver ran down David's back when he recognized Joelle. *Give me a moment. I'll be right there.*

David, you may have the gift of speech, one more time, Joelle replied.

Thank you. He turned to John and Sue. "I think Sue would be a better agent than I ever could be."

"Mr. Liberty! Your voice!"

David laughed. "Yes, Sam. My voice is back, but only so I can say good-bye."

"What? What do you mean 'good-bye'?" John asked. "I don't understand. I have questions. After everything that's happened, you're going to leave?"

"Yes, John. Sometimes it is not for us to understand, but know this: once again God helped David slay a Goliath." David stared into the distance. "'The reward of humility and fear of the Lord is riches, honor, and life.'"

Sue embraced David. Her voice raspy, "I don't understand what happened. I don't know how to thank you. I don't know—"

David returned from his trance. "Shhh. Don't thank me. Just promise to keep your family together."

All that she could muster was a nod of her head.

"John?" David asked.

John nodded and encircled Sue's waist.

"Mr. Liberty?" Sam's voice was soft and low.

"Yes, Sam. It's hardest to say good-bye to you." David knelt and rested his hands on the young man's shoulders. "Always remember, put others first and yourself second."

Sam smiled and fought back the tears. He hugged David tightly and said, "I'll never forget you."

"Nor I you."

David stood and walked out to join the solitary woman. He did not look back for fear that he would not have the courage to continue his journey. He took Joelle's hand and in silence they walked out of the Barnes' lives.

Sam paused when he approached his father's trophy case. He placed one hand on the glass, rested his forehead against his arm, and studied the ball that seemed to glow amidst all the other trophies. Sam read the inscription on the ball like he had for every day since David had left: "John Barnes 400th" and in Sam's writing underneath the inscription were the words: "D. Liberty 800 feet."

His mother called, breaking Sam's trance. "Sam! Your dad and I are ready to play some catch. Are you coming?"

"Yeah, Mom! I'll be right there." Sam smiled and patted the window. He jogged out of the room and glanced back toward the trophy case. "Thanks again, Mr. Liberty, wherever you are."

Book Two

"A heart at peace gives life to the body, but envy rots the bones."

—Proverbs 14:30

Chapter One

DAVID STARED OUT the window of his room in the nursing home. He had returned to the prison that threatened to destroy his spirit, or at least where his spirit chose to die.

Something had changed, and not just the fact that he could move his arms freely. Something was changing in David's heart.

He'd returned last night, screaming incoherent words and thrashing his arms violently. He had been restrained at first, but he sensed a feeling of relief from the nursing staff when they attended to his needs. They seemed glad he had returned, particularly Nurse Wilma, who now entered his room.

"Mr. Liberty, it's so good to see you awake. You have been unconscious for three days. No one could figure out what was going on. Your vitals were fine; we just couldn't wake you up."

What happened? Was everything a dream? I was here the whole time?

"We contacted your daughter. Unfortunately, we had to leave messages. We've not heard back from her yet." Wilma finished making his bed and wrapped the blood pressure cuff around David's right arm.

What happened with the Barnes family? How did I get back here? Where did Joelle go?

"Luckily you're back here with us." She paused and watched the sphygmomanometer. "Just like I expected, you're as healthy as a horse."

Are you going to take me out to pasture then? David touched Wilma on her arm.

Wilma pulled up David's wheelchair and guarded him while he transferred from bed to chair. "Whatever you went through those last three days seems to have done you a world of good. You're actually demonstrating some human qualities." She patted his arm in return. "I'll see you later this morning."

OK, Wilma. Have a good morning. You better let my daughter know I'm all right.

"You know, I better have the girls call your daughter. No . . . better yet, I'm going to call her and let her know you're feeling better." With those parting words, she left David alone.

David wheeled himself closer to the window. He looked out at the blue, cloudless sky and sighed. Being alone with his thoughts could be dangerous. While he was sleeping and dreaming, he did not exist in this world. He did not have to reflect on his past or his future. He hoped his second chance was more than just a dream. *I wonder how John, Sue, and Sammy would have done if I had finished the dream.*

"Has your faith left you so soon?" The reprimand startled David, almost as much as the familiarity of the musical voice.

Joelle? He wheeled his chair around to face the angelic woman before him. *You mean it wasn't a dream? Everything was real?*

"Mr. Liberty, how else would you explain the change?"

What change?

She drew close to David and pointed, pressing her finger against his heart. She whispered, "In here, Mr. Liberty. Right in here."

You mean I really did get a second chance?

Joelle laughed. "If that's how you want to refer to it, then—"

Wait a minute! What about Sam? His parents? Are they . . . will they be OK?

Joelle continued her musical laughter. "Yes. They are great now." She squeezed his hand. "I'm proud of how well you did. You shared love with the Barnes family, and they will continue to be a family once again."

So I did it? I passed the test?

Joelle's tone sobered. "It's not quite that easy."

Easy? You call what happened easy? *I don't understand—*

"David." Joelle cut his thoughts off. "This is only the beginning. The task you completed was the easiest that you will encounter. Do you recall the story of Job?"

David's thoughts raced. *No. I don't recall the story. Is it in the Old Testament?*

"Yes, but no matter. What did you learn from your encounter?"

What? Now you're quizzing me?

"It's important."

Give me a moment. David closed his eyes. He slowed his breathing and called forth the memories of the recent events. His heart warmed when he saw the faces of the new friends he had made. David saw the love renewed in the eyes of John and Sue. He smiled because Sam had seen the look as well.

I learned that pride can destroy a family. That pride, when strengthened, makes an individual selfish and can push us away from those that we love.

"But where does this pride come from?"

David opened his eyes. *It's a tool used by Satan!*

"He used it for what purpose?"

To break up a family.

"How?"

David paused, because the question caught him by surprise. His answer was not confident, and he posed it as a question. *By breaking up a marriage?*

"Exactly."

He didn't understand. Why *this* marriage? *Why did God choose to intervene and save this one and not all the others that fail?*

"Has it been so long that you've forgotten the first rule?" Joelle teased.

I was hoping it would slip your mind. I noticed that you only answer the questions that suit you.

"Let's just agree that the Lord hates divorce, and His assistance in these matters is not always accepted."

So when Satan destroys a marriage, he destroys the family.

"No, but it is easier for him to complete the tasks he seeks to carry out."

You're losing me again.

Joelle nodded. "It's time to prepare for your next assignment."

What? I just got back. How am I supposed to . . . ? David felt drowsy, his eyes began to close. He struggled to stay awake.

Joelle's voice echoed inside his head. *The enemy will be better prepared for you. Recognition will not be as easy this time.*

David did not want to sleep and dream again. *I don't understand.*

"'Where the Spirit of the Lord is, there is Liberty.'"

Chapter Two

DAVID'S EYES ADJUSTED to the dimly lit room.

"Come on, David, we need the lettuce and tomatoes out on the topping bars." The voice came from an adjoining room, where other noises and voices rang out.

David took in his surroundings and realized he was in some type of produce refrigerator. He located the tomatoes and lettuce, scooped up a box of each, and exited the cold locker into a large kitchen area.

"Yeah, I know it's your first day on the job there, Flash, but I need you to pick up the pace a little. There is a hungry crowd out there. We need to keep up with the toppings." David knew the man speaking to him was Thomas, his new boss.

David nodded and cut the tomatoes with the produce slicer. He quickly shredded the lettuce on the same machine. He arranged the tomato slices in four columns in the serving pan and placed the lettuce in a separate pan. He hurried through the revolving door, taking the items out to the bar. Thomas was right. People were waiting impatiently for the toppings.

"C'mon there, Speedy! My hamburger's getting cold!"

Another customer grumbled, "About time."

David replaced the empty containers with full ones and checked the other toppings. Onions, pickles, relish, peppers, spinach, and large, steamy vats of melted cheeses lined the topping bar. He spent the next few hours trying to keep up with the never-ending crowd. It was Friday night, and most of the students who attended Bohning University seemed to be filtering into the restaurant.

David received his first break when the restaurant served its last customer. He did not have a chance to interact with anyone during the rush, and finally was able to use the restroom.

He washed his hands, and was taken back when he viewed himself in the mirror. He shook his head in disbelief. He must be around twenty or twenty-one years old now. He was young again. Talk about the Fountain of Youth!

David dried off his hands, paused once again to look in the mirror, and returned to the kitchen. Tammy and Nicole, twin sisters, were talking to Thomas, his new boss. David accepted the fact that he knew the girls by name and waved to them as he approached.

"Hey, here's our new tenant," Tammy exclaimed. "How was his first day on the job, Tom?"

"I'll tell you what! He's a worker, that's for sure. It's an added bonus that he doesn't talk, gets more work done that way."

Nicole shoved Tom so he almost fell off his stool. "That's kinda mean. Don't be a jerk."

"I didn't mean anything bad by it. I was joking around. You know I was joking, right, David?"

David smiled and nodded. He too leaned against the counter and wiped his brow with an exaggerated swipe to show he was glad the shift was done.

"Yeah, it's always crazy like that on the weekend. Tell you what, David. Since you did a great job on your first shift, I'll clean up and close. Tomorrow night is yours, deal?"

David nodded, clasped and shook Tom's hand. *Deal.* He was beat.

"David, Nicole and I came by to walk you home your first night." Tammy looked at Tom. "Thanks for giving him this opportunity. Now he'll be able to pay us the rent." Her eyes twinkled. "We owe you one!"

"Mmmph. I stopped keeping track a long time ago, girls."

The girls laughed, planted a kiss on Tom's cheeks, and gathered an arm of David's to escort him home.

Tom shouted as they left his restaurant, "I feel sorry for you, man. One of those girls is bad enough, but both of them? God bless you."

I'm certainly praying for God's blessing too, Tom. David smiled and waved good-bye.

The girls bantered back and forth to each other, not really ignoring David, but not including him in their dialogue, which gave David a chance to reflect on his new location. His memory banks opened and he contemplated his new identity.

Tammy and Nicole Stewart were fraternal twins attending the local university. David rented the small apartment above the girls' garage, for he, too, was attending the university. David was majoring in business, as were the girls. Tammy and Nicole had offered to help him in any way they could—perhaps because he was unable to speak. David needed a part-time job to pay for expenses, thus the job at the restaurant. Not much more came to his mind as he glanced at his guides.

The girls appeared as different as night and day. Nicole was brown-haired and brown-eyed. Tammy was blond with blue eyes. Both girls were striking. David could not decide which girl was more attractive and quickly decided he had better not try. Their conversation was amiable, but there was something hidden in their body language. David could not put a finger on it, but something seemed out of place.

"David? David, did you hear what Nicole asked?"

Oops! David shrugged his shoulders and his face reddened.

"Tam, it's all right. David, shall we go to lecture together in the morning?"

With you two lovely ladies on each arm, you bet, David affirmed his decision.

They arrived at the girls' house. Tammy and Nicole said good night.

David went up to his new home. *Here we go, God. I'm still confused, but here I am.*

Chapter Three

THE FIRST WEEK of school took some adjustment. It had been years since David studied for exams or had to do "homework." His current friends consisted of Nicole and Tammy.

Tammy was a member of the cheerleading squad for the football team, and Nicole played field hockey. After much coercion by the two girls, David decided to start workouts with the wrestling team. The actual season did not start until November, but it felt good to weight train and tumble on the mats.

David's first class on Monday, Wednesday, and Friday was an administration course with Dr. Elizabeth Montgomery. She was smart, articulate, a fantastic lecturer, and the first teacher to give her class a pop quiz on the second day of class.

Dr. Montgomery handed back the quizzes to her students. All but two of the quiz papers were returned. She held the two in her hand. "Would Tammy Stewart and Matt James please stand up?"

The rest of the class turned their heads to see the two students rise from their chairs.

Nicole nudged David and whispered, "Isn't Matt the captain of the wrestling team?"

David nodded a quick "yes" and kept his focus on the two students.

"Class, it would behoove you to follow the example of these two fine students. I have reviewed everyone's transcripts . . ."

I have a transcript? David was perplexed, but only momentarily.

"These students have lived up to their expectations. This is the first time in my tenure that not just one, but two perfect quizzes were completed in the first week. Catch on to their shadows, gang. These two are going places. Give them a hand!"

"Oh, brother! Just what my sister needs, a bigger head on her shoulders," Nicole complained. "I see that Matt is smart and a gifted athlete. And drop-dead gorgeous, besides."

David rolled his eyes.

Nicole shoved him coyly. "Better grab his shadow there, boy."

Uh-oh. Here comes the teach.

"Excuse me Miss—?"

Nicole blushed. "Uh, Stewart. Nicole Stewart."

"Ah, yes, the underachieving sister. You could use your sister's study habits."

Nicole shot a nasty glance at her sister, but the professor did not notice. She turned to David. "And, Mr. Conspirator, what is your name?"

David started to write his name on a piece of paper, only to be startled when Professor Montgomery slammed her hand on his desk.

"I will not be ignored, young man. What is your name?"

A voice across the room interrupted. "That is David Liberty, Dr. Montgomery. He is unable to speak"—Tammy moved toward teacher and student—"but he does know sign language." Tammy signed to David, "I've got your back."

David signed in return, "I did not know you knew how to sign." The flashing of his hands were followed by the thought that he hadn't known *he* could sign, either.

Professor Montgomery paused. "Yes. I do recall reading something like that in a transcript."

Nicole burst out laughing.

"What is so funny, young lady?" the professor demanded.

"Apparently *you* don't know sign language." Nicole tried to catch her breath. "David said you're a fat windbag, and my sister said something about a cow."

"That's enough!" Dr. Montgomery roared. "The three of you out! Now!" Her face reddened, and her veins threatened to explode from her forehead. "Get out of my class!"

The three students gathered their books and exited the classroom. Nicole continued to giggle, while David and Tammy were too dumbfounded to respond or fight in their own defense.

Once clear of the classroom, Nicole exclaimed, "That was great!"

Tammy grabbed her roughly by the shoulder. "What are you talking about? Have you completely lost your marbles? Why on earth would you say that to our teacher? I can't believe—"

"Of course you can't, Miss Goody-Two-Shoes. Always perfect. Never the bad apple and always in the spotlight."

"Shut up, Nicole!"

"No, *you* shut up! I'm sick of you being Miss Perfect. I hope you can't rejoin her class. That would be a nice blemish on your record."

"I don't believe you. You're insane." Tammy shoved Nicole so hard that she fell down, landing hard on her backside.

"You witch! I'm going to kill you!" Nicole launched herself toward Tammy.

David tackled Nicole as gently as he could, slamming her up against the school wall. The impact of the brick coupled with his body weight, temporarily knocked the wind and fight out of her. David did not let go once her breathing returned, although he did loosen his grip.

Tammy simply said, "Nicole, I forgive you. I'll see you back home." Without waiting for a reply, she walked away.

Nicole struggled, "Oh no, you don't. I don't want your forgiveness!" she shouted at the back of her sister, who continued to walk away. "I forgive *you*! So there!"

Once her sister was out of sight, Nicole fell limp in David's grasp. "All right, tough guy. You can stop hugging me now."

David relaxed his grip and stepped back.

"Was it as good for you as it was for me?" Nicole smirked.

David signed, "Are you OK?"

Nicole placed her hand on his, stopping him. "Don't bother. I don't know sign language. Only Tammy does. Yeah, shocking, I know."

There was some hearty competition between these two girls, David decided. He pointed in the direction Tammy had walked.

"No. You go on ahead. I'm going to the library to study. I'll see you later." Nicole picked up her books and papers, nodded good-bye to David, and headed toward the library.

David was unsure of what to do. Should he follow Tammy, or should he follow Nicole? There seemed to be a wedge between the sisters, and yet at times they seemed as close as two siblings could be. He made up his mind to follow Tammy. At least he could converse with her using sign language. *When did I learn to sign?*

David and Goliath:
The Guardian Angel Chronicles

Tammy was not home, and David did not find Nicole at the library. He decided to go to wrestling practice and then back to his small apartment. The walk was revitalizing. He was aware of the birds and squirrels, but what really caught his eye were the people. He watched them interact or walk in solitude. He noticed their body language. He had never paid attention before; he did not notice people's lives, unless asked. People—strangers—were outside his circle of concern.

David's reflection was interrupted by the phrase, "It's about time!" Startled, he glanced up his stairway to see Nicole and Tammy waiting on the top step. Everything that had transpired earlier in the day seemed completely forgotten. He made his way up to the landing.

"Where've you been?" Nicole asked. "You weren't concerned about either of us?"

David shook his head and raised his hands in protest.

"Nicole is just giving you a hard time." Tammy jabbed her sister in the ribs.

"Oh, there you go again, spoiling all of my fun."

Tammy ignored her sister's comment. "David, this Friday night there's a Campus Crusade meeting. Nicole and I were wondering if you wanted to go with us."

Before David could respond, Nicole cut in. "If she's going to drag me along, then I'm going to drag you along too. That's all there is to it."

David shrugged his shoulders and signed, "Yes" to Tammy.

"Oh, no you don't!" Nicole grabbed David's hands. "I'll not have you talking to my sister when I don't know what the two of you are saying about me!"

Tammy laughed and hugged Nicole. "We'll meet you here at seven and all go together."

Both girls kissed him on a cheek and made their way down the stairs.

David's face warmed at the physical touch, although he knew the gesture was totally platonic. His face reddened deeper when he overheard Nicole. "Did I tell you he wouldn't stop hugging me after you left?"

The girls laughed, arms entwined, and skipped toward their house.

Chapter Four

FRIDAY NIGHT DAVID went with his two lovely escorts to a small church outside the college campus. The church was unsuccessfully decorated and poorly lit. The musty odor and the atmosphere made him feel that the building was not used for the purpose for which it had been built.

The surroundings did not dampen the mood of the thirty-plus people who milled about. An atmosphere of happiness and excitement flowed as the young adults mingled, laughed, hugged, and conversed with friends and new acquaintances.

David shook many hands when Nicole and Tammy introduced him to their friends and family of faith. David smiled, nodded, shook his head or shrugged, based on parts of the conversation.

Something caught David's attention. He politely distanced himself from the small group and scanned the crowd.

An internal alarm sounded.

His palms grew damp, and his pulse thumped like a runaway freight train. A faint odor of sulfur tickled his senses. *What is that?*

David stepped up on a pew to obtain a better vantage point. He took in the architecture, doorway, pews, and altar, but didn't notice anything out of the ordinary. He stepped toward the rear of the church and again stood up on a pew. He glanced over the many faces in the group. *Nope. Not him. No . . . No . . . No . . . .*

Then he found what he had been searching for—a solitary figure leaning against the wall, completely unnoticed by anyone else in the room. A shadow moved toward the figure and joined him. The two silhouettes blended and then separated once more, leaving just one form in David's field of view.

David felt a rush of pain through his chest, and he realized what was wrong. He remained frozen, standing on the pew, staring at the hidden observer. David heard a voice rise above the noise of the crowd, but he did not take his eyes off his mark.

David and Goliath:
The Guardian Angel Chronicles

"Welcome, old friends and new. My name is Father Brad Maple. I am a pastor down at St. Patrick's Church in Kensington."

David glanced at the man addressing the crowd. The short, stocky man was dressed in black, with white affixed at his collar, signifying his vocation. The priest stepped up on the altar to address the group of students.

David turned his attention back to the hidden stranger, but he could not locate him. David's inner alarm system exploded. At the same time, a tremendous *bang* vibrated through the church.

David's heart skipped a beat. Students screamed and panicked. The priest's body collapsed on the altar.

"Nobody move!" a vicious voice howled. Another gunshot shattered the air. "Everybody on your knees!"

David watched as men and women dropped to their hands and knees. A few had already fallen, whether from fainting or shock. *Where are Tammy and Nicole?*

"Do you see your God has no power here?" The madman, face masked, stood over the priest's body and shouted, "Who will die next for their God?" He sprang from the altar and grabbed a new victim by his hair. He yanked the whimpering boy to his feet. "How about *you?* How's your faith?"

The boy sobbed, face in hands.

Another shot rang out. "You disgust me." He tossed the body aside and reached for another crouching victim.

David's legs carried him off the pew and down the aisle to the scene. *Am I crazy? Where are my legs taking me?*

The gunman pulled a struggling Nicole to her feet. His gaze caught David standing on the fringes of the collapsed bodies of students. He grinned mockingly and placed the gun at Nicole's chin. "What about her, hero? Will your God save her in time?"

A form rose from a huddled position, and Tammy stood defiantly. "My God will save me."

The attacker shifted his gaze to Tammy, who stood three paces away. "Don't worry, sweetie. You'll get your chance next." He jerked Nicole's hair back, exposing her throat. Nicole screamed.

"Take me now if you dare!" Tammy stepped forward with her head held high.

"As you wish." He swung the gun from Nicole's throat and pointed it at Tammy's chest.

Click.

David leapt. Misfire! He reached the gunman and hip-tossed him to the floor.

Bang! The shot and screams echoed off the walls.

David's elbow connected with the assailant's nose. With a resounding *crunch*, the madman's body went limp.

David sat on the stairway that led out of the church. Ambulances, police, and firefighters were on the scene. Tears streamed down David's cheeks while the vivid scenes replayed in his mind. He wished he'd acted sooner. *Dear God, I've failed. Two people have died because I was too slow. I was paralyzed with fear.* He should have approached the gunman when he'd seen him in the shadows.

Do not be afraid. Was it still *his* voice that spoke, or was someone else speaking with his thoughts?

Joelle was right about me, David despaired.

There are lives to be saved. The words sounded in his mind, although they were not from him.

What do you mean? What am I supposed to do now?

"Excuse me. I need to ask you a few questions." The words brought David's head up. "Can you tell me what happened?" The police officer's voice was commanding yet gentle.

David shook his head and looked at the ground.

"Officer, excuse me." Tammy and Nicole made their way over. Tammy's arms were wrapped around her sister. "His name is David, and he is unable to speak," she offered.

"Is he in shock?"

"No, officer. He's always been unable to speak. He communicates with sign language."

"Maybe you two can help me out." The officer focused his attention on the two girls. "What happened in there?"

"We just told the officer over there what happened," Tammy said.

"Please, it would be a great help if you'd tell the story to me, as well. We need as much information as possible if we are going to find the shooter."

Tammy recounted the events that had transpired in the small church. David sat by and listened. Tammy told the story without a waver in her voice. She did not miss a single detail. She described how she stood to save her sister. She told it without any hint of bravado in her words or body language.

David stared at the two girls. He noticed Tammy's embrace tighten around Nicole while she talked about how her sister was held at gunpoint. There was no look of thanks in Nicole's eyes when Tammy stated how she selflessly attempted to offer her life for her sister's.

"We don't know what happened with the shooter. After David knocked him down, the lights flickered, and he was no longer there," Tammy concluded.

Nicole broke free of her sister's hold and sat next to David, putting her arm around his shoulders. Tammy and the officer attempted to walk to the police cars, only to have their progress impeded by the news media.

David stood and held Nicole's hand. They walked down the steps, stealing away from the crowd and commotion, and made their way home.

Chapter Five

FOR THE NEXT couple of weeks, everywhere Nicole looked, Tammy was being honored for being a heroine. Everyone—from the television, radio, newspaper, church, and her classmates—was talking about her courage and her faith. The headline on the morning sport section read, "Local Cheerleader Makes Leap of Faith."

Nicole crumpled the newspaper and tossed it in the garbage. She finished her breakfast, gathered her books, and prepared to leave for class.

"Good morning, sis." Tammy's cheerful voice startled Nicole. "Are you heading off to class without me again?"

"I'm going to a field hockey meeting."

"You've been going to an early meeting every day. Is everything all right?"

"Just fine."

"Are you sure? Do you need some—?"

"I'm fine, Tammy." Nicole changed the subject. "Did you open your fan mail yet?"

Nicole's jab of sarcasm went unnoticed by her sister. "I actually received some invitations for a couple of television talk shows. I'm not sure if I should accept any or all of them. What do you think?"

Nicole stared hard at her sister. "You don't want to know what I think."

"Nicole, I get the feeling that you're angry at me for something."

"Not something, sis. *Everything.*"

"What? I don't get it. I offer my life to save yours, and this is the thanks that I get?"

"Oh yeah. The great and perfect Tammy. Her deeds of selflessness lead to personal gain."

"You can be such a jerk sometimes. What was I supposed to do? Stand by and watch my only sister lose her life? You would have stood up for me."

"No, I wouldn't have," Nicole snapped.

"You wouldn't what?"

"I wouldn't have tried to save you." There was no remorse in Nicole's statement.

"What?" Tammy appeared stunned. "I don't understand. You don't mean that."

"You think you know everything, but you don't." Nicole didn't wait for an answer. She strode to the door and slammed it on her way out. She did not want to hear Tammy's voice anymore.

Nicole went straight to David's apartment. She rapped softly on the door, and without waiting for reply, attempted to enter. The door was still locked, so she fumbled in her purse and fetched a small key. Being a landlord entitled her to certain perks. A quick turn and the door opened.

She stepped into the small apartment, pushing the door wide open to shed more light into the room. She noticed David's books stacked and ready to go, but where was the owner? "David?" Her voice echoed throughout the apartment. She checked his small kitchen, bathroom, and at last, she stumbled on him in the bedroom.

David knelt beside the bed. He appeared to be deep in prayer. Was he even breathing? Nicole was amazed at how peaceful and still he appeared. Cautiously, she extended her hand and touched his shoulder. "David?" she whispered.

He exploded to his feet and whirled into a crouched stance.

Nicole stumbled backward, against the wall. "I-I thought we were going to walk to class this morning."

The flash in David's eyes diminished, and his face relaxed in recognition. He frowned, raised his eyebrows, and let a smirk form as he exaggerated a look at his watch.

"So I'm a little early. Are you ready or not?"

David smiled and nodded.

He tied his sneakers, grabbed an apple, and headed for the door.

"Aren't you forgetting something?"

David frowned.

"Your books?"

David blushed, scooped up his books, and ushered Nicole out the door. After the couple descended the stairs, David and his escort headed toward the campus.

"You don't study much, do you?" Nicole said.

David glanced at her and shrugged.

"You know, it's really not fair that you're doing better without studying than half the class does *with* studying."

David grinned.

"Of course, you're not quite as sharp as Matt." Nicole watched closely for some type of reaction from David, but there was none forthcoming.

Dissatisfied that her tactics did not affect him, she changed the angle of her attack. "Are you wrestling next week?"

She stopped walking, as did David. She watched him pucker his brow and could only imagine what was going through his mind.

"Oh yeah. That's right. Matt's in your weight class, and *he's* the starter. I guess that means you will watch from the bench."

Nicole noticed her jibe strike home. "Hmmm. Looks like somebody may be a little jealous."

David did not know why Nicole was attacking him. *Why you little—*

His thoughts were cut off by a voice that hailed him from nearby. "Hey, David!"

David turned to see the topic of Nicole's conversation materialize from a small group of students. Matt strolled over and slapped David on the back. "This guy is one tough grappler," he said to Nicole. "He's definitely raising my skills."

Oh, great.

"Really?" Nicole glanced from Matt to David. "I heard that he couldn't beat you."

Matt brushed aside the comment with the wave of a hand. "He's going to be a great wrestler."

I was a great wrestler. I'll beat you yet.

"Nicole, are you and Tammy doing anything after classes Friday?"

"As far as I know, we're not doing anything."

"Great! I was thinking of asking your sister if she would go with me to the opening night of *Step Child.*" He paused and slapped David one more time on the back. "Hey, got to run. Nic, thanks for the info, and David, I'll see you at practice." Matt broke away from the couple and headed in a different direction.

David did not wave good-bye. He was focused on Nicole. Her body language completely changed. He could feel her rage. Her jaw clenched, and every muscle in her body contracted. The awful taste of sulfur invaded David's dried mouth.

David touched her arm, and Nicole lashed out. "What do you want?" she hollered.

David jerked his hand back. *I'm sorry; just trying to comfort you.*

"I said, what do you want?" Nicole forced the question through clenched teeth and thrust her face closer to David.

Dear Father, what is wrong with this girl? David did not know how to respond or communicate with the enraged Nicole. He licked his lips.

Nicole regained some self-control and gave David space. "Well, we best keep moving, or we'll be late for class." She walked in the direction of class.

David hesitated. *What the—?*

Nicole glanced behind her shoulder. "Let's go, David."

David followed her to their first morning class. He was in no hurry to walk abreast with Nicole, so he kept his spacing behind her and elected not to sit next to her in class.

The lecture was boring, not only for David—who already knew the material—but also for everyone in class who had read chapter twelve, the assigned work. The professor was reading line for line from the text, and his outline on the blackboard was identical to the chapter outline. To make matters worse, it was a two-hour class.

David lowered his head and held his pen, feigning the note-taking process, and prayed. *Lord, please help Nicole.* Something small struck his head. He glanced around and caught a wink from Tammy. He raised his eyebrows, and she signed. "Boring class."

David responded with his hands. "Yes, it certainly is. And it is going to be a long one."

"How is my sister?"

"I'm not sure. We had an interesting walk." David's hands continued to weave as his eyes scanned for any observers.

"She may need help."

"Maybe." David knew it was not the place to talk about what had happened that morning.

"Friday night?"

"What?"

"There is a play. Go with me?"

David realized she was talking about the play *Step Child*, the one Matt planned to invite Tammy to. For a moment, David thought it would be a perfect opportunity to humble Matt a little. David could take Tammy to the play, and she would have to tell Matt that she was already going with someone. It would be refreshing to see the look of disappointment on Matt's face.

A part of David struggled. *What am I thinking? I have lived my life already . . . but this is my second chance . . . maybe a chance at another life—no, maybe Matt needs a lesson in humility. I could do it to help him.*

David signed his reply to Tammy. "Yes."

Tammy smiled her beautiful smile. "Great. Better pay attention to class now."

The class ended. Nicole gathered her books and strode over to David's desk. "So, David"—she glared at her sister—"what time will we be leaving for the play?"

David glanced at Tammy and then returned his gaze to Nicole.

"I think we should be ready to go by six thirty," she said. Then she left, not waiting for David to gather his wits.

David looked at Tammy, who quickly said, "David, that's fine."

David raised his hands in protest.

"No, really. It would be good for Nicole."

David sighed. A familiar voice interrupted.

"Tammy?" It was Matt.

David rose and left. He did not want to hear their conversation. He was disappointed that his idea to humble Matt was foiled. He did not know how else he could teach Matt a lesson in meekness.

Friday evening David waited anxiously for his date. He could not understand why he felt nervous to the point that "butterflies" circled in his stomach. He took one last look at himself in the mirror, decided that everything was in place, snatched his wallet, and headed down to meet Nicole.

The original plan was that the two couples would ride to the play together. Nicole wanted to be able to enjoy some time alone with her date so she had argued against the idea. David winced when he heard her argument, but he was unable to protest. So Tammy reluctantly gave in to the request.

Matt waited on the front-porch swing. "Hey, David, you clean up pretty good."

David smiled in spite of himself. *And you look rather cavalier as well.* He waved and strode quickly up the four steps, stopping right in front of Matt, who was slowly rocking the swing back and forth.

"Now, as much as I like you, don't get any ideas," Matt said.

David looked quizzically at Matt. *What?*

"I mean, I see enough of you at wrestling practice, so be sure to let Tammy sit next to me, OK?" Matt's tone was light and teasing.

David beamed and playfully made an attempt to dislodge Matt from his throne. *Why, you turkey! You're just as nervous as I am.* David liked Matt. Even though Matt bested him at school, sports, and now women, there was just something likeable about the guy.

Matt struggled to keep from going backwards on the swing, laughing at David's feeble attempt to dethrone him.

"Boys, if you'd rather keep each other company tonight that could be arranged." Tammy's mischievous scolding brought the young men to their feet. The attractive young woman had a better effect on the boys than a drill sergeant.

Matt lightheartedly pushed David one more time and stammered, "You look wonderful, Tammy."

Why, you old dog! David wanted to shove Matt one more time, but he restrained himself. He had to agree with Matt. Tammy was indeed beautiful.

Nicole stepped out into the melee. "So, sis, what are our dates up to?"

David was stunned at the striking figure of Nicole when she placed one hand on her hip, turned her lead leg slightly outward, and postured herself in a position ready to scold whoever needed it. Nicole, in contrast to her sister, wore clothing that was not modest, but emphasized the fact that she was a woman, a very attractive and sexy woman.

David gaped. He caught his breath, and his eyes bulged. He knew he looked foolish, so he tore his gaze away from the stellar form of Nicole. He stole a glance toward Tammy, hoping beyond hope that she had not noticed his drooling. Tammy's face told him all he needed to know. He looked at the ground.

Tammy said, "I do believe, sis, that they were thinking of going on the date without us."

"Really," Nicole began, "I'm sure we could find some other dates . . ."

This time David shoved Matt, nodding toward the girls. He brought his hands to and from his lips signing "speak." *Say something for us, Prince Charming!*

Matt placed his arm around David and pulled him close. "You know, I could do a lot worse than this pretty guy."

The girls laughed. David shook his head and rolled his eyes.

"All right, we'd best be on our way, if we don't want to be late," Tammy said.

Matt offered his arm and escorted his date down the stairs.

Nicole stood defiantly and crossed her arms. "Well! My sister's looks are complimented. What am I? An ugly duckling?"

David stepped toward Nicole and signed how beautiful she looked while privately thinking, *Oh my goodness. She's one gorgeous, jealous child.* He forgot that Nicole was unable to sign.

"My dear sister . . ." Tammy's voice saved David. "Apparently you did not see the drool dripping from your date's mouth when you strolled out on the porch."

David dropped his head in shame, and the temperature of his ears and neck rose. *I'm an immature, bumbling fool all over again. I thought I outgrew this behavior and these emotions long ago.*

Tammy smiled thinly at the effects of her reprimand. "Are we ready to go?"

"I think both David and I agree that we're escorting the prettiest girls to the play." Matt beamed.

Nicole grabbed her escort by the arm. "Come on, I think it's sweet that you are blushing."

This could be a long night.

"Tammy, why don't you and Matt go in Dad's Mercedes; we'll take our bug."

"Are you sure you don't want to ride together?"

"Yes, I'm sure. I don't want my sister's judgmental looks ruining our fun." Nicole tightened her grip around David's waist and nudged him with her hip. "Right, David?"

Please don't leave me alone with your sister! David shrugged and nodded in affirmation.

The couples made their way to the vehicles. When Nicole removed her grip from David, he risked a glance in Tammy's direction.

Tammy was glaring hard at him and signed, "Hands off."

David hands replied, "Hands off."

"Behave. You will suffer."

Already there. David signed to Tammy, "I will take care of Nicole."

Tammy broke their conversation and allowed her date to seat her in the vehicle.

David opened and closed the door for Nicole and made his way to the driver's seat.

Both vehicles headed out of the driveway, the red Mercedes leading the yellow Volkswagen®.

It had been a long time since David had been behind the wheel of a car. It felt like a long-lost friend who had returned from a journey in which there had been no expectation of return. The little bug absorbed all of David's awareness, and he drifted into the simple pleasure of driving.

"David," Nicole said. "Hey, David! Don't let them get too far ahead of us."

David winked at Nicole. His foot depressed the accelerator, and the yellow bug sped toward the leading Mercedes. David felt an old familiar rush when he weaved around the surrounding cars. He kept his speed constant and approached Matt and Tammy.

A barrage of red taillights made him decelerate and apply steady pressure on the brake. The vehicles around him were rapidly slowing down—except one. The red Mercedes' taillights flickered, and the vehicle continued on its path.

David heard the sirens now. A large fire engine was roaring toward the approaching intersection. He pressed harder on the brake as the cold realization struck him that the two red vehicles would hit the intersection at the same time.

David opened his mouth and shouted a voiceless "No!" He threw his hand out, as if it could possibly avert the oncoming disaster. The noise of the impact shook the little bug and vibrated through David.

Chapter Six

DAVID SAT IN the hospital with Nicole. She had not spoken during the car ride to the hospital or while sitting in the waiting room. David tried to forget the scenes, even while they played through his mind. He found himself once more running down the street on the heels of Nicole when she raced to the scene of the accident.

He had struggled to restrain Nicole from trying to get to the vehicle. As fast as they had been, help was already being administered to the shattered Mercedes' occupants. The fireman had the situation under control and acted with amazing speed. An ambulance already waited, eerily inviting, with doors open.

David could still see the vivid scene as it played in slow motion. He could not imagine the number of injuries that had been sustained by the two people being hurried into the waiting ambulance. It had taken all of his energy to restrain Nicole.

Nicole's screams still throbbed in his mind. Over and over she had screamed, "Oh my God! Matt, No!" David was unsure how many times she actually shouted the phrase versus how many times it echoed in his mind. The fact that she called Matt's name did not hurt as deeply as not hearing Nicole call for her sister.

David sat now, in the chaotic waiting room, unable or unwilling, to touch Nicole to offer comfort. He placed his head in his hands and prayed. He struggled at first, but words came.

Lord, I know I haven't always been faithful to You in the past. In fact, I feel uncomfortable even asking for anything. But I ask You to please, please make sure Matt and Tammy are OK. I know I've failed you here, but don't make my friends pay a price for my shortcomings. I still don't know what You want from me.

This is not about you. Was it David's own voice or an actual reply? *Pray for them.*

David prayed. He prayed diligently and with emotion. He prayed for the lives of two friends and no longer inserted the word "I" in his prayer.

He stopped praying and raised his head when a physician approached Nicole. "Miss Stewart?"

Nicole stood. "Is he going to be all right, doctor?"

The physician smiled and nodded. "Your sister is fine. In fact, it's a miracle. There is absolutely nothing wrong except some bumps and abrasions."

David sighed, but Nicole became agitated. "What about Matt James? Is he all right?"

"Your sister's friend is also lucky to be alive, but he was not as fortunate. We had to remove part of his injured leg."

Nicole shook her head. "What to you mean; remove part of his leg?"

"We had to amputate just below his left knee."

David's stomach churned.

"He's going to be fine. You can see your sister whenever you want. Mr. James, however, is still recovering from surgery."

A nurse whisked the young doctor away, telling him about his next case.

Nicole spun on David. "This will make you happy. No more Matt to beat you."

David was dumbfounded. He stared in confusion at the raging woman before him.

"This is unbelievable! Why couldn't she have been the one? It shouldn't have been Matt. It should have been *her*."

David reached out to place a hand on Nicole, but she swiped it away.

"You got your wish. Why didn't I get mine?" Nicole stormed out of the waiting area.

David wondered how many people overheard their conversation. *My wish?* He hadn't wished for this to happen, had he? He didn't want this to happen to Matt.

David wiped his face with an open palm, and his feet carried him down the hall. The doctor mentioned they could see Tammy, so he intended to find her room.

With a few minor difficulties, David found out where Tammy was. He quietly stepped into the small hospital room and noticed Tammy's form, covered with a single sheet, her chest rising and falling peacefully. He stood next to the bed and gingerly stroked her forehead.

Tammy stirred and opened her eyes. "Is Matt OK?"

David signed his response. "Are you?"

"Yes. My body feels like it was hit by a fire truck or something." She smiled with some notable effort. "How is Matt?"

David lowered his head. "He will be fine, but they had to amputate part of his leg."

Tammy groaned and tried to sit up in the bed. "Oh, dear God!" She shook her head and looked around. "Where's Nicole? Is she with Matt?"

"No." David hesitated. Then he signed, "She was really shaken by the news about Matt. I'm not sure where she is right now." He reached out and took Tammy's hand, laced his fingers around hers, and squeezed reassuringly.

"Nicole has been acting strange lately. Have you noticed?"

David nodded.

"I didn't realize she liked Matt. I thought she liked you. In fact, this might sound strange, but I was actually a little jealous that she was going to the play with you."

"You were jealous of your sister?" David broke their holding of hands to ask her the question.

"Right. Maybe the accident affected my head." Again she smiled, with less effort than before. "I guess I was, but right now we should focus on Matt. Do you know where he is?"

David shook his head.

"Why don't you find out where he is and go and see him?"

"The doctor said he's not ready for visitors yet, and I had a difficult time trying to find *your* room."

"Ah, yes. Their inability to communicate with you." Tammy threw the sheets off and sat on the edge of the bed.

David placed his hands on her shoulders in an attempt to put her back into the bed.

"David Liberty! We need to find our friend, and you need me to help."

David crossed his arms and refused to be budged.

"I'm going. You can either come with me or continue to stand there pretending that you know best." She stood and adjusted her gown.

David rolled his eyes and motioned her to wait. He left the room and before long returned with the bottoms and top of surgical smocks. He tossed them on the bed and turned his back to Tammy.

"Good idea," she said.

After Tammy had changed clothes, they left her room and searched for the nearest nurses' station. David steadied Tammy, keeping her upright when she missed a step.

David smiled when Tammy, displaying the utmost confidence, approached the nurses' station. With a few quick questions, she found the room where Matt was located.

David and Tammy walked hand in hand on the way to see their friend. Approaching Matt's room, they noticed a person leaning against the wall with his back toward them.

Tammy recognized the form. "Nicole?"

Nicole turned her tear-streaked face toward her sister. Her sad countenance transformed to anger. "What are you doing here?" she asked through clenched teeth.

"We want to see how Matt is doing," Tammy replied.

Nicole stepped toward Tammy. "Why would he want to see *you*?"

Tammy recoiled from her sister's icy stare. "What's wrong with you?"

"*You're* what's wrong!" Nicole lunged.

David stepped up and latched onto Nicole's arms. He squeezed her—hard.

"Let go of me!" Nicole howled.

David shifted his weight and tossed Nicole against the wall. He held her there by her wrists. He frowned and shook his head.

"David, you're hurting me," she whimpered.

David studied her face and his anger lessened as did his grip. He mouthed the word "why?" *What is going on with you, Nicole?*

"Because it should've been her. She should have been the one, not Matt!" Nicole dropped her head. "Let me go, David. Just let me go."

David relaxed his grip and stepped away from Nicole. He positioned his body in front of Tammy and examined Nicole while she made her way back down the hallway. He watched and he knew. He now knew. It was Nicole who needed his help. Her apparent disdain, contempt, and envy of her sister would destroy Nicole's life. Who else would she destroy in the process? A familiar smell tickled his nose.

"David? What's going on with Nicole? What did she mean when she said, 'It should've been her'?"

David signed, "I'm not sure." *Yes I am.* "I think she is distraught over Matt's accident."

"Yes. That's probably the case." Tammy exhaled. "Let's see how Matt's doing."

David knocked on the hospital room door and cautiously pushed it open. He and Tammy entered the room.

Matt lay with his head propped up and his eyes shut. A single sheet covered him from the waist down. An IV line entered his left hand while a monitor chirped with each beat of his heart. Various contusions decorated his arms and his face, offering a sharp contrast to the white linen that surrounded him.

Tammy was the first to shake off the shock of seeing the extent of Matt's injuries. "We should go," she whispered. "He needs to rest."

David nodded, and turned to leave.

"Aren't you going to say hello?" a raspy voice asked.

David and Tammy rushed to Matt's side, each taking a hand to comfort their friend.

Nicole slammed down on the park bench. Her hands grasped her hair and she pulled herself down into a partial ball. She continued to pull at the roots of the brown hair as her body wracked in rage. She seethed with resentment. "It should've been her!" She forced the words through compressed lips.

"Did it work?" A voice permeated her anger.

She tilted her head to see a figure sitting beside her. "No! Tammy is fine! She's always fine!"

"There will be another time."

"Matt's the one who was hurt. Lord knows I didn't want anything to happen to him." A stream of tears trickled down her cheeks.

A hand rested on her shoulder, but there was no comfort in the touch. "You deserve better. It is not fair that your sister has everything. It needs to be taken away from her."

David lay on his back, staring up at the ceiling, reflecting on his friend Matt. He was amazed at the attitude Matt demonstrated. Matt was truly thankful just to be alive. The fact that he had lost part of his left leg appeared to be no more significant than the bruises that colored his frame.

Matt had asked them what had happened in regard to the car accident. He could not remember a single thing. All he could do was shake his head in disbelief as Tammy interpreted David's story. Tammy's own recollection was obviously not complete. She told them she remembered traffic stopping, the sound of a siren, and their car continuing forward.

Matt was clearly relieved when he learned no one else was injured. His concern was genuine, and he demonstrated only minimal disappointment with his own situation.

David initially thought Matt might be in denial, but the more he talked, the more he realized Matt knew exactly what was going on. He expressed disappointment that he would not be able to challenge the current NCAA wrestling champ. He quickly followed this statement with one that stated how gracious God had been to spare his life.

David had never been that gracious. He had thanked his Lord only when everything was going the way David planned. Matt verbalized and demonstrated his love for God. This observation humbled David. *How ironic. I thought Matt needed a lesson in humility, and it is I who needed one.* His thoughts shifted to Nicole. What could he do to help her? Her envy would destroy her spirit.

David's inner voice responded. *What is the antithesis of envy?* Who asked the question?

I would expect that love is. David replied.

What specific action could demonstrate this type of love?

David realized his answer was not entirely correct. Love in itself could be a tool against all sin, but what specifically could reverse the feelings of envy? Acts of kindness?

He listened for a reply. When none came, he continued his conversation. *But how can I get Nicole to do any act of kindness when she despises her sister?*

You must teach by doing.

But kindness to Tammy will only evoke more jealousy and envy.

Perception is not reality. Nicole perceives you and she are the same.

The last statement sent a shiver down David's spine. *But I'm not at all like her. I haven't demonstrated that type of envy!*

Never?

David covered his face with his hands. After some time his tears dried and he uncovered his features. *I had forgotten. Is this my punishment?*

Chase my heart, David.

That was the last statement he heard. He did not understand why he was given this second chance, but he realized it was his *last* chance. He sat up from the bed.

I will chase your heart, Lord.

Chapter Seven

TAMMY ADJUSTED HER backpack. She tightened a belt so the weight would rest partially on her hips. She resumed walking, and the soft breeze felt good massaging her face. Distracted by her thoughts she was startled when an unseen companion spoke.

"Where are you off to, young lady?" Thomas, the restaurant owner, smirked when Tammy jolted. "Nicole mentioned you were leaving. What did she mean?"

"I'm off to go hiking."

"Where are you headed?"

Tammy glanced to the south. "Away. Far away."

"What? What about your classes and work?" Thomas frowned. "Were you even—"

"Look, Thomas. I'd rather not talk about it. Just leave me alone," she snapped.

"Nicole told me where you are headed. You really shouldn't go alone."

Tammy turned on her friend. "I don't think . . ." She noticed the pack on Thomas's shoulders. "What are you doing?"

"I'm going with you. At least I can keep you company for awhile."

Tammy resumed her brisk walk. "I don't need your company, but it's a free country." She did not wait to see if Thomas would follow.

David did not see Tammy in class on Monday. He did not think much of it until she did not show up for class on the rest of the week. To make matters more of a mystery, Nicole had been in a great mood. It was as if the weight of her demon had left her shoulders. She smiled, laughed, and outwardly demonstrated how "happy" she was. David tried to inquire about Tammy, but Nicole brushed his attempts aside, saying, "Don't ruin the moment."

David struggled to not worry about Tammy for it was time to put his plan into action. Nicole had agreed to a visit with Matt. She and David would drop by Matt's house next week.

He headed home from wrestling practice, and as was his habit, stopped at the mailbox to collect the mail for the Stewarts and himself. He glanced through the various envelopes and paused when he found one addressed to him. It was a personal letter, and David's heart raced when he recognized the handwriting. He stuffed the letter into his pocket and continued up the drive toward his apartment.

He detoured slightly to Nicole and Tammy's house to drop off their mail and proceeded up his steps and into the apartment. He removed the letter from his pocket and tore it open. He read the letter and heard Tammy's voice, as if she were standing right there, speaking the words to him.

"My dearest David,

First of all, do not worry about me. I am fine. I have taken a leave of absence from school for the remainder of the semester. I need time to think, reflect, and pray. I am not sure what I have done to create this chasm between Nicole and myself, but I need to find out what I should do to repair the gap. My journey will help me focus, and I hope to find some answers. I have all the supplies I possibly need. Again, do not worry. I will be fine. I hope you understand. I need to repair this rift before you and I can have any relationship. Please take care of Nicole. I miss you already.

God Bless.

Love, Tammy"

David folded the letter and placed it under his pillow. He was not sure if he should feel happy or distraught at the words she'd written. The feeling that overpowered all others, though, was one of joy.

Nicole met David after wrestling practice on Monday. She had been feeling great, now that Tammy was out of the picture. Nicole was anxious about seeing Matt. She had no desire to see him. She knew she would feel uncomfortable and would not know what to say or how to act. Would she be able to hide her feelings of anxiety?

"Are you ready to go?" she asked David.

David nodded and beamed with his infectious smile.

"Mmph. I know why you are grinning. You no longer have any competition on the wrestling team."

She could not tell how her words affected him, for his countenance did not change. He locked his arm around Nicole's as they headed toward Matt's home.

"Come to think of it, neither of us has anymore competition." Nicole's tone lightened, and she continued. "C'mon. Let's race!" She gave David an impulsive shove backwards and took off running down the sidewalk.

Nicole's head start was enough to allow her to beat David to the front porch of Matt's home. "If you went any slower, you'd be going backwards."

Nicole's jibe made David smirk, and he playfully shoved her away from the door and advanced to ring the doorbell.

The echoes of the chime hadn't faded before the door was flung open. Matt stood in the entry, body supported by crutches, a smile plastered on his face.

"Come in, you two. It's great to see you two. How are you doing, Nicole?" Matt motioned his friends to enter.

"I . . . I'm good. How . . . how . . . how are you?"

"I'm great. But it seems you need a language refresher course." Matt smiled. "I'm joking. Come on in and have a seat."

All three found a place to sit. "How's wrestling practice?" he asked David.

Nicole's mouth gaped when she noticed Matt moving his hands while he spoke to David. She snapped her head toward David, who winked at her and replied with sign.

"I didn't know you knew sign language," Nicole said in amazement.

"I'm learning. David's been teaching me every day since, well, since my accident."

Nicole turned to David. "You've seen Matt every day?"

David nodded.

"Seems I'm stuck with this guy." Matt laughed. "He has been insistent in helping me recover, so I made a deal with him."

"A deal? What do you mean?"

"I told him he could help me only if he taught me sign language. I told him that writing down what he wanted was getting very tiresome, so he agreed."

"But I don't understand. Why is he . . . I mean *how* is he helping you?"

"He massages my leg, preparing it for the prosthesis, and of course we're working out together."

"Working out?"

"Yeah, just trying to stay in shape, so the rest of my body doesn't get soft."

Nicole sat silent for a moment. She couldn't believe David was helping Matt. She'd thought David would be relieved that Matt could no longer compete against him on the wrestling team or in the classroom. "I thought you just wanted to see how Matt was doing, but you have been seeing him all along?"

David signed a response.

"What did he say?" Nicole asked.

Matt remarked, "I believe he is saying that he needs you for backup."

"Backup for what?"

"David's going to show you what he's been doing with my leg, since he won't be able to work with me the next few days. I told him that I'd be fine, but he can be rather insistent. He said you'd be more than happy to help."

Nicole held her tongue. Her face warmed, and she knew she was blushing. She'd been set up; she was trapped. Her heart raced. She did not want to work with Matt. Out of sight, out of mind. She looked out the living room window, trying to figure out how she could escape or refuse the invitation.

She opened her mouth to respond, hoping her excuse would not sound too lame, however David grasped her arms, and gently—but with great strength—pulled her over to Matt.

"David, I can't."

David placed a finger on her lips and placed Nicole's hands on Matt's leg, near where the surgery had been done. He kept his hands firmly on top of Nicole's.

Matt's skin was cold. The very contact with it made Nicole shiver. She tried to withdraw her hands. David's pressure was unyielding, and she could not break contact with the remnant of Matt's leg. In a final attempt to escape, she looked imploringly into David's eyes, while she thought; *Please don't do this to me.*

David's smile was full of warmth, concern, and understanding. He loosened his grip and removed Nicole's hands, resting his own in their place. Nicole's stare was directed to Matt's leg and David's hands that weaved.

Matt hissed in pain. His muscles tightened and his knuckles turned white as he fought the need to pull away from David's touch.

Nicole gasped and stammered, "David, you . . . you're hurting him!"

"It's all right, Nicole," Matt struggled to speak. "David has to desensitize my leg before I can possibly wear a prosthesis or get out on the mat again."

David stopped his work, allowing Matt to talk.

"Desensitize? What do you mean? And what's a prosthesis?" Nicole asked.

Matt relaxed. "Apparently the nerves that were severed are now working overtime, that's why it's so sensitive. A prosthesis is the term used for my artificial leg."

Nicole wrinkled her forehead.

"Normal touch is now magnified, and my nerves report it as pain. The doctor told me I need to keep touching and massaging the area, and the sensitivity should greatly lessen."

Nicole allowed her hands to be placed on Matt's leg. She was too overwhelmed to resist this time. David released his grip once her hands were in contact.

Nicole knelt in front of Matt, frozen. Her hands rested on his newly amputated leg, but she was unable to move or speak.

"Nicole? Nicole!"

She shook herself out of her trance and glanced up at Matt.

"I'll be fine. Look at David."

She looked at David.

David made a massaging motion with his hands. He rotated his thumbs up and down, indicating the type of movement Nicole needed to duplicate.

She knelt there, hypnotized by the motion of David's hands, and her own hands began to mirror the movements.

David winked at Nicole and pointed to her work.

She changed her focus to the motion of her hands. At first her touch was light, but she gradually increased her pressure and manipulated Matt's flesh like a bread maker would knead dough. She worked around the fleshy aspect of the stump and also worked back and forth over his scar.

Nicole felt awkward with the massage and noticed how Matt struggled to keep from jerking his leg out of her hold. He grimaced, tensed, and at times tipped his head back in response to the pain he was feeling.

Wondering if she would ever be done, she felt David place his hand on her shoulder and tug her away from Matt.

David raised a finger to signal "one moment."

He moved over to Matt and knelt at his left side. He placed his left hand on Matt's remaining shin and his right hand on Matt's thigh. David nodded once, and Matt attempted to straighten his knee. David fought the force of Matt's thigh as it drove the knee toward full extension. Once the knee was fully extended, David shifted his left hand to the back of Matt's leg, cupping the remaining calf muscle. Matt attempted to bend and flex his knee as David resisted the movement. The pair repeated this sequence ten times before breaking.

"What were you doing?" Nicole inquired.

Matt's inhaled deeply before he responded. "We're working on maintaining my quad and hamstring muscles for when I start walking with the prosthesis."

"What else?"

"What do you mean?" Matt asked.

"I mean, what else is David helping you with?"

"We're studying together, but right now he's getting me ready to walk. The rest of the exercises I can manage independently."

David signed to Matt.

Matt nodded. "David has one other request."

"Now there's a surprise," Nicole said sarcastically. "What is it?"

"He wants you to learn sign language."

"So . . . he can start teaching me."

"He wants *me* to teach you." Matt looked at his friend. "Is that correct, David?"

David nodded.

"I'm not sure I'll be able to fill in for David anyway," Nicole said. "I mean, I have the work at the restaurant to take care of."

David signed, and Matt interpreted. "Do you have any other excuses?"

Nicole bristled. "That's not an excuse! If it weren't for the restaurant, I'd gladly help out."

David grinned while his hands moved.

Matt translated. "David said he has your shifts covered for the next few weeks. In fact, Thomas has apparently gone on vacation, so it was rather easy to persuade the acting manager to adjust your schedule."

"What about my wages? I need some income! Just because my family is well off doesn't mean I don't need the extra cash."

David reached into his pocket and pulled out a folded piece of paper. He grabbed Nicole's wrist and turned her palm over, slapping the parchment into her hand.

"What's this?" She unfolded the paper.

"David told me earlier that this money order would cover any lost wages."

Nicole glanced down at the money order in her hand. She inhaled deeply and stared at David. "You got me. I guess I'm all yours, but I have one condition."

David braced himself and prepared for a rebuttal.

"Matt, I want you to teach me how to take down your friend here, so I can use his head for a mop and his butt for a broom."

Matt laughed. "It'll be my pleasure!"

David stepped up to say good-bye to his friend. They clasped hands, and David pulled Matt toward him and slapped his back. They broke their embrace and David ushered Nicole toward the door.

"I guess I'll see you tomorrow, Nicole." Matt's voice chased David and Nicole out the door. "And thanks. It means a lot to me."

Nicole waved but did not turn to face Matt when she left.

David and Nicole made their way home. "It's a good thing you can't talk, mister," she said, "or you'd have some explaining to do."

David did not acknowledge that he'd heard a word she said. He continued to stare straight ahead, walking down the sidewalk.

"I don't get it." Nicole shook her head. "I thought you'd be overjoyed that Matt's no longer in class and unable to wrestle. But come to find out, you've been seeing him every day, helping him by studying and working with his . . . with his injury."

David stopped and faced Nicole, who also stopped. He placed his hand over his heart. Then he gently took Nicole's hand and placed it over her heart, patting the hand and nodding his head back in the direction they had come from.

"I'm not exactly sure what you're trying to tell me, but I'll do as you wish for now. God knows why, cause I sure don't."

David smiled and placed his left arm around her shoulders as they resumed walking.

"It's a good thing the two of you boys are so good looking. Otherwise I'd have nothing to do with either of you." She laughed at her own joke and planted a kiss on David's cheek. "I have to get to practice. I'll talk to you tomorrow."

Chapter Eight

NICOLE WAS NERVOUS when she knocked on Matt's door. For a moment there was no reply. Her muscles relaxed and her anxiety dissipated. Maybe no one was home. Her heart skipped, however, when she heard Matt's voice from inside shout for her to come on in.

She pushed the door and saw Matt removing a sock-type sleeve off his amputated leg.

"What's that?" Nicole pointed at the object Matt had been wearing.

"It's is called a 'shrinker.' It's supposed to help shape my leg for the prosthesis." Matt smiled. "And how are you today?"

"Oh, me? I'm good. How . . . how are you?"

Matt laughed. "Hey, I'm not going to bite you. You don't have to help me if you don't want to. David seemed to think you wanted to help."

"It's not that. I do want to help. . . I just . . ."

"I know this is awkward. How about I teach you some sign language while you work on my leg?"

"Sounds like a plan." Nicole knelt before Matt, and taking a deep breath, reached out and placed her hands on Matt's stump. Her hands trembled, betraying the fear that she was feeling. Matt did not appear to notice, so she slowly stroked his skin.

Her hands took in the feel and shape of his remaining limb, and she became hypnotized by the motion of her fingers. Her confidence grew, and she applied more pressure. As she pressed harder with her thumbs, she touched a nodule of flesh that caused Matt to yelp and withdraw his leg in pain.

"I'm so sorry! I didn't mean to—"

"No, no it's all right," Matt replied. "I'm the one who is sorry. I'll try to hold still. Go ahead, try again." He placed his leg back in her hands.

Nicole protested, "I don't want to hurt you."

"Nicole, it has to be done if I want to walk without these crutches. Start again. I'm ready."

Nicole was not sure *she* was ready, but she nodded and worked on his flesh once again. She soon discovered the areas that were the most sensitive. With Matt's guidance, she spent more time massaging these areas, even though they produced the most pain.

Matt taught Nicole sign language.

Although she was unable to mimic his hand movements, Nicole appreciated the distraction. She found that she no longer had to stare at his leg. Her hands had memorized every contour, nodule, and scar.

When she finished, she applied resistance in the way David had demonstrated. Nicole resisted both knee extension and flexion to work Matt's quads and hamstrings. They performed three sets of ten together, laughing and enjoying each other's company.

Matt made a jibe about Nicole's lack of strength. She retaliated by picking up his crutches and moving across the room, threatening to throw them outside.

Matt promptly made amends and stated that not even David could apply such force.

Nicole laughed and called him a liar, but the ploy worked. She returned his crutches to his side and resumed the exercise together.

Time passed quickly. Nicole realized she had to go, in order to be at practice in time.

"Nicole, thanks again. I really mean that. I don't know how I'll repay you."

"It's my pleasure Matt. I'll start running a tab for you, if you want." Nicole flashed a grin and waved good-bye as she opened the door. "I'll see you again in a couple of days."

"You bet. Thanks again, and have a great day!" Matt hollered to her as she left.

No sooner had the door of Matt's home closed, when the back door opened, and David strolled in.

"David, you bum! Are you ready?" Joy raced across Matt's face when he saw David enter the room.

"I'm ready to kick your butt." David smirked and signed, "How did things go with Nicole?" He was still amazed at how rapidly Matt had learned sign language.

"Great! I was a little concerned with what you had confided to me, but I don't think things could have gone any better."

"Good. I'll get the mat out." David unraveled a mat, which covered the living room floor.

"Do you think I could be ready for the NCAA tourney?"

David finished getting the mat ready and signed, "Do you think that you will be ready?"

"After my accident, it didn't matter to me. I was just so thankful to be alive. It was you who instilled the crazy notion that I could still wrestle in the tourney."

"You want to beat Davis. You lost to him by two points in the final last year and you have worked too hard this year not to wrestle."

"Yes, it'd be great to win a national title. It's been one of my dreams since high school, but in the grand scheme of things, the national title is rather a small accomplishment."

"How do you do it?"

"Do what?" Matt joined David on the mat, and both wrestlers warmed up.

"Stay so positive."

"Any other attitude would not be very productive now, would it?"

David studied his friend. His hands moved deftly. "I don't understand why you're not angry or even depressed."

"I thought we talked about this before."

"Tell me again. I have a thick skull—a wrestler, you know. Things have a hard time reaching my brain."

"Yeah, you're definitely a bonehead."

"Are you angry at God?"

Matt stopped his back bridge and rolled over onto his belly. He propped on his elbows to address David. "So you think I should be angry at God for sparing my life?"

"He has taken your leg, and therefore changed your life forever."

"Yes. But why should I assume that he has changed it for the worse?"

David did not respond. He did not know how to convey his own confusion to Matt and his amazement that Matt was just as positive now, after his loss, as he had been before.

"David, if I believed in God and loved Him only when things were going my way, would I really love Him?"

Again, David did not respond. This young man seemed too good to be true.

"David, I'm human. I've felt sorrow and disappointment, but never was I really angry about what happened. Yes, I'm sorry I lost my leg, but I'm still alive. That's what I rejoice in."

"But how could someone who loves us allow these bad things to happen? It doesn't make sense to me."

"Mistake number one is assuming you can think on the same plane as God."

David shrugged.

"Without trying to get into a huge philosophical debate," Matt went on, "consider this simple analogy: My parents took me to the doctor when I was very young to receive a series of immunizations. There I sat, trusting my parents. The doctor came in. Imagine my surprise when the doctor gave me my first shot, which caused me to holler in pain, pain that my parents allowed to happen to me. Their foresight told them that this was necessary to allow me to grow into a healthy young man. In the same way, I believe that the moments of pain we feel in our life allow our spirit to grow in a manner that is necessary for our current and future relationship with God."

"If you say so. How about I inflict some pain on the mat?"

Matt laughed. "Let's get to it."

David and Matt practiced for two hours. They eventually collapsed in exhaustion. Matt rolled over and rubbed his leg in a circular motion. David stretched a hamstring that continued to contract due to dehydration.

Matt gasped. "So, is this training for me or for you?"

"I won't be wrestling in the tourney."

"That's not what I mean."

David stared at his friend. "I'm not sure . . ."

Matt nodded. "If it will help you by helping me, then we can help each other."

David pulled his friend up to a stand. He slapped Matt on the back and embraced him with a bear hug.

Tammy hefted her backpack and kicked out the flames of her campfire. It felt good to be on the hiking trail. It would take her some time to reach her destination, but she was looking forward to scaling the majestic face of the mountain once again. When she had stood at the summit in the past, she had felt close to God in a way that words could not describe. When she reached it she would be able to pray for herself and for her sister.

Her companion had already gathered his gear and slowly made his way down the trail.

Chapter Nine

THE NEXT COUPLE of weeks flew by. Nicole and David worked with Matt, never passing each other in the changing of their shifts. Matt made progress with his sensitivity and his wrestling adaptations.

Nicole looked forward to the days she was able to work with Matt. As he progressed physically toward his goal of walking, she progressed emotionally with her ability to give.

One Tuesday afternoon, Matt was preparing to leave for his appointment with the prosthetist. He maneuvered with the grace of a gifted athlete as he hopped into the driver's seat and tossed his crutches into the seat next to him.

"Where am I going to sit?"

Matt rotated to see Nicole smiling brightly. She placed her head through the passenger window.

"Nicole! What are you doing here? Shouldn't you be at practice?"

Nicole opened the door and flipped Matt's crutches into the back seat and sat down in the passenger's seat. "I decided I felt too sick to make it to practice."

"I guess you're coming along?"

"Absolutely. I have to see if all the work we've done has paid off."

"You don't have to come."

"Just shut up and drive, before I change my mind."

Matt smiled and turned the key. "Aye, aye captain."

They headed down the street and Matt sang a tune. Pausing, he said, "You know, I think my leg is ready to bear some pressure on it now."

"I think it's ready too. But that's not the pressure I'm worried about."

"What do you mean?"

"I mean the pressure on my ears from your incessant singing." She reached over and clicked on the radio.

Matt laughed. He playfully shoved Nicole and attempted to sing along with the radio.

Nicole rolled her eyes and increased the volume, which only caused Matt to screech louder.

They arrived at the medical building. Matt chatted unceasingly while they sat in the waiting room.

After a short wait, a stocky man appeared. "Good afternoon, Matt. Are you ready to try some walking today?"

"You bet I am. Lyle, this is Nicole. She's been helping me prepare for this."

Lyle reached out and shook Nicole's hand. "It's nice to meet you, Nicole." Breaking contact, he motioned to Matt. "Let's get this show on the road."

Matt sat down on a low table, and Nicole placed herself in a chair nearby.

"All right, Matt. Take off your shrinker and place this elastic sleeve over your leg. This form will slide on next and act as a buffer between your skin and the prosthesis." Lyle handed Matt a form that had been molded from Matt's stump. "Now let's put on that new leg." He placed what he called "a leg" into Matt's hands. The top half of the prosthesis was a hollowed, hardened shell of plastic. Its coloring was vaguely similar to that of flesh. The lower half was a metal rod that exited the shell and connected to a workable foot. "Pull it up as far as you can. Then stand up and push your leg all the way into the socket."

Matt pulled on the prosthesis and stood. He pushed his stump down and winced. He stood up and cautiously shifted his weight back and forth.

"Matt, when you are ready . . ." Lyle's words held an encouraging tone.

Matt closed his eyes and took a deep breath as he prepared to take a step.

A loud clap startled Matt. David stood in the doorway, arms crossed.

"David!" Matt exclaimed. "What are you doing here?"

His friend signed, "You weren't planning on doing this without me, were you?"

"Well, get over here then."

David strolled over and squatted down on his heels next to Nicole. "Let's see what you've got!" He reached over and grasped Nicole's hand, giving it a gentle squeeze.

Nicole returned his sign of reassurance and focused on Matt.

Matt took a deep breath. Grinning from ear to ear, he tentatively placed his new leg forward. He transferred all his weight onto the left leg and swung his right leg quickly through to stand on it. He paused in that position.

When Matt paused, Nicole stood and exclaimed, "Matt! Are you all right?"

Matt laughed, and David placed his hand on Nicole's shoulder.

"What's so funny?" Nicole asked.

"I didn't feel any pain!"

"And that is funny how?"

Lyle interjected, "I think he's relieved. Matt, let's take some more steps."

Matt stepped with his left leg and swung through with his right. He continued step by step, standing longer on his right leg and swinging it quicker to avoid too long of a stance phase on the prosthesis. Soon Matt's tempo became more symmetrical as stance and swing equalized from right leg to left.

Mastery of his new limb came quickly. Spinning around, he opened his arms wide, looked toward heaven, and proclaimed a resounding, "Yes!"

Nicole raced toward him, followed closely by David. She flew into his widespread arms. "Matt, you did it!"

Matt spun her around in a circle. "Are you crazy, girl? Testing out all this weight together." He laughed and placed Nicole back on the floor.

"You saying something about my weight, boy?" Her teasing eyes mirrored the joy she felt for Matt's accomplishment.

David placed a firm grip on Matt's shoulder. He clasped his hand and slapped him on the back.

"Nice to see you are left speechless, bud." Matt reached out and hugged his friend.

"Matt, if we had worked faster, you could have wrestled in this weekend's NCAA tournament," Nicole said.

Matt glanced to David.

David signed, "NCAA rules do not allow for a prosthesis on the mat."

Nicole signed back as she looked toward Matt. "Is that true?"

"I'm afraid it's true." Matt shrugged and shared a wink with David.

The two men had not let Nicole in on their secret of making sure Matt was ready for the NCAA tourney. Matt was not sure why David did not want her to know, but he was willing to keep it a secret. He had a suspicion that Tammy was somehow involved, but David deflected any questions.

The three friends were interrupted by Lyle. "All right, we have some instructions to go through. First, let's take off your prosthesis and sock and have a look at your stump."

Matt returned to the low table and sat down. He removed the prosthesis and sock from his leg. He attempted to brush away the sweat as Lyle took the leg and inspected it closely.

Nicole peered over his shoulder. "What are you looking for, Lyle?"

"I need to check where his stump is bearing the weight of his body. That will confirm that the mechanics of this temporary are correct."

"Temporary? Temporary what?"

Matt saved Lyle by explaining, "This is not my final prosthesis. I will use this for a while to confirm the mechanics, and then they will make my permanent leg. Right, Lyle?"

"That's it in a nutshell. Everything looks good. Put it back on so you can walk out of here without those crutches."

"You got it!"

David signed he had to do some studying. With a wave and a nod, he strolled out of the office.

Matt grabbed his crutches and carried them out to the vehicle, Nicole just a step behind.

"Are you sure that you don't feel any pain?" Nicole asked.

Matt tossed the crutches into the trunk. He opened the passenger door for Nicole. "Positive. I can't describe how good it feels to walk again." He stopped Nicole from entering the car, and with sincerity looked into her eyes. "I don't know how I can ever repay you."

Nicole turned a deep shade of red. "Oh, don't you worry. I'll tally up your tab, and we'll think of something!"

Matt chuckled. "I look forward to paying that bill. In the meantime, is there a way I can work off the interest?"

It was Nicole's turn to laugh. "I'm sure there is! Give me a day or two, and I'll think of something."

Matt nodded. He placed each hand on Nicole's shoulder, paused for a moment, and gave her a warm hug. He did not want to let go.

Nicole whispered, "Let's get in the car."

Matt broke his embrace and closed the door for Nicole. He moved around the vehicle and got in. "Nic, do you want me to drop you off at home?"

"Actually, I was thinking of riding home with you . . . there is that matter of interest."

"I'm not going straight home," Matt said.

"Where are you headed?"

"I'm going over to wrestling practice and say hi to the guys. Do you want to come?"

Nicole turned away to stare out her window. "No. Just drop me off at the house."

"Is everything OK?" Matt waited for a response, but none came by the time they arrived at Nicole's home. He slowed the car to a stop.

Nicole reached to open the door, but Matt grabbed her arm, keeping her from exiting the vehicle. She would not look at Matt.

"Nic, tell me, what's up?"

A tear slipped down her cheek. "I guess you don't need my help anymore."

"You mean with desensitizing my stump?"

"I guess."

"What if I just need you?"

Nicole glanced up.

"I don't want to stop seeing you just because you don't have to come over and work with me," Matt said. "Do you want to stop seeing me?"

She did not speak, her tears rolled freely. She shook her head and threw herself into Matt's embrace.

Matt's voice was a whisper. "Shhh. It'll be all right. Are you sure there's nothing else bothering you?"

Nicole pushed free and shook her head. "I'll call you." She blurted out the words and escaped the vehicle, leaving a confused young man wondering at her tears.

Chapter Ten

THE NEXT DAY Matt and David waited anxiously in the locker room. It was the first day of the NCAA tournament, and the competition was being held at Bohning University, the boys' home gymnasium. Coach Sabo had informed Matt three weeks before that the NCAA would allow him to compete in this year's tournament, based on his previous year's record.

The night before, Matt had told his teammates his plan to compete in the tournament. Although the whole team was present, only four other members of the squad would be competing for a national title. Matt would be wrestling in the 167-pound division, with the goal of facing Ron Davis in the final.

Matt's first few matches were easy. He scurried around in a unique posture with left hand and left knee on the mat while his right foot stood in a normal position. He was not allowed to wear his prosthesis but he and David had prepared for that rule. Matt's opponents were tentative, and he breezed through the first few rounds of the tournament.

Over the next two days, Matt amazed more than merely his opponents. The fans became attracted to the underdog who had suffered a potentially career-ending injury. Even the national media followed Matt in his warm-ups, matches, and wins.

After each victory, David ran onto the mat and offered his shoulder for Matt to hold as he hopped off the mat. It was evident that a rematch of the previous year's final was imminent.

Nicole wiped the tears from her eyes. She lay on the living room floor curled into a tight ball. The moisture that accumulated on the wooden floor had not dried. She brushed her hair out of her mouth, nose, and eyes. Her thoughts echoed in her head as she continued to struggle with her recent choices.

She pulled out her cell phone and dialed a number.

"What have I done?" Nicole whined through the speaker.

A voice answered, "You have done what is needed."

"No, it can't be what was needed. Look at David. He chose a different path."

"That's because he's weaker than you, unwilling to do what was needed. He put on a good face in helping Matt, but he's glad that Matt is no longer part of the team. David can now have the glory." The voice was harsh and threatening.

"Is that what is needed? Glory?"

"Your sister enjoyed the glory."

"I'm not sure. I think she got pleasure in doing for others. Could that be true?"

A knock sounded at her door. She ended the call and struggled to her feet. She walked lamely over to pull the curtain back. It was David. Nicole was not concerned about her appearance, and she hurriedly unlocked the door.

"David, I'm so glad to see you! Come on in." Nicole turned, but David stopped her with a quick snatch of her arm.

"What's wrong?" David signed.

"Nothing . . . I'm better now that you're here."

"I need you to come with me."

"I can't go out looking like this." Nicole pointed at him. "Why are you in your wrestling warm-ups?"

David's hands moved rapidly, "There is not enough time. I need you to come right now, so we are not late."

"Late? Late for what? What's going on?"

"Let's just say that Matt and I have a little surprise for you. You must come now!" He grabbed her arm.

"Ouch! Stop pulling so hard. I'm coming."

David released his grip and flushed.

"It's all right." Nicole rubbed her arm. "I mean it's all right that you were pulling on me. We'll see if my arm is all right later." She smiled.

David grabbed her hand. The two ran down the sidewalk toward the university. "David, what on earth is going on? What's the hurry?"

David did not take the time to stop and explain. He ran faster.

David and Nicole were breathing hard when they entered the packed gymnasium. People covered the bleachers and the open floor. David pulled Nicole through the crowd and into the bleachers. There was one spot available. He motioned Nicole to sit.

David started down the crowded bleachers. Nicole yelled, "David, are you wrestling? Is that why I'm here?"

David shook his head as an announcement came over the loudspeaker. "And now, wrestling fans, the finalists in the 167-pound weight class . . ."

The pause was long enough for David to point up and sign, "Listen."

"Ron Davis and Matt James."

Nicole's eyes widened. In her peripheral vision she saw David continue down the bleachers out onto the gym floor. Her focus was so intense on the figure loosening up on the far side of the mat that she was oblivious to the shouts and cheers of the crowd as they called out Matt's name. His warm-ups were still on, and his hood masked his face. A shudder went down her spine when she noticed there was empty space in the left pant leg of the wrestler.

"Matt?" The whisper scarcely left her lips.

She saw it was Matt when he removed his warm-ups, tops first and last, the bottoms, and hopped to the center of the mat.

His opponent quickly joined him. A handshake, a simultaneous nod of the heads, a whistle, and the match was underway.

Nicole saw that David stood mat side, apart from the team.

She watched the two combatants engage and disengage, testing each other's weaknesses. The two men rolled around in a blur. Nicole looked to the scoreboard when the first period ended. She had no idea how Matt was doing, but the scoreboard read "three to three."

The referee motioned the men to assume their positions. Then he blew the whistle, starting the second of three periods.

Nicole watched Matt scramble, then she heard an ear-shattering scream from his lips. His opponent had slapped the fleshy mound of Matt's stump.

Nicole watched in horror for the remainder of the period while Matt fought to escape, only to be blocked by an opponent who cruelly gripped Matt's leg and stopped him cold. She wrapped her arms tighter around herself, as if somehow she could protect herself and Matt from the pain.

Matt no longer cried out in agony, but his facial expression and body language demonstrated how much agony he was in when Ron grabbed Matt's left leg.

Tears welled up in David's eyes. He watched his friend bravely fight until the end of the second period. It could not end soon enough. The score was now in Ron's favor. To overcome the deficit in the third period would be too much to ask. Ron would have the ability to play strictly passive defense, a stalling tactic that would earn him the national title.

David locked eyes with Matt. "Take neutral," he signed. "Be quick and look to me."

Matt nodded and chose the neutral position for the third and final period.

David signed, "Take him down. Fast."

The whistle sounded. Matt exploded forward. Before a screaming crowd, he took Ron down to the mat.

"Turn him to his back!" David signaled the instructions as his mind screamed.

With half the period fading, it was evident that Matt was not going to be able to turn Ron on his back.

David realized they needed to change tactics. He pounded on the floor to get Matt's attention. "Let him up." David's hands conveyed his thoughts

Matt did not second guess, and he allowed his opponent to escape.

Ron changed tactics and went on the offensive. He caught Matt off guard, taking him down to the mat with thirty seconds left in the match.

David saw the hopelessness in Matt's countenance. It was the first time he had ever seen his friend appear defeated. Matt was on the bottom, where his opponent had held him in the second period and dominated.

"Expose your leg and stand," David commanded when Matt looked for help.

Matt's eyes widened, and for the first time in the tournament, he hesitated.

"He reaches for it, and you throw him."

The seconds ticked away. David did not know if Matt had the courage to endure the pain on his leg once again. He watched his friend agonize over the decision. With fifteen seconds remaining, Matt exploded from the floor and stood, exposing his weakness.

Ron reached for the stump.

David's mind yelled, *Now,* just as Ron's coach screamed, "Nooo!"

David watched the end of the bout frame by frame. Ron's right hand dropped to Matt's leg. Matt shifted his weight and tossed his hips, expertly flinging his opponent across the mat and finishing the move by lying chest on chest. Matt had thrown Ron to his back. The seconds expired, and the referee headed over to the scorer's table to tabulate the results.

The entire gymnasium remained silent and eager for the final call.

"Men, shake hands," the referee instructed.

Ron and Matt shook hands in the unusual silence of a packed gymnasium. The referee swept Matt's hand up in victory.

The applause that erupted from the crowd was deafening. People scampered from the bleachers to congratulate the winner.

The announcement came over the loud speakers: "The winner of the one hundred and sixty seven pound title goes to Matt James, with the final score of ten to nine."

Matt was surrounded by his teammates. They hugged and congratulated the national champ. They lifted Matt high in the air and chanted, "Champ, champ, champ!"

"Where's David?" Matt's voice shouted over the crowd that had engulfed him. "David! David, where are you?"

David stood at the corner of the mat, watching his friend shouting his name. He waved his hand when Matt called.

"Guys, put me down!" Matt hollered. With amazing agility, he hopped to David and tackled him. "We did it, David! I can't believe it! You crazy fool, we actually did it!"

The celebratory hug did not last long, for many hands pulled Matt and David to their feet. They stood face to face with congratulatory slaps and questions coming from all directions.

Nicole slipped in between the two friends. She glanced at each man and then stated in exasperation, "What have you guys been doing? I mean, I don't understand what or how . . . ?"

Matt laughed, "Thanks for the congratulations there, Nic."

"What? Oh, you did great, but how?"

Matt put his arm around David and gave him a big squeeze. "This guy has been working to get me ready for this ever since my injury."

Nicole frowned at David. "What?"

"Nicole, Matt is my brother in all but blood, and I love him like a brother." David's hands responded.

The men's embrace was interrupted by the media frantically snapping pictures and asking Matt a hundred different questions.

The distraction allowed David to focus on Nicole. "In helping Matt succeed, I shared in his victory, as did you."

Nicole stared at David. "You really love him like a brother?"

David simply smiled.

Nicole trembled. "David, we need to leave—right now!"

David puckered his brow.

"I've done something awful, and we need to go right now. I need to make it right." Nicole grabbed David and led him out of the gymnasium.

Chapter Eleven

TAMMY SURVEYED HER surroundings and wiped her brow of sweat. Her breathing was labored, and she could feel her heart thumping against her chest. She allowed herself a moment's rest, drank some water, and focused on the path that lay in front of her. She could see the rock face, looming in front of her, which had been her destination these last few weeks.

The Rocky Mountains of New Mexico were gorgeous this time of year. They were known as the Jemez Mountains, the southernmost tip of the massive range extended into the northern neighbor, Canada. A white blanket of snow covered the peaks of the highest mountains and contrasted against the dark evergreen timber that lined the basin. The weather could still pose a problem, but Tammy's mind was made up. Nothing would deter her from reaching her goal.

Tammy had hiked a significant distance since leaving home. Her companion had left her this morning, stating he had a pressing matter to attend to. Tammy did not question his excuse. She was actually relieved that Thomas was no longer with her. Initially he was friendly and a positive companion, but his mood had withered during their excursion. He had become withdrawn and irritated, and Tammy could not figure out why. She did not feel comfortable even looking in his direction, so when Thomas interrupted the eerie silence and announced it was time for him to depart, she did not ask why, in fear that he would change his mind.

The last few days alone had given her the opportunity to pray and open her heart to God. She was still unclear how to confront Nicole in a manner that would not separate the sisters further. She was confident when she reached her destination that God would reveal His plan to her.

Two hours later, Tammy made it to the base of the rock formation she had traveled three hundred miles to climb. She slipped off her backpack and peered up at the massive rock that stood imposingly in front of her. "Well, hello, Goliath. It's been a long time." She spoke to the mountain in a tone that implied that it expected a greeting but would offer none in reply.

She put on her harness and her rock-climbing shoes. The shoes resembled toughened ballet slippers, made of supple leather and sticky rubber soles. She also checked her powder, wedges, nuts, cams, and multiple sections of rope.

Tammy had never climbed Goliath solo, so she would be attempting a free climb. She would use sections of rope as a safety valve for the few regions of Goliath that would present significant difficulties.

After a quick tally of her tools, Tammy prepared herself for the climb. It would take her about ten hours to reach the summit, and that was only if she experienced no setbacks. Taking a deep breath, she cleared her mind, and set her focus on the task at hand.

David, Matt, and Nicole rode in the car in silence. David was glad Matt had managed to catch up with them as they were leaving the gymnasium. Matt had asked for no details, but it was evident that he was going along for whatever ride Nicole was taking them on. Nicole was driving and unwilling to answer any questions. She just mumbled, "I hope we're in time."

After three hours of driving, Nicole stopped at a sporting goods store. The two confused men followed her into the store. Nicole stopped when she found what she was searching for. "See if this fits." She handed David a strange harness.

"Fits what?"

"Over your trunk and pelvis. These straps wrap under and around each leg." She continued to search the apparel that hung on the wall and picked up a harness for herself. "Matt, at the end of this aisle is rope. Pick up four of the hundred-meter length."

Matt nodded and did as he was told while David struggled with putting on the harness.

Nicole stepped up to give him some help, and with a few quick pulls and clicks mumbled, "It fits." She headed away from David and said, "Take it off and come on."

David followed her, nearly knocking her over when he turned the corner.

"What size shoe do you wear?" Nicole asked.

David held up all ten fingers.

"A few more things, and we'll hit the road."

With the quick shopping spree done, the threesome once again found themselves in the vehicle heading down the winding road.

Matt's voice broke the silence. "Nic, at least tell us where we're going. I mean, we're here for you. Can you at least let us know our destination?"

Nicole was silent. When she finally spoke, her voice startled David and Matt. "We're going to New Mexico."

What's in New Mexico? David thought.

As if in answer to his question, Nicole continued, "We are going to see Tammy . . . I hope."

A chill trickled down David's spine. He now had an idea what this was about. Nicole's envy of her sister had sparked some kind of action taken against Tammy. David tapped Matt on the shoulder from the back seat and signed, "Is Tammy in danger?"

Matt wrinkled his brow, but voiced David's question. "David wants to know if Tammy is in danger."

Nicole's silence spoke volumes as did her right foot, which depressed the accelerator. The car's speed rose.

Matt risked a concerned glance toward David. David's hands simply stated, "Pray."

David was unsure how much time had elapsed when the vehicle came to an abrupt stop. It was nighttime, and the headlights shone on a sign that read, "Welcome to the Jemez Mountain National Forest."

"All right. Let's go." Nicole shut off the car, tossed the keys under the floor mat, and popped the trunk. Her flashlight shone brightly, and she tossed each man a pack with the unspoken command of "put this on."

"There are a few hours before daybreak, but we need to get started now."

David and Matt put on their packs and followed the hastily fading light of Nicole's flashlight as she headed up a hiking trail.

Nicole's pace was maddening. David and Matt had difficulty keeping pace. Neither possessed a flashlight, and David was concerned about how his friend was faring with his artificial leg.

Matt stumbled and collapsed. "David, you had better go on without me."

In the darkness, David stopped and helped his friend rise. He felt helpless, for he was unable to effectively communicate to his friend in the gloomy forest.

Matt shoved David, not forcibly, but with urgency. "Don't lose her. My leg can't maintain this pace in this terrain. Go after her. I'll be all right."

The two men clasped hands.

"I'll find you, or you'll find me. Now go!"

David left his friend in the darkness and chased the glimpses of light climbing the mountain trail. *I'll find her, my friend. Nicole, what is going on?*

David closed the distance between himself and Nicole. The journey continued up the mountain. Their breathing labored as the altitude changed.

Day broke, and David's heart threatened to explode from his chest. At last, Nicole stopped and looked back to her followers. Her chest was heaving from the labored breathing and her eyes darted in search of the missing member of their party. She gasped, "Where's Matt?"

David slumped, his hands locked on his knees. Then he stood, wiped his brow on his sleeve, and signed his response. "He couldn't continue. His leg wouldn't tolerate the climb."

"You left him?"

"Technically, *you* left him."

"I can't worry about that now; we have to keep going." Nicole faced back up the trail to continue her ascent.

David grabbed a rock and tossed it at Nicole. The stone smashed against the side of the mountain, stopping Nicole from taking another step. She faced him. "I don't have time for this!"

"No."

"David, we must get to Tammy."

"Why?" he signed.

"I . . . we . . . just come with me. Please!"

"Tell me. It is time."

"We don't have the time."

"What did you do?"

Nicole stared at him. Her jaw clenched, and she trembled. "I did something awful." She averted her gaze. "I cut part of Tammy's safety harness."

David's heart skipped, but his legs carried him the remaining distance to grab Nicole. *Dear God in heaven,* his thoughts shouted, *protect your child!* He shook her shoulders until Nicole lifted her head.

"Let's go." David signaled toward the slope.

"You must hate me." Nicole sobbed and remained frozen. "I know how you feel about my sister."

"How do *you* feel about your sister?"

Nicole gawked at David, unable to respond or move from her trance.

"Lead me. Let's get to Tammy."

Nicole bit her lip, nodded, and seized David's hand. They headed up the trail.

Five minutes later, they rounded a bend, and David stared in awe at the rock formation that jutted before them.

"We're here," Nicole exclaimed. "Wait right here. I have to check something. I hope we're here first." She scampered off toward the base of the rock.

David arched his neck, took in the majestic mountain, and surveyed the scenery that stretched out before him. *God's paint brush.*

His trance was broken by Nicole's voice. "We're too late."

A loud voice echoed within David's mind. *Speak.*

Nicole continued. "Tammy's gear is here. We're too late." Tears streamed down her cheeks. "She's already started her climb. Goliath was not meant to be scaled alone."

Speak!

"She'll never make it." Nicole collapsed to the earth and wailed, "I've killed her, David. I've killed my sister!"

David's voice pierced the air. "Tammy is alive. I can feel it." His ears adjusted to the sound of his newly found voice. "Goliath?" He viewed the mountainous rock that shot up above him.

"No, you don't understand. If she slips while her safety rope is attached to her harness, it will break." Nicole covered her head with her hands. She didn't act surprised that David had spoken.

"Nicole, we need to find Tammy. Do you know the route she'd take?"

"She'll cross through Goliath's Teeth, and"—Nicole turned her head sharply to the left and then to the right—"David! Who said that? Who—?"

David knelt before Nicole and lifted her chin. "Nicole, we need to get to your sister."

Nicole pushed away from David and scrambled to her feet. "What's going on? You can talk?"

"There's no time for an explanation. We need to get to Tammy. Can you take us to Goliath's Teeth?"

Nicole's eyes remained wide, but nodded in affirmation.

"Then let's get going. Let's save your sister."

Nicole whispered, "Tammy."

"You'll have to teach me what to do as we go. I assume that was your plan, anyway."

Nicole cleared her throat. "Yes, it was. Goliath is meant to be scaled by traditional lead climbing." She gathered her wits and opened her backpack.

"Lead climbing?" David asked.

"It shouldn't be too hard. Tammy will have left in some of her bolts for the climb back down."

"OK . . ."

"In the areas that we are unable to free climb, I will lead. When we need to attach to the bolts, we'll take turns leading if I get tired."

"You're losing me. Maybe you can talk me through it as we go."

"I'll try. The first fifty feet we should manage without too much difficulty. Put on your harness, climbing shoes, and make sure your rope is attached. The small fanny pack has some tools you may need during the climb."

"Tell me about them as we climb."

David followed Nicole to the base of the projecting rock. Nicole stepped onto a small ledge, momentarily searched with her hands, and began to climb. David watched her technique. It seemed simple enough. Once Nicole reached about fifteen feet above him, he stepped onto the ledge, mimicking Nicole, and picked his way up the wall of stone. When he reached the height of fifteen feet, Nicole stood sprawled against the face of the mountain, and David rested as well.

Nicole asked, "How you doing?"

"Fine. How long of a climb is it?"

"I honestly don't remember. I'm pretty sure that it will take over five hours to reach the top, and that's where Tammy is headed. If we're lucky, she'll stop at the cleft to rest, and we can gain some ground on her." Nicole paused. "After that, the climb becomes dangerous."

"We'll get there," David said.

"She's a few hours ahead of us."

David grimaced. "How do you know?"

"She signed in at the trail entry. It was logged yesterday, and she wouldn't have begun the climb at night."

Maybe we'll reach her in time. Maybe she won't even have to rely on her harness. David's thoughts remained unspoken.

"One more thing." Nicole resumed her climb. "As an inexperienced climber, don't risk looking down as we get higher."

Down? David glanced down to his starting point. Instantly the world spun, and he was sure his body was about to tumble to the ground. A wave of distant memories flooded his mind, as did his fear of heights.

David gripped the stone so hard that his fingers, under the nails, bled. He could not get close enough to the rock. His breathing and heart rate were so rapid that he was no longer just spinning, but becoming lightheaded. His body threatened to lose consciousness in an attempt to slow his heart rate. Before he slipped into blackness, the pain from his right temple brought him out of his tailspin.

"David! David!" Nicole yanked his hair.

His eyes flew open.

"What are you doing?"

David forced words to his lips. "I forgot. I'm afraid of heights."

"I'll help lower you to the ground. I need you to let go. Let me guide you down."

"Can't . . . can't let go." David shut his eyes and hugged the mountainside.

Sizzling pain shot through his right hand, and then he was falling backwards. He flailed frantically, but a blow to his stomach sent him off of his perch. The descent was short as the climbing rope stretched and then became taught, suspending him in the air.

David bounced like a yo-yo on a string. Nicole promptly lowered him toward the ground, preventing him from getting a firm foot or handhold on the rocks that jutted out.

David's feet touched a solid surface, followed by his buttocks, back, and head. He scrambled to his feet, regaining his senses.

Nicole hollered from above, "Untie your rope!"

David obeyed. He stood transfixed while the rope sprang to sudden life, wound its way back up the mountain, and disappeared where Nicole remained. She waved to David and resumed her ascent up the face of Goliath.

He watched in despair and disbelief. Nicole climbed without him. *I need to be there with her! What's my problem? I need to shake this fear. Dear God in heaven, help me!* Tears of frustration rolled down his face. David made his way back to the first ledge, where they had started their climb. He stood on the ledge and reached up to grab a projection, but was unable to move forward. *No! I must move forward!* But as before, his body betrayed him, and he could not move.

David was unsure how long he stood frozen against the mountain pounding his fist against the rock, before a hand on his shoulder pulled him away from the ledge. His eyes lit with recognition at the face of his friend Matt, who stood before him.

"Hey, what's going on?" Matt asked. "I've been yelling your name for the last few minutes. Where's Nicole?"

"She went up the mountain without me."

Matt lost his balance and almost fell. "What? You spoke. Wait a minute. Say something else."

"Yes, I can talk, for now, but I don't know how long it'll last."

"I don't understand. How can you talk? I thought you couldn't speak."

"I couldn't, and I don't have the time to fully explain why I can talk now. We need to get to Nicole."

"But . . ."

"Please, Matt, just trust me."

Matt stood silent for a moment. "What's going on?"

David quickly summarized the danger Tammy was in. He told Matt how Nicole needed someone to help her access and cross Goliath's Teeth, and how David's fear of heights had caused him to fail both Nicole and Tammy in their time of need.

Matt listened in silence. He didn't ask questions, but nodded every now and then to acknowledge that he understood. "You're afraid of heights." It was a statement, not a question.

David nodded and hung his head in shame.

Matt continued, "You know, I've been afraid. I was afraid once that I'd only be part of a man when I lost part of my body. I felt that in not being a whole man I'd lack in all areas of my life."

"But I thought . . ." David began.

"Wait, David. Let me finish. Yes, I felt blessed that I still had my life, but that did not stop the fear of what that life would become." Matt moved closer and placed a hand on David's shoulder. "But then I met this crazy guy who helped me to believe and hope. More importantly, he—or should I say *you*—helped me face and overcome that fear. It was your love and kindness that confirmed that I was still whole in heart and spirit, and my actions—not my missing limb—defined who I am."

David listened to the self-revelation of the young man who stood before him. In all of David's years of teaching and lecturing, the verbal instructions had never had such an affect on the listeners and note-takers.

"So, I want you to use your love for Tammy and Nicole as a reason to climb the mountain, to face your Goliath, instead of using fear as an excuse for not acting. Do you love Tammy, David?"

David nodded.

"Then show it. I'd go in your place, but I'm afraid my leg could not take anymore friction."

David was amazed. Exactly who was supposed to save whom?

"David, you can do this. I'll stay at the foot of the mountain until you return. My prayers will go with you."

David turned from his friend. It was time for David to face Goliath.

Chapter Twelve

TAMMY SCANNED THE ridges of rock that projected out of the smooth face of the mountain. She had made it to the Teeth. She stood at the last place she would be able to lie down and rest. The small plateau had enough room for three adults to sleep side by side if needed. She and Nicole used to spend a couple of hours resting and relaxing before tackling the protruding teeth of Goliath.

Tammy allowed herself two hours of rest. She had attempted prayer, but fatigue sent her into a deep and dreamless sleep. The chirp of her wristwatch interrupted her slumber. She shook off the mental cobwebs and prepared herself for the task at hand.

Most rock climbers stopped at this point and returned down the mountain. Only the most experienced climbers attacked Goliath's Teeth, and a mere handful scaled the region without a partner. This would be Tammy's virgin solo attempt. Something was drawing her to the top of the mountain. She had felt the tug the moment she'd left her home. There was no stopping now. The summit called.

She took a quick inventory of her equipment. Then, almost forgetting, she removed her necklace and hung it on a small shrub that had burrowed into the side of the mountain. It was a tradition that she and Nicole always performed. They left some small article that they would collect on their return to the ledge.

"Wow!" A voice disturbed her surroundings. "This is quite a view from up here!"

Tammy spun to face Thomas, who stood gawking at the view before him. "Thomas! What on earth? How did you get up here?"

"I felt bad leaving you, so I decided that my engagement could wait."

"But I thought you were not a rock climber."

"I'm not really, but I felt that the way you described your climb, you might need someone in case you got cold feet."

"Cold feet?"

"Yeah, you know. Second thoughts about reaching the summit."

"No, I don't have second thoughts. I don't understand how you got up here."

"So you're still going through with this?"

Tammy, disturbed, nodded.

"Good. Good. You better get going. You don't want to get caught somewhere out here if the sun goes down."

Tammy could not agree more. The fact that Thomas was here on the ledge babbling to her was completely unnerving. She wanted to get away from him just as much as she wanted to reach the summit of the mountain. A strange fear arose within her. She had to get away from him.

Without hesitation, Tammy climbed up and across the Teeth of Goliath. She secured a bolt when necessary and laced her rope through the exposed ring. The sun beat down on her back, and any doubt of her ability to complete the task solo was snuffed by the excitement that grew from her nearing her destination.

She had one more outcrop of jagged stone to move over. Tammy set her rope and groped for a ridge to pull her forward. Finding a shallow edge, she dug into it with her fingers and pulled her knees upward, seeking the shortest route to the summit.

The edge crumbled. Tammy lost her grip on the stone. Instinctively, she grabbed her security rope as she slid down the edge of the last "tooth." She did not panic; she merely waited to feel the rope tighten so she could resume her climb. Tammy's downward slide lasted merely seconds, but her heightened senses seemed to slow the event to minutes. She watched the rope as it went from a parabolic curve to a straight line to her body. The rope continued to lengthen. Her body weight stretched the rope away from her anchor point. Just as the rope reached the apex of its stretch, something gave way under the tension of Tammy's weight. She stared in horror when her body separated from the rope and harness.

David scaled the face of Goliath. His muscles ached from the strain of pulling and pushing and from the internal struggle of his fear of heights. He did not look down, but focused on each precise movement of hand and foot. Any observer would have remarked at his dexterity and strength as he ascended the face of the mountain.

His gaze bore a path up the rock while his mind reminded him of the love he felt for his friends and their need for his help. These thoughts—coupled with prayer—kept his once-fearful body moving upward.

There were various times he slipped, for the route he had chosen was not the best for his destination. He did not know where he was headed, but his inner voice screamed for him to hurry. So he continued moving. Forward, backward, right, or left, David's path was chosen for him. One step upward, two slides backward, and he moved another direction until he slipped or an obstruction caused him to renegotiate his direction. Every slip and recovery chipped away at David's fear.

Dear Lord, let me reach Tammy in time. I have failed You in the past. Give me the chance to help these girls. His prayer was fervent with emotion, and he continued. *Give Nicole a chance to reconcile with her sister and her sister the chance to verbalize her forgiveness.*

David rounded a bend in the stone and noticed a large overhang some distance above him. It was his next destination.

Nicole stood on the plateau before Goliath's Teeth. She scanned the jutting rock formation in front of her and surveyed the plateau. She noticed a glare from a small shrub burrowed into the side of the mountain.

Nicole approached the shrub slowly, as if trying to sneak unseen toward the scraggly plant. Her trembling fingers reached out and clasped the shiny object that hung from the shrub. She freed the necklace from the tiny branches that seemed unwilling to part with their newfound gift. She collapsed to her knees and held the necklace and locket. The locket unlatched and lay exposed. Nicole's eyes misted at the small picture of her and Tammy that had been taken years before.

"Noooo!" Nicole's voice shattered against the rock. She stood and faced the Teeth. "Tammy! Tammy, where are you? Dear God, please, no!" She collapsed, sobbing, and fumbled with her fanny pack, her shoulders wracked with agony at the pain that burned inside her. Unable to see through her tears, she dumped her pack out and shuffled through the items.

Nicole found the small item that she was hunting for, a locket matching the one that hung on Tammy's chain. She placed her locket on the chain with Tammy's and hung it on the small shrub. She stooped and shoveled her items back into her pack and snapped it securely around her waist. Nicole wiped her tears from her eyes and faced the rock formation that loomed before her. "I'm coming, sis." She whispered the words and steeled herself with the resolve to find her sibling.

"You don't have to go alone." The words startled her, and she spun to see their source.

David stood before her with quiet determination.

Nicole rushed to his arms. "Oh, David!"

"Let's find your sister."

Nicole pulled away and bit her lip. "We're too late. She has gone across the Teeth." Tears welled up in Nicole's already reddened eyes.

"We're not too late." David's reply was confident.

Nicole turned her back to David and spoke. "I'll join her, David. We came into this world together, and now we'll leave it together. I'll cross the Teeth alone to join my sister."

David grabbed Nicole's shoulders and turned her around. "I said we're not too late."

Nicole stared at him in confusion.

"Your sister needs us!"

"I don't understand. What do you mean?"

"Yes, tell us," a voice barged in. "What do you mean?"

Nicole and David staggered with surprise at seeing Thomas standing on the ledge with them.

The smell of sulfur burned the airways of David's nose. Recognition touched his mind. "You have no power here," he said to the intruder.

The sinister countenance that shadowed Thomas's grin caused Nicole to step behind David. "Don't I? Doesn't matter anyway. You, whoever you are, are too late. Tammy has fallen, and Nicole is responsible for her death." Thomas's expression darkened. He held out his hand. "Nicole, let's leave now. What you wanted has come to pass."

David felt Nicole's fingers dig into his flesh. Oddly he felt no discomfort as she continued to squeeze and shelter herself behind his frame.

David's heart drummed and he expanded his chest to help hide the girl he protected. Clenching his fists, David spoke to his adversary. "She's not going anywhere with you."

A powerful wave vibrated in David's mind from the wordless thoughts of Thomas. *Ah, yes! I recognize you now. You are but a fledgling. Do you have any power yet? The girl belongs to me. You cannot undo the work I've done.*

David fought against the searing pain in his head. He forced a reply. "I don't know what you're babbling about. The girl is not yours. She has come of her free will to save her sister."

"You lie!" Tom growled. "It doesn't matter. You're too late!"

"No, I believe you are lying. Tammy lives. I can feel her breathing."

"You are misguided by false hope . . ."

David embraced Nicole's trembling body. He glared at the entity that stood before them. "We're through talking." He bent and kissed Nicole's forehead. "Do you want to save your sister?"

"I don't know what—"

"Do you want to save your sister?"

Nicole nodded.

"Then let's get going. Can you lead the way?"

Again Nicole nodded. Her body still heaved from the sobs and fear that had tormented her spirit, but she grabbed David by the hand and led him to the edge of the plateau.

David shielded Nicole from the seething being that stood behind them. He could feel rage traveling through air and stone, but his body protected the feeble girl that stood before him. He knew Tom could not harm Nicole while David remained her guard.

The first few Teeth were not too difficult to traverse. David and Nicole used Tammy's bolts, which still remained in the protruding rocks, to anchor and spot each other.

Neither person spoke of what had transpired on the plateau.

At the third Tooth they ran into difficulty when Nicole lost her footing and tumbled from the mountainside. David quickly grabbed the rope to arrest her fall. His harness was anchored to one of the bolts. He pulled Nicole back up to his secured location.

"Can you do this?" David asked through his rapid breathing.

Nicole nodded and wiped her eyes.

"I can lead," David said.

"No!"

David was taken back by the ferociousness of her voice.

"I can do this. I need to do this, David."

David nodded. "When you're ready."

Nicole closed her eyes and took a deep breath. She gave David a quick glance and resumed her trek over the third Tooth. This time her footing remained and she was able to wedge her hand into a small crevice to pull her over and onto the next rock formation.

David waited at the anchor point. He could tell she was tired, and by the look of the rock formation, she would soon be out of sight. He wanted to call out reassuring words to her but remained quiet, so as not to break Nicole's concentration.

David watched as Nicole resumed her climb around the bend of the mountain. Soon she disappeared out of sight. He waited until he felt a tug on the rope signaling him to climb to the next anchor. A wailing scream suddenly echoed along the mountain and through his soul.

Never in his current life or his previous life did David act with such reckless abandonment as he did when he scrambled across the surface of the mountain. With the desire to reach Nicole fueling his muscles and psyche, David propelled his body effortlessly around the bend of rock, until his body collided with Nicole. His left arm stabilized her limp form against his chest, and his right arm secured both climbers to the side of the mountain.

Nicole lay limp in his arm and David was unsure if she was conscious. He examined the area and saw the source of Nicole's anguish. Tammy's harness and rope hung vacant in the breeze before them.

David, stunned, remained motionless, transfixed by the empty harness that flapped in the wind and the rope that writhed in partial freedom. What seemed like an eternity passed before David was brought back to the present by Nicole's body twisting against his frame.

"David . . ." Nicole mumbled. Then her body lurched back to life, and she screamed. "Nooo!" Her struggle threatened to cast both her and David down the mountain.

"Nicole! Don't move!" David's voice was so commanding that Nicole froze. *This cannot be, I was so sure that Tammy was OK . . . did I not understand . . . something . . . somewhere . . . wait! What is that?* His eyes focused on a discoloration of rock some distance below. He tried to make out what lay beneath him. Gradually, he realized that it was no rock or plant formation that caught his attention.

David's heart pounded faster and faster once he recognized the foreign object. "Nicole . . ."

She did not answer but sobbed and muttered words that David could not understand.

"Nicole . . . I see Tammy!"

The sniffles paused. "You *what?*"

"I see your sister. I'm sure of it, some distance below us."

Nicole wiped her face and blinked away her tears. "I don't see anything. She's gone, David. Face it. I knew we were too late." She pounded on David's chest. "You said we would make it in time. My sister is gone." Her fists struck furiously against David's body and the sobs returned.

David gambled and let go his grasp of Nicole.

Nicole attempted to wrap her arms around him.

He struck Nicole in the stomach, causing her to fall. She dropped four feet before the safety rope tightened and prevented further descent.

"David, help me! What are you doing?" Nicole attempted to climb.

"Listen to me. I'm going to lower you to your sister."

Nicole stopped her climb and stared at David. "Tammy is gone."

"What if she's not? Are you willing to risk going home if there is a chance she's still alive?"

"Well no, but—"

"Then let's make sure."

"But . . ."

"We've nothing to lose. I'm going to lower you down."

After fifty feet, David stopped lowering Nicole. "To your left!" His voice rolled down the mountain.

Nicole glanced to the left. Blond hair glistened in the sunlight and a bloodied hand grasped a fissure in the mountain.

Nicole scrambled to get a handhold on the rock and made her way over to the body.

Tammy lay sprawled against the mount, suspended alongside the very granite she had fallen down.

Nicole was at her sister's side, tears freely falling. She wrapped her arms around her twin. "Oh, Tammy," she sobbed, "what have I done?"

The body that Nicole hugged stirred.

"Tammy! Dear God in heaven! Tammy, are you all right?"

Words escaped from Tammy's lips. "I knew it."

Nicole laughed—a light, hysterical laugh. "Tammy . . . my dear Tammy. You knew what?" Nicole placed her cheek to Tammy's cheek.

"I knew you would come for me. God told me to hang on, and someone would come. I knew it would be you." Tears trickled down both girls' cheeks and they rejoiced.

"We're getting out of here," Nicole said.

Tammy moaned when Nicole moved her. She wrapped Tammy's legs around her waist and hugged Tammy's trunk. She did not need to signal their guardian above. The rope moved, and the girls were pulled up the mountain.

A scream echoed throughout the atmosphere. To those whose ears it touched it was merely the wailing of the wind, but to David's heightened senses, it confirmed the departure of a maddened adversary.

The descent down the mountain was a blur. David managed to pull both girls up and then fasten Tammy to his back with Nicole's help. Nicole led the way back to the plateau and recovered the girls' lockets.

Thomas was nowhere to be seen.

Tammy continued to breathe but had become unresponsive. Her legs dangled along David's sides, while her arms hung around his neck. Nicole and David managed to strap Tammy's midsection to David's trunk; however, it did not prevent Tammy's head from rolling side to side during the climb downward.

Through the hours of descending Goliath, Tammy remained strapped to David's body. Nicole continued to lead and rested at times, allowing David to methodically pick his way down the mountain. His strength never wavered.

With the passage of time, David could see the bottom of the rock face. As the distance closed he noticed two people at the base of Goliath. He recognized Matt, and Nicole waved to him. Matt raised his hand and waved back.

Finally, Nicole's feet struck solid ground, and Matt was there embracing her. "Nic, you made it!"

Nicole kissed Matt then broke the embrace to help David and Tammy.

"David, you old dog. I knew you could do it," Matt shouted up to his friend.

Then there were hands all over David, helping him down and relieving him of his burden. He collapsed to the earth, and hands offered him support. "Don't worry about me. Take care of Tammy."

"Tammy . . . Tammy . . ." Nicole's soft voice called to her sister.

Tammy stirred and opened her eyes. Her pupils were dilated, but she managed a thin smile.

A stranger's voice interrupted the reunion. The voice was powerful and reassuring all at once. "She is hurt but will recover shortly," A woman's musical voice sang.

Matt hastily introduced his companion. "Nic, David, this is Joelle. She showed up when I made out your figures on the rock. She said she is a friend and is here to help."

David looked warily at Joelle. Her eyes greeted him with compassion and sadness. He averted his gaze from her and knelt beside Tammy. He stroked her hair lovingly and absorbed the sight of her angelic face. "She's a friend," David muttered.

"You know her?" Matt asked.

"Yes." David continued to caress Tammy.

Nicole focused her attention on Tammy, who lay in her arms. Her fingers and David's took turns brushing Tammy's hair.

Nicole started when the stranger placed her hand on Tammy's forehead. "Hey! What are you doing?" she demanded.

Joelle did not reply. She remained motionless with her eyes closed, her hand resting firmly on Tammy's forehead.

Nicole attempted to move Joelle's hand, but David grasped her wrist. "It's all right, Nicole. She's a friend. Trust her."

Joelle jerked her hand away from Tammy. Tammy's eyes popped open, and she sat up.

"Hey! What?" Nicole gasped.

Tammy sprang on her sister and embraced her. "Oh, Nicole! I'm so glad you came for me. God truly did answer my prayers!"

Nicole returned her sister's embrace. "Tammy, I am so sorry for—"

Tammy placed a finger on her sister's lips. "Shhh. It's OK. All is forgiven. You came for me. I knew you would."

"Always right, aren't you?" Nicole smirked and winked.

"Well, I . . ."

"Sis, I'm kidding." Nicole hugged Tammy close. She whispered in her ear, "I love you, Tammy."

"I love you too, sis."

The girls' embrace lingered for another few moments before Tammy separated from her sister's hold. Her eyes drifted to the three individuals who stood by. "Matt, it's good to see you." She hugged him and turned to David. "David?"

David's felt tears slide down his cheeks.

"Oh, David!" Tammy threw herself into his arms. "It is good to see you, my friend."

David did not respond. He held Tammy fiercely, secretly never wanting to let go.

"David," Tammy whispered, "Let me go so I can talk to you."

David fought desperately not to loosen his embrace, but his muscles betrayed him. His arms let Tammy free.

Tammy stepped back, spoke, and signed to David, "I missed you."

David bit his lip and signed from force of habit, "I missed you as well."

No longer using her voice, Tammy signed to David, "Your tears. They do not seem to be tears of joy."

David glanced imploringly to Joelle.

Joelle approached and laid a hand on Tammy's shoulder. "My dear child, David has something to say to you."

David's voice trembled as he spoke words to Tammy for the very first time. "It is a great joy to me that you are returned to your friends . . ."

Tammy placed a hand over her mouth in amazement. "David . . ." she whispered.

"And that you and your sister are reconciled," David continued. "But now it is time for me to say good-bye."

Matt responded first to the startling comment. "What? What are you talking about?" Matt and Nicole joined David, Tammy, and Joelle.

Joelle placed her body between David and his three friends. She extended her arm out in front and raised her hand. "David's time with you here is over."

The three friends started to shout in rebuttal, but Joelle silenced them.

"David has other Goliaths to conquer." She grasped David's hand.

David and Joelle made their way back to the face of Goliath. Joelle nodded, and David began his ascent up the mountain with Joelle close behind.

Nicole, Tammy, and Matt stood powerless as they watched their friend return up the mountain. They were unable to move their feet or shout good-bye. The only movement they felt was the blinking of their eyes from their tears. Eventually, when David and his companion were out of sight, the three friends broke free of the spell that held them.

Tammy collapsed sobbing into Nicole's arms, and Matt walked over to where David had resumed his climb.

"Good-bye, my friend. May God go with you on your journey, wherever it takes you. I pray that one day, again, our paths will cross, our guardian angel." Matt turned his back on Goliath and made his way over to Nicole and Tammy to offer his support and comfort.

Matt opened the car door for Nicole. "How's Tammy doing?"

"She's doing great. It's like she was never injured," Nicole replied.

"That's not what I meant."

Nicole's tone became solemn. "I think she's OK. She really misses him, though."

"I miss him, too."

"I know you do. And I will be forever in his debt, for he gave me back my sister. In fact, he gave me back my life by showing me how to love."

"Oh, is that what you call it?" Matt smirked at his jibe.

"Just get your butt in the car and drive, mister," Nicole snapped and smiled.

"Is Tammy going to meet us?"

"She said she'll meet us in the cafeteria for dinner. She wanted to go over to the hospice unit today instead of the soup kitchen."

"I'm glad you decided to volunteer to help cook soup for the homeless," Matt set the trap.

"And why's that?"

"I've tasted your cooking. If you had to do anything above and beyond the boiling of water, the homeless would never get any nutrition!" Matt laughed at his own joke.

"Keep laughing, Romeo. I'll make sure the picture of you in your mother's dress finds its way on the board in the wrestling room."

"Hey," Matt protested, "that picture was taken when I was in grade school. You're not even supposed to have it."

"Blackmail material is always beneficial."

Matt grinned. He started the vehicle and headed down the road toward their destination. A fleeting thought was sent out somewhere, to a friend he hoped could hear his thoughts: *David, thanks again.*

Chapter Thirteen

DAVID'S FINGERS LOST their grasp and his feet failed to find support. His arms waved and flapped in the air while his body plummeted toward the earth. He felt the air rush faster and faster until the sound was a torrent of wind, buffeting against his body.

He screamed a silent cry and his body continued to accelerate. His mind shouted for Joelle, hoping she would hear him and save him from the impending impact that threatened his life.

Then abruptly, calm resonated through his body. He accepted the fate that now stood before him. His only regrets were the unanswered questions and the doubts that still lingered about his own eternity. *It is too soon to end like this.*

The ground rushed up to meet his body, and David closed his eyes. *Father in heaven, Thy will be done.*

His eyes burst open before impact, and he sat straight up in bed. His pupils adjusted to the dimly lit room that surrounded the bed he sat on. Sweat streamed down his forehead and cheeks while his breathing was rapid and short.

David pulled up his bed sheet and wiped the perspiration from his brow and face. He surveyed his surroundings and realized that the room looked all too familiar. David inspected his body and found frail and wrinkled arms and hands. His stomach threatened to unload, as a wave of sickness flowed through his body at the realization of where he now sat. He was back in the nursing home.

David covered his face in his hands and wept silently. *Why must I come back?* Was it all just a dream, or had he lost his mind?

Wallowing in self-pity, David had the eerie feeling that he was not the only person in the room. He peeked over his hands. A figure sat huddled in the corner of the room.

Mary? David's daughter sat asleep in a small chair. Her arms embraced her body, and her head lay awkwardly on a bundled coat that served as a makeshift pillow. *My dear daughter, how long have you been here? How long have I been gone?*

David tried to rise, but his legs would not respond. He moaned and twisted around to grab his pillow. He aimed carefully and tossed it at his daughter.

The pillow struck its target, and Mary opened her eyes. She sat up and her gaze locked with David's.

He extended his arms.

Mary rushed into her father's arms. "Oh, Daddy," she whispered. "It's so good to hug you."

It is good to hold you, my daughter.

Mary slipped away from the embrace. "Dad, how are you feeling?"

David nodded.

Mary's eyes widened. "Dad, I can't believe it. You're sitting without support, and moving your head and arms. I have to get Wilma." She reached across the bed and pushed the call button. "I can't believe you're finally awake."

How long have I been gone? David wondered.

"You've been asleep now for seven days. In fact—"

Nurse Wilma barged into the room, interrupting Mary's words. "What is it, dear? Is everything all right?" Wilma stopped short of the bed when she noticed David sitting and holding hands with his daughter. "Why, Mr. Liberty! It's about time you rejoined us here in the land of the living."

David managed a thin smile.

"Let me get his vitals, dear." Wilma moved to David's side, started the blood pressure cuff, and checked her watch to gain his heart rate. "Everything checks out fine. Let's get this IV out of your arm, and get you out of this bed and into the wheelchair."

David glanced down and noticed for the first time a small tube in the crease of his right arm.

"The IV gave you some nutrients while you were unconscious. Are you up to trying some soft food?"

David shook his head. *I'm not hungry.*

"So you won't eat right now, but I'll be back later, and it'll be time to eat." Wilma patted David affectionately on the shoulder and put her arm around Mary.

"I still think that you should go through with the transfer." Wilma lowered her voice.

"Even with Dad awake now?"

"Yes. I think Mr. Liberty will get better medical attention at Clearbrook. They have some fine doctors on staff and all the modern medical equipment. Besides, we don't know how long your father will remain awake this time. If he falls unconscious again, he may never wake."

Mary sighed. "You're right, of course. It's just that I really trust you, even with the odd things that have happened."

"I'll see to it that the right nurse looks after your father—"

David grabbed the small vase of flowers from his nightstand and threw it against the wall, shattering it into a thousand pieces.

"Dad, what's wrong? What happened?" Mary scampered to his side.

"I'll get a broom and dustpan," Wilma said.

David shouted at Mary in his mind. *I'm not going anywhere!* He folded his arms in defiance and glared at his daughter.

"Dad, what's wrong?"

David raised his eyebrows and nodded toward the door.

"Are you trying to tell me something?"

He nodded "yes." *Come on, Mary. Help me out here.*

Mary fumbled in her purse, and pulled out a pen and paper. She handed them to David. "Dad, see if you can write down what's bothering you."

David snatched the pen and paper but failed miserably when he attempted to write. *Oh my aching head. Figures it wouldn't be that easy.* He dropped the pen and pointed to the door.

Mary glanced in the direction that David aimed. "You want to leave the room?"

He shook his head emphatically and ripped the sheet of paper in half.

"You *don't* want to leave the room?"

David nodded and made a small circular motion with his hands, signaling Mary to continue.

"You don't want to leave nursing home?"

He pointed at his daughter, smiled, and nodded.

Nurse Wilma reentered the room with a broom and dustpan.

"Ah . . . Wilma, seems Dad doesn't want to leave."

"What? Mr. Liberty, is that true?" Wilma asked.

David nodded once and crossed his arms.

"Heaven help us!" Wilma murmured.

I'm hoping.

"You know, I can't remember how long it's been since I have seen Dad this well."

Wilma frowned at Mary and shifted her gaze back to David. "Yes, I have to agree with you, dear. Although he has lost some weight, his mobility is definitely improved. There's something about him; he seems more alive."

Mary walked behind her father and placed her arms on his shoulders. She rested her forehead on the back of David's head and spoke tenderly to him. "I was so worried about you, Dad."

I'm fine, Mary, but it's good to feel your touch once again.

"Mary, you must be famished. Let's grab you something to eat and we can find something for your father, as well."

Mary nodded and allowed Wilma to escort her out of the room.

Once the two women were clear of the room and partway down the hall, Wilma spoke to Mary. "You weren't serious about letting your father remain here. I feel he needs more in-depth medical care."

"I agree. We'll move Dad to Clearbrook. I didn't want him to get upset, with him just waking up and all."

"Yes, dear, but you sure had me convinced in there. Your acting was worth an Academy Award."

Mary smiled. "Dad doesn't need to know that we still plan on moving him. You're not interested in a new job, are you?"

Wilma laughed. "I've never considered a change these last twenty years. This is—and has been—my home for quite some time now. The residents here are my family."

"That is why I trust you. You're one of a kind. I think very few of the staff members actually like their job, let alone care about the residents. That's one thing that I'm concerned about."

"Don't worry. I have some connections over at Clearbrook. Let's get you something to eat."

David wheeled his chair to the window. His thoughts were not on his situation, although his heart had been lightened at the sight and touch of his daughter. His mind drifted to Matt, Nicole, and Tammy. David felt as if part of him had not returned to the room. He knew a piece of his heart had been ripped away.

His shifting gaze focused on a small, black leather book that rested on the lamp stand near the window. The name inscribed in gold letters on the front cover of the book was "Mary Liberty." Gingerly, with trembling fingers, he picked up the small treasure. It was Mary's first Bible. He was sure of that, although he did not recall how old she had been when her mother purchased the gift.

He flipped through the Bible until he came to a section that was marked. The pages lay open before him, and his eyes skimmed up and down the columns until he saw the words: "A psalm of David. Psalm 23." David then silently read the words that followed:

"The Lord is my Shepherd, I shall not be in want.

He makes me lie down in green pastures,

He leads me beside quiet waters,

He restores my soul."

David reread the last line. *He restores my soul?* He continued to read the rest of the psalm.

"He guides me in paths of righteousness for His name's sake.

Even though I walk through the valley of the shadow of death,

I will fear no evil, for You are with me;

Your rod and Your staff, they comfort me.

You prepare a table before me in the presence of my enemies.

You anoint my head with oil; my cup overflows."

A beautiful voice sang, "Surely goodness and love will follow me all the days of my life, and I will dwell in the house of the Lord forever."

David closed the Bible.

"You know, Mr. Liberty, the psalms were meant to be sung."

I guess you weren't listening, or I wasn't singing. One of the two.

Joelle ignored the sarcasm and stepped up to block David's view at the window.

David studied the beautiful figure. *About time you showed up.*

"You weren't so happy to see me at Goliath."

You have to stop doing this to me.

"Doing what?"

Placing me in people's lives and then ripping me away from them.

"You would have rather not known your three friends then?"

That's not what I mean. But yes, it would've been a lot easier to have never known them.

"So you'd rather let the enemy take Nicole, and quite possibly Matt as well?"

144

You know the answer to that.

"Tell me."

David fumed. *I loved all three of them.*

"Especially Tammy."

Is that a question?

"No, simply an observation. Because of your love and your actions you have given each one of your friends a special gift."

What gift is that?

"You're a stubborn man. Has it been that long that you have forgotten that *I* ask the questions?"

No, but I remember that you use that as an excuse not to answer me.

Joelle's musical laughter echoed against the walls of the room and vibrated within David's chest. In spite of David's frustration and pain, he smiled.

"My dear Mr. Liberty. You have given your friends a gift they may share with others. You taught them a skill or—if you will—gave them a tool to fight back against the enemy. Why do you think the enemy tempts us to sin?"

David was not entirely sure what Joelle was searching for, but she did not wait for his answer.

"Sin breaks down our relationship with God. If our relationship continues to disintegrate, then our hope of sharing our Father's eternal love in heaven is lost."

I thought that He loves unconditionally, that no matter what we do, He will still forgive us.

"Yes, you are right. He does love us unconditionally, in spite of our sin. In fact He loved us so much that He gave us the freedom to choose to love Him or to choose not to."

David processed what Joelle told him, but he still had many questions. He knew that asking would not entitle him to an answer, so he chose a different approach. *So God does love us, and because of that love He will welcome us all into eternity?*

"David, can you make your son love you?"

The question caught David by surprise. The flood of memory that the inquiry stirred caused his stomach to churn. *No.*

"Then what is your recourse?"

I tried everything I could think of.

"But you could not force him to love you."

Joelle's statement hit him square in the stomach. He wanted to vomit.

"God will not force anyone to love Him. To say that you love someone is not enough. Words are merely that—words. They cannot convey completely what our hearts believe and feel."

You're referring to actions again. David thought he knew where this lesson was going.

"When the Son walked with us, He told us how our actions toward others would show how we truly felt for our Lord."

I'm not sure I recall . . .

"You need to become stronger in your knowledge of the Word of God. Since your memory fails, I will tell a parable that the Son spoke to the people:

"When the Son of Man comes in His glory, and all the angels with Him, He will sit on His throne in heavenly glory. He will divide the people of nations into two groups, one on His left and one on His right. Then the King will say to those on His right, 'Come, you who are blessed by my Father; take your inheritance, the kingdom prepared for you since the creation of the world. For I was hungry and you gave me to eat, I was thirsty and you gave me to drink, I was a stranger and you took me in, I needed clothes and you clothed me, I was sick and you looked after me, I was in prison and you came to visit me.'

"Then the righteous will answer him, 'Lord, when did we see you hungry and feed you, or thirsty and give you something to drink? When did we see you a stranger and invite you in, or needing clothes and clothe you? When did we see you sick or in prison and go to visit you?'

"The King will reply, 'I tell you the truth, whatever you did for one of the least of these brothers of mine, you did for me.'

"Then He will say to those on his left, 'Depart from Me, you who are cursed, into the eternal fire prepared for the devil and his angels. For I was hungry and you gave Me nothing to eat, I was thirsty and you gave me nothing to drink, I was a stranger and you did not invite me in, I needed clothes and you did not clothe me, I was sick and in prison and you did not look after me.'

"They also will answer, 'Lord when did we see you hungry or thirsty or a stranger or needing clothing or sick or in prison, and did not help you?'

"He will reply, 'I tell you the truth, whatever you did not do for one of the least of these, you did not do for me.'

"Then they will go away to eternal punishment and the righteous to eternal life."

Joelle stopped her quotation from the Scriptures and waited.

The passage is pretty clear. How we treat our brothers and sisters is how we treat our Lord. David responded. The message seemed straightforward.

"There is more to that passage. Review the words I spoke and tell me what was similar about the two groups of people."

David closed his eyes to recall the parable Joelle had quoted. He was unsure if she paraphrased the scripture, but he did recall the story and how a pastor had titled the parable "The Sheep and the Goats." The sheep had performed acts of kindness to others, while the goats had not. *Both groups were surprised at the King's account of their actions, or lack of actions, as they pertained to Him,* David replied.

Joelle's voice tensed. She was clearly losing patience. "But how did they address the King?"

David's brow wrinkled. *They both addressed him as "Lord."*

"So it seems possible that both groups knew Him?" she asked

At that point, maybe all people will know Him for who He is.

"Possibly, but does He ask either group who believed in Him?"

David sensed that Joelle's point would cause him to question what he had been taught and what he had understood about eternity. *No. He did not ask.* An understanding of the passage became clear. *He already knew.*

Joelle smiled, and a light shone around her. "Yes, David Liberty. To believe and not do is not to believe. You see, the sheep performed their actions not out of a sense of duty and slavery but actually with obedience fostered by love. The sheep loved the Son.

"On the other hand, the goats were aware of the Son and possibly His teachings, but they did not love Him. Their actions or—more in line with Scripture—their *lack* of actions demonstrated how their hearts truly felt. Their lives were filled more with selfishness than with self-giving."

Joelle paused and studied her student. "You taught Nicole how to care for others and not just for herself. You helped open a doorway that will allow her to love the Lord, for how could one love the Father if he hates his brother or if he hates himself?"

But I didn't have a chance to really witness to them. I don't even know exactly how to witness to someone. I remember being taught we were supposed to tell people about the Son.

"If a husband is unfaithful one time in his marriage, does he love his wife?"

David's ears burned, and his stomach churned. He struggled for a moment to regain his composure. *We are human. We can and do make mistakes, so I'd say that the man could truly love his wife, even if he has been unfaithful one time.*

"A man is unfaithful twice, three times, and soon too many times for one to count. Does he love his wife?"

Many seconds passed before David responded. *I think then he would not love his wife.*

"But what if he told her that he loved her?"

They would be empty words.

"Yes. I suppose they would be empty. Tell me why."

Because his daily actions showed otherwise.

"So, a primary way to witness is through your daily actions. Words can be meaningless or empty if our actions do not line up with our teachings. That is why you have not been blessed with the ability to speak. We want you to first demonstrate faith and love to your brothers and sisters. We then will have the ability to teach them in earnest about their Father, because they will have the desire to know Him."

Why do I think it may be more complicated then what you described?

Joelle laughed. "Man cannot know the mind of God, but you can know His love, and this you are called to share." She paused. "Were you jealous of Matt?"

David averted his gaze. *Yes. At first I was jealous. He was a better wrestler and a better student than I was. I had already done the work before in my lifetime, and he was still better than I.*

"Were you envious of Matt?"

No!

"What is the difference, then between jealousy and envy?"

David wrinkled his brow in thought. *I'm not sure how to put it in words. Nicole was envious of her sister, while I was jealous of Matt. She perceived that we both had similar feelings, but there was definitely a difference.*

Joelle nodded and remained silent.

I do know that Scripture has referred to God as being a jealous God, so jealousy in itself can't be evil, for it would then contradict the very nature of God.

"Very good. Technically speaking, jealousy seeks out the good in a person, where envy resents it. Envy will seek to destroy it. Jealousy can be good or bad, but envy is always evil."

I was jealous of Matt's ability and strived to be better in practice, but Nicole despised Tammy's talents, personality, and recognition. Nicole didn't want to change herself but rather wanted to destroy Tammy.

"Ultimately, envy would have destroyed her soul."

David was not sure he enjoyed these lessons. In fact, he was pretty sure he did not want any more. The memories and the pain they brought were agonizing.

Joelle placed one hand on David's shoulder and lifted his chin with the other. She stared into his eyes and spoke softly. "Yes, David Liberty, this is a crash course we are attending, but our time is short and the need is great."

The startling power and kindness in Joelle's gaze transfixed David's eyes, and he trembled.

"Your next task will be even harder than the previous ones. You must be strong and meek, and quick and patient." Joelle stroked his eyelids shut.

David felt his consciousness slip away as his body trembled in fear and humiliation. It was not Joelle's power that triggered the involuntary muscle response, but the sudden wave of familiarity that flooded his mind when his eyes became lost in Joelle's gaze.

Book Three

A man of great wrath shall suffer punishment, even if you rescue him, you will have to do it again.

—Proverbs19:19

The diligent hand will govern, but the slothful will be enslaved.

—Proverbs 12:24

Chapter One

THE ROUTE OF the broken cement determined David Liberty's direction while he walked down the cracked sidewalk. He felt like he had awakened from a forty-year sleep. He ran his fingers through his hair and tried to sift through the cobwebs of his mind. There was something he needed to remember. Joelle had mentioned how this next trial would be the hardest to date, but that statement was not what nagged at his core. Her words were laced with a hidden meaning that eluded David's grasp.

A bell clanging in the distance interrupted his thoughts. His feet skipped off the sidewalk and traversed a dirt bicycle path toward the sound of the chiming bell. The grasses and milkweed grew tall along the path. At times David parted the sea of green with his arms while his eyes searched for the source of the musical sound.

The path abruptly ended at another sidewalk. David's gaze traveled across the blacktop parking lot to a small, white building resting on a knoll. Quick inspection of the building revealed a disproportional steeple that rose above the structure—the source of the ringing bell that echoed through David's head.

He watched people casually straggle up the hillside and filter into the church. David's legs carried him forward. The bell, no longer the magnet for his curiosity, had gone silent, but he was intrigued by the structure on the hillside and the patrons who were disappearing inside.

He was the last person to make his way up the gravel walk. He slipped through the open doorway and into a vacant pew in the back of the church. He was sure that his presence in the church had gone unnoticed by the members of the congregation. They were singing a hymn that David recognized, but its name escaped him.

He felt strange in the back of the small church. He did not feel like a visitor but more like an intruder in this place of worship. His heart rate rose and he anxiously glanced around. David wanted to escape from the old building and its inhabitants, but his anxiety and fear became so strong that his legs froze where he stood.

What is the matter with me? What am I afraid of? David struggled inwardly and tried to find the source of his fear. His gaze continued to dart around the room and finally rested on a wooden cross that hung suspended over the front of the church. His eyes misted. *Maybe it's not fear. Maybe I'm too embarrassed to be here. Maybe my failures . . .*

The congregation stopped singing, and David realized that he was one of only two people left standing.

"Good morning, friends and neighbors." A voice carried from the front of the church, where the one other standing person spoke. "Do we have any visitors this morning?"

A chuckle came from the small assembly. The pastor's eyes locked with David's. "Welcome, my friend." He stretched out his open hand in invitation. The entire congregation turned to stare at David standing at the back of the church. "Please, be seated. The peace of the Lord will be with you here."

David glanced at the people who stared openly at him. His legs were no longer frozen; they were his to command once more. His attention drifted to the cross that hung overhead, and his anxiety and humiliation faded away. David smiled and nodded at the pastor and then at the people. He sat down.

The next hour was a blur. He stood when the others stood and sat when they returned to their seats. He listened intently as the pastor read the morning's lesson from Scripture. He called it the greatest commandment. "Love the Lord with all your heart and with all your soul and with your entire mind." The pastor finished his reading by quoting. "And the second greatest commandment is like it: 'Love your neighbor as yourself.'"

David did not hear the rest of the service because he studied the surroundings. The small church appeared to be very old. Rays of light broke through tiny openings in the walls. The stained-glass windows were faded and blurred, making it difficult to distinguish the images that decorated them.

He noticed a balcony above him, but the spaces between its floorboards caused him to doubt that anyone was up there. He counted forty-four people inside the church walls, including the pastor. About half the congregation seemed enthusiastic about worship, while the rest of the group took David's role of mimicking the others' motions.

When the service ended, the people filed out of the church, passing by David with looks of inquiry or complete avoidance of his presence. He nodded and smiled to the few who made eye contact and received only a handful of smiles in return. Everyone seemed content to leave him, uninvited, in the pew where he sat.

Now David sat alone. He stared up once more to the wooden cross. *Guide me now, oh Lord. And I pray that you help me find the desire to love You in a manner that reflects the love You have for me. Your will be done.* He was not sure why he had added the last statement to the simple prayer. He vaguely recalled something important about those four words, but he did not understand their significance.

He stood and walked toward the entrance of the church. He stopped in the doorway and watched the people disperse in all directions. The pastor stood on the dirt path talking with one of the parishioners, and a small boy sat on the top of the stairs fumbling with some marbles in his tiny hands. David had no new memories in this location. He had started his previous encounters as a caretaker and then as a college student, but he currently did not feel as if he had any direction.

For the first time, David glanced down at his clothing and was appalled at his own appearance. Ragged and torn clothing hung from his body; partially-torn gloves adorned both hands, and he realized he was sweating profusely in the heat of the midmorning sun. He wiped the sweat from his unshaven face with the sleeve of his right arm and removed a worn baseball cap from his head in hopes of cooling down. *No wonder everyone avoided me. I'm as disheveled as this building.*

He shook his head, placed his ball cap back on its perch, and noticed the small boy staring at him. The stare was one of wonder, not disgust, as David felt the others had looked at him.

The young boy continued to gape at him until the pastor climbed the stairs and reached out his hand. "Joshua, come here, please."

Joshua stood and moved over to the pastor, grabbing onto two fingers with his tiny grasp.

The pastor inspected the boy and then turned his attention toward David. "Can I help you with something, mister?"

David noticed the defensive posturing of the pastor when he asked the question. He glanced around to find someone to help him communicate in this awkward situation. Finding no help, his focus returned to the pastor. He brought his fingers to his lips while shaking his head no.

"I think it would be best if you continued on your way. Come on, Joshua. We'll let this man go to his home and we'll go to ours." The pastor started down the stairs with Joshua following.

Wait. I don't mean any harm. I'm not what I look like—I mean my name is David. David Liberty. Don't go! David shouted with his mind.

The small, frail boy let go of his hand hold and ran up the stairs to David.

"Joshua, come back here!" the pastor hollered.

The boy grabbed David's hand. "His name is David."

What? How did he know?

The pastor's eyes widened. "Joshua, what did you say?"

Joshua smiled up at David. "David!"

The pastor lunged forward and embraced the boy. "Joshua, my son! You spoke. You spoke!" Tears flowed down his face. He laughed hysterically, rocking the small boy back and forth and mumbling praises to God.

He eventually broke the embrace with his son, holding Joshua at arm's length. "I knew you would talk again, son. Let's go home and tell your mother."

Joshua shook his head and pointed at David.

The pastor frowned. "Son, let's go tell Mom . . ."

Joshua shook his head again and pointed first at his father and then back to David.

David was not exactly sure what was going on, but he knew what Joshua wanted. He moved forward and extended his hand to the pastor.

Joshua took his father's right hand off of his shoulder and motioned toward David.

The men shook hands. "My name is Emmett Brown, and this is my son Joshua."

David smiled and nodded.

Emmett waited a moment and then said, "And your name . . . ?"

David stopped the handshake and pointed toward Joshua.

"David." Joshua said right on cue.

Emmett looked in wonder at Joshua and back to David. "Your name is really David?"

David nodded.

"David what?"

"Li . . ." Joshua began, but David cut him off with a movement of his hand.

David pointed to the black-leather Bible that had fallen to the ground.

Emmett, obviously baffled stooped to pick up the Bible and cautiously handed it to David.

Now let's see if I can remember, David thought as he leafed through the pages. Several unnerving moments passed while he thumbed his way through the worn text. His knowledge of Scripture was limited, but he did recall something in Corinthians. Eventually, his gaze rested on the word that would answer Emmett's question.

David placed his finger on the page, directly under the word he had found. Glancing at Joshua he nodded his head.

"Liberty!" Joshua piped up.

Emmett stared at his son.

David nodded toward the open pages of his Bible. Emmett focused on the word David was pointing to. "Liberty."

"Joshua, let's go home and share this news with Mom. She should be back from the clinic by now." Emmett extended his hand for his son.

Joshua reached out and clasped David's hand.

Emmett sighed. "David, you're welcome to our home. I'm sure you must be hungry."

David realized that he was, indeed, famished. He smiled at Emmett and winked at Joshua.

Joshua beamed with obvious pleasure, and Emmett shook his head in amazement.

Chapter Two

RENEE'S HAND SLAMMED down against the wooden desk as she read the bill that had been misplaced in the mess of papers strewn around her husband's library.

"That irresponsible, lazy jerk! I've told him hundreds of times how much money we lose by making late payments!" She shuffled through the mess that cluttered the desk. Any paper she did not recognize, she tossed purposefully to the floor. Maybe a carpet of papers would help Emmett organize his bills.

The sound of her husband's voice and the closing of the screen door interrupted her tirade. "I'm in your office!" she shouted. "If you have something to say, then come in here to say it."

Shortly, her husband stood in the doorway. A look of surprise crossed Emmett's face. He stumbled to speak.

Renee beat him to the punch. "I found another unpaid bill! How many times must we go through this? Maybe this mess of yours on the floor can now get organized—" She stopped when she noticed another figure in the background standing with her son.

"Renee," Emmett said, "we have company."

Renee made her way toward the doorway. Brushing her husband aside with a wave and a scolding glance, she presented herself to the guest that stood near Joshua. She stared in alarm at the gross figure holding her son's hand. The disheveled man alarmed her more than the smile on Joshua's face surprised her.

The stranger nodded a greeting, and Joshua tugged the bum into the kitchen.

"Emmett, may I talk to you for a moment?" Renee huffed and reentered the library.

Emmett stepped into the room and quietly slid the door closed.

"What is the *matter* with you?" Renee demanded. "Open that door some so I can see if they walk by."

Emmett slid the door partway open. "Renee, I think—"

"No, you *don't* think! That's part of your problem. How on earth could you bring a bum like that into our home and worse, risk our child's health by letting him touch that filth?" Renee dared her husband to offer some logical explanation. She continued her rant. "Do you think he's a lost soul who needs your pathetic guidance or counseling? What's the deal, Emmett?"

Emmett's face blushed, "Are you finished?"

"Finished? Yes, I think we're very close to finished."

Emmett ignored the comment. "Joshua spoke this morning."

"What?"

"Joshua spoke this morning."

"Don't try to divert my thoughts with nonsense." Renee paused. Emmett remained silent, and Renee's curiosity and hope tempered her anger. "Well, what did he say?"

"He said the name 'David.'"

"Are you sure?"

"Yes. He repeated the name three times."

"What? Who is David? Did he say anything else?" Renee's tone changed. She was no longer the angry, vengeful assailant, but now took on the countenance of a loving, concerned mother. Joshua had not spoken since his brother Aaron had died.

"He also said 'Liberty.'"

"Liberty? I don't understand."

"David Liberty is the name of the 'filth' in the kitchen with our son."

"I don't understand. Why would he repeat a stranger's name?"

"Would you let me tell you about our morning? Without interrupting?"

Renee sucked in her lips and nodded her head.

Emmett reached out his hands for his wife's.

Reluctantly, Renee let her husband grasp her hands. She remained silent while Emmett recalled the morning's events.

As far as Emmett could tell, David was unable to speak. "But now that I reflect on what happened this morning, there was something even more amazing." Emmett furrowed his brow. "I know what it is. Our son befriended a vagabond and would not come home without him . . ."

Renee smiled. "That would be like my Joshua."

"No. I mean yes. That part is correct, but he also knew David's last name. Joshua went to speak it, but David stopped him. David then leafed through the Bible and pointed to a word. He nodded to Joshua, who exclaimed

'Liberty.' Then David showed me the word he was pointing to in Scripture."
Emmett waited.

"Well," Renee asked, "what word was he pointing to?"

"The word 'liberty.'"

"There must be some logical explanation," Renee said. "Were you with
Joshua the whole time, or was he alone with this David?"

"Mmm, Joshua was sitting on the steps by himself when David came out
of the church."

"He could have told Joshua his name then."

"But David can't speak."

"Maybe he just wants you to think that."

"I suppose, but there is something going on. I mean . . . Joshua *spoke*. He
talked for the first time since Aaron passed."

"I want to hear his voice. Besides, we probably shouldn't leave him alone
with this David stranger."

Emmett nodded. "You're probably right."

Renee led the way into the kitchen, with Emmett close behind.

Joshua and David sat at the table eating peanut butter and jelly sand-
wiches. Joshua wore a red mustache from the juice that washed down the
sticky combination. He sat next to his guest, having apparently moved his
chair to get as close as possible to the unkempt stranger.

David stood. He bowed slightly and offered his hand in greeting to
Renee.

Renee did not extend her hand. Instead, she surveyed every inch of David's
being.

Emmett interrupted the awkward moment. "David, this is Joshua's
mother, Dr. Renee Brown." He turned to his wife. "Renee, this is David
Liberty."

Renee cast a disgusted glance at her husband and reached out to shake
David's hand. She was mildly surprised at the firm, confident grasp that the
disheveled man demonstrated. The grip caused her for the first time to look
into the eyes of her guest. His eyes belied confidence, strength, and something
else that she recognized but could not describe.

Renee said, "David, you are welcome in our home—today." She stepped
around to kneel by her son. "And how's my boy today?" She stroked the hair
on the back of Joshua's head. "Daddy tells me you talked this morning. Can
you say something to Mommy?"

Renee waited patiently for a reply, and David sat down to finish his
lunch.

Joshua shot up from his chair and clung to David. "No. You must not go! We need you here!"

Renee continued to kneel, unable to move. Her son spoke! Her husband beamed with pride, and Joshua climbed onto David's lap. Renee's mind raced. The struggles and resulting emotions over the last two years had taken its toll on her practice, marriage, relationships, and her decision-making process. She did not know anything about this David Liberty, but she said, "Joshua, Mr. Liberty can stay as long as he likes." *Or as long as we need him,* she thought.

Joshua seemed appeased by his mother's decision. He returned to his chair and the remaining sandwich on his plate.

Renee stood and walked over to Emmett. "Why don't you go get a room ready next door and—"

"I think he should stay here with us," Emmett interrupted.

Renee's eyes flashed with anger. "Why do you always second guess my—"

Emmett stood his ground. "Why don't you ask Joshua what he wants? I mean . . . that's why you're allowing David to stay in the first place."

Renee clenched her jaw.

"Hon, I want my son back, too." Emmett's tone was tender. "I agree we should let David stay, for now, but let's not drive our son back to his world of hiding by fighting or by upsetting him. Don't ask David to stay in the apartment next door. Let him stay here."

The fire dwindled in Renee's heart, and she peeked over her shoulder at Joshua and David. Both had obviously heard the conversation. David kept his eyes averted, while Joshua looked expectantly at his mother. "Well, Joshua. Where should Mr. Liberty stay?"

"Here, Mom, right here!" Joshua yelled. He ran over to hug his mother.

Tears welled up in Renee's eyes at the joy of her son speaking. She blinked and mumbled, "Mr. Liberty, you're welcome in our home for as long as you need a place to stay."

Chapter Three

DAVID FELT LIKE a new man. After he had showered and shaved, Emmett had shown him the guest bedroom and left him an assortment of clothes. Layers of dirt and grime had gone down the shower drain. No wonder Renee and Emmett were appalled by his looks. David shook his head at the irony of how a small child could see past the appearance that had offended the adults.

David selected a loose-fitting shirt and khaki pants to slip into. He threw himself on the bed and fell into a deep slumber.

It seemed like his head had just touched the pillow when a knock at the door robbed him of sleep.

"Mr. Liberty? It is dinner time, if you'd care to join us." Renee's voice trickled through the closed door.

David sat up and shook the cobwebs from his head. He made his way to the door and slowly opened it.

"We're having chicken and . . ." Renee stopped in mid-sentence and gawked.

David smiled warmly. *Yes, I do clean up rather nicely.*

Renee peered closely at David. "At first I thought you were somebody completely different, but now I see that you are the same person." She paused. "Would you like some dinner?"

David nodded and followed Renee to the dining room.

Joshua and Emmett were already seated at the table. Joshua's eyes lit up when he saw David enter the room.

"Mr. Liberty, you may sit next to Joshua. He has been eagerly waiting for you to come out of your room," Emmett said. He motioned to the empty chair next to his son.

"And he hasn't spoken since," Renee remarked under her breath.

David sat down and placed the napkin on his lap, while Renee studied him closely.

"Let's give thanks." Emmett bowed his head.

Joshua reached out, grabbing his father's hand and David's. Renee completed the circle with Emmett and David.

Emmett closed his eyes and said, "God is good. God is great." He smiled when Joshua's little voice echoed the prayer. "Thank you, God, for the food we eat. Amen."

"Joshua, dear, you have to go to see the specialist tomorrow," Renee said. "What are we going to do with your new friend?"

Joshua did not hesitate. "David is going to work with Dad tomorrow." He smiled at David and resumed eating his dinner.

Renee addressed her husband. "You're not going to the appointment tomorrow?"

"My new assistant starts with me tomorrow."

"And you couldn't change his start date?" Renee's voice grew louder.

"I didn't think we both needed to be there."

"It has nothing to do with need; it has to do with want!" Her response approached a shout.

"Listen, Renee . . ."

"Don't you 'listen' me." Renee slammed her plate against the wall. No sooner had the broken pieces and remaining food struck the floor when Renee hurled her husband's plate against the wall. "Don't you want to be with your son?"

Emmett sat stoically while his wife's temper flared.

"You never want to do anything. You're a lazy, selfish excuse for a man!"

"He's not going to tell us anything we don't already know," Emmett replied.

Renee's jaw clenched. "I will not let what happened to Aaron happen to Joshua!"

"The entire community is praying for our son."

"Praying?" Renee scoffed, and she slammed a fist on the table. "Your prayers did not work before. What makes you think that they'd work now? You, who wouldn't even go to the side of our dying son, saying that praying within the shelter of the church would be more effective." Renee eyes flashed with anger as she confronted her husband, daring him to deny her accusations.

Emmett's head hung forward, ineffectively hiding the tears that streamed down his cheeks.

"Your life and your beliefs are all a sham." Renee buried the verbal dagger deeper within her husband's spirit. She turned and left the dining room.

The sudden silence was disrupted by the slamming of a door that vibrated through the house.

The bang of the closing door triggered Emmett into motion. He went to the scattered food and pieces of plate to gather up the mess. He tossed the broken pieces into the trash and chased after Renee.

David glanced at Joshua, who stared into empty space. The boy's color was ashen, and he appeared even frailer than he already was. Joshua turned and looked pleadingly at David. He mouthed the "please" and collapsed.

David sprang to the small boy's side, cradling him in his arms. He secured his hold on Joshua and lifted the limp body. David voicelessly called for help and frantically searched for Emmett, who a second before had been in the room.

Lord, I need my voice! David trotted through the halls and rooms of the house, his pace quickening at the sight of every empty room he passed. He risked a glance at the limp body that bounced in his arms. *Dear God! Don't let this child die in my arms!* Nausea crept into David's gut and an eerie familiarity touched his mind.

He burst outside, hoping Joshua's parents were within sight and that the open air would calm his panic.

David shouted, but no sound escaped his lips.

He could feel the life slowly fading from the child that lay nestled near his chest. There was no more time. David rushed to Emmett's small pickup truck, laid Joshua on the bench seat, and turned the ignition. With one arm stabilizing the small body, David sped out of the driveway and down the street, praying that his memory was correct.

David stayed near Joshua's bed in the small community hospital, watching and waiting for the child to show some sign of life. The nurses and on-call physician had assured David that Joshua would be fine. They apparently knew the boy and were not overly concerned about his unresponsiveness.

David was unsure how long he sat beside the little boy's bed praying and constantly watching the monitor that displayed Joshua's blood pressure and oxygen saturation.

David jumped when people burst into the room. Renee flew to Joshua, followed closely by her husband and two more figures, who slowed as soon as they entered the room.

"Joshua!" Renee's voice was urgent. She glanced at the numbers on the monitor and inspected her son's face, neck, and chest. "What tests have they run?" Not hearing an immediate response, she looked up at David sitting nearby. "I asked what tests . . . ? You!" she exclaimed when recognition struck. "That's the man, officer. He took my son!"

Emmett placed a hand on Renee's shoulder. "Hon, it seems like Joshua needed some immediate care. Let's worry about—"

"Don't you defend him," Renee snapped. "I want him arrested. He took our child." She looked past David. "Michael, I want you to arrest that man!"

Michael was a big, burly figure, but when he spoke, his voice was calm and authoritative. "Now, Dr. Brown, I'm going to find out the whole story before I go slapping handcuffs on anyone."

Emmett interjected, "Renee, shouldn't we be more concerned about our son than what David did or didn't do?"

"Since when have you ever acted like you were concerned about the health of Joshua, or even Aaron for that matter?"

Emmett's face flushed. He redirected the conversation. "Mike, let's take David out in the hall and find out exactly what happened. Hon, page the nurse's station and find out what tests have been run, and check his chart."

"Don't tell me how to treat my son," Renee huffed. "I'd give my very soul for him!"

Emmett walked over to Mike and the still seated David. "C'mon, let's go find out what happened."

David rose and followed Emmett. Mike waited for both men to go ahead of him.

A small, muffled voice froze them in their tracks. "David, are you here?"

Renee bent over her son and stroked his hair. "Shhh, my son. It's OK. Mommy's here." The tenderness she demonstrated with her voice and touch was quite a contrast from the woman who had been shouting moments before.

"David? Where's David?" Joshua mumbled and struggled to open his eyes.

Renee stood, but kept her hand in contact with her son's forehead. "He's here, Joshua. Would you like to see him?"

Joshua nodded feebly.

Renee glanced up to the three men. Her gaze went from Emmett to Michael and then fixed on David.

David noticed the bewilderment on Renee's face. Her body language was very clear. She wanted to know what David had done to her son. Not physically. He knew that she could not fathom the change in her child or Joshua's attraction to him. David was not sure he could answer the unspoken questions.

Emmett placed a reassuring hand on David's shoulder and walked him over to the side of Joshua's bed.

David regarded Emmett's solemn face. It was clear he was confused, as well. David glanced at Renee, who had not stopped staring at him, and knelt beside the bed to hold Joshua's tiny hand in his own. *I'm here, buddy. I am right here.* The old familiar term "buddy" made his resolve waiver, but he allowed no tears to fall.

A thin smile formed on Joshua's lips, while he struggled to open his eyes. "I knew it. I knew I was your buddy."

David could no longer prevent the moisture from streaming down his cheeks. Memories, wanted and unwanted, flooded his mind. *Yes, you are my buddy. I will do what I can to help you.*

Joshua shook his head. "Not me. Mom and Dad."

A chill went down David's spine. This small boy was very special indeed.

Renee stood by, unable to speak, but Emmett voiced the question. "Mom and Dad what, Joshua?"

Joshua ignored his father. "I just need a little more rest. Then I'll be able to go home. Stay with me, David?"

Emmett nodded, but Renee did not demonstrate affirmation or denial.

Emmett leaned over and kissed the sleeping boy's head. He walked around to the other side of the bed, where his wife stood. He wrapped his arm around her waist and escorted her away from the bed and out of the room.

Chapter Four

MARGARET KNEW THAT Dr. Brown was in her office early. The first patient had arrived and Margaret wanted to know what Dr. Brown wanted to do. Margaret was the master of all trades in the medical office, wearing the hats of receptionist, nurse, billing manager, and custodian.

She tapped softly on the closed door.

"Yes? Come in."

"Good morning, Dr. Brown. How are you this morning?" Margaret smiled.

"I'm fine, Margie. What can I do for you?"

"Mr. Thompson is here a little early. Did you want to see him now, or shall I tell him it'll be a short wait?"

"Early? He's forty five minutes early." Renee's irritation showed. "That man can just sit there and wait. He has an eight o'clock appointment, and I'll see him at eight or after."

"OK, Dr. Brown, I'll let him know."

"I mean, doesn't that man have a life? He's in here every other day with some complaint. The best medicine for him would be a good job . . . no, let me rephrase that . . . *any* job—" Before Renee could finish her small tirade, a third voice cut her off.

"Renee, I'll see him. I'm free for the moment." Dr. Jennifer Waits popped her head through the doorway.

"Jen, you don't have to do that. It'd be a good lesson in patience for that man."

"It's all right. I really don't mind."

"You have done enough for me and my patients as it is, covering my caseload for me while I've taken care of my son."

Margaret chimed in, "I'll tell Mr. Thompson that Dr. Brown will see him at eight o'clock."

Dr. Waits placed her hand on Margaret's shoulder. "No, go ahead and put him in room one, and I'll be right with him."

Margaret looked to Dr. Brown in protest, but Renee's head had bent down once more to her paperwork.

"Thanks, Jen. I appreciate your help."

Margaret quickened her stride to distance herself from Dr. Waits as they left Renee's office. She did not like how the balance of patient care had shifted from Dr. Brown to Dr. Waits. More and more of the clinic's patients were now scheduled with Dr. Waits, and Margaret could not figure out how Dr. Waits was able to retain the patients who were once Renee's. "Mr. Thompson, follow me into room number one. Dr. Waits will see you now, so you don't have to wait."

"But I was hoping to see Doc Renee. There's something she needs to know." Mr. Thompson followed Margaret into the first exam room.

"If you don't mind the wait."

"No, ma'am. I don't mind. There's something she's gotta hear."

Margaret smiled. "I'll let her know." She turned to exit the exam room, but Dr. Waits strolled through the open door.

"Good morning, Mr. Thompson. My name is Dr. Waits. Dr. Brown is indisposed at the moment so I will take care of you this morning."

Mr. Thompson blubbered, "Disposed? Disposed? When did that happen? I didn't hear nothing about that!" He panicked. "I don't understand. How'd it happen . . . when did it . . . ?"

Dr. Waits grabbed his arm. "Mr. Thompson!" she barked, and then less forcefully but still very stern, the doctor continued, "Dr. Brown is fine. She is just extremely burnt out right now, having spent most of her energy taking care of her son." She paused, making sure she had his attention. "Do you know her son Joshua?"

"Y-yes. Why yes, I do. How's he doing?"

"He was in the hospital last night. That's why Dr. Brown asked me to see you for her."

"She did?"

"Yes, she did." Dr. Waits glanced over to the bewildered Margaret and snapped, "Margie, can you hand me Mr. Thompson's chart?"

Margaret complied, although hesitantly.

Dr. Waits grabbed the chart. "Can you check my schedule and see when my next opening is on Wednesday?"

Margaret nodded and walked away as Jennifer closed the door. She could hear the doctor's cheery voice say, "I see your first name is Robert. Do you go by Bob?" The response was lost to Margaret as she continued her way to the reception area.

More patients were now coming through the clinic door, signing in, and having a seat in the waiting room. Margaret pulled their files and placed them in an open slot near the entryway of the exam rooms. Dr. Brown believed that the physicians should call the patients into the room. She thought it gave more of a personal touch to the overall office visit.

Margaret checked Wednesday's schedule and noticed that Dr. Waits was almost fully booked, while Dr. Brown had many openings. She shook her head. Two-and-a-half years ago, Renee had made Jennifer Waits a partner in the medical practice. At that time the caseload had grown so large that it was unrealistic for Renee to continue treating everyone on her own.

Jennifer had been a great hire, but things had changed over the last year with both doctors. Renee had become more moody and agitated following the circumstances in her personal life, while Jennifer became more engrossed in establishing a large caseload. At first, Margaret thought Jennifer was stepping up to the plate to do what had to be done with the sudden lapses in Renee's hours. Now, she was not so sure. She could not put words to her feelings, but one thing was sure: change was in the air, and she wasn't convinced it would be for the better.

As arranged, David went to work with Emmett. The men left when Emmett's mother came over to stay with Joshua. The boy was up and seemed to be fine, although he had not spoken since waking.

"I really wish you could speak, because I have some questions for you," Emmett remarked as they hopped in his truck.

David shrugged. He nodded up and down and shook his head from side to side.

Emmett let a quick burst of laughter escape. "Why, I guess you're correct. I can still ask yes-and-no questions. Just like a game of Twenty Questions."

David grinned. *You're not the only one who wishes I could speak.* Being voiceless certainly increased the difficulty of any situation.

Emmett placed the truck in drive and headed down the vacant road. "Are you from around here?"

David shook his head.

"Do you have family or friends nearby?"

No.

"Do you have a destination in your travels?"

That question could be answered either way. *Yes.*

"Why are you here in Smithville?"

David frowned.

"Oh, yeah. Well why . . ." Emmett did not finish his question, because David tapped him on the arm. "What?"

David pointed at Emmett. *Tell me about yourself.*

"I'm not sure what you want." Emmett furrowed his brow.

David put his fingers up and tapped his lips and then pointed to Emmett.

"You want to know about me?"

Yes.

Emmett stared down the road while the vehicle continued to head toward its destination.

After moments of silence, David realized there would be no understanding Joshua's condition with his father unwilling to divulge any family stories. *This communication barrier drives me nuts.*

Eventually the truck came to a stop. David recognized the silhouette of the small white church on top of the knoll. He exited the truck and followed Emmett up the winding gravel path. Emmett led him around the side of the church to a small house constructed of the same material used to erect the church. The outside was weatherworn, and David had the feeling that the inside was as shabby as the church's.

Emmett unlocked the latch and pushed the door open. "This is the rectory. It was built along with the church, as you were probably able to tell. This is where the pastor is supposed to reside, but Renee insisted that she needed to be closer to her office and patients. I think she just couldn't bring herself to live in this dilapidated building."

Can't say I blame her.

Emmett led David into a room and offered him a seat. "I decided to keep my office here with most of my theology books, although I have some at the house. Any appointments with members of the congregation are held here, and this is where they'll call me first."

Emmett pushed the button on his answering machine and an annoying beep sounded. "You have one message," the machine chirped and continued, "Hey, Pastor Brown, good morning. This is Bill Nomed. I'm running late, should be there about nine o'clock. Hope it doesn't inconvenience you. Thanks! Bye." The machine beeped one last time and fell silent.

"I guess we have some time to kill. I wonder why Joshua wanted you to come with me this morning."

David picked up a framed picture off the desktop while Emmett spoke. "Any ideas, David?" he pressed.

Not yet, but I hope I can get you to give me some. David turned the picture around to face Emmett and pointed at the picture, nodding "yes."

"You have an idea?"

David pointed to a child in the picture. It was the only person in the photograph that David did not recognize.

"That is my son Aaron." Emmett offered nothing more.

David sighed and scanned the room. *C'mon. Help me out here, Emmett.* His gaze rested on a pen. *Of course. Why didn't I think of this before?* He put down the picture and scooped up the pen, scratched some words on a piece of paper, and handed it to Emmett.

Emmett read the words. "Tell me about Aaron." He looked up. "Why?"

David tried to stay patient. He really did not know why, but he felt it would give him better insight into the workings of this family. He picked up the framed picture once more and pointed at Joshua.

Emmett's shoulders slumped. He flopped down into his office chair. "Aaron was our firstborn son; he passed away about eighteen months ago."

David sat on the corner of Emmett's desk and waited.

"Probably about the time that picture was taken, Aaron began to develop some strange symptoms. At first, Renee thought they were just growing pains. Then the intensity of Aaron's discomfort continued to rise, and both of us knew there was something wrong.

"Renee ran all the tests she could think of: blood work, x-rays, various scans—from MRIs to bone scans—but we always came up empty. Meanwhile, Aaron lost his appetite and his weight dropped."

Emmett peered out the window, his eyes moist, but he paused only for a moment. "We took him to pediatricians, orthopedics, neurologists, and even a rheumatologist. No one had any answers or could even point us in a logical direction. The neurologist insisted the symptoms were psychosomatic, so in desperation we made an appointment with a psychologist. When I look back on it, that neuro doc was such an arrogant . . . anyway, we saw the psychologist. Long story short, he didn't feel there was any behavioral pathology.

"We returned home, knowing nothing more than when we had before. I had the entire congregation praying for our son. Renee and I were fervent in our prayers. Morning, noon, and night found us on our knees—when we were not obsessed with watching Aaron's every move. Renee took personal leave from her clinic to devote more time to Aaron and our family.

"Interestingly enough, neither Aaron nor Joshua seemed affected by Aaron's waning health. Our family time together was the most joyful I remember, but always in the back of my mind I felt weight and fear of the approaching end of my son. I knew Renee shared the same burden. Aaron and Joshua continued to be the best of friends, even when Aaron became bedridden. He and his brother laughed and played whatever games the boys dreamed up.

"Eventually we had to admit Aaron to the hospital. He was placed in the ICU, and every second of the day I spent in prayer, asking for the miracle that my son would live. I had the confidence that God could heal my son, but now I'm pretty sure I didn't believe He would heal Aaron.

"He soon became unresponsive, and although Renee and Joshua went every day to the hospital, I no longer had the strength to watch my son fade from this world. I couldn't step inside that building anymore. The pain and hurt that I caused my wife was no less than the agony I felt with the unanswered words I prayed."

Emmett brought his gaze around to David, who still sat silently, listening to the story that was being told, unknown by David, for the very first time.

Emmett continued, "Aaron died shortly after. From what I understand, he left this world while holding the hands of his mother and his little brother. If I could change one thing in this life, I'd have been there, holding his hand, as well.

"Things have grown harder with the passing of our son. Joshua stopped speaking the day Aaron died. Lately his appetite is changing, and Renee is in a panic, fearing that our little boy might be following the same fate as Aaron. She's all ready to take him wherever she may need to, in the hopes of preventing a similar fate. I suggested that we travel east to Boston, but Renee no longer will listen to me. She has lost her faith in me as a husband, pastor, and father."

David had no words of consolation or of advice—written or otherwise. It had never been easy for him to convert his thoughts and feelings to writing. He reached across the desk and picked up a black, leather Bible. He raised his eyebrows to Emmett, asking an unspoken question. *What about this?*

"I'm not sure what I believe anymore, David. I don't—"

A knock on the door followed by a "Hello" left Emmett's words hanging in David's mind. The unfinished statement left him with an unyielding sense of dread.

"Come on in." Emmett regained some of his composure, and David slid off the desk and stood up.

A stout figure strode through the doorway. "Hi there. Is Emmett Brown in?"

Emmett offered his hand in greeting. "Good morning. I'm Emmett Brown. You must be Bill Nomed, my new assistant."

The man across returned the grasp warmly at first, but then hesitated as Emmett finished his greeting. "Ah, I see . . . well, this is kind of embarrassing." He glanced from Emmett to David, raising his left eyebrow in question.

"This is my friend, David Liberty," Emmett said quickly in introduction.

Bill nodded to David but directed his question to Emmett. "I think there's been a misunderstanding. Could we have a moment in private?"

"A misunderstanding? Oh, David's fine. He won't talk about anything spoken here today if you don't wish it."

David glanced out the window, not to change his view but to hide the smile that crawled across his face.

The stress that had crept into Bill's expression disappeared. "I don't know how to say this, Emmett, but I think something was lost in the message you received from the bishop's office."

"Mmm, I don't follow you. What exactly was lost?"

"There may have been a misprint in the letter you received from Bishop Brant. You see, I'm not your assistant; I'm your new associate."

Emmett was visibly surprised by the news. He tried to recover by returning the forced laughter. "Yes, that *is* quite a misunderstanding. May I ask why? And what exactly is your role, and mine, for that matter?"

David watched Bill's gaze wander in his direction. It was clear that Bill was uncomfortable broaching these topics, but David didn't move, and Emmett had not excused him.

Bill inhaled deeply, gathering courage to answer Emmett's questions. "There have been complaints from people in your church community about your ability, or clarity in your teaching. In fact, some of the statements the bishop received stated you were no longer able to lead these people." He cleared his throat and continued. "I've been sent to observe, help, and ultimately decide whether or not you are to be relieved of your pastorate."

Emmett slumped in his chair. "I can't believe this."

"Emmett, the bishop understands the challenges you have faced these past months. He is hoping you just need some time off. That is where I come in. I will assume most of your responsibilities over the next couple of weeks, to allow you to regroup and recharge. We will then reintroduce you into those responsibilities and see how things progress."

"Or regressed," Emmett mumbled.

The phone rang. All three men turned to the phone, but no one answered it. The answering machine picked up. "Hi, you have reached the office of Pastor Brown at the Family Bible Church. Your call is important to us, so please leave a detailed message, and we will get back to you as soon as possible."

A soft beep sounded, followed by Renee's hysterical voice. "Emmett, are you there? Where are you? I thought that—"

Emmett scooped up the phone. "I'm right here."

Renee did not lower her voice, and her anger echoed on the answering machine. "I still think you need to come to Joshua's appointment. Just postpone your stupid meeting!"

"I'll be right there," Emmett said.

A pause, "What?"

"I said I'll be right there." Without waiting for a response, Emmett hung up the phone. "C'mon, David. Time to go."

"Whoa, wait a minute," began Bill. "I need to know a few—"

"The office is all yours, Pastor Nomed." Emmett tossed a key ring in Bill's direction, and he and David left the bewildered man standing alone in the room.

Emmett parked the truck. "We're here. Follow me." There was no emotion in his words.

David reached over and placed a hand on Emmett's arm, shook his head, and raised his hand. "Probably don't want to see any more fireworks, huh?"

David smiled thinly.

"Pray for us." Emmett left the vehicle and headed toward the gray stone office building.

When Emmett walked into the waiting area he heard Joshua's name called. Emmett became Renee's shadow, and the family of three walked down the hallway and into the office of Dr. Thomas Johnson, the pediatrician.

They selected chairs that placed Joshua between them, an inappropriate buffer.

Dr. Johnson sat at his desk, concentrating on the work in front of him, apparently not noticing the trio. Finally he spoke, although he still did not glance up from his desk. "Renee, I have reviewed all of Joshua's tests. Everything came back normal." His looked up at the family. "Everything looks good."

"What do you feel is going on then, Tom?" Renee asked.

"I think Joshua is still emotionally affected by the loss of his brother."

"Then why has he recently begun to lose weight?"

"I think it's part of his grieving process. As you know, some people take longer to recover from loss."

"Yes, I know that. I also know that Aaron began to lose weight, and no one could come up with a reason why."

"I don't think the symptoms are the same."

Renee's calm started to shatter. "Look how frail he has become, Tom! I can't let the same thing happen again. I want to see Dr. Curtis in New York. You can get us in."

"Yes, I could, but I'd jeopardize my own good standing with Curtis, sending him a child without any valid symptoms."

Renee stood from her chair. "Why won't anyone listen?" She turned to her husband, "Emmett, are you just going to sit there? Why am I the only one who sees what is really happening here?"

"Now, Renee, calm down. We all want to help you," Dr. Johnson countered. "Has there been any recent changes in Joshua's condition?"

"Of course not. That's what I'm talking about." Renee pounded her hands to her head in frustration. "Why aren't you listening?"

"There has been one change," Emmett said quietly. "Joshua spoke yesterday."

Silence followed the statement.

"Is that true, Renee?" Dr. Johnson asked.

Renee nodded.

"Why, that's marvelous! Joshua, my boy, say something to me."

Joshua glanced at Dr. Johnson and then stared down at the floor.

"Mmm. How much did he converse yesterday?"

Emmett answered the question. "Not much. It was somewhat confusing to me. He spoke in the presence of a stranger we met yesterday. In fact, any words he spoke were in relation to his new-found friend." Emmett told Dr. Johnson the events that had taken place the day before and that morning. He did not mention anything about the new pastor or his subsequent leave of absence from his pastorate position.

"That's interesting. What do the two of you make of it?"

"I'm not sure," Emmett answered.

"All I know is that it's rather irritating," Renee said. "That my son would choose to talk to a stranger—a vagabond at that—and not speak to his mother boggles my mind."

"Is this David out in your truck right now, Emmett?"

"Yes, he is."

"Why don't you bring him in?"

Emmett nodded and left the office.

Renee crossed her arms and rolled her eyes in disgust.

Shortly Emmett returned, with David close behind. "Dr. Johnson, this is David Liberty."

Dr. Johnson reached across his desk to grasp David's hand. "Hi, David, you can call me Tom."

"Hi, David!" A high-pitched voice interrupted the greeting. Joshua leapt up from his chair and hugged David's leg. He looked up at his friend and said, "How was Daddy's office this morning?"

"I see what you mean," Tom said.

"Oh, one other thing I forgot to mention," Emmett said. "David is mute."

While Tom and Emmett conversed, David answered Joshua's question. *I had an interesting morning with your father. He told me what happened with your brother Aaron, but it also seems as if the bishop wants to give your dad some time off. He sent another pastor to help with the church duties.* David patted the small boy on the shoulder.

"Yeah, I miss my brother. Why does the bishop think that Dad needs help at the church?"

David took a step backward.

Emmett stopped in the middle of a sentence and stared at Joshua and David.

Renee moved closer to her son and David. Her countenance reflected her confusion. "What did Joshua say? Did he say something about the bishop?" Renee's glance darted over to her husband.

Emmett bent down and gingerly placed his hands on Joshua's shoulders. He directed his question to his son, but stared accusingly up to David. "Son, what did you say? Did David tell you something when he came in?"

"Emmett," Tom said, "I thought you said David is mute."

Emmett glared at David. "He's led us to believe that."

"Oh, this is nonsense," Renee blurted. "I watched him from the second he walked into the room. He hasn't said anything to Joshua. What on earth are you talking about, Emmett?" She placed her hands on her hips.

For a moment no one spoke. All eyes drifted to the young boy who stood smiling up at his new friend.

David reached down and ruffled the boy's hair. *You definitely can read my mind.* He scanned into the child's deep brown eyes.

Joshua smiled wider. Then his smile faded a little when he spoke to David. "Is everything going to be normal again? Are you gonna help Dad get his preacher job back?"

Emmett's hung his head in humiliation.

David squatted down to Joshua's level. *I'll do the best that I can to see that your Dad gets the help that he needs.*

Renee's voice broke through. "Would someone please tell me what's going on?"

"I'd have to agree that my curiosity has been piqued," Tom chimed in.

Emmett gave his son a quick embrace and then stood to answer his wife. Joshua's little hand grasped Emmett's. David stood off to the side with a firm grip on Emmett's shoulder. Emmett looked at Renee. "It seems the bishop thinks I need a temporary leave of absence."

Renee raised her eyebrows.

Emmett continued, "He has sent a fellow pastor to assume my duties, until I . . . I mean until I'm ready or rested and can resume my role in the church."

Renee's face reddened. "I don't understand."

"I'm not entirely clear. It seems that some of the congregation complained."

Renee's eyes narrowed. "You told our son before you told me?"

"No! You said you saw everything when David and I came into the office. I thought David told Joshua. How could I have told him, when I just found out this morning?"

"That *is* rather curious," Tom interjected. "Who told Joshua?"

David was unsure how to handle the confusing situation. He thought perhaps he should write down on the paper who he was and why he was possibly here with the Brown family. He'd stepped over to the desk, picked up a pen, and found a notepad. He pressed the pen to the paper. *I am not who I appear to . . .* David looked in confusion at the scribble on the paper. He tried again to write, but his pen formed no words. He shook his head and crumpled up the piece of paper. *It figures. I really don't know what I was going to write, anyway.*

Renee's knelt before her son. "Joshua, sweetie, how did you know what happened at Daddy's work this morning?"

Joshua encircled his arms around his mother's neck. He did not offer any explanation. Instead, he looked over his shoulder at David. "And we're gonna need to help Mommy, too."

Renee hugged her son fiercely and allowed her gaze to wander to David. "I don't understand what's going on here, Mr. Liberty, but if you cause my son hurt in anyway, I will make sure that you wish you'd never been born."

I have felt that way before.

Joshua spoke. "David, can we go home now?"

The four adults did not move. It had become clear that although Joshua was finally speaking for the first time since Aaron had passed, he would speak only to David.

Tom cleared his throat. "Renee, why don't you take Joshua home? We can talk another time."

Renee did not respond. She stood with Joshua's arms still wrapped around her neck. She glanced at her husband and walked through the doorway. Joshua stared at David as he left. A smile spread across his face.

Emmett said, "David, go ahead. You can ride with Renee. I'm not going home right now."

The hair on the back of David's neck rose. His body tensed, and his eyes slowly tracked to where Emmett was standing. He was staring off into space. An odd sensation trickled down David's spine. It took all the concentration and effort he could muster to shrug in indifference and remove his presence from Tom and Emmett.

Chapter Five

EMMETT DROVE HIS truck along the winding, bumpy dirt roads of the local state game lands. He had traveled these roads so many times in his youth that every turn and ridge was permanently imprinted in his mind. He had hunted these lands many years ago. As a child he relished that first morning of archery season, when he and his father shared adventures in the surrounding fields and forests. Emmett had never shot that elusive whitetail deer, but he enjoyed the game of tag much more and never really had the heart to release an arrow in the direction of the wonderful animal. His father often thought that Emmett had bad luck or was just not a good woodsman.

He smiled when the memories flooded his mind. He could not hold back the tears, so he decided to let them roll freely, and he continued to drive. It was not far now, and he allowed his senses to take him on an enchanted journey into the past.

He recalled the games he and his friends played in the woods, the crazy war games they invented, all twists on the game of Capture the Flag. He and his friends had used their bows. Years before paintball became a fad they'd padded the ends of the arrows and used them to strike each other as they ran through the forest. Many times they would forego the rules and merely run and shoot at each other in a game of conquest. The game was not always safe. Sometimes the arrow's cedar shaft would break through the padded covering and injure the victim. No serious damage was ever done, however, and the weak-powered longbows, once thought to be useless, were brought to life in these games of war.

Emmett's tears flowed quicker, and he recalled the long walks with the girlfriend of his youth. They hiked the hills together, sometimes playing hide and seek while at other times packing a simple picnic lunch to enjoy on the tops of the large boulders that lay throughout the region. He recalled the joyous times of holding her hand and the first time she had allowed him to steal a kiss. He had known Renee a long time. His childhood sweetheart had grown to become his bride.

The truck came to a stop. Emmett did not consciously recall making all the correct turns, but he arrived at his destination. He turned the engine off, left the keys in the ignition, and exited the vehicle. Emmett patted the hood of his truck and picked up a worn trail to follow into the once familiar forest.

He walked through the woods with a purpose and innate knowledge of where he was going. His feet rarely snapped a twig, and his body moved like a shadow as it had so many years ago playing tag with the deer.

The grade of the trail moved upward and within an hour Emmett stood on the platform that provided an overlook to the waterfall below. The trail branched here at the lookout: one part continued along the rim of the canyon while the other wound its way down the steep embankment to merge with the cascading stream below.

Emmett leaned against the wooden rail. He rested his head on his hands as the roar of the water masked all the other sounds around him. He gazed at the western trail that led down to the pool of water far below. He smiled and retraced the steps he had so frequently walked with Renee so many years before.

The tears fell at the same pace as the water striking the rocks below. Emmett's shoulders shook, and his body wracked with sobs. He glanced upward and, shaking his fist, hollered, "Why have you done this to me?"

Not waiting or expecting an answer, he lowered his fist and continued to speak through his tears. "My son is taken from me, my faith has faltered, I have failed my wife and now, as if in some crude, sarcastic answer to all my prayers, my job is stripped from me and my little Joshua will only talk to a stranger.

"I have utterly and completely failed as a husband, father, and pastor. Renee was right. My faith and beliefs were all a sham. A crutch. Nothing more. It has brought me nothing."

Emmett spread his arms out and braced his palms against the rails. With a quick thrust he pushed his body upward and stood atop the wooden rail. "My son, my son, Daddy will soon join you." Emmett spread his arms outward and bent his knees.

Emmett's muscles prepared to function one last time. He rocked slightly backwards and then sprung from his perch. Searing agony shot through his right leg. A vice-like grip ensnared him, causing his momentum to shift backwards. Emmett's legs collapsed underneath him, and his body pitched forward. His chest slammed against the rail that had once been his perch, knocking the breath from him. He fell, and everything went black.

Renee sat in her office finishing her dictation. She had dropped Joshua at the house with her mother and returned to see her remaining patients.

She was still bewildered by the events of the morning. She did not understand the effect David had on her son. Although she was beginning to feel optimistic, the past still hung heavy on her shoulders. To compound the situation it seemed as if her husband was losing his position at the church, and she did not know if their marriage would survive any more trials. Renee continued to stare absently at the desk before her, deep with thought, when a voice brought her mind back to the office.

"Renee? How are you doing? How was Joshua's appointment this morning?"

Renee looked up to see Dr. Waits standing in the doorway. "Hi. Jennifer. I didn't hear you knock."

"I figured you must have been deep in thought about something, so I decided to step in when you didn't answer."

"Sorry about that."

"It's quite all right. How was the appointment this morning?"

"Good and bad." Renee collected her thoughts, "Dr. Johnson doesn't think there's anything physically wrong with Joshua."

"That's great news! Does he have any thoughts on what could be going on?"

"Personally, I don't feel Tom is correct, so I've asked him for a referral to New York, where Joshua can be further evaluated."

"Does he know someone he could send you to?"

"He does, but he's reluctant to make the referral. Since Tom doesn't feel that anything is wrong, and Joshua is starting to speak again, he doesn't want to burn any of his favors by making the appointment."

Jennifer frowned. "You could make the referral, right?"

"Actually, no. It's a problem that I ran into when we were treating Aaron. All the specialists require a referral from a non-family member. To get our foot in the door we need someone else to make the appointment."

Jennifer went over and sat on top of the desk. "Joshua has started to talk again?"

Renee nodded. "He's not really talking to Emmett or me, but at least he's talking to someone."

Jennifer laughed softly. "Well, we all need an imaginary friend now and then. Sometimes they're easier to talk to then the real thing."

"I wish this person *were* imaginary, believe me."

"What? You mean Joshua is talking to someone in particular?"

"Yup. Some bum off the street." Renee paused, still not believing what she was going through.

"I don't understand. Does this bum have a name? Why are you calling him a bum?"

"Apparently he wandered into church, a homeless vagabond, and my husband brought him home. He was dressed in rags and smelled as if he hadn't seen a shower in weeks. Joshua has bonded to this stranger in a manner that I can't explain or understand."

"Joshua has taken to this man?" Jennifer frowned.

"That is an understatement. I . . . I can't explain his attraction to this stranger, but he talks with him even though he is a mute."

Jennifer was visibly surprised. "What do you mean he's a mute?"

Renee's eyes flashed with impatience. "I mean he can't speak!"

"But you said that Joshua talks to him."

"Yes! I did. I don't understand it, but Joshua talks and communicates with the man."

"What did you say his name was?"

"David. David something."

Jennifer's eyes narrowed. "I don't know, Renee. I would be careful if I were you. Keep a close eye on this man. I don't know if I'd trust him, and I'd especially not leave him alone with Joshua."

"I don't plan to, but the funny thing is I actually trust the man—even like him—which I think bothers me more than the fact that Joshua's talking to him."

Jennifer eyed Renee curiously. "Maybe it should, Renee. Maybe it should."

David's body was sore from the bumpy ride in the back of Emmett's pickup truck. As he rubbed his shoulders and neck he was well aware of the fact that he was not as sore as Emmett was going to be when he regained his senses.

He peered down at Emmett's still but breathing body sprawled on the wooden deck overlooking the gorge. David had arrived on the scene just in time to see Emmett standing on the rail above the waterfall. In three quick strides he managed to grab Emmett's ankle at the precise moment that Emmett had sprung from his perch. An unnatural strength had flowed through David's arm as he snatched his friend from the air and pulled him back to safety.

Emmett stirred. "Ahh . . . where am I?" He groaned. "What happened? Is this . . . ?" He struggled to open his eyes.

David pressed his hand firmly against Emmett's chest.

Emmett collapsed back to the deck with a moan. "Aarg . . . the pain is unbelievable. How is it that I'm still alive?" He blinked and propped himself up on his elbow. "I can't see very well."

David removed his hand from Emmett's chest and stood.

"No, wait! Don't go! What happened? Where am I?" Emmett sat up and rubbed his eyes.

David placed a hand on Emmett's shoulder and let some water trickle on his lips.

Emmett tipped his head back and drank. "Thanks for the water, friend," he muttered after quenching his thirst. "Will you help me stand?"

I will, but I'm afraid that it's going to hurt. David reached an arm around Emmett's back and placed his hand beneath Emmett's arm. Then he stood and dragged his companion to his feet.

Emmett's legs wobbled. He remained upright only by holding onto David. He groaned. "Everything's still blurry. What's your name?"

It's me. David. David used his free hand to tap Emmett's temple repeatedly. *Think!*

Emmett shouted in surprise, "David, is it really you?"

David patted his friend's back in affirmation. *Yes, it's me.* He guided Emmett down the trail, in the direction of the truck.

"How on earth did you find me? What happened? How far did I fall?"

David smiled at the rapid-fire questions and continued to support Emmett's weight. The two men slowly worked their way down the path. *Someday I may be granted the gift of my voice, and then I'll answer all your questions.*

Emmett said, "I don't understand why you are here, my friend, but thank you."

David once again patted Emmett.

Chapter Six

RENEE WAITED WITH growing impatience for her husband's return. She had many unanswered questions bouncing around in her head. With each passing minute she fantasized various improbable answers that her husband would give her. Her anger and frustration continued to rise with each tick of the clock.

Joshua startled her by running into the living room, dressed in his pajamas. "They're almost home. David and Dad are coming!"

"Joshua, you scared the wits right out of me! What on earth are you doing out of bed, young man?"

Joshua continued to speak, but not necessarily to his mother. "Daddy is hurt, but David was there to help him."

Renee looked incredulously at her son and turned her gaze out the window, where vehicle headlights were flashing through the curtains. The lights turned off, and the car doors slammed.

Renee strode over to the door as Joshua hopped up on the recliner to wait.

Renee's frustration returned when she realized she would not be able to grill her husband with Joshua awake. She opened the door and sputtered, "Where on earth have you . . . ?" Her voice quickly rose in surprise. "What happened? Careful, David. Bring him in and lay him on the couch."

David laid Emmett on the couch before him.

"Is Daddy going to be OK, David?"

Renee flew to her husband's side, opening his eyelids to see his unresponsiveness. She inspected the rest of his body and shouted a question at David. "What happened?"

"Daddy fell," Joshua answered for David.

Hearing her son address her for the first time in months caused Renee to gape at her little boy. Her hands, however, continued the inspection of

Emmett's body and drew her stare away from Joshua to the task at hand. Renee grew pale as she recognized the dire shape her husband was in.

She tore open Emmett's shirt to inspect him more closely. Her hand slid to his wrist, and she observed the shallow rise and fall of his chest. He was slipping away. "Dear God, no," she whispered and gently stroked the side of his face.

"Momma, is Daddy going to be all right?"

"Joshua, get the phone and dial 911."

"No, Momma. I'm scared!"

"Sit here and hold Daddy's hand, and I'll call for help."

"But, Momma," Joshua cried as Renee moved to get the phone, "you're a doctor. Daddy needs you to make him better."

Renee hollered over her shoulder, partly in answer to her son and partly in assurance to herself, "Your dad needs more than my help right now."

As Renee disappeared into the next room, David took his place beside Emmett and Joshua. He placed one hand over the little hand that gripped Emmett's hand like a vice. David's eyes swelled with tears while he watched Joshua cling helplessly to his dad.

Renee's voice drifted to David. "This is Dr. Brown. My husband's hurt; he's bleeding internally . . . No, I can't . . . I understand. Come as quickly as you can."

Joshua looked up into David's eyes. "Help my Daddy, David. You're supposed to help us. Please make him better."

David could not remember a time when he had felt so helpless or confused. *What am I to do? Dear Lord in heaven, how can I help this child?*

"Help my Daddy . . ."

David closed his eyes and lost himself to the outside world. He squeezed Emmett's and Joshua's hands as he struggled in silence, talking only to his mind. *Joelle!* His mind hollered. *Help me, Joelle! What do I do? Joelle, I don't want this child's father to die. Help me!*

His mind waited for her sweet voice, but instead his own voice seemed to reply, *Faith the size of a mustard seed will cause the mountain to move from here to there.*

What? I'm not sure. Did I say that or did someone else? David shut out all external senses.

O Lord, my God, I cried out to you and you healed me.

Emmett needs to be healed.

David and Goliath:
The Guardian Angel Chronicles

I ask that supplications, prayers, petitions, and thanksgiving be offered for everyone.

David knew what had to be done. So simple. So powerful. So pure. He sent his prayer forth. *My Lord, My God, heal this man who lies before you.*

A strange sensation coursed through David's body and he felt a power that radiated into Emmett's body. An internal vibration like silent thunder brought David out of his internal trance, just as the medics came bursting through the doorway.

The first man spoke. "Out of the way, please."

"Joshua, you and David need to move, so the men can help Daddy," Renee said.

Joshua glanced up through the stream of tears that trickled down his face. He looked at David and smiled.

David grinned and winked at Joshua through his own tears.

"Joshua, you need to move."

A sound escaped from Emmett, lying on the couch. "Move? Why does my son need to move? What's going on here?" Emmett opened his eyes and rose to a sitting position.

"Emmett! What on earth? Don't you dare move!" Renee hollered. "All right, you two, out of the way!"

Renee's command parted Joshua and David so the paramedics could reach their patient.

The paramedics gave Emmett a thorough examination, but his vitals were within normal limits. Heart rate, blood pressure, breathing rate, and orientation were all acceptable. Emmett struggled with such determination during the examination that the medics were unable to convince him to go to the hospital for further tests.

After much arguing, the paramedics left the Browns' home without taking the patient with them. This had left Renee fuming. At one point she looked ready to carry her husband out to the ambulance herself.

Renee shouted that she would have someone fired for their incompetence. She slammed the door behind the paramedics and continued to rant and rave until she eventually calmed down enough to address Emmett. "I don't understand what's going on here. Emmett, you were on death's doorstep, and now you just sit there as if nothing has happened."

"Honey, I told you I feel fine."

"That's the point. You shouldn't be feeling fine. You were bleeding internally and whole systems were failing. Yet now you sit here talking with me, insinuating that I'm losing my mind."

"Would you rather I were on death's doorstep?"

Renee stopped pacing back and forth, placed both her hands on her hips, and said, "Of course not." Her voice softened. "I just don't understand. I must be going crazy."

"Momma, it was David. He healed Daddy." Joshua said. "I asked him to do something, so he did."

Renee looked down at her son. "Sweetie, what are you talking about?"

"You're a doctor, Momma, and you said that you couldn't help Daddy, that he needed more help. So I asked David."

"Joshua, how could David make Daddy better?" She glanced over to David, as if asking him the same question.

Emmett remained slumped on the couch. He sat upright and asked, "I'd like to know what's going on. I can't remember a thing—just the paramedics barging in here and everyone thinking I was hurt."

"You *were* hurt," Renee countered.

"That's right, Momma. He was hurt, but now he's better."

Renee frowned at David. "Would you care to add any insight to this puzzle? I mean, ever since you have arrived here, things have been far from normal."

From what I gather it's probably a good thing that things are not normal around here. David's unheard sarcasm flowed from his mind, unheard to all but one.

Joshua snickered.

I'd tell you if I could, but right now I'm afraid that I'm supposed to just fit in with your family.

"He just needs to be part of the family, Mom."

Emmett asked, "David, do you know what happened?"

"Of course he knows what happened. He's the one who carried you inside and placed you on the couch," Renee answered

David nodded. *Yes.* He glanced at Joshua, completely aware that the young boy could read his thoughts, at least to some degree. *We were on a hike and you fell.*

"Daddy, you were on a hike and fell. David brought you home," Joshua piped in.

"David, could you write down what happened and what's going on?" Emmett asked.

"Yes, that'd be a great idea, wouldn't it?" Renee snapped. "I've been asking right along for someone to please help me to understand this mess."

David shook his head. *I don't believe I can write that down.*

Renee tossed her hands up in disgust. "That's just great." Her eyes flared. "Then maybe he shouldn't be welcome in our home any longer."

"No, Momma. No!" Joshua hopped over and clung to David's leg.

"Just a minute," Emmett said. "Everyone hold on a minute. Let me talk to David." The firmness in Emmett's voice had obviously been heard so infrequently by his son and wife that they both shared looks of surprise. His voice turned peaceful. "David, do you mean you won't write down what happened or that you *can't?*"

David smiled. *Good man.* He held up his hand and showed two fingers.

"I had a hunch. So you can't write it down, correct?"

David nodded.

"My son has obviously taken to you. He feels you are supposed to help our family somehow."

David nodded.

"Do you know how you're going to help us?"

No.

"I fell when we were hiking?"

Yes.

"Was I hurt badly?"

Renee interrupted. "He wouldn't know—"

Emmett raised a hand to silence her. The gesture worked.

David nodded. *Yes. You were apparently hurt very badly.*

Emmett leaned back. "You know, the only thing I remember before waking up on the couch was a strange surge of, I don't know, a strange feeling waking me up." He refocused his attention to David. "Did you do something to me? Did you heal me?"

Three pair of eyes looked at David.

David raised a single finger.

"Huh?" Emmett looked perplexed. "What does 'one' mean? Do you want me to wait for something?"

Renee interjected, "Emmett, you asked him two questions. He is signaling the first choice."

David glanced at Renee and nodded.

"Oh. Right. Got it. So you did something. Now, let me just ask you this: did you heal me?"

David looked at Joshua and thought intensely about the question and its answer. He tightened his lips and shook his head. *It was not I who did the healing.*

Renee appeared relieved.

Emmett studied David. "For some strange reason I trust you. I can't explain it, but you're not here by chance, are you?"

No, I am not.

Joshua still clung to David's leg and piped up, "He's our guardian angel, Dad."

Renee finished washing up before bed and sat on the comforter waiting for her husband. Waiting was not part of their normal routine. Usually either Emmett or Renee, if the first to bed, would be asleep or feign sleep before the other spouse crawled under the sheets. This had been going on for a months, creating a chasm that was close to becoming impassable in their failing relationship.

Renee did not have the strength to continue their nightly ritual. Her nerves were still shot by the events of the day, and her mind was racing. She intended to talk with her husband, something that was out of the norm and caused her heart to pound faster.

The bathroom door opened, and Emmett appeared. He paused in midstride, cleared his throat, and words tumbled out. "Is . . . is everything all right?"

Renee shook her head and fought the moisture that threatened to burst from behind the wall she had built since Aaron's death.

Emmett moved to Renee's side. He was shaking as he crossed a border that had not been crossed in a long time. She saw the pain and fear in his eyes and blurted out, "Emmett, I thought I lost you."

An invisible barrier still separated husband from wife, but Emmett was able to return his wife's eye contact. He fumbled for words. "I . . . I don't remember what happened. Why were David and I hiking?"

Renee moved closer to her husband. "I'm not sure, but I don't know what I would have done if I'd lost you," she whispered.

Emmett toppled over, clutching his stomach and wincing in pain.

"Emmett!" Renee reached out and caught her husband, successfully helping him collapse backward onto the bed. Renee fell, as well, landing partially on the bed and partially on her husband. "Emmett, what's wrong?" Panic laced through Renee.

"Renee," Emmett whispered, "I'm sorry."

The reply caught Renee by surprise. "What? Should I get you to the hospital or call—?"

Emmett placed a finger against Renee's lips, cutting off the rest of her words. Renee started to push away, but Emmett laced his other arm around her.

Renee froze. Her husband was not physically restraining her from moving away, but his touch implored her not to move. She was afraid. She had come so close to losing his touch altogether. She broke the silence, and her whisper echoed through the bedroom. "Are you sure you're feeling all right?"

Emmett whispered in return, "This pain will pass." He paused and took a deep breath. "But the pain I've caused you, though, is enough for me to wish my life to cease. I've hurt and failed the only woman I've ever loved."

Renee was stunned by his words.

"I've failed you as a husband and as a father for our children. I know I don't deserve your love anymore. I just wanted you to know that I'm sorry for the hurt I've caused you. My only wish is that I could somehow undo the past."

Something inside of Renee crumbled. It was part of the wall that had been built and reinforced during the emotional separation from her husband. Now, as the walls weakened around her heart, she saw the man she had fallen in love with lying before her. A man she had almost lost earlier this day.

There were no more restraints. Renee leaned forward, lips hungrily searching her husband's lips. At first he did not respond, but with some reassurance his passion quickly matched her own.

Sleep was not important that night while a husband and wife began steps forward in reconciliation. Their covenant of marriage had been only on paper of late, but the chasm that existed between them was now much smaller than twenty-four hours earlier.

Chapter Seven

EMMETT DROVE THE pickup truck with a smile on his face. He did not care if David eyed him curiously; he could still not believe the night he had shared with his wife. They talked until morning, covering an array of topics. Their past childhood and courtship dominated the conversation. They had also talked about the possibility that Emmett had been healed by David's touch and about the eerie but wonderful effect David had on Joshua.

Joshua was now talking directly to his parents. It was evident this morning at breakfast. Joshua had informed them that David was to go to work with his father again today.

Emmett tried to persuade his son to follow a different game plan, especially since Emmett was on a leave of absence from the pastorate. Joshua was unrelenting, and Renee also convinced Emmett that he might as well head over to the rectory office to see if Bill needed any help with organization during his first few days at a new location.

Emmett was soon whistling and humming while he and David rode in the truck. David playfully slapped him on the shoulders. Emmett glanced over at his companion and laughed when David plugged his ears.

"What's a matter, David? Don't you think I can carry a tune?"

David rolled his eyes and grinned.

Emmett felt his face warm, wondering what David was thinking. "Now, David . . ."

David struck him again on the shoulder, shook his head, and waved his hands as if signaling that he did not want to know.

Emmett laughed. "Don't worry, my friend, I won't bore you with details."

David wiped his brow, feigning relief.

They pulled into the parking lot of the little church and walked to the rectory.

Emmett hesitated at the door. "I don't know what to do. Should I ring the doorbell or just go on in?"

David reached out and opened the door. Then he stepped back and indicated for Emmett to lead the way.

Emmett took a deep breath and, finding a small reserve of courage, fought against the urge to turn around and head back to the truck. He stepped through the doorway and into the small building, wondering how such a feat that had once been so automatic now made him feel like an imposter. He allowed his feet to take him in the direction of his office and became aware of voices carrying on a conversation.

Emmett peered over his shoulder at David.

David placed his hand on Emmett's back and pushed him forward, guiding him into the room.

Emmett was quick to recognize Lenny Jackson, a member of the church. "Sorry to barge in on you like this." He looked apologetically first toward Bill and then to Lenny. "I thought maybe Pastor Bill might need some help with the organization of the office or with any questions he might have."

Bill smiled. "Good morning, Emmett. I see you brought your sidekick with you. Good morning, David." David nodded a greeting. "I really appreciate you stopping by, Emmett, but I think it would be best if you waited outside until Lenny and I are done; then you could definitely help me out with a couple of things."

"Right. Sorry for interrupting you. David and I will be outside at the picnic table."

Before the men could exit, Lenny Jackson said, "Wait! I think I want Emmett to hear what's going on."

At first, Bill did not reply. Lenny's request had clearly caught him by surprise. But then he nodded. "Yes, that might be a good idea. What do you think, Emmett? Will you sit and listen for a bit?"

"If Lenny would like me to stay, then I'd be honored to sit and listen." Emmett moved into the room but David waited inside the doorway.

Emmett sat down but abruptly stood again. "Where are my manners?" He motioned David into the room. "Lenny Jackson, this is David Liberty."

Lenny and David clasped hands.

"Hi, there," Lenny said. "They call me Lenny. It's short for Leonard."

David nodded politely.

Emmett broke in. "Lenny, David is unable to speak. He's a friend of mine, and I know this is an odd request, but can he stay and listen as well?"

Lenny responded, "Yup. I like 'im. Sit here with us, Dave." He indicated a nearby chair.

Bill did not hide his frown when he spoke to Lenny. "Start again from the beginning, Leonard."

"Uh . . . it's L-lenny, Pastor," Lenny stammered,

Emmett reached out and patted Lenny's leg reassuringly. "Go ahead, Lenny. What's this all about?"

Lenny dropped his head. He ran his finger through his hair three or four times before he looked at the faces in the room. "I know I am gonna disappoint you, Emm, but Sally has left me. She wants a divorce."

Renee's drive to the office was brief. When she arrived, there was a message on the answering machine. Dr. Waits would not be into the office because she was not feeling well. With Margaret away on vacation, Renee would have to handle the office herself.

Because Renee practiced medicine in a rural community, the office could be handled with one nurse-receptionist and the attending physician without difficulties. Since the arrival of Dr. Jennifer Waits, the patient visits had increased as well as the overall number of patients who now belonged to the small, private practice. Today, Renee would have to cover her own patients, Jennifer's patients, scheduling, and collections throughout the day. Things could get really bogged down if a walk-in emergency occurred.

Renee could not remember the last time she had covered the office alone. It had been sometime before the arrival of Dr. Waits. She decided to keep the answering machine turned on and placed the sign-in sheet on the counter. She also printed a sign that read: "We are short staffed today. Will be with you shortly. Thank you for understanding." She placed the sign next to the clipboard, where the patients would be signing in.

No sooner had she put a pen on the sheet when the first patient of the morning walked up and signed in. Renee did not recognize him. "Your last name, please."

"Howard. Dwight Howard."

Renee pulled his chart and waved the man to follow her into the first exam room.

She flipped open his chart and scanned the contents, trying to read the writing that was in her partner's handwriting. "Mr. Howard, I am Dr. Brown. What can I do for you this morning?"

"Do for me? Where's the other doctor?"

"Dr. Waits is not in the office this morning. She had another emergency to tend to."

"I need my wounds checked."

"Wounds? What wounds?" Renee looked up from the chart and peered closely at the man before her. Mr. Howard was a rugged man. His head was partially covered with a gauze wrap, and his right arm hung in a sling. His face was streaked with gashes. Renee was taken back when she saw the shape he was in.

"C'mon, doc. The wounds that are covering my body."

"I mean, what are they from?"

"Isn't it in my chart?"

"Yes, Mr. Howard, I'm sure it is in your chart, but you will save us both time if you just answer my questions. Now, what happened?"

"Haven't you read any of the news around here? I was attacked by a mountain lion."

Emmett sat entranced while Lenny told his story of woe. His wife, Sally, had left him more than ten months before, but Lenny was not clear on why she had left him. Sally had moved back with her parents while Lenny continued to live in the home that belonged to the married couple. There were no children involved. For that, Lenny said he was thankful.

"Lenny, I want you to put yourself in Sally's shoes. Why would she have left you?" Bill asked.

Lenny faltered. "Her . . . her shoes? I don't understand."

"Lenny, what Bill wants you to do is pretend that you are Sally. In other words, if you were Sally, what would you think of Lenny?" Emmett explained.

Bill nodded in agreement and shot Emmett a look of thanks.

"I'm not sure. Sally has not said why she left." Lenny's eyes misted.

"She didn't use words to tell you why she left, but we're pretty sure she has indirectly told you why," Bill said. "Now, just pretend that you are Sally. Tell us how she sees Lenny—you."

Lenny nodded his head. "I'll try."

Emmett interjected, "Take your time."

Lenny did the best he could to describe himself through his wife's eyes. He described a person who was strong-willed and protective. He loved his wife deeply and was probably too father-like to his young wife. There were intimacy problems, not only with a difference in their levels of desire, but the actual physical act was sometimes painful for Sally. She often cried during their lovemaking. Lenny admitted there were occasional spats about this problem, and he often called her names. It was only recently that he found out she had actually heard him call her these names. He always assumed she was asleep. It hurt deeply when she confronted him, telling him how much those words had hurt her—words he'd thought he was saying to unhearing ears. His face reddened.

"Lenny you're doing well," Bill said. "Is there anything else we should know?"

Lenny nodded his head and looked anxiously toward Emmett. "She stopped going to church with me."

Emmett racked his memory of the past few weeks, trying to recall Sally's face in the pews. He flushed, for he could not even remember seeing Lenny in the congregation, one more detail affirming what Bill had told him and fortifying the fact that Emmett needed to change something in his own vocation.

"I'm sorry to hear that." Bill's tone softened. "How long ago did that start?"

"About eight months ago."

Bill turned to Emmett. "What was your response when you no longer noticed Sally at church?"

Emmett was taken back by the change in direction of questioning. He blushed even more at the humiliation.

"It wasn't Emmett's fault," Lenny said. "She just told me she didn't believe in the childish stuff anymore and that she wasn't going to church anymore."

Bill gave Emmett a disapproving look but addressed his next question to Lenny. "So Lenny, when did you stop coming to church?"

"About four months ago."

Emmett's eyes widened. No wonder he could not remember seeing them at the services.

"But now you are seeking the church's help?"

Tears streamed down Lenny's face. "I just want my Sally back."

"What do you think is the best way to get your wife back?"

"I . . . I'm not sure."

Bill continued, "Tell me something that you *think* might help."

Lenny watched Emmett for help, but Emmett's lips remained sealed. He no longer felt worthy to give anyone advice.

"Well, Lenny, you are here at a church . . ."

Lenny answered with hesitation. "Should I pray?"

Bill slapped his hand on the desk in excitement. "Exactly!" The noise caused everyone to jump with the exception of David, who continued to sit, a forgotten observer.

"I . . . I've been praying."

"What have you been praying for?"

"To . . . to get Sally back."

"That's fine, but we need to pray for the reconciliation of your marriage, that is, the healing of Sally's and your marriage. It sounds like Sally may be feeling she's not deserving of your love. The problems you're experiencing with intimacy may make her feel inadequate as a wife. Instead of facing this problem, it was easier for her to run away. So we need to pray for the Lord to rejoin you in marriage."

For the first time, Lenny's face no longer had the appearance of a beaten man. He sat up straighter and leaned closer to Pastor Nomed.

"Lenny, the Lord tells us in Scripture that he hates divorce, so with this knowledge we're going to ask Him to heal your broken marriage. Scripture also tells us that if two of you agree about anything for which you pray, it shall be granted by God."

Lenny listened intently.

"So Pastor Brown, his friend David, and I will pray for the reconciliation of your marriage," Bill continued. "With faith, it shall be granted by God."

Lenny sprang from his chair and reached across the table, shaking Bill's hand vigorously. "Thank you, Pastor, thank you!"

Bill laughed.

Lenny then shook Emmett's and David's hands, thanking them over and over again.

As Lenny left the room on a whirlwind of emotion, Bill shouted to him, "Remember! Pray daily and wait patiently for the Lord to heal Sally's heart and your marriage."

The door to the rectory slammed closed after Lenny left the building. Emmett could not believe the change in Lenny. He spoke to Bill, "You've given him hope. I believe he has left a changed man."

Bill rocked back in his chair. "Yes, he's going to be fine. More importantly, now I think you do, indeed, need some time away from this place. Take some time to sharpen the ax, if you will."

Emmett nodded and sighed.

"I think your family should remain active with the church. That's important, you know."

"My wife has stopped going."

"What about your son?"

"Joshua?"

"Yes. He could join the boys' brigades."

"I'm not familiar . . ."

"We're starting it here at this church. It's essentially like the Boy Scouts, but with more of an emphasis on religion."

Emmett nodded. "I'll talk to Renee about that. I'm sure she would think it'd be good for him to interact with other boys, but isn't he too young for Boy Scouts?"

"Brigades is for young and old alike, I'd love to have him."

Emmett stood to leave. The conversation was emotionless for him at this point. "I'll talk to Joshua and Renee. Thank you, Bill."

"Just take some time alone, Emmett. The same advice we gave Lenny goes for you. Pray. We'll pray for you, as well."

Chapter Eight

DAVID AND EMMETT got into the truck. David could tell that Emmett's mood had changed one hundred eighty degrees from their drive earlier in the morning. He watched Emmett check his rearview mirror, fasten his seatbelt, and insert his key into the ignition.

Speak. The single word echoed through David's mind.

Emmett sighed. "Bill gave Lenny some great advice. He did better than I would've done." He put the truck in drive.

Speak. Your words need to be heard. The confusion on the origin of the words no longer mattered to David. He knew it was time to follow the command. "I don't think his advice was great. It was OK, but I'm sure you could've done just as well, if not better."

Emmett took a sharp glance over his shoulder to the small compartment in the extended cab of the pickup. His eyes shifted right and left, as if second guessing that he had heard anything at all.

"Yes, the sound of my voice is even startling to my own ears," David said.

Emmett stared in astonishment at the source of the words. He remained so captivated by the smile on David's face and the surprise at hearing David speak, that he forgot to take his foot off the gas or watch the curves of the road.

The truck ran off the road into a nearby field. The jostling of the vehicle caused Emmett to crank the wheel to the left and slam on the brakes. The truck's backend swung around, tearing ruts into the hayfield. Emmett gripped the steering wheel, even though the vehicle had stopped.

David leaned over and cut off the engine. "Steady . . ."

Emmett nodded. "You can talk?"

"For the moment."

Emmett shook his head. "What do you mean, for the moment? Have you been—?"

"No. My gift of speech comes and goes, based on the need."

"I don't understand."

"Truthfully, Emmett, I don't understand it fully, either. Let's just say it is part of my penance. Right now we have something more important to discuss than my ability and inability to speak."

"But I—"

"Emmett, I'm serious. You need to trust me and help me address the situation at hand, for I don't know when my gift of speech will fail. Deal?"

Emmett nodded.

"Good. Now what was wrong with the advice Bill gave to Lenny?"

"What do you mean? I don't think there was anything wrong with the advice. In fact, Bill's quotes of Scripture were right on."

"I didn't ask you what was *right* about his advice. I asked you what was *wrong*, or more importantly, what was missing." *A lesson I, myself, am learning*, David added silently.

Emmett hunched his shoulders. "I'm not sure."

"So, you're in complete agreement with Bill?"

"Now that you mention it, I do feel as if there was something missing."

"What?"

Emmett thought for a moment. "The praying for reconciliation does not address the personal problems that each spouse brought to the marriage."

"Correct. We don't know Sally's side of the story, but Lenny was able to paint a picture of himself. Describe the negatives."

"Controlling. He probably misunderstands how to create a desire for intimacy with his wife."

David laughed. "A majority of men fall short there, my friend. What else?"

"Well, with that being the case, I'll go out on a limb and state that they have problems communicating."

"So, why would God simply reunite the two of them if their internal problems have not been solved? Their marriage would just go down the same path all over again, would it not?"

"Yes."

"Both must have the desire to save the marriage. You and I should pray for God to instill that desire within their hearts. Next, Lenny needs to change. But more importantly, he needs to show Sally that he loves her. Words can be just that—words. Our actions define who we are. Lenny's action will show Sally that he loves her. If he truly loves her, then *her* life is more important than his own. If he demonstrated his love, Sally would want to reconcile the marriage, or at least entertain the notion."

"But we don't know Sally's side of the story."

"You're correct. Free will is one of the greatest gifts the Lord has given his children. I'm not as versed in Scripture as you and Bill are, but there is one passage that for some reason has etched its words within my mind: Love is patient; love is kind. It is not jealous, is not pompous; it is not inflated; it is not rude; it does not seek its own interests; it is not quick-tempered; it does not brood over injury; it does not rejoice over wrongdoing, but rejoices with the truth. It bears all things, believes all things, hopes all things, endures all things."

"Yes, that passage was read at my wedding."

"And at my wedding," replied David softly.

"You're married?"

David peered out the window. "I was married . . . once." He turned back to Emmett. "We must help Lenny demonstrate his love to Sally. If he truly loves her, he'd be willing to show her that she's the most important part of his life."

"But what about Bill? I mean, I've been dismissed from my pastorate. Maybe we should explain our thoughts to Bill."

"Emmett, the Lord is calling you to act. No more hiding in prayer and no more relying on someone else to act. Have faith. Move forward with your knowledge converted to action. Only through *your* actions—not Bill's—will Lenny understand how to show Sally his love."

"I don't understand. How do you know?" Emmett asked.

"Your works confirm your faith. It will help you heal as well."

"When do we start? How do we start?"

David tried to reply, but his voice was gone. He turned his palms face up, indicating that he did not know. David pointed to his lips and did a slice motion with his hand.

"Your voice? It's gone?"

David nodded.

"This doesn't make any sense to me. I mean, your voice coming and going. I'd question it more but something tells me not to. Does that make any sense to you?"

David smiled. Yes. *For some strange reason more and more of this makes sense to me.*

"I believe your advice is correct as well. I'll be honest with you. It scares me. It scares me to think that my own marriage is somehow a reflection of Lenny and Sally's."

As was mine, Emmett. As was mine.

"It is curious to think about what you've said. I've always believed that only the Lord can change a man's colors and that prayer for that change can cause change. Otherwise we are continually destined to fight against our unique sinful nature."

David slapped Emmett on the arm in agreement and then pointed at him.

"Me? What?"

David's finger jabbed Emmett's chest, directly over the heart.

Emmett stared at David. "Yes. I know you're right. I need to pray for change in my heart." Emmett shifted his gaze out the window. "In the past I prayed for the healing of my son. That healing didn't happen. I've also prayed for the healing of my marriage, and that hasn't happened. To be honest, I've lost faith. And now I've lost my church. Maybe I wasn't praying in a way that was consistent with God's will. I was praying for Him to fix things, or more importantly, for me to avoid any responsibility."

David patted Emmett on the shoulder.

Tears streamed down Emmett's face, and he fumbled for words. "I remember. Everything has flashed before me. I tried to take my life. I was set to jump." Emmett stared at David, "But you saved me. Somehow you followed me and saved me from myself."

David did not acknowledge yes or no but merely continued to listen.

Emmett broke into uncontrollable sobs. His body heaved, and he wailed, "Dear Lord! Will you ever forgive me?"

Chapter Nine

RENEE COULD BARELY drag herself through the door. It was after ten o'clock when she finally finished at the office. It took her some time to dictate her office notes for the day and finish the charges, but that was not the sole reason she was so late returning. She secretly hoped everyone would be asleep by now, including her husband.

Emotionally, Renee was spent. She quietly closed the door behind her and made her way through the kitchen toward a strange flickering light that guided her way.

She paused at the kitchen table, where a candlewick sputtered and fought against drowning in the melted wax that grew around it. A plate covered with food and clear wrap lay at her spot at the table with a note nearby.

Renee's fingers trembled as she peeled open the piece of parchment:

Renee,

Just pop your dinner in the microwave when you get home. I am heading to bed. It's about 9:30. I'm exhausted. Can't wait to tell you about my day. Remind me to talk to you about brigades. Wake me if you want to talk.

Sweet dreams, my wife.

Emm

A tired smile crossed Renee's lips when she read the last line of the note. She collapsed into the chair, unwrapped her dinner, and answered the call of hunger she had been unable to satiate throughout the day.

When she finished the last crumb on her plate, she reread the brief note. She shook her head, smiling. It was the only good thing that had occurred during her day. Renee could not remember the last time her husband had made a meal and, more importantly, considered her schedule in doing so.

Her smile faded. She reached into her pocket and pulled out a letter that she had read and reread over a hundred times since she had received it that afternoon. The letter had been sent certified, requiring Renee's signature, indicating that she had received the document, which was not unusual in a medical office.

Renee read the letter again while she sat in the dimly lit room, experiencing the emotions of surprise, disbelief, anger, and a feeling of sickness—the same feelings she had the first time she read the document.

The letter was written by an attorney representing Jennifer Waits. Apparently, her partner was intent on buying Renee's ownership of the practice. The monetary offer was incredulously low, but that was not what bothered Renee the most. It was the signatures on the second page that struck a powerful blow.

The second page was a petition stating that the patients listed wanted their care provider to be Dr. Jennifer Waits. The number of patients on the document represented at least seventy-five percent of the practice.

Renee was shocked by some of the signatures. There were names of people that she considered to be close friends. She studied the list of names in disbelief and humiliation. When had she grown so far from her clients? How could she have failed so many of them?

Renee folded the document, shoved it back into the envelope, and stuffed it into her lab coat. Pushing herself from the table, she wearily rose and cleaned up. She removed her lab coat and draped it over the chair. Then she picked it up, not wanting anyone to read the letter. She went outside and tossed the coat into the front seat of her car. She returned to the house and entered the bedroom.

She was thankful her husband was deep in sleep. She slipped into bed alongside him, watching his chest rise and fall. Her eyes misted while she wondered how their lives could continue to spiral farther and farther downward. Renee clenched her jaw, called forth her anger, and fought against her tears and sorrow. Then she reformed the wall that had begun to be torn down from around her heart. It was a long time before she drifted into a restless sleep.

The alarm screamed its wake-up call far too soon for Renee's comfort. She rolled out of bed, and slipped into her shoes. She made her way toward the kitchen. The aroma of coffee caused her to breathe in deeply.

Emmett stood over the table, pouring a cup of coffee and setting it on her placemat. Next to the steaming cup was a plate holding a toasted and buttered bagel, strawberries, and cheeses. Renee stood frozen, watching Emmett prepare breakfast. "What are you doing?" she found herself asking.

"Well, good morning!" Emmett smiled. "I'm getting breakfast ready for you."

"But you normally don't get up for at least another hour."

"Yes, but I no longer want to do the norm. I thought it'd be nice for you to have something to eat before you left for the office."

The stresses of the previous day were lost for a moment. "Who are you and what have you done with my husband?"

Emmett laughed. "I hope he's done being done."

Renee wrinkled her brow. "What?"

"Nothing. Sit down and eat. I want to tell you about yesterday."

Renee sat cautiously at the table as her husband poured her a small glass of orange juice. She was finding it hard to take her eyes off of him. "Dinner last night and breakfast this morning? What has come over you?"

Emmett sat down, visibly excited about something. "I'll tell you. David and I went to the parsonage yesterday and ended up talking with Bill and Lenny Jackson."

"Lenny?"

"Yes. Remember Lenny and Sally? I married them about four years ago."

Renee nodded and took a bite of the warm bagel.

"Anyway, Lenny asked me to stay and listen to the story he was telling Bill, so David and I remained. Lenny told us how his wife wanted a divorce. Bill led the counseling session, giving Lenny what I thought was good advice.

"After Lenny left, Bill informed me that he was convinced that I needed some time away from the church, but he insisted that you and Joshua remain involved somehow. He even suggested that Joshua join the brigades."

Renee pretended to miss the fact that she was being asked to continue in some capacity with the church. "The brigades?"

"Apparently it is similar to Boy Scouts. I think it'd be good for Joshua, especially with him speaking. Maybe being around boys his own age would help him along."

Renee sipped her coffee. In spite of what had happened the day before, her son was still her main concern. She still feared that something was wrong, that Joshua was physically failing. She did not know if contact with other virus-carrying children would be a good idea. "I'm not sure I want Joshua around other children just yet."

Emmett placed his elbows on the table and leaned forward. "Renee, I really believe this would help Joshua. Why don't we leave it up to him? What benefit is it to keep him locked up? Let him be a kid, for crying out loud!"

Renee's defenses rose. "Emmett! I was the only person at the office yesterday, stressed to the hilt, and I really don't want to discuss the matter further. I'm his mother and I will decide what is best for him."

"Don't you mean what's best for *you?*" Emmett countered as he pushed himself away from the table. Turning his back to Renee, he placed his dish in the sink.

Before Renee could retaliate, Joshua bounced into the room. "Good morning Daddy and Mommy!"

Both parents tried to disguise their anger as they bid their son good morning.

David strolled into the kitchen seconds later, offering a big smile and a wave in greeting. He caught Emmett's eye and gave him a wink and a thumb's up, ruffled Joshua's hair, and poured himself a cup of coffee.

Joshua looked at David curiously. "Interrupted?"

Renee's brow furled. "What's that, honey?"

"Nothing, Mommy." He plopped himself on his mother's lap.

Renee looked astonished. It had been so long since her son had voluntarily sat on her lap that she couldn't utter a word.

"Mommy? I think that today David should go to work with you."

Emmett and David froze.

Renee cleared her throat, glanced at both men, and pulled her gaze back on her son. "Honey, I'm not sure that would be such a good idea. Mr. Liberty would be extremely bored. What on earth could I have him do at the office?"

Joshua wrapped his arms around his mother as she tried to gently decline his offer. Without losing his hold, he turned his head toward David. "Could you help her at work?"

David winked and grinned.

Joshua returned his smile and echoed David's thoughts. "David could take patients into rooms, write down stuff, and put their names in your book."

Renee's eyes widened at Joshua's words.

Emmett put in his two cents. "You did say you were short-handed."

Renee shot him a look that said, "mind your own business."

Emmett shrugged. "David, I thought that we'd go and see Lenny this morning."

David shook his head and jabbed a finger at Emmett.

"Test your wings, Daddy," Joshua said.

David tilted his head toward Joshua and then nodded at Emmett.

Emmett whispered, "Well, I'll be a son-of-a-gun." He raised his hands in resignation. "All right, I'm outta here. Renee, I'll be over at Lenny's. David, have fun at the office. Joshua, let's go. I'll drop you off at Grandma's on the way." Emmett left the kitchen.

"Emmett, wait!" Renee hollered. She noticed her son's pleading eyes and turned her glance over toward David, who waited for her reply.

"Momma, you need his help."

Renee gave in with a sigh. "All right, he can come with me, but I'm not sure how much help he'll be, or if I'll have time to show him anything."

"Thanks, Mom." Joshua squeezed her once and hopped off her lap. "Take care of her, David."

David held out his hand for a high-five before Joshua darted past. Hands collided for a sharp slap and David fixed his attention to Renee.

Renee answered the unspoken question. "We're going to go to the office now. We'd best be early, if I'm going to get any use out of you."

Chapter Ten

RENEE CHECKED HER messages. There was the voice of Dr. Waits, stating that she would be unable to make it to the office. She also said she had received the receipt that showed Renee had received the letter. Renee slumped back into her chair. "I don't know if I can handle another day," she mumbled.

"How can I help?"

"I don't know if there is anything you could do." Renee sighed and then sat upright. She shook her head rapidly from side to side. "Sorry, I must be exhausted. I thought for a second that you spoke to me."

David's lips parted into a thin smile. "Well, either you are exhausted, or I'm speaking. I guess both are possible."

"What type of game are you playing here?" Renee's face reddened.

"No game. But it's time for you to listen and for me to talk."

"But I . . ." More words would not come. Renee's eyes widened in surprise. She could no longer vocalize her thoughts! She could not speak, and the panic caused her to run for the door.

Strong but comforting arms enveloped her, preventing any escape. "Renee, everything will be fine. I need you to calm down and let me talk. Will you do that?"

The embrace touched Renee's memories and tension left her rigid muscles. Her mind drifted to the past, when a similar comfort had been found in the arms of her father. Renee's anxiety left and she collapsed against David's chest.

"Sit here for a moment," David said.

Renee sat down in the chair behind her.

David knelt down so his body took on the same height as Renee's. "I know this sounds strange, but the gift of my voice seems to come and go. I don't know how long it will stay with me, so I need you to listen. Do you understand?"

Renee, still in shock, nodded.

"Do you want to keep your medical practice?"

Renee's eyes opened wide. She leaned back in her chair, trying to create space between her and David.

"More importantly, do you want to keep your family?"

The directness of the question struck a blow in the pit of Renee's stomach. Her eyes misted over and she bit into her lower lip to keep it from trembling.

David moved closer and rested a hand on Renee's knee.

She braced herself and prepared to spring from the chair, but David's touch and the concern in his eyes kept Renee from further action.

"Obviously both are rhetorical questions, for I know the answer to both. Maybe I should ask if you would like to know *how* to keep your family and practice."

Renee simply stared.

"I think that if you try, you may be able to talk now." His voice was gentle and reassuring.

"Who . . . who are you?" Renee stammered.

David shook his head. "For now, I'm not at liberty to say. Let's just keep it simple. I'm a friend who wants to help you get your life back together."

The statement triggered Renee's defense mechanism. "Who said I need to get my life back together?" Her voice rose in anger. "What kind of game have you been playing here, Mr. Liberty? I can't believe you have taken advantage of our hospitality. I can't—"

David raised a hand. "I can't believe you have lost touch with your patients to such a degree that you would allow your practice to go to Dr. Waits."

Renee was stunned, but her surprise at David's knowledge did not lessen her anger or suspicion. "What? Are you in on it? Are you trying to disrupt our lives and distract me enough for Jennifer to steal my business?"

David raised his voice. "You're talking nonsense. No more words." He waved his hand.

Renee tried to continue her rampage, but words would no longer leave her lips. Confusion and fear overrode her current emotional state.

David stood and towered over Renee. "If you do not learn to control your anger it will destroy the life you once loved. I'm confident that you don't love the life that you have chosen, but if you continue this path of displaced anger, you will never have the harmony you once had.

"The past is gone, and none of your actions today can change the events that happened yesterday. Your actions can only make tomorrow a better place. That is what you want, isn't it?"

Renee stared at him in horror. Her mind was unable to grasp that she could not speak, but her ears tuned into David's words as if he were speaking into a microphone.

"I know you have lost your faith. Lost your faith in your husband, in medicine, and—more importantly—in the Lord."

Renee broke eye contact and stared at the floor.

"Look at me."

Renee fought with all her might, but she could not keep her muscles from lifting her head to face David. Her heart was pounding so quickly that she thought it would explode out of her chest.

The entry door to the clinic chimed, indicating that the first client of the day had arrived.

David smiled. "I guess we'll have to continue this conversation another time. It's time to care for your patients." David walked out of Renee's office, allowing her body to return to the control of its owner.

Emmett knocked on the door to Lenny's house.

The rustic door squeaked as it was pulled open. "Pastor Brown!" Lenny exclaimed. "Hello. Come in, come in!" His greeting was childlike and full of excitement at seeing Emmett standing on the front deck.

Emmett had been nervous as he approached Lenny's home, but the warm and exuberant greeting calmed his nerves and lightened his heart. "Good morning Lenny. How are you?" Emmett entered Lenny's humble home.

"I'm good. I've been praying. Praying all the time, just like Pastor Nomed instructed me to do."

Emmett patted Lenny on the shoulder. "I'm glad you have been praying. Can you tell me what you've been praying for?"

Lenny looked a little confused. "I've been praying for me and Sally to get back together. Just like you and Pastor Nomed said to."

Emmett smiled. A flicker caught Emmett's eye and he noticed a computer screen in the alcove of the kitchen. "I didn't realize you and Sally had a computer, Lenny. I thought the two of you didn't want computer in your home, let alone being able to afford one."

"We . . . uh . . . we . . . got it about a year ago. Helps with doing the bills, and Sally likes to check the weather." Lenny paused then said quickly, "Would you like something to drink, Pastor Brown?"

"Sure, that'd be great." Emmett noticed the shift in Lenny's mood and moved toward the computer.

"Here's some water!" Lenny's voice rose and his eyes widened as Emmett wandered over to the screen. Lenny hustled over to place himself between Emmett and the computer. He handed the glass of water to Emmett, but in his hurry, he dropped it. Driven by reflex, Emmett and Lenny both attempted to catch the falling glass, but without success. The glass bounced harmlessly off the wooden floor. However, water splashed every where.

Lenny bent forward to scoop up the now-empty glass and inadvertently bumped the chair in front of the computer. The movement was enough to jostle the mouse, and the screen saver went off the monitor.

Emmett's face reddened at the sight on the screen.

Lenny, obviously panicked, reached out and pulled the plugs. The monitor went black.

"Sorry about that," Lenny mumbled and dropped his chin to his chest.

Emmett recovered from his initial shock at what had been displayed on the screen. "Lenny, let's sit down in the living room and talk about how we're going to work on your marriage."

Lenny kept his head down and followed Emmett into the living room. They sat down and faced each other, but Lenny would not lift his gaze from the floor.

"Lenny, I—"

"It's not my fault, Emmett! With Sally gone, I just . . . well, I just don't know what to do."

Emmett raised his hand. "Lenny, stay with me here. We're going to talk about you and Sally. But first, let me ask you something."

Lenny's eyes widened.

"How do you think Jesus feels about the church?"

The question caught Lenny by surprise. He shrugged and mumbled under his breath.

"Lenny?"

"I guess He loves our church. I mean that's why He came, 'cause he loves us . . . I guess."

"Yes, He does love us. Do you know that in the Bible Jesus refers to himself as the groom and the church as his bride?"

Lenny shook his head, indicating that he did not know that.

Emmett continued. "That's how much He loves His church. He used a comparison of marriage to describe his love for us. Do you know He also told us husbands that we need to love our wives as He loves the church?"

Lenny was listening intently, and Emmett smiled. Lenny had always been like a sponge. His education level was only at the eighth grade, but he was eager to learn. His ability to retain knowledge was not the best, but sufficient. "Isn't the wife supposed to be submissive to her husband? I thought the Bible said that the man is the head of the household."

"Very good, Lenny. We're talking about the same passage. If you continue to read that chapter in Ephesians, it tells us we should love our wives so much that we would give our lives for them, just like Christ did for the church." Emmett paused. "Which do you think is harder to do? Obey someone or give your life for someone?"

"Well, to give your life would be harder to do," Lenny replied.

"Exactly. Do you love Sally enough to give your life for her?"

Lenny's eyes filled with moisture. He did not reply.

"I'll answer for you. I believe that you *do* love her that much. I just don't think Sally knows you love her that much."

"What do you mean?"

"If I asked Sally to describe the love—let's say the amount that you loved her—what words would she use?"

"I . . . I don't know."

"I think it's time we show her."

Startled, Lenny asked, "Whadya mean?"

"I mean let's show her how much you truly care for her."

"But Pastor Nomed said we should just pray for us to get back together."

"Yes, he did, but let's think about this for a moment. I'm going to tell you a story. Sit tight and hold any questions until I'm finished." Emmett leaned back in his chair and closed his eyes. "There was a young man named John who worked for a factory that made cars. John's job was simple but important. He inspected the seatbelt latch, making sure it locked in place. Next he made sure the right amount of pressure would release the latch when the button was pressed. John caught any defective designs and flagged them for the factory to fix.

"John worked there for a year when he acquired an interest for antique cars. The problem with antique cars is they require a lot of money, both to purchase and to restore. Soon, John found himself deep in debt.

"He began reading fortune magazines to find an answer to his financial problems. He became so obsessed with his financial problem that his inspection of the seatbelts suffered. John inspected only the front seatbelts and not the back, saving himself some time to read his magazines on money schemes and antique cars.

"As fate would have it, there were a series of car accidents in which the rear seatbelts had failed. As a result, the car factory was sued for a large sum of money. The owner of the company eventually lost the lawsuit filed against the factory, but he vowed to the public that the problem would be fixed and the car's reputation restored.

"The owner stumbled onto something both interesting and disappointing in his search for an explanation of the faulty seatbelts. Video tapes showed John neglecting to inspect the back seatbelts. John was fired immediately.

"As you can imagine, getting fired only worsened John's money situation. With all the publicity, no other company would hire him. Finally, in desperation, he returned to the car factory and asked his former boss for his job back. John begged and pleaded, stating he had learned his lesson and was a changed man." Emmett stopped the story, opened his eyes, and leaned forward to peer at Lenny.

Lenny's curiosity was clearly getting the best of him. "Is that it? What happened? Did John get his job back?"

"I'm not sure. Lenny, pretend you're the owner of the car factory. Would you hire John back?"

"Gosh, no. No way I'd hire him back!"

"Why not?"

"'Cause I don't know if he's changed. He hasn't proven that he can be responsible."

"Then why should God reconcile your marriage if the problem that created the separation has not been fixed?"

Lenny looked like he had just lost his best friend. His lower lip trembled and tears flowed down his face.

"Lenny, the power of God can change us on the inside. Our prayers should ask for this change first. The next step is to demonstrate your love to your wife. Not with words. Show her how much you truly do care for her."

"But . . . but she won't even talk to me."

"I'm not looking for excuses. Let's find solutions. Let's not tell God how big our problems are. Let's tell our problems how big our God is."

The day became a blur to Renee. Once she mustered the courage to step out of her office, David already had things running smoothly. He placed the first two clients into exam rooms with their folders in the slots outside the door. He stood at the front desk, talking to the next person who had just signed in.

He glanced at Renee. "Dr. Brown, room one is ready for you. I wrote the blood pressure and heart rate on the chart. The room number two vaccination is on the counter and ready for you to draw. You have some time to chat with each client, and I will guide you from there." David turned back to the patient.

What is going on? Renee felt as if she were in a dream. She was unsure, however, if the dream was a nightmare or heavenly in origin.

She picked up the first folder, knocked on the door, and entered the exam room. She found her voice. "Good morning, Mrs. Reuben. How are you this morning?" Renee's eyes scanned the chart, and she then looked to Mrs. Reuben.

"I am just fine, dear," the older lady stated. "Such a nice young man brought me in here."

"David? Ah, yes. He is a nice man."

"He seemed to know my husband, Charles, and asked all about him."

Renee felt that nothing else could surprise her this morning. "And how is your husband doing?"

"He's doing all right. It's still hard for me to have him in the nursing home while I'm at home. But you know I just couldn't take care of him anymore. I hope he knows that I still love him."

"Of course he knows. And I'm sure he understands."

"Huh. That's exactly what your guy said. Must be true then."

"Yes, I'm sure it is. Now, let's talk about you for a moment. I've read through your chart and looked at the numbers David wrote down for us. Let me double check those." Renee took Mrs. Reuben's blood pressure and heart rate. The numbers were the same as the numbers David had written down.

"I think there is no need to change any of your medicines right now. I'll have you stop at the front desk to schedule to see us in about four weeks."

"Already did that. David said you would want to see me back in four weeks, so he scheduled that already."

Renee shook her head. "All right then, Mrs. Reuben. You have a great day, and give my regards to your husband."

"I will, dear. And you have a great day as well."

David stood at the reception area when the next person walked through the clinic door. His gaze rose instantly when a familiar odor tickled his senses.

"Who are you?" the woman demanded as she approached the counter.

"Good morning. How can I help you today?" David replied.

The visitor inspected the office and glared at David. "Who are you? What are you doing here?"

David smiled politely and fought the urge to gag. "My name is David, and I'm helping out in the office today."

"No one brought this to my attention." She slammed her fist on the counter.

David knew who he was talking to. "How are you today, Dr. Waits?"

Her eyes narrowed. "Who *are* you?"

"I told you, my name is David."

"I heard what you said your name is. Now tell me who you are!"

"I don't understand the question."

Dr. Waits turned her back. "It doesn't matter. Renee will see it's best for me to have the office." Without further words, she left the clinic.

The day passed quickly, most of it in a whirlwind, with all the disadvantaged patients that came to the office. They needed something extra; there were untimely phone calls; patients asked irrelevant questions and needed a sympathetic ear. Three walk-ins were worked into the schedule, but somehow David and Renee handled them all.

Although they interacted strictly as professionals, David knew that Renee watched him every moment she had available. David took the brunt of everything, softening any encounters for Renee. He laughed and enjoyed himself through it all and knew there was a time when she had done the same.

Before he knew what time it was, the last patient left the office and only the remaining paper work needed to be completed.

Renee spoke. "David, thank you for all your help. I still don't know who or what you are. I really don't know what else to say but thank you."

David nodded. "You're welcome. There is something you should know. I talked with the patients today who signed the petition. It was their perception that what they were signing would allow Dr. Waits to treat them if you were unavailable."

"I don't understand. You mean that it's not a petition relieving me of care for those who signed it?"

David shook his head.

"Why would Jennifer do such a thing? How did you know about the petition?"

David shrugged. *I can no longer answer your questions in the way you would like. I hope today was enough to get you headed down another path.*

"Why won't you answer me?"

David shook his head, shrugged, and drew an "x" on his throat.

"Your voice is gone?"

A single nod.

"You did say that it came with need. There is no rational explanation for today's events. I hope I don't wake up in the morning and find out this was all a dream."

David smiled and gave her a wink. He waved her to follow as he set the remaining charts down and walked out the doors of the clinic. *I didn't get the chance to tell you of one other visitor that you had this day, but it's probably best that you didn't know.*

Chapter Eleven

RENEE AND DAVID returned home. David headed to his room while Renee walked to the kitchen. A plate with dinner sat on her placemat, and Emmett and Joshua were just finishing their own dinners.

"Momma!" Joshua hopped off his chair and ran over to give his mother a big hug. "How was today?"

Renee grinned and squeezed her son. "You were right, my son. David was a big help today."

Joshua looked up at his mother. "I knew he would be. I'm going to take him his dinner. He is too tired to come out of his room."

Renee did not ask how her son knew that. "Go ahead. Take him some food." She ushered Joshua away and collapsed in her chair.

"So your day was good?" Emmett ventured.

"No, it was great. It was scary. I don't know what it was, really. You wouldn't believe me if I told you."

"So David spoke to you, too?"

The question brought Renee into an upright posture. "You knew he could speak, and you didn't tell me?"

"I tried to tell you this morning, but we got sidetracked."

Renee recalled the morning and said, "I'm sorry Emmett. You did want to tell me something, but I was more interested in, well, what I was more interested in."

"No biggie."

"No, it is. You've been trying, and I haven't. Tell me what you wanted."

Emmett recounted the previous day's events. He told Renee about how David had told him that he was able to speak only if the need was great. He told Renee about the advice he had received from David and what he did today.

"I took Lenny over to Sally's parents. That's where she's staying. We didn't knock on the door, just stood outside. Lenny had brought his guitar, and he played and sang.

"Sally stuck her head out the window and yelled for him to go away. That's when I gave Lenny a wink, and he played a song that he wrote especially for Sally. It was beautiful! He sang with such passion and conviction that I knew Sally would be touched.

"When he was finished he placed two roses, one red and one white, on the porch with a simple note. It read: 'Dear Sally, I have hurt you in such a way that I know I do not deserve your forgiveness. I am sorry. Love, Lenny.'"

"You've been busy these last two days," Renee said. "Your actions surprise me. I can't believe that you were able to persuade Lenny to serenade his wife."

"I merely helped him come up with the idea. He just needed someone to take his hand."

Almost as if requested, Renee reached out and took hold of her husband's hand. "My day was just as amazing. To me even more so than yours." She recounted the entire day, leaving out a couple of details until the end.

"Emmett, yesterday I received a letter from an attorney stating that Jennifer wanted to buy my share of the clinic. I was so hurt and humiliated that I couldn't bring myself to tell you."

"I haven't been the husband that you could confide in."

She shook her head and ignored the statement. "There was a petition signed by many of my patients stating that they wanted Jennifer to be their primary care provider. David found out that it is fraudulent. They thought they were signing a different document. Don't ask me how he knew about the petition. I didn't tell him about it. There is something very strange going on."

"That may be so, but I think a better adjective is 'wonderful.' There is something wonderful and amazing happening in our lives right now."

David and Joshua sat on the bed together while David ate his dinner.

"You've done it, David. I knew you could help our family."

Something tells me we're not out of trouble yet.

"What do you mean?"

I'm still here, which I think means there's more work to be done. We've just touched the tip of the iceberg with what your family will have to go through.

Joshua frowned.

David ruffled Joshua's hair. *Don't you worry, bud. As long as I'm here, together we will face whatever attacks your family.*

"But it's all better now."

David furrowed his brow. *Your parents are talking again. Yes, that's good. But I have a feeling that the real storm is coming. The real storm is on the horizon. And it will be a strong one.*

Two figures sat in silence in a dimly lit room. Shadows flickered about the area from the few lit candles. The room was unnaturally warm, and if someone were to observe the flames closely, they would notice that the candles could not be made of wax, for they would have certainly melted from the surrounding temperature.

One of the figures spoke. "Things are not going as planned." The voice was that of a woman.

"What do you propose we should do?" The man's reply was hesitant and shaky.

"If you had done what had been asked of you earlier, we would not be having this discussion."

"It's not my fault that his friend David saved him from jumping."

The first figure stood abruptly, pointing a finger to her affiliate. The shadows bouncing throughout the room hid her face, but the tone of her voice was enough to make her anger visible. "You were supposed to be here months ago. What delayed you?"

"I had loose ends that needed to be tied up." The reply was feeble, but the truth.

"Bah! Things were going well until that homeless whelp David interfered. He is more than just a bum."

"How are things going on your end?"

The woman sat down in the chair.

When it was apparent that she would not reply, the man continued the conversation. "What do you want to do?"

"We were so close." The words were barely audible. The woman stood again and continued in a normal voice. "We'll let them enjoy this harmonious but temporary moment, and then we finish this nonsense."

The man still had not moved, and did not reply to the woman's statement.

"We will break them apart by affecting what they both love."

"I'm afraid I don't follow—"

"The child, you idiot! The child."

Chapter Twelve

THE NEXT FEW weeks were the best that Joshua could remember. At least, the best by far since his brother Aaron had died. He noticed the affection between his parents. The smiles, the touches, and the holding of hands seemed to denote the return of his family.

Joshua felt better. His energy level and his appetite returned. Even though he was a young child, he was able to understand intuitively that his own health seemed reliant on the health of his family. His mother no longer looked at him with anxiety in her eyes. The fears and concerns that she had imposed on her remaining son were slowly fading away. Renee even agreed to let Joshua join the boys' brigades. He thoroughly enjoyed interacting with boys his own age and even older.

Renee returned to church with her family. And although Emmett was not leading the congregation for the time, it was good to be back to worship together. David attended services with the Browns, but preferred to sit in the back alone, where he leafed through the pages of Scripture at an unprecedented rate.

Lenny Jackson returned to church as well. Sally was still not with him, but he and Emmett were working diligently to change that. Lenny looked and spoke like a new man. Neither Lenny nor Emmett shared with Pastor Bill what they were doing, but they did not think it was necessary since things were going so well. Sally was talking with Lenny again, and they had even gone on a date together for the first time since their troubles began.

Renee's medical clinic was running smoothly. David had been a trooper. He had helped Renee until Margaret and Dr. Waits returned. If Dr. Waits had been surprised that Renee handled the clinic on her own, she did not express it. However, she had been unable to hide her surprise and anger when Renee and David presented her with a signed petition that nullified Dr. Waits's own petition. Renee did not discuss the fraudulent document with Jennifer; she just handed her the new petition. Dr. Jennifer Waits stormed out of the office shouting that her attorneys would be involved. A few days later, she resigned her partnership with Dr. Renee Brown.

Renee's schedule changed as she now had to cover the office by herself. The practice was large enough that it needed two physicians. Renee did not complain and seemed to thrive with the busy work life that she was able to balance with her family.

Emmett continued to counsel Lenny and other members of the church and community. Not only did he instruct them on actions, but he also put them into practice within his own marriage. He and Renee were becoming an equal partnership.

David helped out whenever needed. He helped at the medical clinic, and he helped Emmett counsel others. In the evenings he sat with Joshua and read books with the happy child. David tried not to infringe on family time and often excused himself to his room, where he picked up the Bible and read. It seemed like forever since his first meeting with Joelle, and he decided since he had time he would try to become more familiar with God's Word. He had not been able to speak during this time, but for the most part he was able to communicate with those around him. David was able to talk with Joshua, who still seemed gifted to read his mind.

On one particular rainy Sunday, the Browns invited Pastor Bill Nomed over for dinner. Pastor Bill showed up at the doorstep with an umbrella in one hand and a bottle of wine in the other.

Emmett greeted Bill. "It's nice to see you this evening. Come on in."

Bill left his umbrella outside and offered his gift to Emmett. "A little dinner wine for us. Boy, that weather out there is not even fit for a duck!"

Emmett chuckled. "It's a good thing you don't have feathers then, my friend. Come on in to the dining room. Dinner is ready."

Bill followed Emmett and took the seat offered to him. "Ahhh, something smells wonderful!"

Renee greeted her guest. "Yes, Emmett cooked a wonderful meal for us. Hello, Pastor."

"You mean Emmett made this meal?" Bill scanned the layout with obvious surprise.

"Yes, he did. He has turned out to be quite a chef these days."

Emmett blushed. "Enough idle chatter. Let's say grace and eat before my masterpiece gets cold."

Everyone laughed and bowed their head.

Emmett said softly, "Joshua?"

Joshua folded his hands and led the prayer. "God is good. God is great. Thank you God for the food we eat. Amen."

"Amen!" the adults said in unison.

After the food was passed and the plates were full, Bill spoke. "Thank you so much for inviting me. It's rare that I have a warm meal for dinner. To be honest with you, I'm just too lazy to cook for myself."

Renee smiled. "I've been spoiled lately. I can't recall how long it's been since I cooked dinner." Her gaze drifted to her husband.

Emmett returned her smile. "Bill, I have an ulterior motive for inviting you for dinner."

"Yes, I know what you're thinking," Bill said. "You're wondering if you'll be reinstated as pastor."

"No, not exactly. I wasn't wondering *if*. I was wondering *when*."

Bill set his fork on the table and took a deep breath. "I see. You know I've heard whispers in the congregation that you essentially disobeyed my request to take a mandatory vacation away from the responsibilities of the church."

Emmett set his jaw but did not respond.

"I know that your intentions are good and you have helped Lenny and Sally Jackson with their situation. I think you're just about ready to come back to your position."

Emmett's face lightened, and he glanced to his wife. "That sounds great, Bill! When do you think—?"

"Hold on. Let me finish, would you?" Bill chuckled. "As you're aware, this coming week I am taking the boys' brigades on our first camping trip. I was thinking that when I returned we would welcome you back into the church as my assistant."

Emmett's body deflated. "Oh."

"In due time, if things go well, you will be reinstated in your church."

"Honey, that's still the news we're hoping for," Renee said. "Who cares that it isn't in the timeframe you were hoping. At least it's a step in the right direction."

"I suppose you're right." Emmett was unable to hide his disappointment. Renee reached over and patted his hand in reassurance.

Bill interrupted the silent communication. "So, Joshua, are you ready for our big camping trip in the mountains?"

David, who had been sitting quietly throughout the meal, noticed Bill's instant slip in body language. He caught the narrowing of his eyes and the discoloring of the face as Bill watched Emmett and Renee. *That is strange. Is*

Bill jealous of Emmett? No. Something else. What's going through your mind, Bill?"

Joshua glanced at David then shifted his gaze back to Bill. "Yes, Pastor Nomed. I can't wait. David and Dad have already helped me pack. I have my compass, flashlight, matches, sleeping bag—"

"Whoa! Sounds like someone's excited about this trip." Bill clapped his hands in approval.

"Bill, I just wanted to say thanks." Emmett changed the subject. "Thanks so much for giving me a second chance. It seems that I've gotten an awful lot of them lately."

Bill nodded. "You're certainly welcome. Come now, let's finish this superb meal so we can get to dessert!"

"Dessert? Who said anything about dessert?" Renee teased.

Bill chuckled. "Listen here, Dr. Brown. One does not invite the chubby pastor over without offering dessert!"

Everyone laughed heartily at the pudgy man's jibe at himself. Everyone, that is, except David. David pondered at the brief window Bill had opened. A window that David could not see clearly through.

Joshua hiked along a well-trodden path through the forest. He was in the company of six other boys and Pastor Bill Nomed when they headed off on their grand adventure. His little body was coated in a thin layer of sweat from the load of his backpack and the steepness of the climb.

The small band had left early in the morning, with a goal of setting up their campsite before noon. They left their parents waving cheers and good luck to the boys while they headed off on their own. Joshua had a tough time saying good-bye to his mom and dad. Tears dribbled down his cheek as he fought to gain some courage to break the hug his mother gave him. Lastly, he hugged David good-bye. David ruffled his hair and tapped his little chin upward. The gesture was followed with the thoughts of "be strong," and Joshua forced his legs to walk away from his family and join the other boys.

The hiking was difficult, but Bill did his best to keep the boys interested in the surrounding nature. Joshua studied everything that Bill pointed out. He learned the names of various birds and trees, as well as little tidbits of information about them.

"Can anyone tell me the name of the bird making that racket?" Bill asked.

A boy named Adam quickly answered, "I think it's a blue jay."

"Very good. Now, why is he making that racket?"

Joshua thought for a moment. None of the other boys offered any suggestions, so he piped up. "Maybe he's saying something to other blue jays."

"Why yes, he is, Joshua. When something begins moving around on the forest floor the blue jay will holler out his cry. The bird is protective of its territory and will make the jeering noise at intruders."

"You mean like a mountain lion?" Adam asked.

Charles, standing next to Adam, shoved him. "Don't be scaring the younger boys, Adam. Mountain lions do not live around here. My Dad told me that."

Adam shoved back his assailant. "Yeah, well, my Dad was attacked by one, right here in these mountains."

"Boys! That will be enough pushing." Bill stood between the pair. "Adam, your dad's right. There are no mountain lions in this region."

"But my Dad—" Charles blurted.

"Your dad ran into something up here, Charles, but the sheriff didn't confirm that it was a lion."

"But—"

Bill grabbed him by the arm and hissed into his ear. "Charles, that'll be enough. You're scaring the younger boys. There are no mountain lions here, so just drop it." Bill let go of Charles arm and spoke to the group of boys who were scanning fearfully through the trees. "Boys, blue jays will often squawk when a deer moves underneath them or even a person. There is nothing to be alarmed about. Let's keep moving."

Rob, another of the boys, spoke up. "Pastor Bill? It's getting close to lunch time. I thought we'd be setting camp up before noon. I'm really getting hungry."

"We'll stop shortly to eat lunch, but I've changed my mind about where we'll set up camp for the night."

There were moans from all the boys. Adam asked the question that popped into everyone's head. "How much longer do we got to keep hiking?"

"Of that I'm not sure. Depends on how slow you boys are. I hope you can keep up with a fat man like me." Without looking back, Bill headed up the trail.

Some chuckles were mixed in with the groans, and the boys followed their taskmaster. Joshua's little legs ached, but he was determined not to be left behind. He took a quick swallow from his canteen and hustled after the group.

It was late in the day when the group reached their destination. They had left the trail about three hours earlier and trudged after their leader. Bill never seemed to tire or break into a sweat. The boys took rests more and more frequently throughout the day. Although Bill was eager to reach their destination, he allowed the boys to rest when necessary.

The boys collapsed in a clearing on the forest floor, moaning and complaining about every muscle.

"Congratulations, troop, we made it." Bill's smiled proudly. "Who wants to help me gather some firewood?"

Everyone groaned, but no one volunteered.

"Very well, then. Joshua, set your pack down and come help me."

Joshua took off his backpack, drank the remainder of his water from the canteen, and slung the container around his shoulder. "Coming. I need to refill my canteen anyway." He rose to his feet and followed Bill out of the clearing.

It was difficult for Joshua to keep up with Bill. He kept losing sight of the pastor. Huffing and puffing, Joshua ran through the forest, trying to keep pace until he slammed into Bill.

"Joshua! There you are. Try and keep up. Let's come this way, I want to show you something."

After the pair walked a few minutes, the wall of trees abruptly disappeared and the two hikers stepped onto the rim of a vast ravine.

Joshua had never seen anything so high or vast in size. As he glanced precariously downward, he was grasped unexpectedly by his shirt and thrust out over the edge of the canyon rim.

"No!" a sharp voice commanded from the forest behind.

"But I thought . . ." Bill's voice responded.

"Put the boy down!" The female's voice was not to be disobeyed.

Joshua felt the ground beneath his feet. Bill still held onto him. Joshua was too frightened to struggle or protest.

"What's going—?"

"Silence!" The shadows of the forest parted, and a lone figure approached. "Do not speak again! Follow me, and bring the boy."

The woman wore a large hat that kept her face hidden and hiked with an ornately-carved walking stick. She passed Bill and Joshua and continued farther north along the lip of the canyon.

Joshua felt Bill tug on his shirt as they followed the strange guide. After a short time the trio stopped at the foot of a bridge that spanned the width of the canyon. The bridge was largely constructed of rope, only wide enough to allow hikers to cross in single file.

Bill shook his head. "What are we—?"

The guide struck Bill's shoulder with her walking stick. "I said to be silent!" she warned.

Bill toppled forward, losing his grasp on Joshua and clutching his shoulder.

The woman addressed Joshua. "If you wish to leave this man, now's your chance. Cross the bridge and he won't follow."

"What are you doing?" Bill hollered and attempted to stand.

The woman hammered Bill with her staff, driving him to the ground. "You must go now! And hurry! I don't know how long I can keep him away from you." The tone in her voice had changed from a military commander to a concerned mother.

"But . . . but I don't . . ." Joshua's stammering was interrupted by his apparent rescuer.

"Joshua, you must hurry now. This man means you harm."

Hearing his name gave flight to his feet. Joshua scrambled onto the rope bridge and made his way across the unstable structure. As his little hands grasped the rope rails to assist his crossing, Joshua heard the whacking resume on Bill. The howls and screams that followed chased Joshua faster across the swaying bridge.

Finally, his feet landed on solid ground, and the unexpected steady surface caused him to topple onto the dirt and rocks that lay strewn about. He scrambled to his feet and risked a glance back from where he'd come. His breath caught at the sight. The rope bridge swung downward across the chasm. The ends had been severed from the anchor points on the other side.

Bill and the woman walked away from the rim of the canyon.

"Why did you keep hitting me?" Bill rubbed various parts of his injured body.

"I had to make it real. I needed the boy to react in fear to get him across the bridge."

"I don't get it. Why not just let him fall over the rim?"

"I'm not convinced that the grieving process of losing another child would divide the Browns' marriage. They seem to have regained too much ground of late."

"What has this accomplished?"

"You fool! Don't you understand? With their son lost somewhere in the wilderness, their minds will race with endless outcomes. They will view each other as not doing enough to find the lost boy. Their prior fears and anger can then drive a wedge between them. At the height of those emotions they will finally find their lost son, except by then it will be too late. Too late for everyone."

"How do you know Joshua won't be found?"

"I'll take care of that. Now get back to your little band and head down the mountain."

"But it'll be dark soon. How will I get that group of boys—?"

"Listen, you idiot. You've just lost one of your boys. Get back down the mountain and contact the sheriff's office!"

Bill struggled to his feet. "But what do I tell them?"

"You tell them that Joshua fell into Hammond Canyon."

David sprang out of the chair where he had been reading Scripture. Joshua was calling out to him. Something had gone terribly wrong on the hiking trip. David could hear the fear in Joshua's call. He could not make sense of the words, but the boy's fear became David's. He raced for the door, but just as he reached for the doorknob, everything went black.

Chapter Thirteen

EMMETT AND RENEE walked into the sheriff's office with hands entwined. The telephone call they received early in the morning had been disturbing. Nothing was stated over the phone, but the tone of the sheriff's voice when he had asked Emmett if both he and Renee could report to the sheriff's office immediately left a feeling of dread in both parents.

Also unnerving was the fact that David was not in his bedroom. All of David's possessions were in the room, but the room had been empty when Emmett had entered. It distressed Emmett deeply, although he did not voice his concern.

Sheriff John Davis greeted them when they entered the building. "Good morning Mr. and Mrs. Brown. Come with me to my office."

The feeling of dread continued to build. They followed John into his office. Oddly, Pastor Bill sat in one of the office chairs.

Renee could keep silent no longer. "Oh, dear God! What has happened? Where is Joshua?"

Emmett laced his arm around Renee as they both stood trembling.

Renee repeated her question. "Where is Joshua?"

John motioned to the empty chairs. "I think you should both sit down." His voice was calm and filled with concern.

Emmett tried to usher his wife toward an empty chair, but Renee broke free of his grasp. "I will not sit down. Where's my son?" Her gaze went to Bill and then back to the sheriff.

John inhaled deeply. "I'm afraid I have bad news."

The words paralyzed Emmett. His heart stopped as the sheriff continued his statement.

"Apparently, Joshua took a fall."

"A . . . a fall? What do you mean?" Emmett asked.

John wiped his brow. "Joshua fell into Hammond Canyon."

"Dear God! What are you talking about? Hammond Canyon? What on earth were they doing near Hammond Canyon?" Emmett turned his gaze to Bill. He continued to speak but was aware of his wife weeping beside him. "You were up near Hammond Canyon, Bill? Is that true?"

Bill did not make eye contact but nodded.

Emmett grabbed the stout man by the shoulders. "You never said you were going to the canyon. What happened?"

A steadying hand from John pulled Emmett away from Bill. John said, "Near as I can figure, Emm, the boys decided to go a bit farther than originally planned. Bill here still seems to be in some sort of shock, but I was able to figure out that Joshua slipped off the canyon rim. We already have a search party on the way up there."

Emmett pointed at Bill. "What's he still doing here? Shouldn't he be taking the search party to the spot where Joshua fell?"

"Yes, he's going to. But look at him, Emm. He needed some rest. Plus I figured that you and Renee would want to make the trek with us."

Emmett nodded. He moved closer to his wife and placed an arm around her. Her body heaved as she sobbed.

Joshua sat down against a moss-covered stump. He was slowly recovering from the shock that his mind and body had been put through. His throat was dry and his lips were parched. His tongue had doubled in size, and it was difficult to wet his lips.

Gradually his breathing and pulse returned to normal. His eyes scanned the surroundings, searching for something that might assist him in his predicament. Nothing triggered any ideas, so Joshua closed his eyes. *David, are you out there?* Joshua paused, hoping for a response. *Can you here me, David? I need you! I'm lost somewhere in the forest. David, why don't you answer me?*

Joshua waited a long time before he decided that David was unable to answer his call. Realizing that he was alone, he whispered a prayer. "Dear God, please help me. Send me my guardian angel."

Joshua struggled to get to his feet. Every muscle in his body screamed in pain. His legs trembled as they tried to hold up his body, and the sudden nausea that swept over him threatened to knock him back to the ground.

He was not a stranger to the woodland environment. His parents had taken him and Aaron on many hiking trips. Their vacations had consisted of camping in national forests. That had been some time before, when Joshua was young. Those memories kept Joshua from being fearful of the sounds and sights that surrounded him.

Joshua picked up a fallen branch to use as a makeshift walking stick. He glanced back toward the canyon and then allowed his feet to carry him farther into the woods.

He needed to find water to quench the fire that burned in his mouth and throat. That is what he set his focus on. Little feet and stick crunched the leaves that carpeted the forest floor. The odd cadence of rustling warned the inhabitants that something strange was moving along the woodland. The disturbance was enough to cause the local blue jays to begin jeering at the intruder that entered their domain.

The light within the canopy of trees quickly faded. Joshua was not interested in stopping. He continued to struggle forward, even as the shadows loomed within the forest walls. The darkness continued to envelope the surrounding trees and plants and even the noises throughout changed in tone and magnitude.

Joshua continued walking, not understanding that the only way he would find water in total darkness was if he fell into some. His steps became shorter and shorter. Either his foot caught on an exposed root or his muscles finally fatigued, for Joshua collapsed to the forest floor.

Darkness.

David struggled to open his eyes. Why was it so hard to open his eyelids? It required all of his energy to finally open his eyes from the blackness that had overtaken his body.

His pupils adjusted to the surrounding shadows, and his mind shouted out in fear for his little friend. *Joshua, where are you?* The rest of David's body awakened, and he struggled to rise from his back. He propped his arms shakily behind his body to help support his weight. Shaking his head, he tried to clear the fog and focus on his situation.

His head throbbed, and David reached up to rub his forehead. Something stung in the crook of his right arm, drawing his focus away from his head to the sensation near his elbow. David stared in bewilderment at the tube that was inserted through his flesh and at the wrinkles that covered his arm.

A steady beep drummed in his ears, and he panicked. Eyes darting to the nearby wall where the source of sound emitted, he noticed a monitor registering blood pressure and heart rate. *No!* Voiceless, he hollered in shock and denial when he recognized his environment.

David realized he was home, back in his prison, both body and room. But no, something was different. He held his breath and tried to calm down. He surveyed the room more closely and realized that he had been moved.

There were two windows in the room, both covered with blinds. There was a different chair and table. His closet was on the wrong wall. *Where am I?*

David tried to swing his legs to the side of the bed, but they would not respond to his command. *Dear Lord! Why now? What's going on? I need to get back to Joshua. Can anyone hear me? Send me back. Joelle, help me get back!*

There was no answer. David grabbed each leg and moved them to the edge of his bed. He yanked out his IV line, not caring that it would trigger an alarm at the nurses' station somewhere. He needed to see something.

David lowered his body to the floor, collapsing to one side. He rolled toward his belly and dragged his body toward the closest window. He reached the wall and pulled himself up to a seated position. Placing a hand on the nearby chair, he struggled to pull himself up farther and with a little luck, into the chair.

His muscles failed him. He no longer had the strength to do what his mind desired. His frail body collapsed into a slumped position against the wall. His breathing was labored and his heart pounded. Tears flowed down in frustration and despair. *What is happening?*

A click and the opening of his room door caught his attention. A young nurse strolled in, humming a tune and checking a chart. She mumbled, "What triggered the alarm this time?" She stopped at the foot of the bed, still engrossed in her paperwork, and then looked up at the monitor.

Her eyes widened when she noticed the empty bed. "Oh, my word! Mr. Liberty?" She checked the other side of the bed first. Her anxiety clearly rose as she scanned the room. There, slumped against the wall, sat her patient.

"Mr. Liberty!" she howled in surprise. "How on earth did you get there?"

I flapped my arms really fast. Old frustrations returned. *Where exactly am I?*

The nurse approached. "Are you OK?" She inspected her patient.

David nodded.

"Thank goodness. Let me get some help."

David grabbed her arm and shook his head.

"What? What do you want?"

David pointed at the chair.

"You want to sit in the chair?"

David nodded.

"Let me get some help first." The nurse tried to pull away.

David held fast. He shook his head and pointed once again to the chair.

The young nurse sighed. "All right. Try and help me."

Although it was a struggle, the nurse managed to get David into the chair. "Here we go. I'm going to let my supervisor know that you are awake."

David grabbed her arm. He pointed to the window.

The nurse smiled and drew the curtains back. "Don't go anywhere. I'll be right back."

I'll be here. David didn't recognize the scenery outside his window. A cold shiver trickled down his spine. *Where am I? Am I lost to Joshua? Joelle!*

Thirsty. Joshua was thirsty and exhausted. He sat upright and reached for his canteen. It was empty. There was not a drop of water to be found.

The surrounding forest stood in shadow, and Joshua found it hard to see more than a couple feet in front of him. Reflexively, he wrapped his arms about his torso. He was not cold, but the action brought him some comfort. A tear formed at his bottom lid and Joshua called out with his mind. *Please, dear Lord, help me. Where did my guardian angel go? I know you sent David to me. I just know it. Please, dear Lord, I'm so scared!*

"Joshua?"

The voice startled Joshua and he attempted to leap to his feet. He scanned the area for the source of the voice. His gaze fixed on a beautiful young woman who sat a short distance from him. Her very presence emitted a light that brightened the surroundings.

"Joshua, do not be afraid. I am a friend."

"You . . . you're a friend of David's?"

The beautiful woman smiled. "I see you are a very special little boy. Yes, I am a friend of David's."

Joshua struggled to his feet in excitement. "You're going to help me get home?"

The smile on her face faded. "Joshua, I cannot help you get home right now, for you are still sleeping."

A puzzled look stole across Joshua's face. "You mean I'm dreaming?"

"Yes, my child. You are dreaming."

"Why are you here? And where's David?"

"I am here because you were praying."

"But I'm sleeping?"

"Yes. I was sent to give you comfort in answer to your prayer." The figure reached out, offering a canteen.

Joshua grabbed the container and let the precious liquid wet his lips and throat. He had never felt such a wonderful sensation as the cold water quenched the terrible thirst throughout his body. After he was satisfied, he wiped his mouth asked, "Where's David? I can't feel his presence. Am I too far from him?"

The light that shone from the woman dimmed, and she looked away. "Yes, Joshua. We are both too far from him. Even I am not sure where he has gone."

"But you should know. You're just like him. You said you're his friend."

"My sweet child, I am afraid that I do not know everything."

"But I don't understand. You could help me."

"Shhh, little one, listen for a moment. I am here for this brief moment as a small answer to your prayer. And I need your help for David."

"How can I help? Why does David need my help when I need his?"

"Your lives both require the assistance of each other. David needs you to believe."

"To believe? But I already believe."

"Yes, Joshua. You do believe. Now I want you to have faith that David will come back to you."

"Is that the only way that I'll see him again?"

The womanly figure was beginning to fade. "Yes. I am afraid that is the only way David can be found. Through your faith and prayer."

"That's it? That'll be easy!" Joshua's face brightened. "He doesn't know, does he?"

The figure became transparent as the light from the coming sunrise pierced the walls of the forest. "No, he does not know . . . yet."

Joshua knew the time for his encounter had come to an end. "Before you go, will you tell me your name?"

The figure had completely faded, and the last wisp of her light was about to blink away. "Joelle. My name is Joelle."

Joshua awoke with a start. Something small and creepy was crawling across his neck. He brushed frantically at his exposed skin, trying to wipe away the unwanted guest. He shivered with the chill of morning and noticed that the sun was making its way up into the sky.

He pushed himself up to a seated position and recalled the unusual dream from the night. He remembered every detail. Amazingly, he realized that he was no longer parched; in fact, he was no longer thirsty. He struggled to a standing position and bent down to grab his canteen. His muscles uttered a small cry of surprise as they pulled on the now-heavy canteen.

Joshua stared at the object. It was no longer empty. He smiled, and without checking the contents, slung it over his shoulder. *Thank you Lord. Thank you for the drink this day. I ask you to help me find my way home and, just as important, help David find his way back to me.* Joshua smiled and walked along the forest floor.

Chapter Fourteen

EMMETT, RENEE, JOHN, and several others were unsuccessful in the exploration on the canyon floor. No sign of Joshua could be found. On the rim above two deputies and Bill searched.

Radio contact confirmed that the area on the canyon floor was directly below the spot where Joshua had fallen. There was no sign of the fallen boy anywhere in the basin or along the steep walls of the canyon. Binoculars continued to survey every inch of rock and earth that projected skyward while other eyes scanned for some clue on the canyon floor.

Sheriff Davis depressed the call button on his walkie-talkie. "Put Pastor Bill on."

"Yes?" Bill's weary voice projected from the hand-held communicator.

"Are you positive that we're in the area where Joshua fell?"

"I'm not one-hundred percent sure, but I think this is about right."

Emmett inched closer to John.

"Something's not right," John mumbled. "Put Larry back on," he snapped as he talked into the small black box.

"Yes, Sheriff?"

"Do you see any signs that the boy or anyone was up there?"

"Just a minute, sir." Sixty seconds passed before Larry was heard again. "No, sir. I didn't notice any sign that someone was here before us. I don't think Bill has us in the right location. He seems somewhat out of sorts."

The sheriff sighed. "Been a long thirty-six hours for him, I'm sure. Larry, I want you to have Bill take you to where the boys were going to set up camp. Maybe from there the area will look different to him and we can try again."

"Yes, sir. Larry out."

"Radio me when you're there. Over and out." John placed the walkie-talkie back on his belt. "Let's continue to look." John pointed to people in the search party. "You. Travel downstream. The rest of us will work upstream."

He shrugged at Emmett and Renee. "Travel whichever direction your gut tells you."

Emmett nodded and glanced toward his wife. They spoke no words when their eyes made contact. Emmett could not even find the courage to smile to reassure his wife. Renee had not said a word since they'd left the sheriff's office. "Let's go upstream," Emmett finally said.

Renee did not acknowledge the statement with any words or facial expression, but her legs carried her upstream.

The small party fanned out and scoured the east side of the large stream that ran through Hammond Canyon.

An hour had passed when John's radio beeped.

"Sheriff? Come in, Sheriff."

"Right here, Larry. Have you had any luck?"

"No sir, we haven't. I think we may have to go farther down to find where the boys and Bill left the trail. Unfortunately I think Bill needs to rest. He might need a doctor."

"Great. Get him back down the trail. Have Derrick see if he can find the boys' camp. After you take care of Bill, maybe some of the older boys will come back up the trail with you. Hopefully their memories are better than his."

"Yes, sir."

"We'll continue to search here. I want you to get some supplies sent up the canyon so we can camp here during the night, if necessary."

"Yes, sir. Anything else?"

"No. Over and out." John glanced at Emmett. "Let's keep looking, Emm."

The small party continued to search the region. Renee looked straight ahead, never scanning the floor or the walls of the canyon. Her face carried a haunted look. She managed to navigate the rubble and debris in the basin without glancing down to see where to place her feet.

Emmett's eyes hurt from the intensity of his search. His eyes checked everything within a tight radius, scanning, probing, searching for some clue that his son had passed by. He weaved in a tight pattern, edging toward the stream and then back to the canyon wall. Once he returned to the canyon wall he systematically viewed its surface with his bare eyes and then with binoculars.

David sat staring out the window. The feeling of helplessness threatened to drive him mad. He sat doing and thinking nothing. He was unaware that someone had entered the room behind him.

"Dad, it's true. You're awake!"

The familiarity and surprise of the voice caused David to jerk his head in shock to better focus on his visitor.

"It's so good to see you." Mary rushed over and threw her arms around her father.

Mary, you need to get me back to my old nursing home. Take me back to The Waters. David's gaze sought the eyes of his daughter as he pleaded silently to her.

"Oh, Daddy!" Mary looked into the eyes of her father, eyes that danced with life in a way she had not seen for many years. "I knew we had to get you out of that last nursing home. And just look at you! You're already doing better."

David made the sound of a loud raspberry. He struggled violently for a moment, trying to dislodge himself from the chair.

Mary took a step back as her father struggled in the confines of his chair. "Dad? Why are your arms tied down?"

David stopped struggling and opened his hands. He looked to his daughter and then back down at his restraints. *Mary, you must untie me!*

Mary returned to her father's side. Her fingers fumbled clumsily to untie him. "I don't understand. Why were your arms tied?"

"Whoa!" A voice echoed from behind father and daughter. "You better put those restraints back on, miss. Doctor's orders. Mr. Liberty is to remain restrained for his own protection."

David's eyes narrowed when he heard the orders come from the man walking into the room.

"Why? I don't understand. How is it for my Dad's protection? It seems restraining him will do more harm then good."

"That's not for me to decide, ma'am. I'm just a floor nurse. That's something you need to take up with the attending physician."

"I'm not going to tie my father's arms back up."

The nursed sighed. "It'd probably be easier if you did, ma'am. He may not struggle so much if you did the tying."

Mary glared at the nurse and then glanced at her father. "I . . . I can't tie his hands."

"Then I'm going to have to get some help. He is one tough old bean, and it'll take more than me to get those hands restrained." The nurse shrugged and left the room.

Mary peered at her father who returned her stare.

You must get me out of here. Something isn't right. I need to get back to Joshua. Aarrgg! Why can't I speak when my need is great?

Mary reached her hand out and stroked her father's face. Tears rolled down her cheeks as she gingerly placed David's hand against the chair to tie it back in place. "I'm sorry, Daddy," Mary whispered. "I don't want them to hurt you. I'll get to the bottom of this. I promise. I don't know what's going on here. It must be a mistake. I'm going to go and figure this out." She finished tying down David's second arm and hugged him fiercely. "I love you, Daddy."

David watched his daughter stand and go. *I love you too, baby*. He flexed his arms against the resistance of the ties, testing them unconsciously. He stared out the window and pondered his dilemma.

Moments after his daughter left, he heard the soft padding of someone walking into the room.

"Ah, David Liberty. How nice of you to join me at my new facility."

A chill crept down David's spine, and he fought to recall the familiarity of the voice that spoke to him. *What do you want?*

"You mean you don't know?"

His memory triggered, David turned to study his antagonist. *What are you doing here?*

The female laughed. "You don't seem surprised that I hear your thoughts. I'm ensuring that my investments are not spoiled by you."

You can't keep me here.

Again a soft chuckle escaped her lips. "Oh, I wouldn't be too confident of that if I were you. You see, I'm now your physician, and with the right prescription you won't need those restraints." She paused. "Of course you won't be awake anymore either."

Why are you telling me this? Why not just get it done then? Or, Dr. Waits, if that is truly your name, are you just trying to get me to believe you first?

Anger flashed across Jennifer Waits' face. "Think you're clever, don't you? I'll tell you why. I want to enjoy your horror as you fade into a coma knowing that you won't be able to help your precious Joshua. His life shall be lost, and I'll claim his mother and father for my own."

David tensed every muscle in his body and tried to break through the restraints. *If you hurt that boy—*

"You're pathetic." Dr. Waits sprang forward and slammed a needle into David's neck.

David shrieked in silent rage from the searing pain at his neck and the grip on his heart. He fought hopelessly as his mind slowly closed. He focused his last thoughts on the only One who he could turn to. *Dear Lord, my God, Your will be done.* A blinding light sheared through the darkness as David's consciousness was snuffed out.

Chapter Fifteen

JOSHUA PICKED HIS way carefully through the underbrush. He was not sure what direction he was heading, but he hoped he was making his way parallel to the stream that flowed through Hammond Canyon.

Briars and sticks tore at his clothes, slowing his progress. He noticed a clearing a few yards in front of him and looked for the easiest path to exit his entanglement. Joshua moved a few steps, only to discover that the path he had chosen quickly disappeared, swallowed up by the multi-floral rose bushes that redirected his feet.

The terrible maze did not have an exit, and Joshua could not find his way back in the direction he had come from. The canopy was sparse, allowing the growth of the miserable briars and the heat of the sun to drain Joshua's limited energy.

He sat down in frustration, able to see the clearing through the water in his eyes but unable to reach it. He wiped his teary face and stared through the bars of his prison at the open space that lay teasingly out of reach. A soft breeze whispered through the branches and assisted in drying his wet cheeks and eyes. Joshua blinked the remainder of the tears away and enjoyed the cool breeze that struck his face. He closed his eyes, allowing the wind to massage his face.

The snapping of a nearby branch caused Joshua to open his eyes and scan his surroundings. The noise did not seem to be from the infrequent dropping of a twig from an overhanging branch. A small movement in the clearing caught his eyes. At first he had no idea what he was looking at. The sunlight and shadows seemed to create a subtle movement of something back and forth. The movement was hypnotic, and Joshua continued to stare for several moments.

He was aware of how silent the forest had become. The birds were no longer singing, and there were no sounds from the furry little mammals that scampered across the dry leaves on the ground. Joshua was sensitive to the rhythmical movement and the wind steadily caressing his face.

The sharp cawing of a nearby blue jay made his heart leap, and the movement that he had been watching stopped. Joshua wanted to kneel for a better look, but the muscles of his legs were unresponsive. He placed a hand on the ground to give his legs assistance and froze as a new movement caught his attention.

Out of the shadows emerged an enormous cat. He had never seen an animal as large as the one that stood mere yards in front of him. The cat's tail twitched and Joshua recognized the rhythmic movement as the one he had been watching dance in the sunlight and shadows seconds before.

Caw! Caw! The blue jay hollered its distress in the trees above. The cat twitched its ears toward the alarm in irritation to the bird's calling. The cat lifted its head slightly, testing the currents that flowed through the air. *Caw! Caw!* The jay sounded again directly above the great cat. Whether it was agitated by the bird above or driven by its appetite, the mountain lion loped out of the clearing and back into the shadows of the forest.

Joshua did not move, even after the cat disappeared into the forest. He still had one hand planted on the ground and his legs remained folded underneath his small frame. His heart continued to race at an alarming rate. He could feel the beat of it within the pit of his stomach.

Eventually, Joshua collapsed to the ground. He wrapped his little arms around his chest and trembled.

Sheriff Davis nodded and spoke to Emmett. "Yes, I'd agree. That's the track of a large cat."

"I believe it's from a mountain lion," Emmett replied.

"Now, Emm, we can't be sure of that. I mean it's a large track, but the moisture and elements could have changed its size."

"No, it's still fresh. It's from a mountain lion. I'm sure."

The sheriff sighed. "Well, even if it is, it won't bother a party of this size."

"I'm not concerned about us. I'm concerned about Joshua."

John Davis glanced at his friend. "Emm, why do you—?"

"Joshua is alive, John," Emmett interrupted. He lowered his voice as he glanced toward Renee who sat on a small stump staring blankly somewhere ahead. "I'm sure of that. If he had really fallen anywhere in this region we would have seen some sign."

John stared at Emmett. He nodded once and answered, "I've been thinking the same thing. I didn't want to say anything, but I need to talk with Bill. Would he have any reason to kidnap Joshua?"

"I'm not sure. I don't think he's telling us exactly what happened. I had my doubts at your office, but now that we've seen no sign of Joshua, I think his story was a lie."

"That settles it. We're going to head back to town and see if we can pull the truth out of him."

Renee walked up. "I'm not going back."

Both men started with surprise when Renee spoke. John was the first to gather himself, "Renee, we need to talk to Bill again. Joshua isn't here. Let's find out what really happened."

"Yes, you need to talk to Bill again, but I don't. My son's out here, and I intend to find him."

"Renee, you can't possibly do any good out here. Come back with us. Besides, it wouldn't be safe for you out here alone."

"Just like it's not safe for my son out here alone. You go; I'll keep searching."

John's face reddened. "For gosh sake's, Renee! We don't even know that Joshua is out here. I won't let you stay here alone, even if I have to carry you!"

Emmett placed a steadying hand on his friend's shoulder. "Sheriff, take your men. Talk to Bill. Renee and I will continue looking."

"Emm, you're both being crazy!"

"Leave me your radio and call me as soon as you know what happened."

John shook his head, but handed his radio to Emmett. "I won't argue with you anymore, Emm. I'll call you as soon as we know something." John walked away from the couple. Without glancing back he said, "Be careful."

Renee and Emmett watched the sheriff and deputies make their way back down the canyon.

Emmett felt he would be able to persuade Renee without John's help. Her color had returned to almost normal, but her eyes were still hollow. He reached out to hold her hand. "Renee? Shall we keep looking? I think we should go talk to Bill. He's not telling us everything."

"We'd be too late."

"What do you mean?"

"By the time we got there and talked to Bill, it would be too late."

Emmett frowned.

"Emmett, Joshua is here. I know it. We need to find him before it's too late."

"Why do you think Joshua is out here?"

"You wouldn't believe me if I told you. I'm not sure I believe it myself. We must find him before the mountain lion does." Renee walked upstream.

Emmett followed. "You heard me talking to John about the mountain lion? I didn't want you to hear that."

"No, I didn't hear you."

Emmett waited for more of an answer, but none came. As they continued to walk, he questioned her further. "Did you see tracks?"

"No."

"Then how do you know there's a mountain lion here?"

"You confirmed that there was."

Frustrated, Emmett grabbed his wife by the arm. "Maybe we should go back to town."

Renee stared at him. "I told you we would then be too late to save Joshua."

"How do you know that?"

"The same way that I know a mountain lion is hunting our son. Someone told me in a dream."

David's body floated, or maybe it was not his body but his mind. He could not be sure. It was difficult to formulate any consistency with his thoughts, for they too seemed adrift, as was his body.

Visions of Joshua and others flashed in and out of focus. Mary, his daughter, was holding a newborn child that she had just given the name Jimmy David. Tammy hung precariously off a ledge as Nicole struggled to save her sister and herself. His wife's words "I do." Sam watched his father hit a home run. Joelle's beautiful lips moved when she talked to David.

Through the black and silent void, other images, not as pleasant, came in and out of focus. Dr. Stevens smiled as he tore a necklace away from its owner. A priest was shot by a gunman. David's wife cried while her husband walked away. Jennifer Waits plunged a needle into David's neck. Joshua crouched in the brush, and a mountain lion hunted the forest, while David stood by helplessly, unable to help the little boy.

A musical melody stopped the array of visions. "David? David, can you hear me? David, please answer me!"

David's mind struggled with the blackness and confusion that surrounded him. *Joelle, is it really you?*

"Yes, David. I am here."

I can't see you. Am I dreaming?

David sensed Joelle smile as she chided him. "You crazy man, remember that I ask the questions."

Joelle, you must go to Joshua and help him. I'm lost here, and he needs you.

"No, Joshua does not need me, David. He needs you."

I'm trapped here. You must go in my place.

David perceived Joelle's emotions change. "I cannot help Joshua. He is not my charge. Only you can help him."

How can I help him when I can't even help myself?

There was no answer.

Joelle?

"David." the volume of Joelle's voice faded to barely a whisper, "I am not permitted to answer your question."

David's panic switched to anger. *Then ask me a question.*

"Why do you wish to save Joshua?"

The question caught David by surprise. His mind reeled in confusion. He obviously cared a great deal for the young boy, but he did not feel that this was the answer Joelle was searching for.

"Suffering will come to all, David. Why must you save this boy when he is already saved?"

An answer escaped David's mind before he could reason it out any further. *By saving Joshua we will save Emmett and Renee as well. I don't think that either would recover from the loss of their son. Not at this point in time.*

Joelle's voice became stronger. "'God wills everyone to be saved and to come to the knowledge of truth.' This is written in Scripture and so you have been called to help and pray for those who need prayers and petitions."

Apparently I've been called to do more than just pray.

"As we all are, David."

I need to get to Joshua.

"I cannot help you while you are here. Only He can."

I understand. I've been reading the Word, and I read something about the ability to move mountains.

Joelle did not respond, but David knew she was smiling. He could feel her stroke his face.

David's eyes fluttered open to see his daughter Mary gently stroking his face. "Mary, you must get me out of here." David's vocal cords had atrophied from the lack of use and his voice was raspy and brittle.

Mary's eyes widened. "Daddy, did you say something?"

David struggled to keep his eyes open. He reached up and grabbed his daughter's shoulder. "Mary, you must get me out of here and return me to The Waters."

"Oh, my word! You did speak! I can't—"

David pulled Mary toward him. "I was not the best father, Mary. But if you ever did love me, I ask you to get me to The Waters. Now."

"I don't understand." Mary stepped back.

"Mary, my dear sweet Mary. I'm afraid that I don't have the time or the energy to explain this to you. As it is, I feel the drug's strength returning, and I will once again slip into darkness. You're my only hope." David eye's closed and his arm went limp.

Mary's trembling hand reached out and touched her father's face. "I'll get you back to The Waters. I promise, Daddy." She kissed him on the cheek and skirted from the room to fulfill her promise.

Emmett and Renee continued their search through the strewn rocks on the canyon floor. Emmett scanned the ground while Renee searched above. They did not walk together step by step, for one would stop and study an area while the other continued to move up ahead. At one point Emmett had gone a significant distance before he realized that Renee had not moved for an extended period of time.

Emmett made his way back to his wife. "Renee, what's wrong?"

"I'm not sure. But something doesn't seem right." She did not look at Emmett but scanned the cliffs above.

Emmett turned his gaze upward, trying to distinguish what was troubling Renee. After a few moments he mumbled, "What are you looking at?"

"That's the problem. I don't see anything, but something doesn't seem right."

"Wait a minute! That's it! The rope bridge is no longer spanning the canyon. I wonder when that fell down."

Renee stepped toward her husband. "I don't think it fell down. I think it was cut down. See? There it hangs on the west bank. It was cut from the east side, where Joshua was!" Renee could not contain her emotion.

"How do you know it was cut?"

Renee ignored the question. "Joshua is up there, Emmett. We must get to him."

"It's too dangerous to climb that bank. We need to go back down and then up."

"No!" Renee's eyes sparked with rage. "There won't be enough time. I'll go alone if I have to. I will save my son."

Emmett stared in disbelief at his wife. He peered up at the steep bank that loomed before them and watched his wife approach the side and pick her way up the bank. He walked over to where his wife struggled and boosted her up to where she could get a handhold. "Let's get moving. We don't have time to waste."

Husband and wife did not share anymore words. They worked their way up the bank, at times side by side and at other times front and back. Physically and emotionally the task was monumental, but they managed to scale the cliff and eventually found themselves standing on the rim of the canyon wall.

Emmett did not rest to catch his breath but immediately went over to the hanging bridge of rope. Tentatively he pulled up the structure, unsure if he wanted to confirm Renee's premonition. His heart skipped as his hands came to the end of the ropes. No fraying or wear had caused the bridge to fall. A sharp object had cleanly sliced through the braided strands. "Scan the ground for footprints, anything," Emmett said.

They searched the earth before them. Renee spoke for the first time since their ascent. "I know Joshua is here. We mustn't waste anytime. We have to find him!"

"Here! See how these stones have been disturbed? This twig was broken!" Emmett stooped and moved aside the debris that had attracted his attention. He gasped, "Renee, there's a small handprint. I think you're right. Joshua was here!"

Chapter Sixteen

AT THE WATERS, Mary and Wilma tucked David under his bed sheets.

Wilma said, "I don't understand, dear. Why have you brought your father back here? I thought we decided he would get better care at Clearbrook Nursing Home."

"I know we did, Wilma. I can't explain it. You wouldn't believe me, anyway. I thought he should come back here to The Waters."

Wilma placed her hand on Mary's shoulder. "Dear, you can tell me."

The concern on Wilma's face was reassuring, and it prompted Mary to speak. "Dad woke up at the other nursing facility, but some things did not seem right. Apparently he had gotten out of bed and made his way over to the window of his room."

"That sounds like excellent progress to me."

"So I thought, but when I came in to see him for the first time after he was awake, someone had his arms restrained."

"Restrained? I don't understand."

"Neither did I. They tried to tell me it was for Dad's own protection, but that sounded strange to me. And after I left him for just a short time, he slipped back into his unconscious state, similar to his previous episodes, but something was different."

"Different?"

"Yes, but I couldn't figure out why he seemed different."

"But he's sleeping now, even as he was when you brought him in."

"I know that he sleeps now, but when he woke before, he spoke to me."

"He spoke? I've never heard that man speak a word the whole time he has been with us."

"He talked to me. He made me promise to bring him back here, and that's why we've returned."

"What else did he say?"

Before Mary could answer, a strange, melodious sound filled the room. Mary watched as a woman, a striking woman, walked into the room and stood alongside the bed where her father lay. "Who . . . who are you?" Mary asked. The stranger looked familiar, but Mary could not place her.

Wilma piped up, "Now what kind of question is that, dear?"

The beautiful stranger's lips parted, and words flowed into Mary's mind. "The nurse cannot see or hear me. Only you can. Make an excuse for Wilma to leave."

Mary stared in wonder at the woman across from her. She glanced at Wilma, who was completely oblivious to the fact that someone else was standing in the room. "Wilma? Did you hear anything?"

"Just you asking me who I was."

Mary felt unsteady on her feet. She placed her hand on the bed and sat down next to her father. Reaching up, she rubbed her forehead. "Wilma, I don't feel so good. Could you get me some aspirin, please?"

Wilma patted Mary on the shoulder. "Of course. I'll be back in a minute." Wilma exited the room.

Mary rubbed her forehead and then her eyes. When she found the courage, she glanced up to see if her illusion had disappeared. The woman still stood at the side of the bed, but now she was holding David's hand.

"Now I recognize you. You're the mysterious physical therapist. What was your name?"

"Joelle."

"You look different. What are you doing here?" Mary asked. "And why didn't Wilma say anything to you?"

"I told you that Wilma could not hear or see me."

"That's ridiculous. What do you take me for, some kind of fool?"

"Watch."

Wilma returned to the room carrying a small cup of water and two buffered aspirin. "Here, dear, this should help."

"Thank you so much." Mary took the aspirin. "Wilma, who is standing next to Dad's bed?"

"Why you are, dear. Why do you ask?"

"No, I mean besides me."

Joelle interjected, "She will think you are losing your mind if you continue."

Wilma remarked, "Are you sure that you're feeling all right? Maybe you should head home and get some rest. Your dad will be fine, and if he should wake, you know I'll call you."

Mary's face wilted and her legs buckled. She placed her hand on the rail of the hospital bed to keep from falling. "Wilma, I'll be OK, but I will take your advice and head home in a moment." She risked a peek toward Joelle, who stood by the bed. Mary turned to Wilma and forced herself to smile.

Wilma patted Mary on the arm. "You get some rest. I think it's long overdue." She waited for Mary's response, but when none came, she left Mary alone with her father.

After Wilma left, Mary resumed stroking her father's hair. She studied the hard lines of his skin and the contour of his face. Somehow her father had changed. Not daring to look at Joelle, Mary said softly, "Who are you and what do you want?"

"I want your father to remain in this room."

The answer caught Mary by surprise, and she stared at the stunning figure. "I don't understand."

"There are many things that are not meant to be understood. Our meeting is one of them. I am asking you not only to leave your father in this room, but also to keep him here no matter what it takes."

Mary's legs could no longer bear the stress that was weighing on her body. She collapsed to a seated position along the motionless body of her father. "I must be losing my mind. At first my father talks to me in a manner that he hasn't done in I don't know how long, and now I'm talking to a hallucination."

"Your father asked you to return him here to The Waters."

"Yes."

"Promise me that you will do everything that it takes for him to remain in this room."

"I don't understand."

"Promise me."

"Who are you?"

"Promise me."

"What will happen to him?"

Joelle's expression softened. "As long as he remains within these walls, I can watch over him."

Mary shook her head slightly and laid herself onto the chest of her father. "None of this makes sense."

"Mary, I understand that this is all somewhat overwhelming. Your father still has a very important purpose that he must carry out, and only you and I can help him."

Mary lifted her head. "What purpose could my father possibly have when he is unable to function?"

"Through God all things are possible."

"What things are you talking about?"

"I do not have time to discuss this further. Your father is needed, and I must awaken him. Please stand behind the curtain so he does not see you. Watch, listen, and most importantly, be still."

Mary got up from the bed and moved to hide from her father's sleeping form. She felt as if she had no control over her body as she wrapped the curtain around her frame.

Joelle spoke. "David Liberty, it is time to awaken. I am here." Joelle's voice was laced with a tenderness that did not go unnoticed by the hidden observer.

David's body stirred and his eyes opened. "Joshua!" he said aloud. "I need to find Joshua!"

"Yes, you have been procrastinating far too long, Mr. Liberty."

David's frail frame pushed itself to sitting position. "Humph. About time you showed up. What took you so long?"

Joelle's laughter brightened the room. "Yes, it is good to see you too. Still asking questions though, aren't we?"

David tried to shake the cobwebs from his head. "I was drugged. I still feel way out of it. My thoughts are not clear."

"Your daughter was able to bring you back to your room at The Waters."

"Mary?"

"Do you have another daughter?"

"I see that I've been a bad influence on you."

"It is time."

"Past time."

"Yes, you are correct. Close your eyes."

"Hey, why am I talking?"

"Still asking questions, David Liberty? Be still. Joshua needs you."

Mary trembled behind the curtain as she listened to her father's voice. Everything within her shouted for her to jump out and embrace the man that had raised her, but she was unable to move. A long moment of silence passed before Mary realized that Joelle was once again addressing her.

"You may come out now."

Mary stepped out from behind the curtain. Her father lay as he had when she first hid herself. "I don't understand."

"Promise me."

Mary's lips trembled and her mind raced with possible explanations for the events that she had just witnessed. Nothing made sense, yet she found herself compelled to answer Joelle. "I promise."

His legs were full of strength and vigor as David tore through the undergrowth of the forest. His body once more restored, he rejoiced at the energy that flowed through his veins.

David slowed to a walk and scoured the earth, searching for some clue that would help him find the trail of his little friend. Focused on the ground before him, he wandered into a small clearing.

The crisscrossing of many tracks made it difficult to distinguish how much time had elapsed since they had been made. The tracks themselves were confusing. Two sets of adult tracks entered from the east side of the clearing and then headed south out of the clearing. Large cat tracks also entered the clearing from the east and headed south. What seemed the most unnerving was the two sets of child prints. One set exited south, while the other left the clearing southwest.

David studied both prints made by the small children. They were identical. David could not tell the difference between the two. In fact, he felt that there was no difference between them, that they were indeed the same print made from the same shoe. Even the depths of the tracks were too similar to differentiate if they were made from two different children.

David was not sure which set of tracks he should follow. Were there two boys who were lost in the forest, or was someone trying to lead him in the wrong direction?

David reached out. *Joshua, can you hear me?* David held his breath and waited for an impossible response. It came, as if from crossing a vast ocean.

Joshua's mind called out in reply to David. *David you're here!*

Yes Joshua, I'm here. But where are you?

I'm in the forest.

Joshua, I need you to help me find you. Do you remember a small clearing in the forest?

I've seen many clearings.

David thought for a moment. *What else have you seen?*

A pause before the answer followed. *A very large cat. I think it was a mountain lion.*

David's heart skipped a beat. If Joshua had seen the great cat, then it was only a matter of time before the cat found Joshua. *Did you see the cat at one of the clearings?*

Yes. I made sure I went in the opposite direction.

David frowned. Neither set of shoe tracks went in the opposite direction from the tracks that the mountain lion had made. *Joshua, do you know which direction you headed?*

Do you mean like north or south?

Yes.

No. I was so scared. I just wanted to get away from the—

Joshua can you hear me? David waited anxiously for a reply, but none came. *Joshua, where are you?*

There was no reply.

David took a deep breath and chose a set of tracks. He moved quickly down the trail, realizing there was not much time. He only hoped the adult tracks were those of someone searching for Joshua, so he had chosen to take the other trail. He hoped someone would find the little boy before the mountain lion did.

Joshua felt better now that he knew David was somewhere in the forest. He was confident David would find him and that it would be only a matter of time.

His canteen was empty, and his throat longed for water. He had drunk the last drop some hours before, and now his lips were dried and cracked. The energy that Joshua exerted during his journey quickly lowered his hydration.

He collapsed next to the trunk of a hemlock tree, no longer feeling the urge to find a way out of the forest. Joshua let his head collapse against the bark for support. "David will find me," he whispered and closed his eyes.

The screaming of a blue jay startled him. His eyes flipped open and his head jerked forward. The bird hollered over and over a short distance away. A chill crept down Joshua's neck and back. He scrambled to his feet and stepped up on a rock, enabling him to grab one of the lower branches of the hemlock tree. Heart racing, Joshua hurriedly pulled himself up branch by branch.

The cawing of the jay was nearing, and the intensity of the bird's distress cries matched the pounding of Joshua's heart. The bark roughed up his small hands as he grabbed and pulled, propelling his body farther and farther from solid ground.

The jay's cry stopped. Joshua wrapped his arms and legs around the trunk of the tree and held his breath. The only sound he heard came from the pounding inside his ears; the rest of the forest had gone completely still.

The silence was interrupted by Joshua's gasping. His breath came short and quick. Then a new sound reached his ears. Its eerie proximity caused Joshua to grip tighter around the trunk of the tree. The creaking and clicking of the tree bark being disturbed caused Joshua's mind to call out in desperation, *Hurry, David! Please hurry!*

David's eyes were riveted on the ground. He followed the tracks for a short time but something tugged at the back of his mind. Something was not right. David's anxiety grew. Time was running out.

He knelt down to study the small prints that marked the trail before him. What was wrong? He stared at the tracks, trying to figure out what was bothering him. Then it hit him. The tracks had become easier to follow, but not in a way that seemed natural. Obviously, fresher tracks would be easier to recognize, but there was something strange about how fresh these tracks were.

David traced his fingers around the outline of a print and then jerked his hand back in surprise when the footprint disappeared. He stared in shock at the smooth ground where the track had once disrupted it. He snapped his head back to study his trail. Only *his* passage was marked; no longer did he see any trail of a little boy.

He'd been tricked! These tracks were not Joshua's. He took a deep breath, made a decision, and ran, following the forged trail that shone like a beacon before him. His heart told him he would be too late if tried to backtrack. Maybe he could buy Joshua some time if he could find the source of the false trail.

David's legs spurred him through the forest at a pace that even the white-tail deer could not match. Each stride carried him over many feet of ground as he raced against time. Branches and thorns tore at his clothes and skin; other jagged obstacles promised to impale themselves into David's flesh if he stumbled. He gave these no attention while his focus remained on finding the end of the trail.

His pace slowed when the trail stopped. He surveyed the area quickly, noticing a strange rock formation that loomed all around him. He realized there was only one way in or out of this unnatural gully. The way out was behind him; a trap lay before him.

He walked deeper into the walled cage. *I'm here. Show yourself!* his mind shouted.

A soft chuckle echoed off the rocks. "So you are here. A little sooner than I expected, but no matter, it won't change the outcome."

Show yourself, you snake!

"Your wish is my command." The reply was laced with sarcasm.

David turned to his left as a figure appeared on the top of the stone wall. *You?*

Jennifer Waits smiled. "Who did you expect? Surely you didn't think I'm limited to any particular environment. When you left the nursing home, I left as well. You will not ruin my plans. I knew you would return for Joshua."

And I will save him.

"I don't think so. Even if you survive this encounter you will not be in time to save the little boy. In failing the boy, the parents will become mine. The horror they will witness will turn them forever more from your Lord."

David clenched his hands and set his jaw. His eyes scanned the rocks for a way up to his foe.

"Even more rewarding is when you fail the boy and die in my trap, you will learn what it is like to truly suffer before my master."

Your overconfidence will be your undoing.

"And your faith in your Lord will be yours!" The devil's handmaiden stretched forth her arm. "Enough! I tire of this conversation. I must observe my victory. Goliath, awaken!"

A deep, guttural growl came from behind David. He turned to see the source of the rumble. An immense bear rose out of the earth and stood between him and the exit. The bear towered at least nine feet tall on its hind legs. It glowered at the small man before it.

"Meet Goliath, my dear man, except in this story it will be Goliath that slays David. Kind of ironic, don't you think?" Jennifer called out over her shoulder as she turned to go. "It'd give me great pleasure to watch, but I'll see you when this is all over. Goliath, my pet, it's dinnertime."

The large bear dropped down on all fours, preparing for its death charge.

An eerie calm came over David, and he knelt down to one knee. His mind and soul spoke a psalm that had been written in ages past. *"To You, Lord, I call; my Rock, do not be deaf to me. If you fail to answer me, I will join those who go down to the pit. Hear the sound of my pleading when I cry to You, lifting my hands toward your holy place."* David's arms reached toward the heavens. *"Do not drag me off with the wicked, with those who do wrong, who speak peace to their neighbors though evil is in their hearts. Repay them for their deeds, for the evil that they do. For the work of their hands repay them; give them what they deserve."*

David rose, and his head and gaze followed his arms that extended skyward. Something long and sleek materialized within the palm of his right hand. *"Blessed be the Lord, who has heard the sound of my pleading. The Lord is my strength and my shield, in whom my heart trusted and found help. So my heart rejoices; with my song I praise my God."*

The satanic agent faced David when he finished his prayer. "My master rules this kingdom. The world is ours. Your words are like the babbling of a brook as it wanders aimlessly wherever the earth shall guide it."

David bent forward and selected three smooth stones from the ground. He placed the first stone securely within the cradle of leather that joined the two cords of the sling together. Deliberately and methodically he twirled the weapon in the air. *Does not the water make its own path as it cuts through the earth?*

"You're such a fool! That measly toy will not harm the bear. It's no man that you face but a beast. Your stones will enrage Goliath all the more, and I will stay to watch him devour your flesh."

David quartered his body toward the womanly foe who stood on the rock above him. He accelerated the speed at which the shepherd's sling twirled. His gaze locked with his antagonist. *The first stone is not for the bear that stands beside me but for its master that chimes above me.* David released his grasp on one cord and the missile streaked toward its mark.

Jennifer Waits stood frozen with shock while the small stone sliced through the air, gained momentum, and sped toward her forehead.

Chapter Seventeen

A SCREAM VIBRATED through the woods, and Emmett and Renee rushed through the underbrush. Emmett took the lead. His wife followed closely on his heels as he sprinted toward the sound of his son's voice.

He neared the source of his terror and noticed a large cat at the base of a tree, a few yards ahead. His looked up the trunk and saw the plight of his son.

Joshua was trying to climb farther up the trunk, and a second mountain lion was inching its way closer to the boy. The lion was several feet below where Joshua struggled through the thinning branches.

Husband and wife screamed, "Joshua!"

Emmett accelerated and bowled into the surprised cat at the foot of the hemlock tree. His momentum caused both cat and man to roll over and over. Emmett's arms grabbed onto the lion, determined to keep it from his son and wife.

Emmet felt the claws rend his flesh, and he collapsed to the ground.

Renee screamed.

"Daddy!" Joshua shrieked, "Help me!"

The lion in the tree eyed the prey above it. Instinct kept the cat from climbing higher, as the preservation of its own life outweighed the desire that pushed it toward its quarry above.

The mountain lion on the ground stalked the source of the new noise. The screaming lady was an easy target. It crouched lower; its tail switched back and forth. The muscles in the lion's frame rippled with expectation, and it prepared to leap.

"Daddy, don't let it get Mommy! Help her, Daddy!" Joshua screamed.

Emmett, bleeding profusely, intercepted the lion that leapt toward Renee and tackled it. This time, Emmett's arms encircled the neck of the beast, and he squeezed.

The pain that wracked Emmett's body threatened his consciousness, but he continued to squeeze. The great cat's claws raked through his flesh. The cat struggled to back its head out of the trap, but Emmett squeezed. "God, give me the strength to hold on!" He squeezed harder. "I . . . will . . . not . . . let . . . go!"

Emmett's mind raced, reviewing his past, his unwillingness to take a risk, being frozen with fear and unable to act. His thoughts were separate from his body, and yet they invigorated the need to hold on.

He would not let the beast hurt his wife. He would not let go. His failures were in the past. He was finally able to let God be the God of his life. God gave Emmett strength, the gift of strength to beat the physical and spiritual foe, and the inability of his mind to register pain.

Fangs sank into his forearm and claws ripped through muscle to the bone, but Emmett squeezed harder.

Emmett knew his son and wife would be all right, and he smiled. The ferocity of the great cat was subsiding, as was Emmett's consciousness.

"Emmett!" Renee screamed as the combatants' movements stilled.

Emmett's gaze found Renee. He smiled one more time.

The thrashing of the entangled bodies stopped. Lion and man lay, intertwined in a motionless struggle in which one fought to preserve its own life and the other fought to preserve the lives of the ones he loved.

The stillness was shattered by a figure leaping from the woods. The whirling of a sling stopped, and the third stone arced skyward to the last target. The stone struck the lion between the eyes, and it fell lifeless to the earth.

David stood behind the crowd while the bishop finished the funeral ceremony. His eyes, clouded with moisture, watched first Renee and then Joshua place a rose on the casket before it was set in the ground. David could not bring himself to be near Renee and Joshua, or the friend whose body now rested silently in the casket before him.

Tears streamed down his cheeks when he remembered Joshua screaming to heal his father. He could still feel the tiny fists beating against his thighs. But Emmett remained still. David could not heal his friend. The echoes of Joshua's words rang through his ears. "I thought you were my guardian angel. How could you let this happen? I hate you! I hate you!"

If David had only followed the other set of prints in the forest, the outcome would have been different.

A hand grasped his while his shoulders shook in agony of his failure and loss. A musical voice echoed in his mind. He looked at the person who now held his hand.

The outcome would have been worse, Joelle thought to David.

David tried to pull his hand away. *Get away from me!*

David, the outcome would have been worse.

How could you possibly know that? Oh, wait, I'm sorry. That was a question. How stupid of me. Let go of my hand.

Two people are alive because of you.

And Emmett? He saved them as much as I did. He gave his life. What did I give?

He could show no greater love. He gave his life so his wife and child would survive.

David whirled. *But he's dead, Joelle. My friend, Renee's husband, Joshua's father, is dead.*

No, David. You could not be more wrong. He lives now with our Lord.

David tried to jerk his hand away, but Joelle would not let go. *You protected the child and thus his parents. That was what you were meant to do.*

Joshua hates me. He knew his dad had been healed before, but I couldn't do it this time. David succeeded in breaking her grip and grasped Joelle by both shoulders. *Why couldn't I heal him a second time, Joelle? Tell me why.*

Joelle's countenance changed when David confronted her. Her eyes narrowed. *It is not for you to ask.*

Then it must have been His will. That's all I know.

It's time to go home.

No, I will stay here. I will take care of Renee and Joshua. I won't go with you.

You do not yet have the power to refuse.

Chapter Eighteen

DAVID'S EYES OPENED when the faint light caressed his face. He reached up to rub the grit from his eyelids and wondered when he had finally stopped crying. His arms were wrinkled and flabby, and he realized that he had returned home, home to the nursing facility and to his dying body. The intense pain within his chest triggered the memories of the past few weeks that he had shared with the Brown family.

David wrapped his arms around himself in an attempt to warm what could not be warmed. *Dear God, what have I done to deserve this pain? I don't want to do this anymore. I don't want to share in the suffering of others. I don't want to make new friends just to leave them after I have grown to love them. Why is this happening to me?*

The shade covering the window flipped up, and a blinding light cascaded into the room. David blinked as his eyes tried to adjust to the intense light that filled the room.

Joelle waited by his bed. "Hello, David, it's good to see you."

I'm not sure I can say the same.

Joelle's broad smile diminished, and she lowered her voice. "I understand how you feel."

Then why do you continue to do this to me? I grow to love these people, and then they're ripped away from me, or I'm ripped away from them.

"Is it not better to have loved and lost than never to have loved at all?"

David glowered at his tormentor.

"Would you rather have not met Joshua? Would you rather his family had been lost to the enemy, to suffer an eternity of torment and pain? Are you that selfish that you are more concerned about your pain than your friends' fulfillment in life?"

David did not answer. Instead, he turned his gaze away from Joelle and stared out the window. *I don't know if I can continue to handle the loss I feel. I want to see these people again. I want to know how they're doing with their lives, to see if I really made a difference.*

"Did you make a difference with your own family? Yes, you loved them in a sense, but you always put your own needs and desires first. You did not seek them out later in life to see how they turned out."

David's shoulders slumped. *Why do you torture me so? Things are different now.*

"And how is that, David Liberty?"

I'm not sure. David faced the beautiful woman. Tears streaked his face. *If I could just see them one more time. To have some peace of mind that all is well with their lives, and maybe to see if I was as important to them as they were to me.*

Joelle looked away. "What you ask is not permitted."

I'm sure it's not. David rolled to his side and pulled the bed sheet over his shoulders. *Please, leave me alone. The pain is too great. I still feel Joshua's tiny fists when they struck my legs.* David closed his eyes, not waiting for a response.

Joelle moved to the side of the bed. She reached out to place a hand on David for comfort, but her arm remained frozen in the space above him. Her eyes glistened with moisture. "For you, David," she whispered, "I will do this for you."

A jolt coursed through David's body, and his mind lost consciousness.

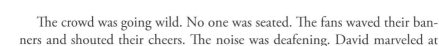

The crowd was going wild. No one was seated. The fans waved their banners and shouted their cheers. The noise was deafening. David marveled at the amazement and energy that pounded through the ballpark. *Where am I?*

The man next to him clasped David on the shoulder. "Can you believe it, buddy? Bottom of the ninth in the seventh game of the World Series, and it all comes down to this at bat?" The excited fan shook David and raised a fist up in the air. "Come on, Sam! Let's hit that ball!"

A voice crackled over the loudspeaker, "And now, this year's batting champ, your own Sammy Barnes!"

Sam? The same Sammy whose family I helped? David stretched up on his toes to get a better view of the man coming to the plate. David could not identify the batter who stepped up to the right side of the plate. David was in the bleachers, out behind left field, a distance far too great to recognize any player who stood at home plate.

The scoreboard read Yankees six, Padres five. The bases were loaded, and there were two outs. With Sammy coming to the plate, there were three possible scenarios: an out would end the game, a walk would tie the game, or a hit would win the World Series for the San Diego Padres.

The excited fan who had grabbed David said, "Sam's due. He hasn't had a hit all game. He's due, I'm telling you!" The fan turned back to the action out in the field.

Everything around David grew dim. The noises faded, and the images that surrounded him clouded. The movements of everyone slowed. David's senses focused with surprising clarity on the young man who stood at the plate.

The batter was poised. With the smooth swing of his bat he sent the leather-bound ball over the left field fence and into the outstretched hands of his former friend, David Liberty.

Chaos erupted. The shouts and clamor of the fans caused the foundation of the stadium to tremble. David was mobbed by men and women alike, some congratulating him and others hitting and striking him, trying to get their hands on the ball he held.

Miraculously, he slipped away from the mass of people and made his way down to the floor of the stadium. His hand still grasped the ball firmly. He could not believe what he had seen.

David worked his way through the crowd, his mind set on a particular destination. The badge that he wore on his shirt made the security guards open the gate to allow him to pass without question. Shortly he found himself in the press room, where reporters and VIPs swarmed in a more organized mob.

The clamor subsided as coaches, managers, and Sammy Barnes came to the podium. The flashes and clicking of cameras echoed throughout the room. A hundred hands rose, and questions from the reporters swarmed the room.

"One at a time! One at a time," shouted the manager.

David peered closer and smiled. The manager of the Padres was none other than John Barnes, Sam's father.

"John, can we talk to Sam?" someone from the crowd hollered.

John smiled at his son. "I suppose you can. But one question at a time." John slapped Sam affectionately on the shoulder and ushered him to the microphone.

Sam pointed to one of the waving hands in the crowd. "Yes, Stan."

"Sam, how does it feel to come out of your mini-slump to hit the Series-winning homerun?"

"I'm still in shock right now, but I'm sure by tomorrow I'll be feeling pretty good about the team's accomplishment overall." Sam pointed to another. "Rebecca?"

"Yes, Sam. What type of reward are you willing to offer for the ball you hit? From what I understand, no one knows where the person disappeared to. What's the value of that ball?"

"To be honest with you, it's not the ball that has any worth, but the action that's associated with the ball. My memory of feeling that moment is something you can't put a price on." Sam pointed again.

"That has to be the farthest hit of a baseball I've ever seen. What's your take on the hit? Is it the farthest hit ball you've seen?"

Sam smiled. "Not by a long shot."

"What do you mean? What's the farthest you've seen?"

Sam smiled. "You wouldn't believe me if I told you."

A voice yelled from the crowd. "I'd guess that it was eight hundred feet."

The reporters and VIPs broke out in laughter.

Sam scanned the crowd. "Actually, that's the distance. Who said that?"

The crowd grew silent. Everyone looked to his or her neighbor, trying to find the source of the statement.

John Barnes moved up to stand next to his son, as did Sue. She was wearing a Padres uniform and remarked, "I've seen a ball hit that far, as has my husband." Sue glanced at John, who frowned slightly at his wife but did not make any comment.

"Come on, Sam," Rebecca began, "you can't possibly—"

Sam cut her off. "Just a moment. Who guessed eight hundred feet?"

David smiled. Hidden in the back of the crowd he replied, "Sometimes a bunt can be just as important as a homerun, right, John?"

No one could pinpoint where David's voice was coming from. The Barnes family scanned the crowd of reporters and VIPs, hoping someone would step forward.

"Please, who said that?" Sam asked.

"It's good to see you again, Sam. It's good to see you give credit to your team and acknowledge that a baseball is just a ball. It is your actions that define you. Catch!"

From the crowd a ball flew into the outstretched hand of Sam Barnes. Sam turned the ball over and read the inscription: "Yankees 6, Padres 9. Nice hit, Sammy —D.L."

Sam's eyes misted, and he handed the ball to his mother. "David?"

"Yes, Sammy. It was a great game. It's good to see your family together."

The crowd mumbled and searched for the person who was conversing with Sam.

"You can't stay?"

"I'm afraid not. But know that you and your family are always near my heart and in my prayers."

"As you are in ours."

A single figure stepped away from the crowd and nodded to the Barnes family. David smiled and said, "Keep your priorities, keep your faith, and know with God on your team you, too, can hit an eight-hundred-foot home run." David turned to leave. A slim, womanly figure grasped his arm and both disappeared in the crowd outside of the conference room.

David's body hunched over the cane that supported him, his legs wobbly and his back unable to straighten, as he shuffled down a paved walkway. The sun shone brightly, and the air was warm and comforting. David made his way to a nearby park bench and collapsed in exhaustion. *Where am I now?*

He surveyed his surroundings. People were everywhere in the park. Couples were walking hand in hand, children were running and playing, exercise enthusiasts were biking, jogging, or walking. Everyone seemed to be smiling.

David doubled over in pain and coughed, confused at his current physical state. His body jolted with pain.

"Sir?" A female voice touched his ears through his coughing fit. "Can I help you? Would you like some water or something else?"

Perhaps some cough medicine might be in order, David thought while his cough subsided. He wiped his chin on his sleeve, and his gaze drifted up to focus on who was speaking to him. Another shock went through his body when he recognized the face of Tammy Stewart. She was a few years older than when he had helped rescue her from her fall off the mountain, but he recognized her instantly. He wondered if Nicole and Matt were around.

Tammy knelt down and placed a reassuring hand on David's shoulder. "Is there anything I can do for you, sir?"

David became lost in her eyes, unable to respond to her question and not wanting to break his gaze.

"I'm going to get you some help. Wait right here, I'll only be a moment."
Tammy stood to leave, but David grabbed hold of her wrist. She tried to pull
herself free, but David snapped her down to her knees.

Startled, Tammy cried out, but David placed a finger to her lips to silence
her. He winked at her and removed his finger from her lips. He let go of his
hold on her wrist and signed, "Where am I?"

Tammy shook off her surprise and signed, "You're in the Liberty Memorial
Park."

David replied, "Why the name 'Liberty'?"

"I—it was named after a very special man."

"You own this park?"

"Oh no, the county owns the park. My sister and I donated it to the
county." Tammy paused for a moment. "Why did you think I owned the
park?"

David ignored the question. "How is Nicole?"

Tammy wrinkled her brow. "You know my sister?"

"Did she marry Matt?"

Tammy's eyes widened. "Yes, she married Matt about five years ago. They
have two children, a boy and a girl."

David's hands continued to gesture, now more rapidly. They matched the
rate of his heartbeat. "And you? Have you married?"

Tammy closed her eyes and whispered, "No, I haven't."

The bizarre conversation was interrupted by a child's voice shouting,
"There's Aunt Tammy, over at the bench."

Tammy looked up just in time, before two children tackled her to the
ground.

"David Bryan and Beth Ann, you let your aunt up off the ground this very
minute," a woman's voice said sternly.

David craned his neck. His heart leapt with joy at seeing Matt and Nicole
walking toward him hand in hand. When they reached their children, Matt
pulled them off Tammy, holding each child like a sack of potatoes. Nicole
helped her sister regain her feet.

Nicole nodded toward David, sitting on the bench, "Who's your friend,
sis?"

Tammy stuttered, "I'm not sure, his name is—"

David tried to stand, and Tammy quickly supported his weight. He welcomed her assistance and signed, "My name is David."

Nicole and Matt frowned and glanced at Tammy.

Matt set his kids down, directing them to the playground, and offered his hand to David. "My name is Matt."

David smiled and returned the handshake, squeezing Matt's hand firmly before releasing it. "It's so good to see you all."

Nicole stepped closer. "Do we know you, David?"

David ignored the question. He fought to keep his eyes from watering and resisted the urge to fall into Tammy's arms. "How is life's journey?" he signed. "Are you placing others before yourself?"

The adults nodded and stared at the old man.

David scanned the park. "Why did you give this place to the county?"

Tammy did not hesitate. She spoke like she had answered the question a thousand times. "This park is more than the trees, benches, and playgrounds that you see here." She pointed to a building on the east side of the park. "The structure you see to the east is a shelter. It provides meals for those who are hungry and a roof for those who need a home. The park in which we stand is merely an extension of the shelter, but we donated it to the county so all could enjoy it, not just those who needed the shelter."

David tried to blink the tears away. *You truly have done an amazing thing, my friends*, David thought.

When his eyes were able to focus, he saw a familiar form slip away from a nearby tree. A simple nod told David it was time to say his good-byes.

He studied his three friends. "It is good to see that you are helping His children."

Matt stepped closer to offer David support. "Maybe you should come to the shelter, David. I'm sure you would at least enjoy a nice meal."

Tammy nodded. "Yes, and if you need a place to stay, there's always room."

Nicole smiled and put her arm around her sister. "She always says that, David. If we had to put you up in our own house, there's always room."

Tammy blushed and smiled at her sister.

David grinned. The two sisters' lives had truly been changed by a stranger who had passed through their lives for a moment in time.

David's voice returned. "Thank you for your generous offer, but things are not always as they appear. Isn't that correct, Matt?" David reached out with his cane and tapped Matt's prosthetic leg.

The hollow rapping caused three jaws to drop.

"I'm glad to see you all again. May God's peace be with you, no matter what mountain you must climb." David dropped his cane and turned to leave.

Tammy stooped and picked up the cane. She cradled it in her arms and said, "Are you going to leave me again, David Liberty?"

David stopped, but did not make eye contact. He signed, "Some journeys must be taken alone. Where I go, you may not follow."

Tammy took another step forward. "Take me with you."

"Remember this: your actions define you. Your actions are a reflection of the person that you are on the inside. My actions were not, so I must make this journey alone. This is my mountain to climb. You may not come with me." David resumed his walk toward the solitary figure that waited for him.

Tammy watched David leave. Clutching the cane intensely with both hands, tears flowed freely down her cheeks. She glanced at Matt and Nicole, who appeared to be in shock.

Tammy peered down at the cane. To her surprise, there was an inscription: "I carry you always within my heart —D.L."

Tammy surveyed the park for David, but the figure of a man had disappeared from her sight. "Come back to me," she whispered.

A reply softly tickled her mind. *I will come back. Somehow I will find a way.*

The church bells rang throughout the valley. The chime was so strong that it vibrated the ground where David stood. His body had changed, and vibrant energy coursed through his veins. He searched for the source of the bells and focused on a building that stood apart from the homes around it.

The musical sound beckoned him forward, and he ran with an urgency he could not explain. Shortly he found himself before the crowded doors of a church. "What's all the excitement about?" David muttered as his shoulders bumped into strangers on either side.

A gentleman heard his question and answered, "Don't you know? Joshua is getting ordained today."

David's heart leapt. *Joshua? Little Joshua, my buddy?*

He forced his way through the crowd and found an empty seat three quarters of the way in the back.

David could feel the anticipation ripple through the air around him. People were smiling, waving hands, and embracing each other with an enthusiasm that was contagious. He had never seen a church so crowded. The crowd continued to grow, and bodies shoved themselves into any available space.

Then the clamor of the multitude decreased to a low hum. The ceremony had begun. David craned his neck to watch the small parade of robed figures take their places on and before the altar. He recognized the face of Renee, also robed in a ceremonial garb, take a seat on the altar. A young, handsome man sat down next to her, grasping her hand.

David's heart leapt when he recognized the young man. Joshua!

An elderly, father-like figure made his way slowly to the podium. He adjusted his garbs and placed his eyeglasses on his face. His soft voice projected across the church through a sound system that magnified the speaker's voice. "Ladies and gentlemen, we thank you for coming to this wonderful event today. Through your support by your physical presence and your constant prayers, Joshua will be blessed by the vocation he has chosen within the church."

The old pastor continued to speak, but David's mind closed his ears, and memories flooded through him. It was not the images that made him nauseated, but the feeling of failure that returned to his mind. He remembered Joshua's tiny fists beating against his legs. He remembered bending over Emmett, silently pleading with the Lord to heal the man. He remembered the words that crushed his heart: *I hate you! I hate you!* David shook his head. Tears trickled down his face, and his attention returned to the voice of the speaker.

"I would like to introduce a very special guest." The old priest motioned as his voice crackled. "This next speaker is Pastor Renee Brown, Joshua Brown's mother."

Renee glided to the podium. She smiled and nodded at the intense applause, and after a moment, she raised her hand in a gesture for silence. "Thank you. Thank you so much. It is a great honor to be here today. It is a great honor to share with my son as he devotes his life to the Lord in a manner that is designed to teach other's about Christ's gift to His children.

"Everybody is called to devote his life to the Lord, but each path we choose may be different. Whether doctor, teacher, janitor, or pastor, we are all commissioned to love God first, above all others. Above money, above power, above recognition, above any person, God needs to come first.

"Secondly, but equal to the love and devotion that we show the Lord, we are called to love our neighbors. Our love for the Lord is reflected in the manner in which we treat His children. Christ commanded us to be like Him.

Christ loved all. This was demonstrated by His actions. For what greater gift of love could be shown? He died, that we might live." Renee paused, as if trying to collect her thoughts.

Not a sound could be heard in the congregation while everyone waited for her to continue. Renee discreetly wiped her eyes and smiled. She scanned the faces. "My son has demonstrated an enthusiasm for the Lord and for all his children. I won't take anymore time from his special day." Renee returned to her position, and the old pastor stepped forward.

The ordination proceeded, and David stretched to his toes to view the ceremony. He was unable to hear the exchange of words, for no longer was the sound system projecting the voices.

After a short time, the elder returned to the podium, and without any change in his tone, said, "I now introduce to you, for the first time, Pastor Joshua Brown."

The congregation erupted with applause. Mother and son embraced on the altar as the claps and whistles echoed throughout the church. Joshua kissed his mother's cheek and walked up to the podium. He adjusted the height of the microphone and addressed the congregation with zest in his voice. "Good morning, Church of Christ!"

The assembly shouted in unison, "Good morning, Pastor Brown!"

"I am honored to be your servant." Joshua raised his hands, asking for silence. Then he pulled out his notes and studied them for a moment. Shaking his head, he crumpled the paper and stuffed it into a pocket. "For months I've been preparing what to say to you on this day, but the Spirit of the Lord has asked for a different message." Joshua reached into his pocket and removed his wallet. He unfolded the leather and removed a faded piece of paper.

"I found this poem in one of my father's Bibles. His name was Pastor Emmett Brown. Although the poem is not a quote from Scripture, I will tie in its message after I read it to you. Ironically, the author is unknown. The only reference written on the poem is the name and address of the Daughters of St. Paul." Joshua read:

"When things go wrong, as they sometimes will,
When the road you're trudging seems all uphill,
When the funds are low and the debts are high,
And you want to smile, but you have to sigh,
When care is pressing you down a bit,
Rest if you must, but don't you quit.

Life is queer with its twists and turns,
As every one of us sometimes learns,
And many a fellow turns about
When he might have won if he stuck it out.
Don't give up though the pace seems slow;
You may succeed with another blow.

Often the goal is nearer than
It seems to a faint and faltering man;
Often the struggler has given up
When he might have captured the victor's cup;
And he learned too late when the night came down,
How close he was to the golden crown.

Success is failure turned inside out—
The silver tint of the clouds of doubt,
And you can never tell how close you are,
It may be near when it seems afar;
So stick to the fight when you're hardest hit,
It's when things seem worst that you mustn't quit."

Joshua folded up the piece of paper. "You see," he began, "God knows what He is doing." He placed his hands on the podium and the passion he felt was conveyed in his words. "Do you have the faith He knows what is best?"

He left the altar and walked down on level with the congregation. "What storms are in your life? What storms await you in the future?" Joshua's voice was intense. "There's one thing for certain: you will have storms in your life!

"In the book of Matthew, Christ tells a short parable about a wise man who built his house on a rock and a fool of a man who built his house on sand. The rain fell, and the floods came. The wind blew and buffeted against both houses. The house on the rock didn't collapse, for its foundation was built strong. The house on the sand collapsed and was ruined, for its foundation was not stable and it couldn't stand against the storm."

Joshua clenched his fist. "What is your foundation? Is Christ your rock, or have you built your life on the sand? You see that the storm struck both houses. Having Christ as the foundation did not exclude the man from the coming storm, but it did ensure that the house remained standing." He looked across the congregation. "The house represents your life, your soul, your very being. What have you built your life upon? Is Christ your foundation?"

Joshua's voice lowered, and his mood changed. "Make no mistake about it, my brothers and sisters. The storms will come. These storms are not addressed in Scripture as being either good or bad, but I will tell you this; the storms will affect who you will become and what path in life you choose to travel. As physical exercise stresses the muscles and causes them to adapt and change, so will these storms stress your spirit, causing you to grow and develop into the person God needs you to be for the people He has surrounded you with.

"But only if He is your foundation. For only He has the power to carry you through the storm. Without Christ, your house will be forfeited to the storm. His promise empowers us to continue the race, to never give up, to never surrender. Let's not be the man that turned around because of adversity, to lose an eternity of salvation that might have been obtained with just one more step."

Joshua turned his back on the congregation but he continued to speak. "It's not for us to understand the nature of the storm. It is for us to have faith that through Christ we will emerge from the wind, the rain, and the floods. In my own life I have seen these storms."

He turned back to study the faces within the crowd. "I watched my father give his life so that my mother and I could live. I was just a child and didn't understand why he had to die. I didn't understand why the Lord did not save him, but I understand today that because of my past I have chosen this path. If my father had not died, I wouldn't be standing here before you. Of that I'm sure.

"For quite some time I held resentment in my heart. Not toward the Lord, but toward one of his children. His name was David. He was my friend, a very special friend whom I blamed for the death of my father. I blamed him for the death of my father because David was unable, not unwilling as I thought, to save him. I thought David was my guardian angel and he'd make everything all right, but there was no miracle to be seen that day, and my father's life passed from this earth." Joshua surveyed the crowd before him and focused on a figure whose face remained covered by the light and the shadows of the candles nearby.

The figure rose slowly to an erect position, and his voice carried effortlessly through the assembly. "But there was a miracle that day," David said aloud.

No one dared to look for the source of the voice. All eyes stayed locked on Joshua and his reaction.

Joshua smiled broadly. "I suppose there was a miracle. My father acted in the way that his Lord and Savior did. He gave his life so that others could live."

"And you and your mother have realized a dream that at one time must have been your father's."

"Yes, the Lord truly has a bigger plan. Through my father's sacrifice, many people have been given the chance to know the Lord. It was not just my life and my mother's that were saved."

David nodded his head. "I've heard it said that God knows what He's doing."

"He does. Unfortunately we too often forget that He is in charge." David did not respond. "David? I must ask something of you."

David's body stiffened.

"I want to ask for your forgiveness."

David felt his heavy load lighten. "There's no need to ask. You've done nothing—"

"No, I have. I resented you for quite some time, and although I have prayed for forgiveness for these feelings, I'm compelled by the Spirit to ask you for forgiveness." He waited a moment. "David, will you forgive me?"

David humbly nodded his head, "Yes, Joshua, I forgive you."

Joshua grinned. "It is truly good to see you again, even if for one moment, my friend." A hand came to rest on Joshua's shoulder as Renee moved close to her son.

David felt a tap on his own shoulder and noticed Joelle standing by his side. Her expression told him that his time had run out. David nodded and turned to go. *Good-bye, my little Joshua. I'm sure your father is proud of what his son has become. I'm proud of you, too.*

Good-bye, my guardian angel. Joshua replied silently. *Know that your moment in my life shaped its course, as did my father's.*

It's good to know that God does have a plan.

Joshua watched David and another figure make their way out of the church. He was not sure if his friend could hear his final thoughts. *I will pray for you, dear David, for like me, your work has just begun.*

The end of novel one: David and Goliath
The Guardian Angel Chronicles